HELLO AGAIN

BOOK YOUR PLACE ON OUR WEBSITE AND MAKE THE READING CONNECTION!

We've created a customized website just for our very special readers, where you can get the inside scoop on everything that's going on with Zebra, Pinnacle and Kensington books.

When you come online, you'll have the exciting opportunity to:

- View covers of upcoming books
- Read sample chapters
- Learn about our future publishing schedule (listed by publication month *and author*)
- Find out when your favorite authors will be visiting a city near you
- Search for and order backlist books from our online catalog
- Check out author bios and background information
- Send e-mail to your favorite authors
- Meet the Kensington staff online
- Join us in weekly chats with authors, readers and other guests
- Get writing guidelines
- AND MUCH MORE!

Visit our website at
http://www.kensingtonbooks.com

HELLO AGAIN

DORIS JOHNSON

Dafina
BOOKS

Kensington Publishing Corp.

http://www.kensingtonbooks.com

Acknowledgments

Thank you to my editor, Karen Thomas, for providing me with this opportunity to tell this story. You are truly a gifted visionary.

To Pattie Steele-Perkins, my agent, a special thanks for your support and encouragement.

To my husband, whose love, wisdom, and right-on comments, is priceless.

To my sons and their wives, Mark and Alison, Rod and Bonnie, thank you for your patience and listening to my plot and for answering my endless questions on what young folks are up to these days! Rod, thanks for steering me to your cycling friends.

To Kim Snow for her savvy input on marketing and advertising.

To all the biking enthusiasts who took the time to answer questions about the world of cycling: Derek Maillard, Allen Washington, Jacques Karteron and Sal Bellitte of Bellitte Bicycles who gave me a tour of his shop. Guys, if you see any "oops!" they're all mine.

To all the readers who continue to support me. Thanks for sharing.

A tribute to Marshall W. "Major" Taylor who didn't allow racism to end his dream. And to all the current black competitive cyclists looking to make their mark.

And most of all to God, who continues to bless me with time, health, and talent to write my stories.

Chapter One

5 25 13 20 7 31.

Once in a lifetime. Only once, David Blackshear mused as he placed the plaque bearing those numbers back in its prominent place on his dresser. The solid gold numbers on the onyx marble background had changed his life five years ago on this thirty-first day of the month, his birthday. Showered, naked, smelling like Calvin Klein's Escape, he opened and closed the drawer after removing fresh underwear, then stepped into black boxer briefs and pulled on a matching tank undershirt. He sat down on the white chaise longue that occupied a corner of his huge bedroom and pulled on a pair of black silk calf-length socks.

A small smile touched his generous mouth but disappeared quickly as old thoughts brought frowns to the caramel-tan skin of his forehead. Exactly what and where would he be now if not for fate? So many factors had been in play that day he'd played a lottery game he'd rarely bothered with. He'd graduated from St. John's University after seven grueling years of night school. The 7. It'd been his thirty-first birthday and he'd splurged those thirty-one dollars he could not afford. The 31. He'd vowed to open a business in five years. The 5. The remaining numbers were birth dates of his brother, best friend, and a random one for luck.

David slipped into black slacks and a gray silk shirt. No tie. He tied on polished black shoes and slipped a charcoal gray wool-blend jacket off a hanger, shrugged into it and left the bedroom. In the library of his Queens, New York, spacious five-bedroom, four-bath Tudor-style home he walked to the bar and cracked a bottle of Cristal champagne and filled a crystal flute. He toasted a similarly styled plaque as was in the bedroom. Only there was but one number: 49. The amount in millions that he took home—after taxes. From struggling working man to drunkenly, dizzyingly wealthy man with the fateful dropping of some balls.

Now on his 36th birthday he couldn't help but reflect on his life and how it'd changed. But had he changed in these last years? He didn't think so. His looks were the same he thought as he stared in the mirror behind the bar. He saw a tall black man at six feet, weighing in at about 198 pounds: slender build, firm, not overly muscular. He'd always thought his wide forehead was too high and overshadowed his high cheekbones in his heart-shaped face. A few times he'd sported facial hair trying mustaches, beards, fades and goatees. But now he was clean shaven. His coarse black hair was close cut with a receding widow's peak. He always gave thanks for his excellent health.

As he stared, David mused that one always did not see what was on the inside. He looked fine, but was he really? People saw what they wanted to see. The trappings of wealth. Fine houses. Expensive clothes. The best restaurants. A plethora of businesses that made him even more money. They didn't see when he bid them good night, entered his home and closed the door, that he was alone. Except for his housekeeper who came and went to her own family every night, he was alone.

David never admitted to himself in all these years that he was lonely. Not until one day he looked around and realized that he *was* alone. Not until the day he saw something that he wanted and was jolted into the realization that there was a prize he could not have. Being told no in the last five years had become foreign to him. It wasn't until that day that he looked inside and saw longing and felt the emptiness. Him? With all his bounty? He'd laughed aloud it was so unthinkable. All he wanted was a woman, something that any average Joe had. Not any woman, the kind he could have with the crook of a finger; the kind who'd swear undying love only to assuage her gold-digger desires. They were as flies he had to bat away akin to a dog trying to scratch away fleas. But he'd wanted that one—the one he'd seen that day. With just a glance he'd known she was something special. His body had reacted before his brain did. In his cool dude frame of mind he'd acted the fool and she'd blown him off. In a flash she was gone, and since that day of awakening in January he'd tried to fill the hole in his heart.

David turned away from the bar and walked to the large mahogany desk. In his burgundy swivel chair he looked around the room where, if necessary, he spent some time managing problems that arose in his businesses, but limitedly, for he needed the peaceful refuge of his home.

His glance rested on the framed photos: his parents, his older brother, Jonathan. That was it. No significant other—as in an intended or the beautiful woman of the moment. His reflection showed in the glass frames and he wasn't surprised at more frowns marring his features. Though he'd tried telling himself that he was happy and wanted for nothing he knew the telling of the lie. He wanted another photograph sitting beside his loved ones. Not just anyone. The face he wanted to see was seared in his mind and try as he would there was no way he could erase it. Not with the women he wined and dined casually, or the women who provided a natural physical need. There was no way on God's green earth that he could find her. A face in a crowd. A voice even in its sharpness he'd wanted to hear again.

The phone rang but he didn't pick up the receiver. Instead he listened to his brother's voice, sounding almost surprised that he was talking to a machine.

"David, I hope you're showering or somewhere else in that house, man, because my driver will be there to pick you up about seven-fifteen. Ten minutes, David. Don't even think about backing out of this birthday party. People want to see you, plus, got a surprise for you. Later."

Surprise. David grimaced. He could imagine what Jonathan planned to spring on him. About five-foot three, curvy, and all wrapped up in foxy-wear, meant to impress. Velvet-touch skin and smelling like the fragrance of the month.

That image didn't fit the one that was fixed his mind. Slender. Taller. Five-foot six. An unbuttoned winter coat had hid the shape but he saw a medium bust and had envisioned the slim waist and shapely hips. Skin the color of a toffee candy. Oval-shaped face, and round, espresso dark eyes flashing dire warnings. A whiff of summer breezes tantalizing his nostrils.

He shook off the vivid vision in response to the ringing doorbell. In the shadows of the frosted glass double doors he saw the shape of one of Jonathan's drivers. He turned off lights, set the alarm and left the house. On the steps he inhaled the warm air of the last day of May. The sky was dimming as late evening would soon turn into dusk. He liked dusk, the time of day when the friskiness of business had wound down and the action of after dark was about to start. Settled in the back of the black Mercedes he contemplated the night ahead. He'd told Jonathan not to make a big fuss but he knew his brother wouldn't listen and would plan his own show. So he'd resigned himself to whatever was going to be. The twenty-five minute ride to the downtown Brooklyn art gallery was normally hampered by traffic so he made himself comfortable for the nearly hour-long trip. His cell phone was off and he intended to keep it that way—at least for the next hour. He couldn't think of an emergency that arose that his capable associates couldn't handle if he was unavailable.

To him this was a milestone birthday and he wondered just what the final hours of his natal day would bring. A pensive smile crossed his lips. At least he knew what wasn't going to happen. He hadn't tempted fate by buying himself another lottery ticket.

He'd been right about the surprise package Jonathan had presented soon after he walked into the gallery, hosting at any given time, at least a hundred and twenty people. There was nothing unpleasant about the pretty, twenty-something woman, nothing he absolutely detested. She appeared to be nice, polite and well-spoken. After an hour he was bored. Vivacity was lacking in her voice and her eyes were expressionless. Unexciting was a generous description of her. He extricated himself and mingled, smiling across the room at his brother's inquiring eye and mouthing a "No, thanks."

He, like other guests, ate from the sumptuous buffet, sipped drinks from passing waiters, walked around expressing opinions about the photographic art lining the walls on both levels of the spacious gallery. Similar in design to the Guggenheim Museum in Manhattan the sloping floor ascended to a balcony space where more of Jonathan's works were displayed along with other artists'. He dutifully danced, was entertained by comedians and singers, and reluctantly made a speech after the cutting of the cake. The many-tiered sweet confection rivaled the finest wedding cake, but it was decorated with every shape of bicycle imaginable.

"You like that?"

David ate another piece of cake before answering his brother, who was also finishing some of the delicious dessert.

"You know sweets are my downfall. Can't get enough. Delicious," David said between forkfuls.

"I meant the bikes," Jonathan Blackshear said, looking in amazement at the decorations, some now strewn on the table.

"You look surprised," David said. "Wasn't that your idea?"

"Not really. I just told Val what you were extreme about and she took it from there." He picked up a miniature decoration. "Never knew there were so many kinds. Thought I saw them all in your shop."

David smiled. "You never went through a catalog." He looked at a woman who seemed to be in charge and nodded toward her. "Is she the one responsible?"

Jonathan followed his look. "Yes. That's Valeria."

The tone of voice caused David to look at his brother and back at Valeria. He saw a pretty, brown-skin woman, about five-foot four, voluptuous, with killer legs and a beguiling mega kilowatt smile. He turned back to his brother who was still staring, looking much like a man who was interested. Very interested. David was filled with surprise. It'd been six years since his widowed brother had given a woman the time of day much less the look he was giving Valeria now.

Jonathan, feeling David's stare, said, "She owns her own catering business. I've used her before for openings here and people love her. Did you like everything?" He gestured at the buffet tables still looking as fresh as when people first dived into the vast spread.

"Couldn't say a bad thing about it if I wanted to. Everything was the bomb." David set his plate down on the tray of a passing waiter and Jonathan followed suit. "Keep the number for me. I could use her."

"I've got it."

That tone of voice again. "You really do?" David watched his brother's expression. "I mean, like that?" His eyes darkened as he thought of his dead sister-in-law, Cynthia. The pain she'd caused had left her widowed husband a zombie. Until now. Was Jonathan ready to live again? he wondered. David turned to stare at the beautiful caterer, then stopped himself. No, he wasn't going to do that. To compare the living to the dead.

Jonathan nodded. "I'm thinking on it," he said, watching for a reaction.

After a moment, David said, "Then don't wait on it too long. Things tend to disappear when you don't really mean for them to."

"Like four months ago?"

"Just like that," David said, quietly. He shrugged and gazed around the room. "Wes left?" Changing the subject was safe.

Understanding, Jonathan left it alone. "Probably in my office where he's hunted down a wrestling station." He looked after his brother walking across the room looking quite content and happy on the outside but he knew the real deal. He jammed his hands in his pockets and sighed deeply. *Just as he knows the deal with me.*

The betrayal of his wife was a deep wound that had closed, but smoothed to a nearly invisible scar. It was as a metal plate implanted in the body: it only hurt on rainy days. He searched the room until he found her. Maybe this was his time. His blood ran hot whenever he saw her. Their eyes locked and they both smiled, she moving away to tend to business and he turning to answer a question about his work. Yes, maybe this was his time, Jonathan thought. But he worried about his brother. Everyone had loved Cynthia and David had idolized her. What she'd done had turned David into a bitter man, distrustful of women and vowing never to marry. Maybe this Jones he had for a stranger was finally bringing him to life. If only there was some way Jonathan could help, the cost would be as nothing if it brought joy into David's life.

"Better put those dogs where they belong or you'll hear it from here to Space Mountain." David sat down on the wide black sofa across from the man, whose feet were propped up on the walnut desk, watching the wall-to-wall plasma TV screen where four men were mauling one another, complete with the appropriate grunts and groans.

Wesley Gray adjusted his body, saying, "Great party," without taking his eyes from the screen.

"How would you know?" David took in the action and grimaced as a body slammed to the floor was immediately pounced on by another three-hundred-pound block of flesh. "Ouch." He flinched as if he'd been the one getting the sneak attack whack to his back.

"This is the second rate stuff. You just missed the headliner. Now that was something to behold." Wesley unglued his eyes from the screen. "Too much partying? It's only just past midnight." He studied his friend. Since David had walked into the gallery earlier, Wesley had noticed the absence of gaiety and happiness in the man about to be feted for his birthday. He told himself that it was just temporary, that friends would put the light back in his eyes, and bring lightness to his steps. He'd watched for a few hours and it hadn't happened. He knew why. He picked up the remote and turned off the TV.

David looked surprised. "You had enough, too?"

"Hire me," Wesley said, not a smile in his voice and a serious look in his dark brown eyes.

"What?"

"You heard. Hire me."

Frown lines wrinkled David's forehead and he sat forward on the sofa. "What's wrong? The business in trouble?" Years ago, Wesley had been one of the beneficiaries of David's good fortune. Thinking that he was the next best thing after Shaft, he'd used his sudden wealth to found Gray's Investigations. Success was in the cards apparently because Wes had soared in business. Now there was a financial problem? David was worried.

"No," Wesley said. "You're in trouble."

"What are you talking about?" Relief cleared his brow as David settled back, crossed knee over knee and played with the sharp crease in his slacks.

"Hire me to find that woman." Wesley shrugged. "I'm only the best and your only chance at happiness." He turned a solemn look on David. "I mean it. You're a changed man since that day in Penn Station. It took us so long to make good on that bet and now I wish we'd never gone through with it." He shook his head. "Fate is a you-know-what."

"You plucked the thoughts out of my head," David

said. "But forget it. You know as well as I do that my money would be going to no good. A woman passing among hundreds in a crowded station and you can find her? No name, no business address. Nothing. I don't think so." He looked shrewdly at his friend. "Trying to pick my pockets, Wes?"

Wes feigned hurt. "Never," he said solemnly.

David grinned. "Forget it. Your suggestion is hopeless. Never happen in a million years. Turn that thing back on. Let's see what's on the market watch."

Wesley complied with a grunt. "Business? It's Sunday morning, man. Do like the rest of us and take a break. It is the seventh day you know."

"When you do," David said with a grin. He grew serious when he watched the commercials, always looking for one that caught his eye. His high-end bicycle business and passionate hobby, was long overdue for a new look, different, appealing print and visual ads that said something and stayed in the head, making a viewer a potential customer.

Turning to channel surfing he stopped with interest as a spot that'd caught his eye days ago came on. He smiled, and then seriously gave thought to what he was watching. All too soon the commercial ended and another jingle came on but he still thought about the previous ad, even remembering the product name.

"Now, that's what I want," he said, slamming a fist in the palm of his hand. "That's it."

Wesley turned from the TV to his friend and back again. "Cat food?" he asked, bewildered by his friend's interest in the silly antics of a few felines.

"No," David said with impatience. "The previous ad." He gave him a look. "Do you remember what it was? The product?" He waited expectantly.

"Sure. I buy that stuff all the time. Makes me smell

good and apparently the ladies like it too," Wes said. "Why?"

David was thoughtful. "Exactly. You remembered the ad after it was gone. You use the product." He sat on the edge of the seat. "Did you use it before or after you saw the commercial?"

Trying to remember, Wesley said, "I think I used it before, but after the ad made it sound so good, I recall thinking that I'd gotten the jump on a lot of people." He stared at his friend. "What's up?"

David sat back on the sofa, a wide grin lighting up his face. "Now, you're hired," he said.

Wesley stood up. He was six feet, same as David, but weighed in at two hundred and five. Many people thought David and Jonathan were brothers as they were almost always together and had similar body builds. His earth-brown, square face and round chocolate brown eyes fringed with long black lashes made him a favorite with the ladies. His black hair was close-cropped and he sported a thin mustache over his full mouth. He walked over to the sofa, stood in front of his friend and stared down at him. Reaching inside his jacket pocket he pulled out a handful of jelly beans and began popping them into his mouth. "Are you okay?" he asked. "Not feeling edgy about this birthday, are you? We wake up every morning. We get a little older. That's the way it is, man." He frowned.

David smiled, knowing Wes was agitated when the jelly beans appeared. "Relax, man, I'm fine." When Wesley sat beside him but still stared suspiciously, he said, "That commercial says it all. It works. I want the same lightness, effortlessness and quality for Champion Wheels."

A deep sigh made Wes's shoulders droop. "That's it? You've already got ads."

"They're stale. No oomph. I want something like that and even better." David felt suddenly rejuvenated.

"So I'm hired for what?"

"Find the creator of the commercial."

Wesley laughed. "Your assistant can do that just by picking up the phone." He winked. "I will be picking your pockets then," he said, still laughing.

"No," David said, shaking his head with emphasis. "Not the company. I want the person who came up with the idea. Its creator. From idea to storyboard to what I just saw on TV. I want a name."

"That's it?" Wes said as if all he'd been asked to do was find out the name of the mayor of New York City.

"That's it," David said, flipping channels again in hopes of running across the same commercial. "That guy's work is in my head. He can put life in the campaign I've decided to plan before the cycling season ends." He shook his index finger up and down with vigor at the TV. "Champion Wheels will be on the lips of everybody, even non-riders." He looked at the door as his brother opened it and entered the room.

Jonathan looked at David and then at Wesley who shrugged. "Something put that smile on his face and it obviously wasn't anything or any*one* out there," he said, jerking his head toward the waning crowd in the gallery. To Wesley he said, "Bicycles?"

Wesley nodded. "Nailed it."

"This is going to be something else, guys," David said with enthusiasm, his mind already racing to when he could speak with the adman. He checked his Omega watch for the date and mentally counted the months he had left. He splayed a hand. "The season is already here, but it doesn't matter. If the ad is that good it'll stick in the mind until Christmas and into next season. Business will boom around the holidays so no sense in putting off a campaign for months," he said, looking up and glancing at the two men who were watching him with identical looks. Definitely one of affection for the man they both knew so well.

"What?" said David, his smile fading. "You don't think it's possible?"

"First of all," Jonathan said, "I don't know what you're talking about. But whatever it is if it brings you back to life, I'm all for it."

"Seconded here," Wesley agreed.

Briefly, David explained his plans to Jonathan and when he finished said to the private investigator, "You can start on that right away, can't you, Wes?"

"You'll have the name tomorrow, man." He grinned. "Talk about picking pockets." He paused. "Only one thing. Those agencies usually work with teams of creative geniuses. You might be getting a slew of names."

"I know," David said. "But someone had to dream it up initially. *That's* the name I want."

Jonathan didn't understand Wes's crack but he knew from experience that the two men often spoke in code, something they'd both been doing since they'd met in their first year at Springfield Gardens High School in Queens where they all grew up.

"David, get out there and say good night to the last of your guests." In the doorway, he shook his head. "I told the people to come empty-handed but folks just don't listen. What in the world could they possibly get that you don't already have?"

"Man, you'd be the first one to go attitudinal if you didn't get a birthday gift," Wesley said. "When your thirty-ninth gets here in a few months I can fete you empty-handed, right?"

Jonathan winced, and then laughed as he closed the office door. "Ouch, got me," he said, and then eyed the corner table where the colorfully wrapped boxes filled a table.

David looked. His brother was right. People just don't listen.

"Well," Jonathan said, "while you two are bidding your adieus, I'll see to getting these things loaded up."

"Okay," David answered, his mind on other things as he left the room, absentmindedly saying inane things to people as they were leaving, everyone promising to "get together soon," yet, they rarely did except at more invitational affairs where they wound up echoing the same refrain.

Once home he helped the driver unload the trunk and the backseat of the Mercedes. Inside he left the gifts on the floor in the hallway and immediately went to the library where he booted up his computer, enthused over starting his campaign.

It wasn't until three in the morning that David left the room, shedding his clothes on the way to the bedroom. On the king-size bed, dressed in navy silk pajama bottoms, he lay staring at the ceiling in the dark room. He closed his eyes with a smile on his face. In seconds he opened them.

For hours he hadn't thought about *her*.

He closed his eyes again wondering if after all, love just wasn't in the cards for him. Or wondering if he'd finally gotten over Cynthia's betrayal of his brother. He'd loved his sister-in-law, thinking that one day he'd find her clone and marry her. After her death he'd turned a bitter eye on women and marriage. No one had suspected that the beautiful Cynthia had been living a lie, killing the souls of the loved ones she'd left behind. But he thought if after six years Jonathan was willing to put the past behind him, he could too. Then again, maybe love wasn't for him. It was like that for some people he knew. As his brother and best friend Wesley thought, his true love really *was* his work—his passion for his one-time cycling hobby, that had become a worldwide lucrative business. What woman could—or even would—want to compete with that? But behind the lids of his closed eyes, instead of the darkness, he saw that face again and wondered where in this world she could be.

Chapter Two

"Come, live in the world you deserve." The sultry voice of the female commentator faded as did the commercial, with the beautiful model gazing up at the man of her dreams basking in his appreciation of the scent of her, as if her skin was the elixir personified.

Margo Sterling was fuming, as she did each time the commercial aired. *Four* months and it was still going as strong as it had when it appeared the first week in January.

"I hate that commercial." The words were a gurgle in her throat, but balling a fist she shook it at the thirty-two-inch television screen in her living room. "I hate you Tyrone Henderson," she added, not as an afterthought, because her former colleague was never too far from her thoughts and her wrath. If he ever crossed her path she'd try to wrap her hands around his beefy neck and wring until he begged for his life, she thought, smarting all over again. That smart sophisticated perfume ad had been her idea and he'd stolen it. Robbed her talent!

"Aargh," she grunted, getting it out of her system at least until the next time the spot aired. She got up and went to the kitchen in her sixth-floor roomy two bedroom cooperative apartment in Jamaica, Queens. She poured a mug of coffee, the second of the morning, and carried it back into the living room. It was already past eleven o'clock on this Sunday, the first day of June, and she meant to have a lazy day doing nothing but relaxing although she knew the real word for it was sulking and worrying. Too keyed, she wasn't even going for her three times a week walk as was her habit after work and at least one morning on weekends. On Friday, the ominous feelings that she'd carried as she left the office were still present, cloaking her in a cape of gloom.

For the last four months she'd been on edge, walking around the office as if on eggshells. Lawrence Pearsall, her boss, had not taken too kindly to Ty's betrayal of her, thus the firm. Her saving grace had been another idea of hers, a commercial that had aired a month after the perfume ad. As her stolen idea was, it'd been just as successful and was still running strong. But that triumph, though it should have exonerated her in Lawrence's eyes and boosted her own self-esteem, hadn't, and she was perturbed by his disgusted look whenever she caught him staring at her. She no longer felt secure in her job or her skin. Confidence shaken, she slowly realized that something was happening. Accounts she'd been overseeing as associate creative director were being given to other colleagues. She often felt that if it were not for her latest success with the male cologne client, she would have been asked to step down from her hard-won present position, or worse, be fired. She stilled her heart amid rumors that she's halfway out the door. Thoughts of how long Lawrence was going to keep her dangling got in the way of her creativity and she could think of nothing but what she'd do when the dreaded summons to his office came.

Still dressed in robe and pajamas, she tucked her feet beneath her on the long navy sofa, scrunching down in the many pillows. Like the woman in the perfume ad, she snuggled, but instead of against a handsome man she was quite content with the sofa, finding the pillows more appealing. Men! Betrayal was still sour in her mouth as she thought about Ty's using her.

Margo had achieved her professional goals at least to the point she'd estimated she'd be when she first graduated from New York University with her degree in advertising. Her gaze settled on the mantel where plaques and statuettes of awards she'd received were placed prominently. At twenty-nine she was full of pride and satisfaction and sought nothing but to achieve higher status, one day making top VP. She enjoyed her company and the relationships she'd formed. She felt the scowl forming. Friends and relationships?

"Hah!" Tyrone had been a friend, a good friend with whom she worked well. She'd been pleased when he left the company to join a competitive firm with a respectable title and substantial pay increase. She hadn't been envious because she knew that one day she'd be rewarded in time in the firm. Though their business is a competitive one, she felt that she and Ty could share and thrash out ideas together on various projects as they did with other team staff. After Ty left she was curious and hurt that he did nothing to keep their friendship going. It was she doing all the calling and e-mailing until she finally stopped wondering if his new status had gone to his head. One day, her assistant excitedly called her into her office to come watch a commercial.

Margo had stood staring in amazement at the eye-appealing perfume ad. Hers! The one she'd dreamed up and commiserated over with Ty who'd doubled over with laughter, saying it was beneath her talents, and to forget about bringing it to a team meeting. He'd stolen her idea, taken it to the competition where he'd been elevated, all on her back!

She finished her coffee and kept herself from slamming the mug down on the glass-topped end table, instead placing it down gently. While channel surfing, her mind wandered back to that dreadful day.

It was cold, in the teens, as she left her office, walking for blocks, bracing the wind, head down, not caring who she bumped shoulders with until a surly man threatened to knock her silly as he yelled for her to watch where she was going.

"Sorehead Knicks fan," she muttered as she hustled her way down people-laden Seventh Avenue and back to Two Penn Plaza, the building in which she worked. But instead of taking the elevator up to the fourteenth floor she passed Madison Square Garden and headed down the stairs to Penn Station where she sat at an outdoor café drinking hot java, although her preferred drink after morning coffee was any kind of herbal tea. She'd ordered the strongest coffee bean they'd offered, and wished it was a smooth cognac, burning the murderous thoughts from her brain.

Seething at her friend's betrayal she sulked, looking mad at the world, and with an evil eye, dared anyone to even think about occupying the other seat. Ty Henderson's image was implanted in her brain; and an image of her gleefully sticking pins in a male doll's head was delightful. She'd been drawn to him when he'd first joined the firm only months after she did. She remembered he was so eager to learn and her ego was puffed that he hadn't minded that she was female and in a position to teach the ways of the company. Betrayed!

As she sipped her coffee she couldn't help but feel the stare and she lifted her eyes to that of an AMTRAK baggage handler in his red cap giving her the eye from the next table. From his two grinning redcap friends she could see that they were egging him to make a move and to her astonishment he flashed his smile and began walking toward her. *No, he's not!* she exclaimed to herself. When he stopped in front of her and said hello, she eyed him for a long moment before dropping her eyes and busying herself with retrieving her purse, all the while thoughts of the male species and betrayal bursting like rockets in her head. The redcap wasn't the only red she saw, almost laughing at the image that suddenly raced across her mind. He was the princely matador bravely waving a red cape at a maddened bull. She stood and stared directly in the man's eyes, almost taken aback by his strong masculine handsomeness. "Not in your *wildest* dreams or on your *best* day," she said tightly, and walked away.

A familiar jingle brought Margo back to the reality of her living room and she stared at the screen, a slow, mood-lightening smile touching her generous mouth. Her reason for existing and the reason, she believed, that she was still employed, pleasured her eyes and ears. Like that green lizard in an ever-popular commercial she'd worked her own tail off redeeming herself in her boss's eyes, who was still irked at Ty absconding with a moneymaker of an idea. With a shrewd eye and keen ear she listened to her now-popular commercial that was probably selling plenty of cologne for her client.

"Gotcha, Ty," she said, feeling mollified every time she saw the commercial. "Now let's see you steal your way to something like this!" She sometimes wondered how many other successful ads he'd given his new firm. Of course, it'd be easy to find out, but she was too bitter to even bother. One day he'd learn he'd made a mistake she reasoned, and then where would he turn? She couldn't help envisioning another willing female taking him under her wing and her lips curled. Somehow she wished she could warn the unsuspecting, too-nice woman, whoever she might be.

Margo was suddenly too keyed to settle back down. She flipped channels anyway hoping to see her ad again and was pleased when it aired almost back to back on the same station. Her client had obviously been pleased with her work, and she couldn't help but bask in the knowledge that a small fortune was behind her project. Only money, she thought, suddenly wishing that if money were no object she'd really go all out for a client. Many of her ideas were somewhat panoramic and as her boss kept reminding her, budget, budget, budget so as not to turn off potential accounts. Maybe one day she'd have the gumption to start her own business.

Calmed down, she suddenly remembered the words her assistant had whispered to her on Friday—that there was a buzz that her latest effort was award worthy. All she could think of was one of the coveted industry awards for commercials. To receive such recognition was a coup for anyone, but she hadn't taken the rumor to heart. Not when she was feeling uptight about even being in the industry in the coming months. She knew that to get to the top of her game again, showing Lawrence and everyone else she still had what it took, she had to work even harder.

Her gaze scanned the mantel again and she studied the photo of her retired parents. They were proud of her, calling and praising her after they'd seen the new spot. She'd promised that she would visit them in Miami, Florida, but not until the winter, the thought of the oppressive summer heat making her sweat in anticipation. Her eyes slid to another picture, that of a beautiful young teen, a happy grin splattered over her face, dressed in baggy pants and oversize shirt, posing daringly on a new skateboard. The face was the image of hers and Margo ignored the mist feathering her eyes as it sometimes did. The passing of time lessens the ache

of absence but she'll always miss her twin sister, Kai.
That picture was taken only weeks before Kai's death.
Struck as she sailed out of Manhattan's Damrosch Park
in Lincoln Center on her skateboard, she never saw the
vehicle. She was fourteen. Months after the funeral, her
parents moved out of the Lincoln Houses project right
behind the arts center, unable to live with the memories
of Kai in the neighborhood, a place she'd been since
birth. They settled in a rented house in St. Albans,
Queens, later buying it, staying until Margo was grown,
and eventually relocating to Florida.

Margo sometimes thought about how differently the
twins had lived their lives. Kai was exuberant in everything she did. Early memories had them in the bathtub
where Kai was forever being scolded for ducking under
the water making like a submarine while Margo tried
desperately to save her. It was Kai who took them to for-
bidden places and innocently remained noncommittal
while Margo truthfully told where they'd been with
Margo receiving the punishment. She was perfectly
content to stay at home reading, writing and drawing,
while Kai was the tomboy daredevil challenging her
young male admirers to keep up with her tricks.
Margo's eyes clouded when she thought of that fateful
day when Kai didn't come home, refusing her twin's request to come watch a new trick she was going to show
the guys, laughing that it was the mother of all moves.
Margo refused, knowing she'd just close her eyes at the
pivotal moment scared that her sister would take a trick
to the extreme. Afterward, Kai's number one fan told
Margo that Kai had excelled, making his and the other
guy's jaws drop in admiration. She'd been looking back
laughing and smiling at her triumph when she'd sailed
into the street into the path of the truck.

Margo wondered what Kai would be like now, nearing

thirty. Would she have made a name for herself in extreme sports or in nontraditional women's boxing? Would she have become a few and far between black astronaut? Would she already have achieved her brow-raising first or even third Olympic Gold in skiing, downhill racing or speed skating?

Threatened by encroaching melancholia, Margo shrugged away the pillows and pressed the power button on the TV remote and walked to her spare room used as her office. It was a glorious day, not meant for tears, and if she continued in this vein she'd be no good to meet the challenging stare of her boss in the morning. Kai would only laugh and tell her to suck it up and move on. *There's a whole world waiting to be discovered.* Margo smiled when remembering those very words Kai had used and Margo had told her to stop dreaming, that there were no new worlds to discover. Kai had replied "Is there no Red Planet? Where oh where is Atlantis?"

By dusk a pleasantly tired Margo pushed away from the desk, rolling her tired shoulders and eying her work with a critical stare before turning off the table lamp.

"Mission accomplished" she murmured, thinking about the onset of earlier doldrums. She'd shaken them by blocking out the world, doing what she frequently did—drawing illustrations and writing tales to match. She'd often turned to thinking up tales, things she remembered that she and Kai had done or said. Over the years she'd amassed pages of stories and pictures meant for her eyes only, because they'd become her refuge when she was feeling blue. The situations she put the young characters in brought a smile to her lips and rare sounds of laughter to the silent room. She'd even named the headstrong little girl Kai and the admiring young boy, Antoine. The little peacemaker, Chloe, was herself of course. She read the tale she'd just finished, a teaching lesson for Kai's selfishness, and was pleased.

She gathered the drawings and pages of text and put them in a folder with dozens of others. On the desk was a favorite framed illustration. It was of the Kai of her imagination; a precocious ten-year-old with an impish grin and long black wavy pigtails flying in the wind as she fearlessly tumbled over and over down a grassy hill. She didn't give the drawing her twin sister's face, yet Margo knew in her heart the tales were based on Kai's ever adventurous spirit, each funny story dear to her heart. It was in a way her tribute to a free spirit whose light went out far too soon.

The two quick rings of the doorbell moments after Margo had showered and dressed in a loose-fitting peach lounging slacks set, had her smiling in anticipation as she walked down the short hallway. At nearly eight o'clock on a Sunday evening she could have but one visitor. She opened the door.

"Hey, Rhonda," Margo said, stepping back and letting her neighbor waltz inside.

"Hey, yourself," Rhonda Desmond said, handing Margo a foil-wrapped plate. She sniffed the air and shook her head. "I don't know why I bring you dessert knowing you haven't even cooked yourself a meal." In the kitchen she looked at the spotless stove and shook her head again but noticed the mug in the sink. "At least you had coffee. Was that it for the day?" She sat down at the kitchen table looking at the younger woman with a raised brow.

Margo laughed while removing the foil. It was half a pineapple upside down cake and she grinned broadly, her taste buds watering in anticipation of the first mouthful. "No, I had a boiled egg and toast with a couple of mugs. For lunch and dinner I had a frozen Hungry-Man Roasted

Turkey Dinner and a glass of apple juice." Knowing her friend's penchant for tea she put on the kettle. "You'll join me, right?" she said, sitting across from her friend.

"Lunch and dinner," she snorted. "If it'll put something in your stomach before morning, I'll join you." Rhonda noticed the lounging outfit and said "You didn't leave this house today, did you? No walking?"

Margo smiled at her friend who was her senior by only thirteen years. At forty-two, Rhonda could be one of the *Essence* models in the magazine's spread on the glamorous older woman. She looked thirty, was trim with an athletic body, not an ounce of flab anywhere. She wore her jet black hair cut short and tapered with feathery tufts on top. The style complimented her round face, highlighting her big dark brown eyes that flashed with humor and intelligence.

"I had a relaxing day," Margo said, childish pranks and images flashing in her mind. "First in a long time." She got up to get plates and utensils and poured hot water in their mugs over Orange Zinger tea bags. After the first bite of the sweet confection she said, "I don't know how you fit domestic stuff like this into your busy life. You've got a power job, a zillion church committees, and not to say anything of socializing." Her eyes danced. "How was the jazz brunch today with, ah—?"

"With the group," Rhonda cut in. "And yes he was there and no, he's not Mr. Right," she said quickly before Margo hit her with a barrage of questions about her admirer. "He's got the message," she said, letting out a deep sigh. "Finally."

Margo smiled knowing that Rhonda was truly happy that a male choir member who wouldn't take no for an answer was finally relieved of his agony. Rhonda was a beautiful woman, a successful bank vice president, a community activist, and a divorcée with a twenty-year-old college student daughter.

"I told you to buy a ticket, you'd have enjoyed the music and the choir group is not as stuffy as you think." Rhonda finished her sliver of cake and sipped her tea while giving Margo a keen eye. "You're not still having a time of it with old Larry are you?" she said with bemusement.

"Lawrence," Margo said with emphasis, "would kill you for calling him out of his name." She wrinkled her nose. "He'll be uptight until Christmas in July," she said and cut another piece of cake. After savoring a mouthful she stabbed at the air with her fork. "He acts as if it were *his* brains that were picked!"

Rhonda watched the cloud settle over the pretty oval face, and the round brown eyes darken, and she frowned. "I don't know why you stay there putting up with his nonsense. You can make vice president anywhere else with your talent. You know that, especially with this last idea of yours."

"Yes and how many more years would I have to struggle in order to do that?" Margo said, a dull ache pounding her chest with the thought of starting over. "I'm nearly there with Mirken and Prusser. They're one of the tops in the business."

"And you can go someplace else and put them *at* the top," Rhonda replied with impatience. "It's not like you're pushing the hell out of sixty and ready for the rocking chair."

Margo raised a brow. "Who do you know who rocks anymore," she said wryly, but she smiled. She liked her neighbor and considered herself lucky in knowing her.

When she'd bought the co-op five years ago she never thought that the single mother and her daughter Brenda who lived just across the hall would become her closest friends. Always working, making no time for socializing, she was happy when Rhonda, an astute businesswoman, recognized a young workaholic and befriended her. Over the years they'd traveled together, had dinners out, and Margo was treated as family, attending Brenda's milestone events and expected to be present at the young woman's college graduation in two years.

Rhonda stood and cleared the table. "I'm just telling you that you're way off base if you think you can't make it elsewhere. I know talent when I see it. Remember that. And tomorrow when you walk in that office ignore that grudge-holding joker and keep doing your thing. He knows what he's got in you." She pointed at the wrapped plate. "Don't make yourself sick finishing that tonight. I made some Cornish hens. If you get hungry, knock."

When Margo walked off the elevator on the fourteenth floor of her office building the next morning, there was a smile on her face as she waved to Lawrence Pearsall, her boss, sailing by his glass-walled office with pep in her step. She held back the giggle that threatened when he gave her a "what's gotten into you" look and a scowl settled on his craggy face.

But moments later, shock sent ice water pouring through her veins as she read her morning e-mail. The warm feelings Rhonda had left her with were gone with just the click of a mouse. One stark memo from Lawrence Pearsall had her insides whirling like a child's spinning top. Another of her accounts had been reassigned.

"No," Margo murmured. "Not another one!" She rested her arms on her desk and stared at nothing as her entwined thumbs made circle after circle as her brain went numb with disbelief.

Never knowing how she'd made it to Thursday, Margo dispiritedly cleared her desk in preparation of leaving for the day. A glance at her watch brought a sound of dismay; it was not even six o'clock. Her confidence was badly shaken. All week whispers ceased when she appeared or walked by. Her assistant was doing double duty, assigned to someone else so Margo hardly saw her. After all, there was no need, was there, with so few accounts and unimportant ones at that. For the first time she actually thought about spiffing up her résumé. She looked up sharply at the rap on her open door and watched her boss stride in with a folder. The look on his pale hard face was undecipherable and she held her breath. *Here it comes,* she thought as the word "fired" seared her brain. Giddily, she wondered how many ways one could say "you're dismissed" before a folder was required.

Minutes later her head spun like a deranged puppet as she watched his jacket flapping in the air as he strode from her office. Not fired, not fired, not fired sped through her brain, making her dizzy. She stared at the folder that Lawrence had left with her to study. A new account. Hers alone. She looked at it again. "Obviously your last endeavor caught an important eye. He's insisted on working with its creator, and no one else. Don't bungle it up." Lawrence's stinging words was an assault on her ears.

A huge account and he had given it to her. Of course, silly, he had no choice she thought, stopping short of chortling; the client had spoken. She smiled at the sweet revenge of it all but then bent her head to study the contents of the folder.

"David Blackshear" she said the name aloud. "You

certainly seem to know what you want." The client was very specific in his demands, she was thinking as she perused the rough workup Lawrence had done, but she knew that she could deliver. Though not a sports freak she was talented and had done a successful tennis spot, years ago. She drew in a breath as she noted the ten A.M. meeting with the new client. Without missing a beat Margo put her purse back in the drawer while logging back on. The ideas tumbled from her brain and she speedily captured them, smiling with the feeling of new life surging inside.

When Rhonda heard the soft click of the apartment door closing across the hall, she noted the time from the TV cable box: eleven twenty-one. She narrowed her eyes thinking that her friend had given that ungrateful man another day and night of her life. "Wake up, Margo, life is for living," she murmured as she turned her attention back to the late news.

David stepped off the fourteenth floor elevator at Two Penn Plaza at exactly nine fifty-eight and was met at the reception desk by the man he'd spoken with two days before, Lawrence Pearsall. After the usual greetings and small talk in the man's glass-walled office, David was impatient with the man's effusiveness and guile at snagging a huge account. He wanted to meet the artist, the woman who he'd be working with. Margo Sterling, he mused.

When Wesley had gotten the information for him only a day after he'd requested it, he'd been surprised that the person behind the commercial he'd admired was a woman. So why did he think it was a man, he'd asked himself. Chauvinist, he was not. Waiting for her boss to summon her to his office, David could only think how intrigued he was by her work and wondered if she'd done anything with the ideas he'd had delivered to her boss. Hoping he wouldn't be disappointed, he waited, thinking positive, and standing when he saw a woman walking their way.

Margo was as nervous as if this were her first job interview, though she willed herself to appear calm. Lawrence stood, smiling, with the firm's newest client. To see the look on his face she thought, you'd think he'd gotten a sheik's account. She stepped inside the office with a serene smile and an outstretched hand. It dropped just as the pleasant greeting on her lips froze as she stared at the handsome man.

David had stepped forward but stopped mid-stride. It was her. The videotape that played in his mind since that cold day in January was reeling away. Her look. The scent of her that had reminded him of soft summer breezes. That warm, toffee-shaded face! All he had to hear was her voice but no, that wasn't true. She was that woman. Margo Sterling was his fleeting stranger. Here she was not five feet away!

The redcap from Penn Station! Margo was flabbergasted. How could this be? she wondered. This was a million-dollar account she was being handed. Speechless, she could only stare while Lawrence Pearsall looked from her to the silent David Blackshear. When Lawrence cleared his throat making an attempt at introductions and when Margo would speak, her new client beat her to it.

"Hello, again," David said. This time there was no charming, accompanying smile.

Chapter Three

Recovered, Margo offered her hand, a forced pleasant smile on her face, fully aware of Lawrence's preposterous stare.

"Mr. Blackshear."

David took the outstretched hand, his mind willing his body to remain aloof in response to the soft firm clasp of her hand.

"Ms. Sterling, my pleasure." Was that a sardonic look? she thought as she quickly broke contact, refusing to give thought to the sudden pulsing in her veins. Not knowing him well enough to read his eyes, Margo was a good enough judge of character to know that he found her humorous. She tried to keep her face from flaming as she could guess why.

Lawrence Pearsall's light gray eyes darted in frustration from one to the other. His laugh was nervous as he said, "I wasn't aware you two've met. So no introductions needed I guess." He threw his employee a cryptic look but only said, "Well, Mr. Blackshear, I'll leave you in Ms. Sterling's capable hands. I'm sure you'll be pleased with what she has to offer you." With another glance and nod at Margo he watched with darkened eyes as she led the millionaire to her office. No sooner than they were out of sight he went to his desk and picked up the phone, the wheels in his head turning like a windmill in a gale.

Alone with him in her office, Margo squared her shoulders. Might as well get this over with now, she thought miserably, wondering how long it would take her to find another job. "Mr. Blackshear"—she gestured at a chair in her tiny conference area—"please sit."

Not usually rattled, David struggled with the war inside. How was he to conduct a million dollar business deal with the woman he'd been dreaming about bedding? Bravely, David took the indicated chair at a small table while she took the seat across from his. He watched, curious, as she struggled to say something.

"Mr. Blackshear," Margo said in an uneven voice. "I'll understand if you request to work with someone else."

"Why would I want to do that?" David said, suddenly the businessman. He gestured at a picture of her latest commercial hanging on a wall behind her desk. "Isn't that your work?" Impatience tinged his voice.

"Of course it is," Margo answered with heat.

"I asked specifically for the person behind that advertisement and here you are. I see no problem with that unless, of course, you can't deliver the same intense and impeccable quality that I'm expecting."

"You didn't expect to be working with a person who acted extremely rude to you four months ago," Margo answered, recognizing but ignoring the challenge.

"No, I didn't," David replied. He gave her an intense stare. "But here we are. If you're ready to get to work, so am I." *Four months,* he thought, the warmth in his belly belying his outward calm. She knew the exact amount of time that had passed since their discomfiting meeting. Could that mean—no, he refused to read anything more into that than what it was—she dissing a stranger, a man dressed in working blues with a red cap on his head. Her silence left him wondering but he said, "So what's it going to be? Can you make my bicycles fly across the TV screens of America? The choice is yours." He held her gaze. "If you can't, or prefer not to, I'd appreciate your saying so now and we won't waste any more of each other's time. I'm sure Mr. Pearsall will find another client more to your liking to work with as soon as I'm out of your hair."

Margo was sitting back in her chair with entwined fingers, her thumbs going circle over circle while she listened. There was no arrogance, no cocksureness in his voice or manner, just straight talk. His voice was grudgeless and nonaccusing. Suddenly, all pressure oozed from her like toothpaste sliding smoothly from a tube. At once she felt both weightless and energized. Instead of responding to his inquisitive stare she picked up two folders, handing one to him: the result of burning the midnight oil.

"Thank you," she said quietly, pointedly, not referring to what she was thanking him for. She felt the man with the intense, intelligent brown eyes already knew. "This is the preliminary sketch of what I have in mind for Champion Wheels," she said, watching him open his folder as she did the same. "If you'll look it over first and tell me if I'm headed in the right direction, we can go from there."

David was silent as he studied the pages of ideas she'd come up with complete with illustrations of one of his popular bike models. After five minutes he pulled his chair around so he was sitting beside hers, frown lines wrinkling his brow as he pointed out something. For the next half hour they sat together going over her plans, he disagreeing with some things and nodding thoughtfully over others, while she disagreed with one or two points he made. Pleased, David closed the folder and stood. "There's nothing wrong with your direction, Ms. Sterling," he said, thoughtfully, tapping the folder. "You visited my Web site," he stated. At her nod, he said, "Very thorough. May I keep this?"

"Of course," Margo replied, her heart pounding wildly in her chest at his acceptance of her hastily put-together ideas.

"Thank you," David said, his mind spinning with plans. "I'll be seeing Mr. Pearsall now and cementing the arrangement. I like your work and I'm certain we can make this a success." He lifted a shoulder. "I had no timetable for this, but since you've picked up my wavelength I'm thinking that now we can get this done in a short period of time, say three months. Too fast for you?" His gaze was intense.

Margo could feel his enthusiasm and it was catching. "That would not be a problem," she said firmly, meeting his direct stare. "Just let me know the time frame you have in mind for each phase so the team of necessary people can be in place. If you decide to go with the African-American consumer as you're undecided or the general market, or both, I'll need to know as soon as possible. Also, if you're seeking a high profile black to tout the product, yesterday is better to have started." She was standing just inches away and as he bent to open the briefcase and put in the folder, she caught a whiff of his scent. Subtle, like clean fresh-cut wood shavings, she thought, making an effort not to noisily inhale.

"All good points," David said. "I'll give you my decision on the way to proceed when we meet again." He paused. "The virtual tour of my shop and the factory is very good but nothing like seeing the places in the here and now. I'd like you to put that on your schedule, say in a day or two, possibly Monday?"

"Yours is the only account I'll be working on, Mr. Blackshear," Margo said as she walked with him to the door. "So anytime is fine with me."

She accompanied him to Lawrence's office and just before he entered David stopped and looked at her. "I'm not all that formal, Ms. Sterling," he said, giving her a direct look. "We'll be working closely together and I prefer David; and if I may use your first name too, the job will be done without uncalled for pretentiousness."

"I haven't a problem with that, David." Her tongue glided over his name as if she'd been saying it all her life. It felt—comfortable. She held out her hand and he took it. "Thank you again and I look forward to a successful campaign for Champion Wheels."

Almost with trepidation, David took her hand, knowing the surge of emotion that was going to hit him in his solar plexus. He wasn't wrong. He inwardly exhaled and they dropped hands. "If it's not a problem, I'll call you later with an idea I have. Also, I can give you the time my driver will be picking you up on Monday for the tour."

"You're the client, call anytime you like with suggestions or complaints," Margo answered. "That's how Mirken and Prusser has kept long-time satisfying relationships."

"Until later, Margo."

In her office, anxious to learn about this mysterious man, Margo accessed the Internet and instead of typing in Champion Wheels as she'd done before, she typed in David Blackshear. Almost an hour later she pushed away from her desk virtually in shock. Her client was a multimillionaire! And he was her account! She was ecstatic and dizzy all at the same time.

She printed out copies of all she'd found, from his beaming face in a newspaper article holding up a check

for his millions and his myriad enterprises to pet interests and charities, and his philanthropies. His life at a
glance. Lawrence had given her the account only because he'd asked for her. What if he hadn't? Would she
still have a job? Feeling grateful to David Blackshear
she had to willfully stop the shaking of her legs under
the desk.

When the euphoria of it all wore off, Margo's brain
went into overdrive as she was hit with a stomach-
cramping thought. Why had the man she'd insulted
months ago asked for no one but her? she wondered;
there were others on the creative team, and to have
sought out Mirken and Prusser from all the top ad agencies in the industry, what did it mean? She looked at the
date of the newspaper article showing his big win. Five
years ago. He'd been as wealthy as Midas for the last
five years.

So why in January, only four months ago, was he
parading around Penn Station in a red cap? She'd
thought she was turning off a smart-alecky handsome
blue-collar worker who would flash his pretty smile, get
next to her and score big in front of his buddies with a
hardworking woman. Another guy trying to make it on
the back of an unsuspecting female, she'd thought.

The knot tightened in Margo's stomach as her
thoughts went wild. With his millions he could have
anything he desired: crazy, in-your-face commercials,
Super Bowl quality, airing all over the world. Then why
her? She was nobody in the big scheme of things, still
trying to scratch her way to the top.

Fleeting images of that day flashed by. She scanned
David Blackshear's face, after she had put him down—
the dying smile and the odd quirk of a brow. She saw the
gleeful looks of his buddies and heard their laughter.

Margo shuddered. It wasn't her talent after all she

thought, with a dull thudding in her chest. He wants me. David Blackshear after four months, with all his millions, had tracked her down. For his pound of flesh. His manly revenge.

"Margo, David Blackshear, here," he said when she picked up. She listened to the low even voice she'd liked when they were talking so earnestly together this morning. Now, she answered evenly, "Yes, David, is there anything wrong?"

David frowned as he heard the even tone, almost dry, so different now. "Not really, but I'm afraid there's a scheduling conflict and Monday is no good for the tour. But Tuesday would be fine if that meets your schedule."

"Tuesday is fine," Margo said, still even-toned. "As I told you, yours is my only account."

"Perfect," David answered. "My driver will pick you up at ten-thirty."

"I'll be waiting." Margo replaced the receiver softly, and then sitting back, began methodically twirling her thumbs.

David stared at the phone for a long time. The woman he'd just spoken to was not the same one he'd left earlier. Her excitement with a new challenge, the vivaciousness he'd heard in her voice, was absent. She was all monotones and he was baffled. Instinct of dealing with all sorts of people, especially in his old job as a Long Island Rail Road conductor, told him that something was wrong.

Frowning, he rehashed their conversation and could find nothing that would bring about this sudden distancing. He thought of her boss, Lawrence Pearsall, and

dismissed him as an overbearing, full-of-himself chauvinist who was the type to cut an employee's throat and
immediately treat himself to a five course steak dinner
at Peter Lugers. But he was careful in seeing to it that
the million-dollar account was in the bag, so to speak,
before the client left the building.

Not given to pacing, David got up and walked to the
window of his fifteenth floor Harlem office building.
This location was one of two that he maintained for its
accessibility to the community, the other being on
Madison Avenue for its convenience to out-of-towners.
He smiled at the thought of passing former president
Bill Clinton on the street on his way to his offices in the
Harlem State office building on 125th Street or around
the corner in The Bayou restaurant, famous for its Cajun
cuisine. Never in his wishful thinking as a struggling
blue collar worker and night school student had he
thought of being where he was at today—in the position
to give, to employ, to help wherever he could and to
enjoy his life to the fullest. He would get tickled sometimes when he was in his favorite place, his bike shop in
Brooklyn, just thinking about his good fortune. Once,
cycling had been his hobby, indulged in only sporadi-
cally when he got a break at work or in between classes.
A weekend of biking, joining a tour or even managing
to buy on credit a power bicycle had been hard won
pluses in his life before five years ago. Now his hobby
was his passion and a big time business. He had no
shame in indulging in the sport with complete abandon
and competitiveness.

He turned away from the window and sat back down
at his desk where he'd had those disturbing thoughts
about Margo Sterling. What had happened? When he'd
left her earlier, for hours he'd had to pinch himself. He
even laughed when he thought about calling Wesley and

Jonathan. They'd be ready to get him a shrink when he reported he'd found her. Not even Wesley's sleuthing could have turned up the impossible. The joy of the telling would have to wait until he had them in front of him to watch their disbelieving expressions.

In four months and even after their meeting his thoughts about her were unchanged. Just as he'd known since that day he'd tried to talk to a stranger, Margo Sterling was the woman he wanted. He knew it in his gut. No figment of his imagination she was as real to him as the warm blood running through his veins. When he left her this morning not only were her brilliant ideas in his head but she was there as well, the woman herself. Cool, beautiful, and a woman about her business. After her initial discomfort of remembering where they'd met, she'd been the total professional, working with him, putting him at ease with the knowledge that his money was going to be well spent with a pleasing finished product. Once, he'd gotten off track with a non-business remark and she smoothly sidestepped the offer of lunch, bringing him back to the business at hand.

That had thrown David momentarily. The disdainful woman of Penn Station had turned up her nose at a mere worker yet almost annoyingly dismissed the opportunity of getting to know a wealthy client a little better.

Margo Sterling, David decided, was a woman of mystery. Yet he knew that now he'd found her he would have only three fleeting months to learn all there was to know about the woman who'd painted searing pictures in his brain for almost half a year. But deep down he hoped that the flesh and blood woman met all the expectations of the fanciful visions that had haunted his days and nights.

Though one thought bothered him he chose to ignore it as the face of his dead sister-in-law appeared briefly, dredging up the awful pain and sorrow thrust upon his family. No, this woman couldn't turn out to be deceptive like Cynthia. His inner feelings told him that she was the one he'd been waiting for—the one who could make him believe in love again.

On Sunday, Margo had a dream that woke her in the middle of the night. Ill, foreboding feelings kept her awake and when she left the house on Monday morning, rushing the three blocks to catch the subway, she wished that she was boarding a train to the ends of the earth, because all that awaited her at number Two Penn Plaza was chaos and confusion, the kind associated with the explosion of a doomsday machine. She could almost feel the fallout from the flak that was about to give her a one-two punch in the stomach.

No sooner than she shed her lightweight jacket, a buffer against the cool June morning breeze, she was summoned to Lawrence's office.

Through the glass wall Margo could see another associate creative director, Eddie Logan, chatting amiably with her boss. Eddie? What was he doing here? she wondered, a frown wrinkling her forehead. He was ferocious in his rise to the top and was her fiercest competition. He had accounts up the kazoo and begged for more but he always delivered in exemplary and over-the-top fashion. They both rose as she entered the office.

"Margo," Lawrence said, taking his seat and gesturing for her to do the same. "First, as we all know, your excellent work of the past has fallen short of the firm's commitment to continue to produce pristine work. You are also aware that the firm has been going through some reorganization." His pale gray eyes darkened as he looked from Margo to the smug-looking man seated beside her. "Unfortunately some of the positions we could not save, and I'm sorry to tell you that yours is one of them."

"What are you saying?" Margo said, feeling her body go limp. Right now she couldn't stand and run from the chilling words if all the creatures of Hades were after her. "You're firing me?" Her voice was just above a whisper. "Not even the decency of a private discussion?" She looked at Eddie Logan who appeared to be enjoying himself to her further confusion and shock.

"Oh, come, Margo, we're all family here and besides, you've known Eddie since you two have worked so well together. He's part of what I have to say so no sense wasting time in two separate meetings."

Margo's state of confusion did not hamper her sharp eye as she noticed the familiar folder on his desk. Her copy of the one she'd made for David Blackshear. She looked at Lawrence in shock and from him to Eddie. "You're giving him my new account?" she said in disbelief.

Lawrence looked away from the accusation in her eyes. "Correction," he said. "It is no longer your account because you will be gone as of today, no time at all to complete a job. Eddie has read everything you and Mr. Blackshear talked about and where you're going with the project. He's here so that you can bring him up to speed in case you didn't include anything you and Mr. Blackshear discussed."

"But Mr. Blackshear specifically asked for me," she blurted, believing that she was walking through someone else's nightmare.

With an impatient shrug Lawrence said, "That was because he doesn't know we've someone more competent to do a superior job."

Betrayed again, she thought wildly. Ty Henderson's laughing face floated before her like a dreaded specter. "You can't be serious with all this," she finally managed.

In answer, Lawrence picked up an envelope and handed it to her. "Obviously you're going to make this more difficult than it needs to be," he said dryly. "You'll find your severance package is more than generous." He stared at her with unblinking eyes. "Before you leave, please apprise your assistant of any matters that need immediate attention." He half-smiled, knowing that the most important thing in her life was in Eddie Logan's hands. He stood. "Good-bye, Margo."

Later, Margo never knew how she'd made it out of Lawrence's office, feeling his and Eddie's cocksure looks boring into her back as she left. She recalled that a trip to the washroom where she splashed her face with cold water was met with pitying looks from her coworkers who quickly gave her space. In her office she looked around in a daze. Who comes to work in the morning prepared to cart home seven years' worth of collected memorabilia, knickknacks left over from office celebrations, plants, and a can of tuna from her bottom desk drawer?

The ride home on the nearly empty F train at midday was one of the longest in Margo's life as she walked the three blocks to her apartment building carrying a filled Macy's shopping bag. She held back what would have been a hysterical laugh thinking that the last years of her career were in that bag. Strange coming home when the sun was still high in the sky, she thought. Long days turning into fifty-hour weeks rarely allowed her to see the sunlight.

Inside her co-op, alone, and out of sight of laughing eyes, she let loose. Pent-up emotions emerged when she fled to the bathroom, slamming the door, shedding shoes and clothes, almost ripping them from her body, until she was standing naked looking at herself in the mirror. Her usually serene exterior was as wild-looking as the hair she'd pulled loose from its neat bun flowing about her face in long wayward wisps. She felt the yell coming from the bowels of her soul and did nothing to stifle the full-blown scream that pierced the small room, bouncing off the walls and stinging her ears. It waned to a moan and then a soft whimpering cry as she licked the salty tears on her lips. She stepped into the bathtub and turned on the shower. Vignettes flashed by of her life at Mirken and Prusser. Happy times, sad times, exhilarating times. And then there was today, the end. She saw the smugness of Logan. And the crafty, vindictive, meanness of Lawrence Pearsall. And long before, there was Ty. And was Blackshear a part of it all in his own sadistic way?

Feeling assaulted, closing her eyes against the hurt, she let the tepid spray try to cleanse her mind of the evil thoughts she had against those who had betrayed her. They'd have given better treatment to a vicious cur about to rip their throats out, she thought.

It was after six when Margo awoke. Earlier, weakened and overwhelmed after her shower she'd slid under the welcoming coolness of her sheets and closed her eyes, praying she would not dream. She felt empty inside, not from lack of food but spiritually, and she wished the feeling was not so all-consuming and would soon dissipate. The glass of orange juice she poured settled in her stomach in a chilling pool, sending shivering waves over her body. She left the kitchen and padded to her workroom.

It was midnight when Margo turned out the light, leaving Kai and her friends with an unsolved riddle.

* * *

On Tuesday morning at ten forty-two when his driver reported that Margo Sterling was not at work, David was on the phone with Lawrence Pearsall. What the man was trying to tell him did not compute and by eleven fifteen he was in the offices of Mirken and Prusser.

"You signed a contract with Mirken and Prusser, Mr. Blackshear," Lawrence said, a stern but confident look on his face, though inwardly he was fervently hoping to avoid a confrontation with a multimillion dollar account.

David had refused a seat when he strode into the man's office and now he looked down at the five-foot nine or so man who was drawn up to his full height, doing a Herculean job of meeting David's intense look. "I don't know whether you read your own contracts, Mr. Pearsall," he said, "or perhaps you don't bother with the small print. I specifically asked for Margo Sterling and the paper I signed in this office adhered to that stipulation, otherwise we do no business together." He continued to stare down the man who'd turned crimson. "If you want to make a federal case out of my withdrawal be my guest," he said. "But you'd better be darned sure that your reorganization plans didn't include letting her go before I walked in your door with my business." He turned to the other man who Pearsall had introduced as Margo's replacement. He had no words for the pink-faced man who appeared to be in shock, but he looked him over and then said to Pearsall, "Be damned sure."

"I can't believe you, man. You're yanking our chain, right?" Wesley looked from David to Jonathan who was in awe and back to the angry man sitting tensely behind his desk. They were all in the office of Champion Wheels at David's sudden behest. He had news. Not knowing what to expect from the man they both loved and ready to defend him in anything, they both dropped everything and arrived within minutes of each other. They were met with a sumptuous spread of Chinese food and they ate as David talked.

Jonathan stopped eating and looked at his brother. "You found her on Friday and you're just now telling us on Tuesday?"

"And you lost her again?" Wesley said, breaking off a piece of spring roll and popping it into his mouth. He shook his head in disbelief. "Why didn't you say something then? I could have gotten the skinny on her by now."

"I'm hoping you can still do that, Wes," David said quietly, pushing away the rest of his pepper steak. He'd lost his appetite. "I want her."

Jonathan and Wesley exchanged looks.

"To do my campaign," David said sharply. "She's as good as I thought the person behind that ad was. It just happens to have been her. Whether she's hooked up with a big firm or freelances, it doesn't matter. I want her." He looked at Wesley. "Can you find her for me?"

The private detective had a glint in his eyes. "You're paying?"

"Of course," David said with an impatient look, and looked as his friend elbowed him to the edge of his desk. "What?"

Jonathan was smiling, knowing what Wesley was about. His brother, always annoyed by the appearance of masses of information, usually gave researching stuff on the 'Net to his associates. He drank some seltzer and sat back watching the show.

Wesley was at the computer and online in a flash and

after a few quick taps on the keyboard a smug smile appeared on his face as he hit the print key. He pointed to the printer at David's elbow and said, "There she is." When David snatched up the page, Wesley grinned. "You can bill the agency," he said, and sauntered back to his chair.

"Now, Brother, what was that worth," Jonathan said before erupting in laughter. Wesley joined in.

"Okay, you guys, you had your fun," David said but joined them in laughing at himself. He stared at the page and he went still. "This is for real?" he said with amazement. He looked at Wesley. "Jamaica Estates?"

"And you're right in her backyard in Holliswood," Wesley said, getting a kick out of watching his buddy.

"All these months," David murmured. "How could I have missed running into her?" he said, staring at the smiling men.

"Let's see," Jonathan said with a mock-serious look at the ceiling. "How many times has David Blackshear ridden the subway in the past few years?" He leaned over and took the paper from David's hand. "Or," he continued, "strolled down Midland Parkway of an evening in the middle of rush hour? Or shopped on, what's that main shopping area? Jamaica Avenue? Or visited the Queens Central Library on, let's see, Merrick Boulevard?"

"Or," Wesley chimed in, "haunted Cunningham Park watching every woman who jogged by?"

David rocked back and forth in his chair, waiting for the comedy act to subside, but when they would go on and on he held up a hand in stop sign fashion, a grin on his face. "Okay, okay, guys, I got the message."

Jonathan was quiet as he looked at his brother. There was a sense of calm about him now that had been subtly missing for months. He wondered if fate really was being kind in this turn of events. He knew that David would seek this Margo Sterling out. But telling himself that it was *all* business was the wrong thing to do. Jonathan knew without a doubt that this woman had gotten under his brother's skin like no other woman ever had. He knew it with all his heart and soul. He'd had a love like that once. Thinking about it brought a pang to his chest but he shrugged it off. That was a long time ago, he reminded himself. You've moved on, said the voice in his head.

David saw the wheels turning in Jonathan's head and guessed what he was thinking. "Things are going to be all right Jonathan," he said. They looked at each other and no further words were needed.

Wesley understood what was going on and what went unsaid between the two brothers. He didn't relate to it but stood and said, "If that's all the work you got for me today, I'll be getting on back. A job just as easy might have come in." He winked and chuckled softly.

David threw him a look but said quietly, "Thanks for coming over here, Wes. You too, Jonathan. I needed you guys to help me get my head back on straight after listening to that pompous joker this morning. Thought I was going to lose it there."

Jonathan stood. "We're always here, you know that." To Wes, he said, "You drive?"

"Yeah, commandeered a company car. Need a lift?"

"No. I was about to make a run when I got the call, so my driver's waiting."

Both men waved, and on their way out of the office David heard them laughing and joking with his staff. With their departure he felt sane again knowing that with them in his corner he'd never have to spend a dime on shrink fees.

He stared at the name and address on the paper and

questions loomed in his mind. What kind of reception would Margo Sterling give him the next time he saw her? he wondered. Whatever it was she'd better be strong. Now that he'd seen her again he knew that his feelings still ran deep. He wanted her. She would have the devil of a time trying to get him out of her life.

David also knew that he was readying himself for the fierce battle between his head and his heart. Would good sense rule, telling him to walk away from Penn Station's woman who wouldn't give a working man a second glance? Who now might harbor devious thoughts about the wealthy redcap? How could he be sure of who she was? That little voice in his head screamed, *Beware, danger.*

But David knew that all his practical thinking was futile, and he was already losing the battle. Little did Margo Sterling know that on a frigid day in January she'd captivated a stranger's heart forever.

Chapter Four

Funny how the days just flew by. She'd thought that without the hustle of readying for work every evening, flying out the door by seven A.M., putting in twelve hours, dragging herself home after dark, she'd be in a quandary as to what to do with herself. It'd been one week and two days that she'd last acted like an employed person scurrying along Seventh Avenue like the rest of the drones of the city.

The quiet was strangely peaceful: not only of the inactivity and lack of movement in her building, but in the neighborhood itself. She'd taken to walking almost every day and she marveled at things she'd never noticed before. As a working woman she'd done it begrudgingly to keep energized for an expected grueling day; it had been a duty to keep her vessel healthy. Now she stopped and looked. Had that old gnarled tree in front of her building with its lumps and age bumps and inviting leafy branches always looked so majestic? Had she always mechanically lifted a hand in greeting to the elderly man standing in the doorway of his florist shop? He'd seemed to know her and she returned his friendly smile. Two blocks down and across the street—when had the vacant lot become four new homes? In Cunningham Park the expanse of green fairly hummed with life on a midweek day. It was only Wednesday and she wondered if there were really so many people unemployed like herself. But no one seemed to be walking with hangdog looks and hunched shoulders. There was laughter and smiles and teenage lovers forgoing the last days of school before summer vacation started.

Feeling tired but good after her long walk, Margo entered her building with more life and pep than she'd had in the past week. It was nearly four o'clock when she got off the elevator wondering if Rhonda had returned from her bank conference in Chicago. Deciding to stop, she rang the bell but there was no answer so she stepped across the hall and opened the door to her apartment.

The day after Margo had gotten fired Rhonda had stopped by that evening to tell her that she was going away. When she saw the red, puffy telltale signs of tears, Margo blurted out the story, and when she was finished Rhonda went dumb. When she recovered she went ballistic, swearing up and down on the failings of the male species. Her antics and choice of words had Margo laughing as she looked at the absurdity of it all. She'd gone to bed that night with fewer evil thoughts weighing on her chest.

Showered and finished preparing a light dinner of a broiled lamb chop she'd left in too long, frozen spinach, a salad, and iced tea, she took her meal to the living room and turned on the TV. To escape the inevitable commercials she flipped to a cable movie station where she began watching for the third or fourth time an old Wesley Snipes movie, *Murder at 1600.* She never would get over the deviousness of powers that be and their successes at master cover-ups. She should be so devious, she thought. She'd be somewhat of a power by now.

* * *

David was at home in his library and for the third
time he reached for the phone and let his hand drop. For
a week he'd wanted to call her but each time he seethed
thinking how she'd been treated, guessing that the sound
of his voice would probably result in a resounding click
of the receiver in his ear.

It hadn't taken Gray's Investigations long to get him
the information he'd requested. When the report was
sent to him he'd felt like a dolt after looking at the re-
cent history of his prospective employee.

That day in January when she'd shot him down she'd
had every right, David thought, and it was that one moment in time that he'd chosen to give her the come-on.
That was the same day she'd learned of a creature
named Ty Henderson's thievery of her ideas. It wasn't
long after that that Lawrence Pearsall had started giving
her the business, making her pay every day for what he
perceived to be her act of disloyalty to the firm. David
snorted. As if she'd intentionally given her hard thought
out idea to a jerk! He inhaled and pressed in her number and waited, hoping that she would hear him out.
Talented, young, unemployed, she was probably anxious
to be back at work. And she would be if she'd only listen to him. His was an offer she could hardly refuse.

Margo frowned at the interruption and refused to answer the phone on the second ring. Wesley Snipes was
chasing an intruder from his apartment, slipping and
sliding over back alleys, getting soaked in a serious
downpour. She glanced at the Caller ID display and her
brows shot up. Shock mesmerized her and the answering machine started before she picked up. "Hello." She
pressed the "mute" button on the TV remote.

David couldn't read anything into that one word. He breathed deep.

"Hello, Margo," he said. "David Blackshear, here. How are you?"

She could have laughed. "As well as can be expected," she replied dryly. With a thought, frown lines appeared. "If you are calling on behalf of Logan because he's hit a wall with my ideas, you can forget it. I've had enough of my brains being picked and displayed for the world to see."

"Logan?" David frowned.

"My replacement," she said impatiently, wondering what was wrong with the man. He must have been working with Eddie Logan all week.

"Oh, the man with Pearsall last Tuesday when I severed our relationship," David said. He vaguely remembered the man's face.

"What?" Margo's chest was pumping and she suddenly felt flushed all over. "You did what?" Last Tuesday was the day he would have sent his car for her. Somehow that thought made her weightless and she tried not to think ahead.

"I withdrew my business from Mirken and Prusser," David said. "I believe I told you that I wanted you to do my campaign. I still do. That's why I'm calling." He paused. "I'd like to offer you the job if you're still interested and I'm hoping you haven't committed your time and talents to another firm. Am I too late?"

Margo was almost numb. "You still want me?" she said in a small voice.

"I do." David closed his eyes at her innocently spoken words.

"I—I don't know what to say, Mr. Blackshear. I will be looking for another job but I haven't begun to . . ."

"David."

"What?"

"We agreed on first names, remember?"

"Oh, yes," Margo answered, her head swirling with questions. *Why does he want me?* she wondered. Old thoughts about revenge and vindictiveness crowded her brain. But deep down did she really believe that anymore? He sounds so sincere and businesslike. Could he be for real? "I'm sorry, what did you say?"

"Can we meet to discuss my proposition?"

"Proposition?" she repeated and almost laughed. *Pull it together,* she scolded herself. "Well, I don't know," she said, wondering why she didn't know. She'd love to see her initial plan to fruition. She'd been excited about it and she knew she could give him what he wanted.

Feeling her indecisiveness, David didn't give her a chance to say a flat out "no." He said, "You don't have to decide this minute, Margo. I have a contract drawn up that I'd like you to look over. I can have it delivered to you tonight and you can give me your answer after you've looked it over." He paused. "Would Friday be time enough? We can meet and discuss your answer informally over dinner if that would put you more at ease. If the answer is yes, I will be delighted. If no, I will be disappointed, but then we both would have enjoyed a harmless and I hope delicious meal together." Before she could answer he said, "I'll let you get back to your evening and I will make the arrangements for the delivery in the next hour. It's been my pleasure. Good night, Margo."

Her head was spinning as she watched the muted movie play, feeling as mystified and as shocked as Wesley Snipes as he dived for cover, missing the barrage of bullets that just killed White House Security Chief Spikings.

At his word the package was delivered before the

next hour was gone. It was just after seven thirty. Margo took several pages from the large envelope and settled down on the sofa to read. Seconds into reading she sat up straight, some of the pages sliding to the floor. She read again the opening paragraphs identifying the job in question and the compensation.

"Compensation?" she said, staring at the lottery-winning figure. After the initial shock she picked up the fallen pages and continued reading. When she finished she went to the kitchen and put the kettle on. Warm tea rolling around in her belly would take care of the queasiness, she thought. "But what am I going to do about these?" she said after a half laugh as she bent to hold her shaking legs. "Now I know the sound of knocking knees."

On Friday, Margo refused David's offer to come pick her up, preferring to meet him. It was a business meeting after all, she'd told herself. She did own a car that she kept garaged in her building and had gotten more use out of it this week than she had the past year. She drove herself to his choice of restaurants, one that she was familiar with and had always enjoyed the Indian cuisine. Being on nearby Queens Boulevard was an extra plus.

Inside, she was led to the bar where he was waiting. When he saw her he stood. Margo drew in a breath. Both times that she'd seen the man the situation hadn't called for her eyes devouring him. But he was a handsome man, though she got the impression that he thought otherwise. Some men had a way of letting you know what they thought of their good looks. David Blackshear was so unassuming. She liked looking into his almond shaped, deep dark eyes with those long jet eyelashes that uniquely shielded his thoughts when he so desired. His face was heart shaped with high cheekbones that probably spoke of undiscovered Native American heritage.

"I'm glad you decided to come, Margo," David said when she was near. He gestured to the maitre d' and they were led to a table that afforded them privacy.

When they were seated, Margo said, "I'm intrigued by your offer, David, and I'm one for satisfying my curiosity." She looked around and inhaled the aroma of spices that was synonymous with the cuisine. "Do you come here often?" she asked him.

"One of my favorites," David answered. "I try to get here frequently."

Surprised, she said, "You live so close?"

"Holliswood." His eyes glinted.

"Then, we're neighbors?"

David could see the wheels turning and he wasn't surprised. People thought that millionaires, especially the nouveau riche, had to live with pretentious glitz and glamour. Though in his community, the guy next door shoveling his walk could be the owner of a billion-dollar dot-com firm. "I'm sure you know by now who I am," he said. He plastered a big grin on his face and held up his menu close to his face, pointing at it.

Margo got the message and laughed.

"I wish they'd burn that silly picture," he said, and shrugged. "But it's theirs to do with as they will." He cocked his head. "I just want you to know that yes, I did the bit with the buying of this and that, houses that I didn't need or want but bought because I could. Spending days in one, a month in another, flying to wherever to sleep overnight in an empty mansion. It was crazy time, money protruding from every pocket." He shook his head. "I'd have clothes sent to the cleaners and they'd be returned with an envelope with cash they'd found in my pockets. Silly stuff like that."

Margo was listening intently trying to imagine the staid, intelligent man sitting across from her acting like a foolhardy kid. "Then what happened?" she asked.

"I woke up," David answered. "After a year of that nonsense, I shed those properties stopped my perpetual vacationing and became a businessman like I always wanted. I kept the house in Holliswood, which I've made almost completely over to suit me, and which I use as my main residence in the city. I have others in places where I vacation." He gave her a mock glare. "So you find that picture of me amusing, huh?"

"It's of the moment," Margo said, smiling at his discomfort. "I'm sure there are thousands of pictures just like yours." She picked up the envelope she'd brought with her. "Which reminds me. I feel like my picture should be right up there with yours given the salary I'm being offered for one little job."

Taking the envelope from her hand David put it on the vacant chair beside him. "What do you say to food before business?"

"Okay," Margo answered and opened her menu as did he. She was hungry. But more than that, she honestly felt that she could talk to David Blackshear all night, and it didn't have to be about business at all.

Surprised at how the time had flown, Margo was unprepared when after their coffee was served, David placed her envelope back on the table.

He tapped it, and after taking a sip of coffee, stared at her intently. "I don't think of it as a *little* job, Margo," David said, with emphasis. "I feel the work you're going to do for me, if you choose to take the job, will be worth every penny. And because I want you to give it your sole attention, without any worries, I've included the health insurance package like any employer would do to hold on to a valuable employee."

Never being one to mince words, thinking that direct was the best, Margo said, "Then I accept your offer, David. I like the challenge of working solo, with no one to pass judgment—other than you of course." Then she frowned, suddenly feeling a bit overwhelmed at the prospect of undertaking such a huge important project. She'd never freelanced before and now she wondered if she had what it took to put the scheme together and come out smelling sweet, with a satisfied client to boot.

He noticed her sudden hesitation. "What is it Margo," he asked quietly. "Second thoughts?"

"No, it's just there are so many entities within a firm, the talents of other professionals supporting a project as a team. I'll need . . ."

"You'll have all the resources that you require at your disposal. All you need do is ask," David said. "You've been in the business long enough to know who and what you must have to make it work. Just make your calls and don't worry about a budget."

Margo's head spun. Was she living a dream, or what? she asked herself. "Yes," she said. "I have contacts."

"What about Monday for a start date?" He'd signaled for the check and it was brought. So soon, David thought, wishing that he could extend the evening. She was so easy to talk to and he yearned to know more about her. It seemed that during dinner he'd been the one giving information. He just realized that other than her revelation that she lived in an apartment building that had gone co-op and the fact that she was a product of New York University, he knew little else. Had there ever been anyone serious? Was she seeing someone? No rings on the appropriate finger attested to that fact and he felt relieved. He saw the flicker of her lashes and the slight droop of her shoulders. "No good?" he asked.

"Oh, no, Monday's fine," Margo replied, hating to waste two days, her thoughts already in gear for the campaign she planned. The thought of working again had given her a rush. She'd entwined her hands and her thumbs were rapidly going circle over circle.

"Then what is it? You're disturbed about something." Now how would he know that? David asked himself. He'd noticed that little habit of frustration in her office. Or was it nerves because of him?

"I was thinking that I've already done quite a bit sight unseen of your product. I would very much like to visit the shop in Brooklyn, get hands-on." Her thumbs stilled. "If you will give me directions and alert your staff of my coming, that would be a great start for me."

"Tomorrow's Saturday," David said, but he was having a difficult time breathing easy. He'd thought that Monday was just too long to wait to see her again. He didn't know how he'd gotten this far into the evening without coming off sounding like a complete idiot. Her voice was mesmerizing with its deep inflections when she was excited about a point she was making. "I'm not a taskmaster, Margo. Don't you want time to catch your breath or get ready for that big weekend date?"

A smile flitted across her generous mouth as she answered. "I've had a week and four days to get it together David, and no I'm not seeing anyone if that's what you're asking. So no big date tomorrow or in the foreseeable future." Date? What was that? she mused to herself. She probably would be a disaster trying to make flirty conversation. She gave him a direct look. "But I can understand if you're tied up weekends."

Returning her stare and tiny smile, David said, "My

weekends are my own if that's what you're asking." He added, "For the foreseeable future."

A sense of warmth tingled Margo and it wasn't from the one glass of pinot grigio she'd had earlier during dinner. That feeling was long gone. "Then you won't mind if I start tomorrow?"

They were outside now in the parking lot and he was walking her to her black, late model Mazda. "Not at all," David said. "It's my habit to get there at least by noon. If you'd like I can pick you up and we can drive to Brooklyn Heights together. It wouldn't be a problem." He saw her hesitation. "Margo, we live less than a mile apart, practically neighbors. We'll be in the shop for the better part of a day working and when we're finished we come home. What's wrong in traveling together, at least tomorrow?" He shrugged. "Other days you can come on your own if you prefer."

She opened the car door and before getting inside, she said, "Okay, David. I'll be waiting outside at eleven. Is that good?"

"Perfect," he said. "I'll be there."

David watched her pull out of the parking lot and head east on Queens Boulevard before walking to his own car. His head was filled with thoughts of Margo Sterling. She was more than he'd dreamed she would be. He'd only seen the outside of her and now he'd seen more of what was on the inside. She was hardworking, striving to make it in her dog-eat-dog world. She'd had her lumps and they'd thrown her for a loop. But with his offer she was all too ready to eagerly jump into the fray again. He could see it in her eyes and sense in her attitude that she was all about work. Never once did she convey to him that in him she saw sugar plum fairies and a vat dripping with gold and jewels for the taking. She'd never once given him a come-on. But why? he asked himself. During their conversation he'd given her opportunities to show her gold-digging qualities, something he'd assumed of the woman in Penn Station a few months ago. Was she playing a game, one he'd yet to catch on to? How could he be so sure that she was genuine? he asked himself. If he pursued her and she turned out to be false—he didn't even want to dwell on that.

Margo was creaming her freshly cleansed face, staring back at the person whose eyes seemed glazed. She'd mentally slapped herself awake since she parked her car in the garage and rode up on the elevator in a stupor. Dangerous, she thought when she entered her apartment. Though the building boasted a doorman and surveillance apparatus, one always had to be vigilant, no matter the circumstances. But she remained in a euphoric state even as she prepared for bed.

All those months ago, David Blackshear had tried to pick her up, a stranger who hadn't the slightest clue as to who she was. She could have been a fugitive on the run, she mused. Now that they were acquainted he hadn't made one overt pass except for the offer of lunch the first day they'd met, which could have been a veiled opening for something more. What was wrong with that picture? she asked herself. Though she was pumped that he wanted her for her talent and brains she wondered if all her hard work over the years had made her a very dull girl. He apparently was no longer interested in her as a woman but in what she could produce for his business. She concluded that he definitely wasn't looking for revenge for her shrewish put-down that day; she'd been in his company long enough to discount that notion. Then what? She sighed and turned off the bathroom light and went into the bedroom. But soon her thoughts went from the personal to the professional and nothing but bicycles flashed across her vision before sleep claimed her.

Margo was in awe. When she first walked into Champion Wheels she tried not to show her ignorance to the friendly staff who welcomed her with smiles. She'd imagined a bicycle store of the type she'd seen as a child on Tenth Avenue in Manhattan. Her father had taken her and Kai to the shop to have the training wheels on her bicycle adjusted. She was six years old. It was a small dark place with bicycles hanging from the ceiling and lined in a row along one wall. Four people including her and Kai made it look like a crowd inside and they soon moved outside in the summer daylight where the repairs were made. Because of her dislike of scraped knees and fear of falling she'd never been as enthusiastic for bikes as Kai had been. Later, when they'd been twelve, she'd passed on a birthday gift of the popular ten speeds that everyone else had.

David was speaking and she turned to him. "I'm sorry," she said, looking at the woman standing beside him.

"I'd like you to meet my manager, Cindy Walden. Cindy, Margo Sterling."

"My pleasure," Margo said, extending her hand to the woman and returning the pleasant smile. Young, early thirties, and pretty, she wore her tinted red hair in a long, fashionable upswept ponytail and behind her stylish, rimless eyeglasses were warm, smiling brown eyes. Her handshake was firm, suddenly reassuring Margo that she was really welcome. On the ride to Brooklyn, she sensed that David was trying to put her at ease when he began talking about his workers. He said that she wouldn't meet a more cohesive or friendlier bunch of people who were looking forward to her visit. He'd been right, she thought, as she warmed to the manager's greeting.

"Same here," Cindy said. "Glad you could come today. We're generally very busy on Saturdays so you'll see a lot," she said.

David said to Margo, "Cindy knows everything and can answer all your questions about the business and then some. In a bit, she'll be back to take you around." He nodded when Cindy excused herself. He looked at Margo. "So you look surprised. Doesn't meet with your expectations?"

She looked at him. "Surely, you're joking, right?"

David tilted his head. "Why?"

Splaying her hands, Margo gestured toward the enormous store that was like an anathema to a reformed chocoholic who'd wandered into someone else's chocolate dream. The place was big, the floor holding many bicycles, some kinds she'd never seen or heard of before; road bikes, mountain bikes, hybrid bikes. She definitely had to study up on a comfort bike. The bikes she'd seen on the Web site didn't compare to the real deal and she knew she had to learn about them all. She could only imagine what a tour of the warehouse and factory would be like. She pointed to a section of floor. "Folding bikes?" she said. "Why?"

David laughed. "For people who travel on trains and planes to bike tours. Or for those who hate renting bikes on vacation and prefer the comfort of their own."

"Oh," Margo said, wondering where she'd been. Thoughts of Kai came and went as she knew that her sister would have known all about things like this. She thought of all those people whizzing by her on her walks; had they been riding a Champion Wheels product? She needed an education—fast, she thought, and was grateful that she'd be in the capable hands of Cindy Walden.

David watched her walk away, studying and touching the colorful bicycles, stopping and staring at one that brought a smile to her face, and when she turned back to him and shook her head in amazement his heart thumped wildly. Hadn't anyone ever told her about her man-killing smile, her mouth widening to show even white teeth and her eyes crinkling at the corners hinting of sweet mysteries? Cindy walked up to her and they began talking and walking around.

He watched, his eyes roaming over her perfect figure. She was dressed in comfortable black slacks with a long-sleeve, light blue pullover sweater that stopped at her waist. The V-neck was not plunging but showed just enough shape of her ample breasts to cause wonder about the rest. She'd removed a clipboard and notepad from her pouch shoulder bag and was jotting down notes as Cindy explained. Margo obviously felt his stare and she looked up with a curious glance. Their eyes locked for a moment and she bent her head to write but David saw her thumb tapping up and down on the pad.

He turned and went into his office. An unsatisfied customer of his high-end product would be arriving shortly and David meant to turn a negative into a positive. He'd learned to do that extremely well in his businesses and selling his bicycles was no different.

With knitted brows, David looked through the open blinds at the woman who'd intrigued him for months. Not counting January, this was his third encounter with her. More than ever he was determined to know her better. He already loved the package she presented but there was more to her than good looks and a brain. David had seen a few times the shadow that came and went so quickly that he was second-guessing whether it'd ever appeared. Today he'd watched her stare at the bicycles and when she'd turned to him, that same quick shadow in her eyes was but a flicker. What had she been thinking of? he wondered. Or who was it that made her look so sad in those moments? If it was up to him to chase those shadows away, so be it.

But a voice said *caution*. Only days before he'd wondered about the actions of a beautiful stranger. Now he was ready to throw caution to the wind and make her his—come hell or high water. He was ready to share all that he had, his life, with her. On what basis? A beautiful face? A hypnotizing voice? He shushed the voice.

He recalled what his brother had gone through and thoughts of a betraying woman caused bile to rise in his throat. David had seen what love could do to a man when it was snatched from him so despicably.

He stilled the voice, because no way could he have obsessed for months over a stranger only to learn that she was a mere figment. Deep down he sensed that this woman was meant to be in his life. If that meant coming to know heartache he was up for the challenge. When all was said and done he'd know whether his body had been talking, or his heart. Sooner than later, he intended to have Margo Sterling in his life.

At close to four o'clock, David and Margo left the shop that was still crowded with customers anxious to find the right bike.

Margo felt tired but exhilarated as she climbed into the car and buckled up. Her head was spinning with all that she'd learned about the world of bicycles. She'd never imagined the scope of the sport. Whenever she'd seen Lance Armstrong and others riding in the Tour de France, to her they were just so many men on identical bikes. Wrong. She smiled. She'd indeed had an education in more ways than one. To her surprise she learned of the many black cycling clubs throughout the country. Her world hadn't been such that she'd ever thought of a black man making his mark in the sport of bicycle racing. Cindy had explained much about a black man who'd become famous in the sport many years ago. Marshall W. "Major" Taylor, a nineteenth and twentieth century cycle racer, overcame racism by becoming the national American sprint champion in 1900. Though always plagued by racism he was undaunted and went on to hold several world records and for many years raced throughout Europe.

African-Americans were nearly nonexistent in the Olympic sport and thoughts of Kai being a pioneer brought a pensive smile to her lips and a funny feeling. Why lately had her dead twin been so ever present in her thoughts? Was it their milestone birthday that was drawing so near that was nagging her? What was Kai trying to tell her?

She shrugged—thoughts of David intruding. She'd had the opportunity to see another side of her employer. The man who had everything he desired was as genuine as the real McCoy, as unpretentious as anyone she'd ever met. In his tan slacks and chocolate brown shirt open at the neck he was laid back and professional. He was neither arrogant nor uppity with his workers and treated his customers willing to part with big bucks for their hobby with friendliness, humor, and down-to-earth courtesy. They all left smiling. She saw the joy on his face and the animation when he explained a particular function of a certain bike. Over sandwich lunches in his office she saw the easy camaraderie and trust in each other that he and Cindy had. She saw that his respect was high for his manager and her knowledge of the business. She settled back with a sigh and closed her eyes but opened them when David spoke.

"Tired?" he asked, glancing quickly from her back to the road.

"Mm," Margo answered with a nod. "A happy tired."

David smiled. "I'm glad," he said, taking another quick look at her. "What was that smile for a minute ago?"

"Just thinking about the whole other world I discovered." After a soft laugh she said, "You know, a bike is a bike is a bike kind of thing."

"I know exactly what you're talking about," he said. "I used to hear that a lot. But with my new campaign I hope to open a lot of eyes to the sport."

"For myself, I can't imagine zipping along at how many miles per hour?" She shook her head. "Flying on the ground," she said in amazement and shuddered. "I'll take my trike, thank you very much."

"A feeling you can't describe," David said. Then her words sank in. He said, "Your what?"

"My tricycle," Margo answered with a curious stare at him. "Why?"

"When was the last time you were on your two-wheeler?" he asked, giving her a strange look.

"I've never had one," Margo said simply.

"You what!" David was stopped at a light and he was looking at her as if she'd just materialized from thin air. "You're kidding me."

Margo laughed. "I kid you not, sir, except for exercising at the gym, I've never ridden a bicycle," she said. "Have I committed a crime?"

"Major," he said and began driving at the prompting of the annoyed motorist behind him. "This is serious stuff I'm hearing here," David said solemnly, shaking his head.

Margo sat up, her laughter dying at hearing the different tone. "What do you mean?" she asked quietly, wondering what was wrong.

"You didn't read your contract?"

"My contract?" Her voice was small.

David nodded. He pulled into a spot, yards away from her building, and parked the car. He turned to her and nodded again, a sobering look on his face. "Yes," he said, "The part about your knowing how to use the product." Her eyes widened. "It was there," he said. "I don't know why people tend to overlook the small stuff. It usually is the most important part of an agreement." He looked worried.

"But I didn't see anything like that," Margo said, her brow furrowed, trying to remember what she'd missed. Had the overwhelming salary boggled her mind that much? She turned to see a tiny smile flicker across his lips.

"David Blackshear," she said, hitting him on his arm with a balled hand. "You're lying to me."

Laughing, David caught her fist. "That's assault, lady. I can make a citizen's arrest."

"And I can keep pummeling you until you apologize for scaring me to death," Margo said, pulling away from him. She didn't realize how much she'd been alarmed. She knew that losing the job was not the only reason. Not being around him anymore she realized would be like, like . . . she couldn't even describe her sudden feeling of loss. He was like someone she'd known forever—he made her feel so comfortable; there wasn't an ounce of phoniness or arrogance one would expect from a wealthy man. He was like a friend already and she'd only been in the man's company just three times in her life. Once the job was completed there was no reason to continue seeing him. That knowledge hit her like a bomb exploding in her belly.

"Margo?"

She looked at him. "I was only teasing, Margo," he said quietly. He wanted to reach over and smooth the wayward wisps of hair from her cheek but dared not. Touching her softness would leave him feeling more deprived than he was, already suffering the effects of being so close to her all day. He'd look up from his desk and see her and Cindy laughing over something, and he'd harden as he imagined his lips covering hers until they were kiss-swollen. Over a casual lunch he'd nearly leapt out of his skin when she licked a bit of mayonnaise from the corner of her mouth, so unaware of the precarious position he was in behind his desk.

"I'm sorry if I upset you." *Does the job mean that much to her?* he wondered. Then he realized that this was her big break, her moment to shine without the backing of a huge firm. Her first freelance project was important to her and he'd made light of it. *Jerk,* he said to himself. After a moment, David said, "Would you like to learn to ride? It's not terribly hard."

Margo thought about Kai and what she would say about this: learning to ride a high-powered bicycle at damn near thirty.

David saw the shadow on her face and knew that she was thinking about whatever it was that made her sad. "Margo?"

She heard the concern in his voice and she looked at him. "Yes, I'd like to learn. It looks like fun," she said, and smiled. "Sorry for going at you like a banshee, but I'm not used to being teased." Margo laughed. "Next freelance job I'll make certain to ask about prerequisites."

Relieved that she was relaxed with him again, David said, "When would you like the first lesson?"

"Tomorrow," Margo blurted and then looked at him quickly. "No, forget that. It's Sunday. Monday will be soon enough." He was probably thinking she had no social life whatsoever. Boring!

Easily, David said, "Can't think of a better time to

learn to ride than in an empty park early on a Sunday morning. No dogs, no tykes on trikes." He smiled. "How about eight o'clock?"

"But I don't have a bike."

"I'll have Cindy deliver the perfect size for you to my house and I'll meet you here at eight." He'd watched as Cindy explained about fitting a bike and had seen Margo straddle one. He'd had to turn away from the delightful sight of her firm, tight buttocks rise and fall on the saddle.

"I'll be waiting." Margo opened the door and he stayed her hand and got out of the car. When he opened the door for her and reached for her hand, she was bemused and wondered just how long it'd been since she was on the receiving end of good manners. How long had it been since she'd been in a car with a man? Sometimes with a client it'd been her doing the driving to a restaurant or to a meeting. How out of touch she was, she was thinking as David walked with her to her building.

She saw a private service car pull up. The driver got out, opened the trunk and removed some bags while Rhonda emerged from the backseat with two more shopping bags.

Rhonda looked from the good-looking man to Margo and her eyes glinted. "Hi," she said, turning back to give the man another once-over. What she saw pleased her and she smiled at her friend. She held up her bags. "Called you to join me but you'd already gone."

Margo eyed the bags from Target and Bed Bath & Beyond and smiled. "Gateway Plaza, again?"

"It's a habit now. Besides, couldn't pass up the linen sales."

"Rhonda, this is David Blackshear. David, meet my friend, Rhonda Desmond."

Rhonda put a bag down and extended her hand.

"David," she said, "Pleased to meet you." She stared a second. "Sounds like a line, but you look familiar." She nodded toward the building. "We're neighbors? I wouldn't be surprised. Everybody runs into everyone else on weekends or in the elevator."

He didn't miss the subtle scrutiny but David smiled at the friendly woman. "You've probably seen me around. Holliswood is not so far." He looked at Margo who'd yet to establish their relationship so he left it alone. How she chose to introduce him to her friends was her business. To Margo he said, "Tomorrow at eight?"

"I'll be waiting," Margo answered.

"Ms. Desmond," David said. "My pleasure." He nodded and walked away.

"Oh, no," Rhonda murmured to his back. "All mine!" She looked at Margo who'd picked up the bags left by the driver and was walking inside the building. Rhonda followed. Once in the elevator she said, "Holding out on me honey?" Her eyes sparkled. "Where have you been keeping that dream?"

"He's my boss."

Rhonda nearly dropped her bags and sputtered when the doors opened and they exited the elevator. "I thought the jerk's name was Larry!"

Laughing, Margo said, "Pick your chin up off the floor. Larry!" She spat out the name as if a gnat had landed on her tongue. She dropped Rhonda's bags in front of her door. "No. David is my new boss. As of this morning." She unlocked her door and looked as Rhonda unlocked her door, quickly pushed all the bags inside and locked the door again.

"If you think we're going to say so-long-see-you-tomorrow on *that* note you're sadly mistaken," Rhonda said. "If you haven't eaten yet I'll whip us up something at your place. Come on, scoot, inside. Let's get this saga going. I'm ushering tomorrow and I've yet to press out my uniform."

While Margo washed up she could hear her pots rattling in the kitchen, and the smell of peppers and onions wafting her way made her mouth water. Never one to just rustle up something from whatever's in the fridge, she was amazed at people who did that and she considered it a special talent.

Over a quickie meal of hash brown potatoes, knockwurst and Caesar salad, Margo told her story while Rhonda listened, not uttering a word until she was through.

"A multimillionaire! Well, I'll be damned." She stared at Margo. "I noticed the absence of the all-important ring," she said.

Margo smiled. "You were quick. The man was in your sight for only an instant."

Rhonda smoothed back her short black hair and with a serious look said, "I told you I'm not immune to trying it again so I just happen to notice the little signs of availability." She narrowed her eyes. "So is he taken or not?"

"He says he's free for the foreseeable future," Margo answered in a droll tone.

"An available multimillionaire," Rhonda said in awe. "I wonder if he comes with strings."

"Why would you say that?" Margo asked, wondering herself. Divorced? Relationship gone bad? David Blackshear didn't give any indication that he was looking for a long-term relationship or for a wife. Could he be a workaholic like she was? she wondered. She'd read his background, the organizations he belonged to, his charitable activities. There must be women he relates to almost daily in these places who must want to put the hooks in. Why hasn't he been caught?

"I see I've set your wheels to turning," Rhonda said

as she got up to clear the table. She shook her head. "I don't know about you Margo," she said, stopping and giving her friend a stern look. "You're going to be thirty years old next week and I bet you haven't given it a thought. I bet you don't even know how it got here so fast." She scraped the bit of remaining salad into the trash. "I'm willing to bet that you're even going to pass it up without a thought and work your fanny off to give this assignment a piece of flesh."

"It's on a Saturday, Rhonda. I'll be home."

Rhonda sniffed. "So what's that got to do with anything? You were working today weren't you?" She tilted her head. "Or were you?"

Margo's cheeks flamed at her earlier thoughts about David. Helping to clean up, she said, "Working. Apparently my new employer isn't interested in anything about me except what I can do for his company."

"You think so?" Rhonda said, remembering the way the wealthy man had looked at Margo before he walked away and her friend hadn't given him a glance. When the dishwasher was humming softly, she pulled off a piece of paper towel and dried her hands. "Life is for enjoying, Margo," she said. "Don't let it pass you by."

Chapter Five

When David pulled into his driveway at close to six o'clock, after dropping off Margo, he wondered why he hadn't invited her out to dinner. He probably would have if they hadn't bumped into her neighbor. It was just as well he thought because his feelings were in overdrive and at least he'd have the rest of the night to recover in time for their meeting in the morning.

Opening the door the good smells meeting his nostrils made him realize that those sandwiches were long gone and his stomach was feeling it. Sounds coming from the kitchen told him his housekeeper was still here.

"Hey, Inez," he said, walking to the stove and lifting the pot cover. "Goulash." His stomach grumbled. "How'd you know that this would hit the spot?" The short, brown-skin woman in her mid-fifties was setting the table as he spoke.

"Did the sun come up this morning?" Inez Lyons grinned at her employer and went to get the salad out of the refrigerator and set the bowl on the table. "Iced tea, hot tea or soda?" she asked as she filled a salad plate.

"Pepsi," David said, calling to her from the bathroom as he washed up. When he returned the food was on the table and Inez had her keys in her hand ready to leave.

"Tomorrow's dinner is in the refrigerator," she said,

watching with satisfaction as David filled his plate. "If you need anything give a holler," she said.

"Good night, Inez. Enjoy your day off," David said firmly. It would be just like her to come when he called, he thought. He wished he *would* disturb her.

Inez smiled, waved and left through the kitchen back door.

David washed his few dishes and utensils and instead of leaving them on the drain board he dried and put them away. He shook his head in amazement at himself. After all these years he was still very much aware that he'd grown up without having others serve him and never took them for granted. But with his hectic schedule and the necessary dinner parties he'd had to learn to let others do for him.

It was Wesley's mother who'd put him straight and had hired Inez Lyons for him. Now, after four years, he didn't know how he'd ever done without the woman who cooked and cleaned and planned his dinner parties. She didn't want to live in the big house with him and had insisted on coming and going every day from her home in distant South Ozone Park where she lived with an elderly aunt. Once during a much heralded impending snow storm forecast, David canceled a planned business dinner but had forgotten to inform her. She'd arrived laden down with needed items for the party even after the snow had started to fall. Feeling foolish and guilt-ridden at her loyalty David kicked himself from there to Sunday. Six months later she was living next door. He'd built a covered pathway between their two houses and she came and went as she needed.

The doorbell rang and David went to answer it thinking that the delivery was earlier than expected. He'd called Cindy from his car telling her what he wanted and she promised the delivery would be within two hours. "Early," he said, but was surprised to see his brother and stepped aside to let him in and closed the door.

"Hey," David said, leading the way to the study. "What brings you out this way?" Jonathan lived in Park Slope not too far from his gallery and visiting his brother in Queens instead of being out on the town on a Saturday night was a surprise.

Jonathan, the same height as his brother, wore his hair in the same short cropped manner. Similar in looks with the Blackshear heart-shape face, he was different in that he sported a thin mustache. There was no denying that they were related.

"Have you eaten?" David asked. "Inez's goulash calls for seconds, which I didn't have and she made enough for five, as usual." He gave his silent sibling a quick glance. "Something up?"

Jonathan had propped one hip on a bar stool but he looked at his brother and said, "You know what, that sounds like a good idea. I think the last thing I ate today was a cheeseburger at two. Bring on the goulash." He slid off the stool and walked from the room with David following.

When the food was heated and on the table with salad, rolls and butter, David, who'd prepared a small plate of the veal stew for himself sat across from Jonathan watching him closely as he ate. "You didn't answer me," David said after a while. "Something up?"

"Yeah," Jonathan said, "Something's up. I . . ." He was interrupted by the ring of the doorbell.

"Put a pin in that," David said with a frown. "Be right back." He looked with satisfaction at the new sky blue bicycle Cindy had selected, tipped his employee who'd brought it and closed the door, leaving the bike propped up against the hall wall.

In the kitchen he said, "Sorry about that. Bike delivery. What were you saying, man?"

"A delivery at the house?" Jonathan frowned. "Must be something special."

"It's for Margo," David answered. "We're going riding tomorrow."

Jonathan raised a brow. "Is that a fact?"'

"It's for the campaign," David said impatiently. "She doesn't know how to ride and I thought she'd get a better grasp of things if she learned."

"Oh, I see," Jonathan said with a small smile, but it didn't reach his eyes. He said softly, "Is she the woman you wanted to find, David? Really?" He remembered the bleak look in his brother's eyes for the last few months. That look was gone now but replaced with something else. Doubt? he wondered.

David didn't answer right away as he finished his food, regretting now his greed and was paying for an overly full stomach. He pushed the plate away and looked at his brother. "I believe she is."

"You're not convincing me," Jonathan said. "Why?"

"You're going to push this?" David said, quietly knowing his brother had his best interest at heart.

"I am. Obviously something's bothering you about the woman otherwise we wouldn't be having this conversation."

David thought about the moment he'd seen her in Pearsall's office and his world started spinning. "I guess I didn't know how I'd react if I ever found her," he said. "That day, after she dissed me, I should have gotten her out of my mind. Just forgot about her kind who wouldn't give a blue collar worker the time of day. You know, the woman holding out and praying that a big fish would come her way; that fairy-tale Prince Charming girls are taught to dream about." He paused, while remembering. "I could have chalked it up, said oh, well, and continued to date myself silly with all the available women who grin up in my face everywhere I go." He threw his brother a look. "You know exactly what I'm talking about." When Jonathan grimaced and nodded, he continued. "But, as you and Wesley know, I couldn't get her out of my mind. She could've been the biggest gold-digger known to man yet in an instant she'd gotten under my skin so bad I couldn't be with another woman without seeing her face."

"You had it worse than I thought," Jonathan said. "So, is she?"

"What?"

"Only after your money and not you."

David shrugged. "That's it," he said, giving Jonathan a blank look. "She's not that woman who turned up her nose. She actually apologized for her behavior that day. Called it rude. In her office she was even willing to turn the job over to someone else if it made me uncomfortable being around her."

"You're right. Doesn't sound like the same Penn Station woman," Jonathan agreed.

"It's a mystery." David rested his elbows on the table and dropped his chin into his clasped fists and stared at his brother. "She seems to be all about work. Shows no interest in me as a man. I think she was actually annoyed when I invited her to lunch and she refused. She didn't even want to meet over dinner to discuss our business deal. Drove herself to the restaurant so it wouldn't seem like a date."

Jonathan smiled. "Strange. Doesn't sound like a woman who'd bark like a dog on command and jump through hoops to snag a wealthy brother. Appears that she wants to do her job and move on to the next challenge."

"Exactly," David said, relieved that he was being understood. "I was beginning to think that I was on the wrong page." He stared at Jonathan. "Do you think it's all a game, one I haven't caught on to?"

"What? As in another way of playing hard to get?"

"Something like that."

Jonathan shook his head. "Doesn't sound that way from what you've said," he replied thoughtfully. "More like she's intimidated by what she's stumbled into. As though she's trying to stay focused so she can do her best." He tilted his head. "*You're* the distraction."

Feeling a weight drop from his shoulders David sat back in his chair. Maybe he was trying too hard, suspicious of every little uttered word or unexplained nuances of expression. He already knew that he was going to do his damnedest not to lose Margo Sterling again, but in doing so he was really scaring her away. Why, she'd probably run like crazy as far away as she could get once the job was finished, he thought. His brother was probably right. She could actually be afraid of him.

"Feel better?" Jonathan said as he observed the relaxed shoulders.

David nodded. "Actually, yes. Thanks for the insight."

"Not a problem," Jonathan answered. He got up and cleared their plates from the table.

"I'll take care of those later," David said, gesturing for Jonathan to follow him from the kitchen. In the study, he went to the bar and reached for a bottle of Hennessy VSOP. At Jonathan's nod, he poured two glasses and gave him one. "Your turn," he said.

Jonathan knew exactly what David meant. Before the arrival of the bike and the turn of conversation he'd been about to say what was on his mind. "I'm going away for a week or two," he said. "Venezuela."

"There are problems with that?" David asked. It wasn't so unusual for Jonathan to travel hither and yon to capture the glorious photographs for which he'd become famous. It was expected to find his beautiful pictures in *National Geographic* and other respected world-known publications. As David had done with his bicycles, Jonathan would dabble in his own hobby of picture taking while working as a struggling lawyer in the criminal justice system. But since David's windfall had become his brother's, Jonathan was able to use his gift of millions to turn his hobby into his career.

"It's Valeria," Jonathan said, sipping from his glass and savoring the nip of the amber liquid as it slid down his throat.

"As in the caterer?" David asked quietly. So there was something there, he thought, as the image of a beautiful woman crossed his mind.

"Yes. Valeria Kimball," Jonathan replied, watching his brother. "You suspected?"

"Sorta, yes," David replied carefully.

"I've seen her a few times." Jonathan rubbed his forehead and then stared at the man who was watching him so closely. "This is the first relationship that I've wanted to be serious about in six years. Since Cynthia."

The look in his eyes was hidden by his action of staring down into his glass, so David couldn't be sure of anything. "You've been with many women since then," David replied. "Are you so sure this is different?"

"I'm sure." Jonathan looked up. "I'm so sure that I want to ask her to accompany me."

David sputtered on a swallow. Wiping his mouth he said, "Whoa."

"I agree," Jonathan said.

"After only a few dates?"

Jonathan stared at David. "Is it any different from your wanting a woman for four months and when you've found her you're looking for a way to keep her in your life forever? You've never even had a date with her."

After the words sunk in, the brothers looked at each other and they both laughed at the absurdity of their situations.

David spoke first. "If she's all you think she is, what's two weeks of absence? Is there someone else in the picture?"

Jonathan hesitated but finally said, "There was, but she said it was finished months ago. He calls every now and then."

"Oh," David said, realizing now what was bothering his brother. He poured another drink but Jonathan refused a refill. "Cynthia dying in that jewelry store robbery six years ago wasn't your fault. She was in the wrong place at the wrong time."

"No. She was in the right place at the right time, with her lover," Jonathan spat, closing his eyes briefly in remembering that dark period. "What do you think I'm thinking? That Valeria is going to play footsie with the old boyfriend while I'm gone?"

"Aren't you?" David asked quietly.

"No."

"I think you are," David said slowly, hearing the defensive tone. "Why do you think you haven't trusted a woman in all these years?" He took a deep breath but said the words his brother had to hear. "We all grieved with you when you lost your wife, Jonathan," he said. "I was with you in the hospital that night when you learned she was pregnant but hadn't told you. We all thought that she was just waiting for the right time as women like to do."

"You know as well as I do, why. That baby wasn't mine," Jonathan said, bitterness causing his voice to go hoarse. He rubbed his forehead and closed his eyes against the memory of that day that was still so vivid. He looked at his brother and shook his head as if to clear the spidery webs clouding his brain. "That night of my birthday party when I confronted her about not wearing the jade butterfly, I couldn't accept her explanation of the color not being right." His short laugh was full of pain and anger. "Hah," he blurted. "What did I know? That tanzanite pendant she chose to wear was from her lover."

"Don't," David said, his eyes growing dark, feeling his brother's pain as he too remembered. Before Cynthia was buried they'd learned that she'd been in the jewelry store with her lover. He'd been buying her a tanzanite bracelet to match the pendant he'd bought for her. Her boss, and lover, who'd been standing beside her, had been killed in the same hail of bullets. David remembered clearly the surviving store clerk's account to the police of who had been in the store and why.

David had convinced Jonathan to attend the funeral for the sake of their parents, who had been devastated by Cynthia's death. They, like everyone else, had loved the beautiful, intelligent woman. When she walked into a room she owned it as if she were an African queen. It was weeks later that they were told the truth. He'd watched at the grave site, as Jonathan tossed the tanzanite jewelry, the jade butterfly, and any other costly jewel that he hadn't bought for her, onto the flower-draped casket.

Jonathan looked bleakly at David. "The baby wasn't mine," he repeated.

David's lips thinned. "You'll never know that." Cynthia's infidelity had devastated Jonathan, but news of the baby had been a shocker. The doctor had dropped a bombshell without being aware of the import of the news.

"I wanted to know," Jonathan whispered. He stared at David. "I never told you but I always wanted to know. Before I left the hospital that night I saw that doctor. I wanted tests."

David raised a brow.

"It eats me up sometimes that I could have had a son." He nodded at David's surprised look. "Weeks later I found out. It would've been a boy and it wasn't mine."

"Man," David said softly.

Jonathan grunted in disgust. "What kind of man wouldn't know that his wife was three months pregnant? We lived together, made love and I didn't suspect a damned thing? Was I so into myself and my job that I couldn't tell whether my own wife was carrying a child? What did I do that drove her to start an affair?"

"Only Cynthia knew what was in her mind, Jonathan," David said wearily. He'd been as flabbergasted as everyone else. Cynthia had played the part of the deceiving wife well, he thought, because he sure as hell didn't suspect she was cutting out on her husband. "What happened happened. You have to move on. If you have strong feelings for Valeria, don't blow it by letting your past get in the way of starting something good."

Jonathan released the glass he'd been playing with. "I'm scared as hell, David," he said somberly. "I have feelings for this woman, as strong as those that I had for Cynthia. Maybe more. What if I mess up again? What did I do wrong with Cynthia that I might repeat with Valeria? I don't think I could go through that a second time."

"How the hell do you know that *you* did anything wrong?" David said. "Cynthia is not here for you to give the third degree. You can't bring that baggage into a relationship with Valeria either. It wouldn't be fair to her."

"Just like you can't bring baggage into a relationship with Margo," Jonathan said. He knew it was his own dead wife's actions that had soured David on women.

David looked taken aback and then gave his brother a rueful smile. "You're right."

Jonathan stood and smiled. As he walked toward the front door, shaking his head, he said, "Aren't we a pair? Guess only time will tell whose advice was the best, Brother."

David was double-parked outside Margo's building at five minutes before eight, two bicycles anchored in the back of a small SUV. After his brother had left last night he thought about what he'd said about intimidating Margo. He promised that he'd look for those signs because he sure as hell wasn't going to be the one to chase her out of his life. Not now. Not before he realized her true feelings—and his. When he saw her coming he pushed away from the car and his eyes widened in amazement as she neared. He couldn't stop the big grin that splashed across his face but held on to the laugh that was caught in his throat.

"Good morning, Margo," he managed.

Margo stopped and stared. She felt the flush in her face and wondered what she'd done so hilarious that he could hardly contain his laughter. "What is so funny, David Blackshear?" she said, stopping in front of him with her arms folded.

Unable to contain himself any longer, the pent-up laughter burst from David in a whoosh. "Margo," he said, "biking is not a contact sport."

"It is if the ground rises up to meet my behind," she said indignantly. She looked down at herself. "What's wrong with me?" She was wearing long khaki pants, heavy socks and sturdy boots. Over a long-sleeve shirt she was wearing a tan leather vest. On her hands were tan leather gloves.

"Nothing, except you're going to burn up before we're through. You're dressed for a nippy fall week-long bike tour in the Adirondacks." David smiled and reached inside the backseat of the car and pulled out a helmet. "This is all you need for protection." After putting it on her head and adjusting it, he stepped back with a satisfied murmur. "It's the correct size," he said, and then removed it, tossing it back inside the car. Margo hadn't uttered a word and when he looked at her again he could have kicked himself. She was embarrassed. *Careful, David,* he told himself.

"I'm sorry if I laughed at you," he said and stuck out a hand. "Forgiven?"

Understanding a veteran cyclist's humor in the situation, Margo smiled and took his hand. "Forgiven," she said.

Five hours after they'd arrived at the park, David was resting on a bench, exhausted. He shook his head in awe, disbelief covering his face. "Margo Sterling, you are something else," he said, his voice filled with admiration. She'd disappeared again leaving him panting on the bench.

The first two hours had been rough, David trying to get Margo to get over her fear of falling, and learning to balance. After strapping her wide-leg pants to keep them from impeding her pedaling and watching her adjust her helmet, he could feel her apprehension but saw her determination. Once she'd learned to balance the low-powered machine he'd selected for her he saw the fear in her subside and he felt encouraged. She'd fallen twice when she stopped short when applying the hand brakes but she swore and climbed right back on. He saw a light blue and white helmet in the distance and watched as she pumped her way toward him. The movement of her legs and hips affected him the same way it'd done earlier when he was following behind her. He'd hardened and stayed that way until he drew his eyes away from her and began riding alongside her.

Margo could see David sitting with his long legs stretched out, arms folded across his chest as he watched her approach. Even from where she was she could see the proud expression he wore and her heart swelled at his approval of her progress. He'd dressed in black bike shorts and a black short-sleeve spandex shirt that hugged his body. The gold and black helmet that rested on the bench beside him matched his shiny, high-powered black bicycle. When he was showing her the mechanics of her bicycle and demonstrated mounting and dismounting, she found it hard to keep her eyes from straying to places where the sun didn't shine. He had strong muscular legs and she could see the ripples beneath his shirt and the strength in his arms. His firm butt moving back and forth had sent her thoughts everywhere but where they should have been, reminding her that it'd been more than three years since she'd ran her hands over a man's derriere.

"Hi," David said, camouflaging his telltale feelings with his helmet. He willed his body to behave as he watched her dismount and he swallowed as her rump rose and fell inches away from him. "Had enough for one day?"

Margo parked the bike and plopped down beside him. "Yes," she said breathless, looking at him with a big smile. "You?"

David nodded, inhaling her musky scent of perspiration and summer breezes. He felt himself rising and moved, adjusting his body away from her. "For now," he said.

She sat back against the bench and breathed deep, exhaling slowly. She stretched her arms high up in the air and wriggled her shoulders. "Umm," she said. "That feels good."

He couldn't take his eyes from her. She'd ditched the leather vest and the gloves hours ago and had rolled up the sleeves of her shirt. The neck was unbuttoned and he watched her heaving breasts strain against the thin material. She was damp with perspiration and her long hair had come loose and little tendrils clung to her neck. Steeling himself from reaching over to whisk them away, David swallowed.

Margo took another deep breath and then turned to him. "I've had a grand time, David," she said. "Thanks. I've never had an experience like this." She looked away from him and gave the bicycle a strange look. "Takes you places, doesn't it?" she murmured.

He had the oddest sense that those words were meant for someone else, they were spoken so softly. But when she looked at him again that feeling was gone as she smiled and said, "I'm starved."

"You said the right words and I know just the place to go to cure our hunger pains." He stood and held out his hand, pulling her up. "You're really starved, huh?"

"Famished." Margo felt the strength in his hands and

was hard put to release him. She had the same thoughts she'd had earlier about his derriere; it'd been a long time since she'd felt the strength in a man's hands. "Lead the way," she said softly.

They mounted their bikes and rode slowly side by side out of the park and to the car where David strapped them on the SUV. When he climbed in beside her, he smiled at the relaxed woman who was nothing like the person he'd met over a week ago. She was resting with her eyes closed, a tiny smile on her lips. She looked content. His heart swelling, he drove away, his mind going a mile a minute, wondering what his next move was going to be. Yet another meeting with her and he was convinced that he was right. He wanted her in his life.

Margo opened her eyes when ten minutes later David stopped the car, wondering what restaurant he'd gotten to so quickly. She could have easily done with a Big Mac, she was so hungry. Tea and toast at seven this morning with a glass of apple juice was hardly enough to have sustained her through the vigorous exercise she'd done. She'd no idea that she would have willingly stayed on a bicycle for so many hours. Her body was paying the price for her foray into a world she'd never envisioned was so much fun, her limbs balking whenever she moved them.

The car was parked in a driveway beside a huge, two-story brick mansion-like structure. She'd driven by some of the homes in her own area of Jamaica Estates and had been through Holliswood going here or there, but never had the opportunity to visit any of the houses since she didn't know a soul who lived in one of the pricey properties. "Your home?" she asked.

"Yes," David said, watching her closely. "Do you mind?"

Thinking about that, Margo answered slowly, "No,"

and then smiled at the serious look on his face. She thought he looked uncomfortable waiting for her response. She'd never seen him when he wasn't so sure of himself. "As long as you have food," she said, wanting to put him at ease.

"I have food," David said, unbuckling himself and getting out of the car.

She hopped down very gingerly and groaned. "Ouch," she said as she sought support against the vehicle.

David came around grinning widely at her inability to walk. "Rubber legs, huh?" he said, catching her arm.

Margo nodded. "Why didn't you warn me?" she said, grateful for the support of his arm as they walked toward the house. "A gym bike it definitely is not."

"No, it isn't," David agreed solemnly. He unlocked the door, pushed it open and let her lean on him as they walked inside.

Stopping, Margo looked down the long wide hallway. Straight ahead and to the left was a stairway leading to the upper floor. Just ahead was what she could see of the kitchen and to her right was a living room. To the left was a large formal dining room. With the exception of where she was standing in the foyer all the floors were hardwood covered with area rugs. She followed David down the hall, her rubber-soled boots hardly making a sound over the gray stone flooring.

David inclined his head toward a room off the kitchen. "In there is everything you need to freshen up," he said. "I'm going to do the same upstairs and then I'll get us fed." He held back the grin as she nodded and walked slowly in the direction of the bathroom. He left, taking the stairs two at a time.

Margo opened the door and, taken aback, wondered if she was in a spa. "Strange place for the master bath," she murmured, looking over the spacious room. There was a whirlpool on the far wall. A stand-up glass block shower to the left, the toilet and double sink to the right and next to the whirlpool was a six-foot rack filled with fluffy towels in a rainbow of colors, and an assortment of perfumed soaps and lotions. The whirlpool looked so inviting that her body ached to be soothed and she fought the feeling of turning on the jets and hopping in. Instead, she indulged herself in stripping, washing like a bird at one of the sinks, and luxuriated in toweling herself dry with a soft baby pink towel. Tossing the linen on a hamper she selected a mango-scented lotion and lathered her body. Feeling invigorated she gave the room another once-over before leaving, admiring the polished and gleaming stainless steel fixtures amidst the soft gray ceramic appointments. The tile floor was done in huge squares of maroon and light gray, matching the smaller tiles on the lower half of the walls. She saw with whimsy that the design behind the whirlpool resembled a set of numbers and realized that her employer had a sense of humor. She left the room and was met with mouthwatering smells from the nearby kitchen.

David was setting the table and when he saw her coming popped the biscuits into the microwave. "Hi, take a seat. Everything's ready." He removed the bread and put the dish on the table. "Find everything you needed?" he asked, getting a whiff of the fruity scent of her skin as she passed by him. She'd tied back her hair but stray strands fell loosely on her cheeks.

"You're kidding, right?" Margo said. "I was tempted to dive into your whirlpool and you'd not have seen me for the rest of the day," she said. She looked at him. "Why did you put the master bath on this floor?" she asked.

"That's an extra bath," David said. "The master's off my bedroom upstairs."

"Oh." Margo was properly embarrassed wondering why she couldn't have realized that. His money could buy him as many master baths as he wanted. "Just wondered," she said, coughing to hide her faux pas.

"There's no need to feel funny for asking, Margo," David said, observing her discomfort. "I told you I liked the area and made living here as comfortable as I could. The house was almost rebuilt from its original design." He took a butter dish from the refrigerator and set it on the table. "And the whirlpool is there to be used," he said. "Anytime."

Margo could feel her color rise. "I'll make a note of that," she said.

He wondered if she was suddenly remembering his wealth and it was making her uncomfortable. Her reaction was not what he would have expected from someone who aspired to putting the hooks into a multimillionaire. Feeling encouraged about who she was, he turned his attention to the food.

"I thought you were famished," he said, removing the covers from the dishes, letting smells waft through the air.

Her stomach groaned and she looked up, giving him a sheepish smile. "There's your answer," she said.

"Dig in," David said, helping himself to the spread Inez had prepared for his Sunday dinner.

Margo eyed her favorite, candied yams, with the glaze so thick her mouth watered and she did as invited and dug in. Although out of her element in the kitchen, but a critic of fine cooking, she had no problem in recognizing carefully prepared food. She helped herself to generous portions of the roast leg of lamb, spinach and onions, and guiltily, a bit more of the yams. She slathered butter on a hot biscuit and bit into it, the flaky dough melting in her mouth. "Um," she said, tasting the

rest of the food. "Delicious." Between bites of the succulent lamb, she said, "I didn't take that long in the
bathroom, did I?"

"Sorry?" David looked at her inquisitively.

"For you to whip up a *lunch* like this," she said with
emphasis, waving a fork at the bountiful table.

He laughed. "Even if you stayed in there for a day
and a half I couldn't have done any of this," David said,
amused. "But I can put together a mean peanut butter
and jelly sandwich." He smiled. "Even make it with
marshmallow when the urge hits."

She raised her brow. "A brother who can't cook?" she
said.

"You found him," David said between bites of the
herbed roast lamb, giving her a playful wink. "Even
after night school I'd come home and try to do the right
thing by eating healthily, but most times my efforts had
me swearing off food for life," he joked. "So I mastered
the art of building the sandwich." He grew serious.
"Ever have an asparagus and cheddar cheese on toast?"

"You're joking," Margo said skeptically, and then noticed his laughing eyes. She laughed and he joined her.
"Well, whoever made this can cook my yams anytime.
They're the best I've eaten," she said, finishing them off.
"Reminds me of Rhonda's cooking and she can deal in
the kitchen. Guess I'm like my mother," she said with
a shake of her head. "She can't cook either."

"Either?" David said with surprise. "You can't
cook?"

"Why does that amaze you?" Margo asked. "Another
prerequisite that was in the small print?" she said with
a mock-horror look.

David smiled and said, "No. No small print." He
shrugged. "Just thought that modern sisters had all that
together. You know, doing it all. Superwomen, my mother

calls them. They have the high-powered job, the wardrobe to go with it, the gym, able to prepare the gourmet meals to impress and to entice." He lifted another shoulder. "Thought that was what women were about these days, presenting the whole dynamite package."

Pondering his words as they applied to her, she raised her eyes to his. "That was me until two weeks ago," she said quietly. "All except for the gourmet cooking."

He noticed the somber tone and the shadow that crossed her face and he knew what she was thinking. "You're still that woman Margo. Only you're your own boss now." To lighten her mood he said, "Who knows, cooking school may be in your future yet."

"No, I don't think so," Margo said, shuddering at the thought of her blundering about the kitchen. "I think I'll be content to find someone to do this, just like you did. Any chance of sharing your secret?"

"Sure. Inez Lyons, my housekeeper," David said. "Sunday's she's off but she always leaves something in case I'm eating in."

Margo flushed. "You just fed me your Sunday dinner?"

David laughed. "Don't be so upset. There's still enough left for a crowd. Inez knows that sometimes my brother and my friend drop by. And they're always looking for a meal." He threw her a look. "If you're really that upset about taking food from my mouth you can make amends."

She looked around and spotted the appliance. "No problem," she said, "I know my way around a dishwasher. Cleanup's on me." She saw his frown. "Okay, then cleanup's not on me. What are my dues?"

"Dinner out tomorrow."

Margo looked at him. "As in a date?" Suddenly the lightheartedness in the room somehow changed.

"As in a date," David echoed and watched for her reaction. He was ready for her refusal even though he'd never seen her so relaxed around him. He waited.

She mulled over his request then finally said, "You're my boss."

"Employer."

"Semantics don't change the way things are," Margo said simply.

"I know," David said, his impatience showing. "Am I to believe that in the months we'll be working with each other that dinner out together is verboten? Out of the question?"

"But, it's not necessary," Margo said.

David's eyes darkened as he stared at her. "Necessary?"

"I mean that whatever we have to discuss about the campaign can be done over the phone, e-mail or a quick meeting or two. I pretty much know where I'm going with this."

"Am I that hard to take that we can't share a meal unless we're discussing your job?" David asked pointedly.

"It's not professional," she finally said. "It would be like dating Lawrence Pearsall!" she exclaimed and with the thought, let the laugh erupt. She saw his expression and her humor grew. "Oh, please excuse me, David," she said, trying to rein in the laughter. "I didn't mean to imply that you were anything like that that . . ."

"Idiot," David supplied, glad that she could laugh at the situation but miffed that she wouldn't eat out with him unless it was about business. Maybe Jonathan was right, he thought. She was intimidated or was plainly just not interested in him as a man. Yet he had to wonder about the last few hours they'd spent together and her uninhibited demeanor, even agreeing to have lunch in his home. So what was that all about? he asked himself. He answered his own question when it hit him that this morning had been all about work; she'd been learning all about the product she was going to produce.

"Yes," Margo agreed with his assessment of her former boss but she was watching his face harden. What could he be thinking? "What's wrong, David?" Margo asked.

"Nothing," he replied as he watched her, still surprised at the conclusion he'd reached. "I think I've worked you long enough for one day," he said as he began clearing the table. "Time to get you home." When he stood, he looked down at her. He said easily, "Planning to work tonight too?"

Where was all this coming from? Margo asked herself. He'd done an about-face on her in a split second. All because she wanted to keep their relationship professional? She stood and helped him clear the table. "No, I hadn't planned on it," she said tersely. "Why?"

He shrugged. "Just wondered when you spent time doing for Margo," David answered. "That's all."

"I've had plenty of time lately doing what I have to do for me," Margo replied. "I thought the whole idea of freelancing was to make your time work for you at your convenience. Am I wrong about that?"

"You're right on the money," David remarked drolly. "On target." The food had been put away and the dishes stacked in the dishwasher. He looked around. "I think that about does it," he said. "If you're ready, I'll drive you home now. Just give me a second to unhook my bike and put it in the garage."

Margo was outside watching him work swiftly in unhinging the bike and disappearing with it. She realized that he left the borrowed blue and white one in place. He was back in seconds and when he beeped the remote, without waiting for him she hopped up into the car.

"I think I know the bike pretty well, David," she said. "I won't need it anymore."

David looked at her and then turned away, concentrating on maneuvering onto the street. "Just consider it as a tool for your on-the-job training," he said, knowing that if the word "gift" left his mouth he'd get an instant negative response. "Is there a problem keeping it in your apartment?"

"No."

"Then it's yours to keep." He saw her quick look. "When the promotion is finished you can return it." He turned away. "There's always a kid out there who'd be happy getting a used bicycle from Champion Wheels. Agreed?"

"That'll be fine," she answered.

The ten minute drive to her house was made in silence as each was lost in thought.

At the curb in front of her building, she took the bicycle from David. "Thanks, I'll take good care of it," she said. "And thanks for the lessons," she added. Before leaving him she said, "I'll need a few days to pull everything together but should you want to check on things I'll be here."

"Check on things?" David gave her a hard look. "As with all my associates I hired you because you know what you're doing, Margo," David said. "If I thought you had any doubts about your talent we wouldn't be having this conversation, would we?"

"Well, I guess you're right about that, David," Margo said, her lips tightening, as she grasped the handlebars of the bicycle. "Then just call as you will," she said stiffly, "I'll still be here." She turned and walked away.

David left before she entered the building, driving

with a little more speed than he should have. He slowed down to avoid being stopped by the patrolling private security force. When he reached home he knew he'd ended a perfect day on a sour note. In the shower he racked his brain as to what went wrong with the way he'd approached her, and why she'd been so turned off, but he came up blank. Margo was an enigma.

He wondered if he was ignoring his sixth sense to danger he'd developed during the last five years. If that danger was Margo Sterling, then he was lost. He could no more ignore her than he could ignore the cardinal rule of survival. *Save yourself.*

Chapter Six

Margo found a place for the bicycle along a wall in her office and before leaving the room glanced at it in awe, a feeling she'd had for most of the day. Never had she imagined that she would take pride in being able to master the machine or that she would have liked it. She really liked it! She eyed the picture of a grinning Kai on her skateboard, and Margo sat down at the desk, a smile touching her lips. "Takes you places, doesn't it?" she murmured in a pleasantly surprised voice.

Now she thought she knew something of the feelings that her sister experienced zipping around on those daredevil boards, defying gravity as she flew in the air. Margo could see Kai's long black hair flying every which way in the wind, shrieks of laughter left behind in her wake. It was that way with the in-line skates, the ice skates and the bicycles. It was the same when their parents took them on a skiing vacation and Margo had deferred, leaving the skiing to her family. She'd watched her parents and sister come sliding down that steep hill along with a dozen other people, all of them smiling and yelling like it was the most joyous activity in the world. Margo had felt safer and content sliding down a snow-covered baby-size hill on a round tin pan, close to the ground with not too far to fall at all. Now she knew.

As if with no will of her own Margo picked up her

pen and sketch pad and started drawing. The three friends emerged, Kai, Antoine and Chloe. Her pen flew across the pages drawing and writing. She always wrote rough and then typed the completed text in the computer, saving it to disk. Before she knew it hours had passed and Margo dropped the pen and sat back, staring with tired satisfaction at what she'd created. Another adventure with the crew. A bicycle adventure.

A new character had insinuated his way into the life of the three friends. A rich kid named Dixon who loved Kai but gave Chloe grief. "Hmm," Margo said. "I wonder how that happened." She stood and stretched her weary limbs, a frown puckering her brow as she closed the pad and left the room. "Dixon. David Blackshear. Hmm."

By the following Thursday, Margo had completed as much as she could without the assistance from some print people. Those resources were needed now and she had to clear it with her employer before engaging other talents. She called David at his home and was frustrated with the news from his housekeeper that he was out of town. She left a message and was surprised to receive a call within a half hour.

"Ms. Sterling, my name is Barbara Olivera, I'm an associate of David's and he asked me to give you all the assistance that you require while he is away."

"Oh," Margo said, taken aback. David had never mentioned a trip out of town. So that's why she hadn't heard from him, she thought. "Thanks for getting back to me so soon . . ."

"David left instructions to assist you in any way that I could, Ms. Sterling," Ms. Olivera interrupted in a brisk tone. "Now if you'll give me all the particulars, I can get started right away. Let's start with the names and numbers so I can set up their accounts."

Twenty minutes later, Margo hung up the phone, her head in a tailspin. Dizzied with the very efficient Barbara Olivera's manner and the money and resources that were already at her disposal, she could only shake her head. She knew that money talked, having been around the corporate world for many years, but she'd no idea how inconsequential it was to the wealthy. No bandying or hemming or hawing over salaries or the expense in getting needed resources. That adage "money talks" rang true.

Satisfied with all she'd accomplished in four days, Margo decided to come up for air. Her bones were stiff at the inactivity all this week and she was paying for it. She hadn't even taken the time to go for her morning walks, giving her all to designing the layout for the print ads. She laughed aloud when she rubbed her behind. One thing she was going to stress in the sidebar was to find the correct size saddle for that part of the anatomy. One thing she did find out in her research was that women's saddles were normally wider than usual. "Hmm, wonder what they're trying to say?" she chuckled softly.

She dressed comfortably in a short-sleeve navy T-shirt tucked into black spandex workout pants, remembering how David had to tie down her flapping pant legs, and knew a shopping trip for proper biking apparel was in order. She wore sensible soft black sport shoes—never sneakers—as Cindy had admonished, and had pinned her hair securely on top of her head. Snapping on her fanny pouch and retrieving her sunglasses, she headed to the door with her bicycle. Borrowed bicycle, she corrected. She'd miss it when the time came but already knew she'd be buying another one. A Champion Wheels was in her life to stay.

The ride to the park was her warm-up exercises but once inside she let herself fly. It was not yet noon and she practically had the lanes to herself. She zipped along feeling the warm summer breezes on her skin and she could feel the big grin on her face as she sailed along. She couldn't help but ask herself where this sport had been all her life. Oh, what she had missed she thought. Such a feeling of being unfettered!

She was resting on a bench after tiring herself to the point of exhaustion and thirst. She'd forgotten to fill the plastic water bottle that was attached to the frame and would have given a mint for a drop. The thought made her smile and as she unbuckled her helmet to lay it beside her on the bench, she turned to see a handsome brother resting on his bike, grinning at her.

"Water?" the smiling stranger said.

Margo looked at the man who was half astride a bicycle that she recognized immediately as a Champion Wheels product. She felt a kinship with anyone who had the good sense to own the high-end product that she was promoting.

"You couldn't be more right," she said, smiling up at the man. "I see *you're* prepared." He was holding his half-full plastic bottle in his hand. She waved at her empty one. "Forgot to fill it."

"You look like you're about to perish." He reached inside a black leather pouch and pulled out a bottle of Poland Spring water. "I always carry more than I need," he said. "You're welcome to quench your thirst. Please don't say no," he added firmly. "I'm not going to be responsible for refusing to come to the aid of a damsel in distress." He tapped his cell phone clipped on his hip. "It's call 911 or drink." He held out the bottle.

Good sense and caution made Margo examine the bottle with its unbroken seal and she took it.

The man noticed her quiet inspection and smiled. "You're right to be suspicious in this day and age," he said. "It's never been opened."

Margo broke the seal and drank deeply of the refreshing liquid. More than gold she thought as the water slid down her dry throat. She had to smile because the thought reminded her of David. Wonder how much *he'd* give up for a drink of life's saving fluid? But she pushed her absent employer from her mind. *That's all he was after all,* wasn't he? Her boss?

"Thanks," she said and capped the half empty bottle. She held out her hand. "Margo Sterling."

"Zachary Dixon." He took her hand in a firm clasp and raised a brow at her sudden strange stare. "You know the name?"

"Uh, uh, no," Margo managed without bursting into laughter at the man's questioning look. "I—I just recently met someone with your surname," she said. *Are you wealthy?* she said to herself and the humor of the situation caused a tiny smile to appear but she quashed the flood of laughter that threatened. Oh, the humor in life, she thought.

"Oh, it's a fairly common name," Zachary said. He parked his bike and sat down beside her. "I see we enjoy a quality product," he said, looking at her bicycle. "I never look at anything else. Comes through for me every time, but I see yours is spanking new. First time owner?"

Owner? Margo thought. "Uh, yes. This is my first and I'm pleased. It was highly recommended," she said.

Nodding with smug satisfaction Zachary said, "You had good advice." He smiled and relaxed against the bench. "You ride here often? I've never seen you before."

"Actually I'm just beginning and I feel safer here for the time being. Not ready to give high traffic streets bike lanes a try yet."

"I've been watching you and I think you're wrong," the good-looking man said. "I wouldn't have pegged you as a beginner." He cocked his head. "You haven't done any touring?"

"Touring?"

"Yes, with a group," he replied. "It's the greatest. Hundreds of bikers with one aim. You start out on a small scale. Five miles, ten miles graduating to twenty, thirty, and sixty miles and then the granddaddy, the century. Lots of fun, good exercise, and good company."

"The century?"

"A hundred-miler."

"Sounds like fun," Margo answered, remembering the pictures of laughing groups in David's bike shop. He'd been in a lot of them and she guessed that he probably went on many tours. *Is he on one now?* she wondered.

"I know the perfect baby tour for you and it's coming up this Saturday, the twenty-eighth." Zachary slapped his knee. "Perfect," he exclaimed. "It's about fourteen miles or so, for beginners. You'd love it."

"Where?" Margo asked, very interested in a new challenge.

"In Brooklyn. We start out at Canarsie Pier. There's a mile of street biking and all the rest is clear for bikers and we wind up in the old Floyd Bennett Field. There's refreshment and entertainment before starting back. It's a great time."

"Why are you involved with beginners?" Margo asked, curious at his enthusiasm.

"I'm involved with a group of volunteers. The owner of Champion Wheels is a guy named David Blackshear," Zachary said. "I've met him once or twice and he seems like a great guy. He's always doing something for the neighborhoods around the city. Well, this year he gave his bikes to some beginners in the hopes that they'll have been introduced to a new experience in their lives. Blackshear is involved in many tours and we volunteers go along to lend support and guidance."

"Sounds like more of what the city needs," Margo said. She'd read of David's philanthropic efforts but hadn't seen biking among them.

Zachary looked puzzled. "I'm surprised that you weren't informed about the beginner's tour when you purchased your bike. The salespeople are trained to be cognizant of new riders." Dismissing the oversight, he turned to her with enthusiasm shining all over his angular face. "So what do you say about achieving your first badge by joining the tour?" Zachary said. "You'll meet a group of nice people, all ages, from teens to grandmas and grandpas."

It's my birthday, Margo thought. Her thirtieth and she was spending it alone. The milestone day would probably have come and gone had she still been employed at Mirken and Prusser. In years past she'd be swamped with work and the day would pass overlooked. Sometimes she'd come home and Rhonda would be waiting with a bottle of champagne. That would be the only observance of her natal day.

"Margo?" Zachary was waiting for her answer.

Oh, why not, Margo thought. She thought of her sister and could imagine Kai grinning and egging her on. "Okay," she said to Zachary, who nodded at her reply. "I guess I have to get my street legs somewhere some time," she said. "Where will the group be meeting and at what time?"

Margo rode home slowly and carefully, watchful of the cars zipping by her. There were no bike lanes here and she wished that there were so she'd be more assured of herself come Saturday. But one thing she'd have to get and that was a rack to anchor her bike for the drive to Brooklyn. Suddenly the excitement caught and she couldn't wait to get home to plan her very different birthday celebration.

It was hours later when Margo returned home after buying all she'd need for her new venture. She'd purchased a new biking outfit, a treat for herself. White jacket and pants with navy blue trim. While eating a salad with grilled chicken chunks she'd bought from the prepared foods section in the supermarket, the bell rang and she let her smiling neighbor in.

Rhonda looked at the meal and grunted in satisfaction. "Looks nourishing enough," she said. "At least it isn't a peanut butter and jelly sandwich." She looked up. "What's so funny?"

"Not a thing," Margo said and wondered how many times today she was going to be reminded of her employer. "What's new in the *Amsterdam News*?" she said, looking at the Black weekly Rhonda had placed on the table.

Opening it to the page she marked, Rhonda pointed to a picture and the caption. "Just that," she said.

Margo looked at a picture of David and a beautiful woman draped on his arm. David Blackshear, out on the town, the caption read. She went on to read the brief story. Apparently David was in San Francisco to complete negotiations of the buying of a building for displaced families. The government's continued involvement with its commitment of matching funds for the successful running of the operation was a major victory according to the reporter's viewpoint. Live-in staff would be provided offering needed social services, including health care that the families so badly needed.

So that's where he'd been, Margo thought, pushing the paper aside but not before taking another look at the beauty on his arm.

Rhonda saw her friend's look. "Is that his lady, do you think?" she asked.

Margo shrugged. "I have no idea," she said. "Could be."

"Well, I don't think she is," Rhonda said in a firm voice.

"Why not?" Margo finished her food and pushed the plate away.

"Because I saw the way the man looked at you last week," she said.

"Oh, really? And how was that?"

"Interested. Very interested."

"You must have been seeing things," Margo said. "He's never given me any indication that he was interested in anything other than my brain."

"He hasn't?" Rhonda was skeptical. "Not once?"

Margo twirled her thumbs. "Except that he wanted a date last Sunday, if that's what you mean."

Rhonda looked at Margo as if her friend had suddenly lost it but also noticed the nervous habit. "Yes, that's what I mean. A date?"

"Yes, but I didn't think it was appropriate. I'm working for the man for God's sake." Margo stared at the older woman. "Would you date your boss?" she said.

"Lord, no," Rhonda said, wrinkling her nose in distaste. "Besides the fact that he's separated and he's asked several times I can't get past thinking of feeling his walrus mustache all over my fine brown, delicate skin. But that's a different situation."

Margo laughed at the image. "Well, you know what I mean," she said, suddenly somber.

"No, I don't know what you mean," Rhonda answered. "You're going to be thirty years old on Saturday and what are you doing to meet that husband you told me you want someday? And the kids? They're not going to get here like that famous infant did once upon a time and long ago."

"I have time," Margo answered firmly. "Now that I can see the world beyond Mirken and Prusser maybe I'll think more about that part of my future. But it's not going to happen right away, I'll tell you. I've a business to build." She smiled. "Why, I haven't even given my company a name yet. There are contacts to make, and supplies to buy. I have a mountain of stuff to do and can't really dive into it until I finish this project for Champion Wheels."

Rhonda made a sound and rolled her eyes. "And by that time, my dear, you'll be past child-bearing age."

Margo made a face. "I intend to be established long before I'm forty, Rhonda. Where's your confidence in me?"

"I don't know where it's going but it's going fast," Rhonda answered. "Look, I know you haven't planned anything for your birthday. Why don't you let me treat you to a fancy night out? You've been talking about going back to Vong for the longest. What about it?"

Margo demurred. "I don't think so, Rhonda," she said. "I'll be sore as the devil when I get back from my tour and I'll probably be spending my birthday night soaking in the tub." Visions of luxuriating in the whirlpool in her employer's *extra* bathroom swirled in her head.

"Tour?" Rhonda looked puzzled.

"With a biking group in Brooklyn. I met this man in the park today, and . . ."

"Stop right there," Rhonda said, giving her the hand. "You met a man in the park today and you're dating him on Saturday?" Rhonda had serious doubts about Margo's frame of mind since being fired. She was worried now.

"It's not a date," Margo protested. "And don't look as if I'm ready to be committed."

"Convince me," Rhonda said, listening intently as Margo began her story. She didn't interrupt but was fascinated at the vigor and sparkle in her friend's eyes at the mention of biking. She didn't see that much enthusiasm when she talked about her new freelance situation.

"That's it," Margo said when she finished.

"Zachary Dixon, huh?" Rhonda pursed her lips. "So what else do you know about this man?" she asked. "Are you certain that there is such a group?"

"Oh, why would the man lie about something that can be easily verified," Margo answered. "It's not as if he plans to abduct me at nine o'clock in the morning in a public space with hundreds milling about."

"Stranger things have happened as you well know, Margo. I never believed you thought you lived in a vacuum." She thought of her own young daughter living a life as a single woman so far from home. Not a day went by when she didn't say a prayer for her daughter's safe comings and goings.

Margo knew what her friend was thinking. "I'll be fine, Rhonda," she said. "Don't worry." She patted her friend's hand. "Thanks for the offer of dinner but I think I'll settle for one of your famous decadent German chocolate high-riser cakes and a bottle of Bollinger's or Taittinger's. That will probably be all the celebration I could handle. What about it?"

"Oh, certainly my dear, I have a wide selection of champagne already chilling just for you," Rhonda grumbled but she smiled with relief. "I'll be over around seven. You should have soaked the knots out by then." Before she left, she gave Margo a look. "Don't think I'm not going to look this bike tour thing up on the 'Net, though." She waved at Margo who was watching her safely into her apartment before closing her door.

David was back at home in Queens by late Friday afternoon after stopping by his midtown office in the morning where he'd taken care of some business. Barbara had all the papers prepared that needed his signature for Margo's expense account. He could see that his newest associate had all her ducks in a row and he was more impressed than ever with Margo's efficiency. She knew who and what she wanted to get the job done.

In his study David sat staring at her dossier, the one Wesley had gotten for him it seemed like weeks ago. Something had been nagging him for the past few days and he was annoyed by his thoughts. Even with the women throwing themselves at him so shamelessly in San Francisco, he had thoughts about the woman he'd left behind in New York. David knew he'd been wrong in leaving her the way he had. He should have gotten in touch with her but had put it off.

Looking at the papers on his desk David figured he had a reason to make contact now though it wasn't about business. What should be so hard about calling to wish her a happy birthday? he groused thinking that she'd even take umbrage at that. Their last meeting had ended on a sour note and he'd kicked himself for going off without calling, acting like some little boy who'd gotten his pride injured. *Unlike Cynthia, she doesn't sleep where she eats,* he thought. *And isn't that a good thing?* he warred with himself. You were the one who wanted to know what her story was. So now you know, brother.

But David closed the folder without picking up the phone, telling himself that since tomorrow was her special day he'd call her then. With another thought he picked up the receiver. Minutes later a satisfied smile touched his lips. "Surely she wouldn't object to that," he muttered.

At seven thirty on Saturday morning, Margo was driving to Brooklyn's Canarsie Pier. She'd left in plenty of time so as not to miss the group that was assembling by nine o'clock. She felt strange attired in her new clothes, the shiny helmet on the seat beside her and her bicycle anchored securely. Yesterday she had to get one of the maintenance men in the building to assist her in installing the rack. She'd remembered to fill her bottle with water and had stashed an extra sixteen ounce in the pouch under the saddle. She felt so ready to tackle this new venture. "Happy birthday, Margo," she said, grinning in the mirror at herself. *This is a new year and new doings,* she thought happily.

One thought bothered her and that was that David wasn't here to share this with her. But she'd surprise him when he returned from his trip. Something Rhonda had said rang true. Yes, she did want to meet a wonderful guy and marry someday. To have children was also in her future. Since her uninitiated layoff she'd had time to think of such things. She never went anyplace to meet men and had no desire to since she'd immersed herself in her job. The relationship she'd had more than three years ago was just that, a go-nowhere relationship. She knew it was partly her fault because she had no interest at the time in slowing her career moves for serious, personal commitment. The parting had been mutual and she'd actually been glad when it was over so she could give her all to her work.

Yet when Zachary Dixon had appeared she noted that he was a handsome guy. He was pleasant and likeable. She hadn't noticed any rings so she believed that he was available and not a player. So why hadn't she looked upon him as a potential suitor? When he'd held her by the hand pulling her up off the bench there was no warm tingling sensation; nothing to indicate a spark of something to come, maybe a little romance. Nothing.

But yet when she'd felt David's touch that first day they'd met, her body had been flushed with a warmth that had surprised her. Womanly places that had been dormant for so long tingled in anticipation. Had she deprived her body for that long? she'd wondered.

And now here comes Zachary Dixon. She knew he was probably hoping that this day would turn into something more, after all, he was a man wasn't he? Otherwise why had he stopped to introduce himself and go to the trouble of this day if not for his future gain? It was his way of making a move on her. But she didn't care about seeing him other than in this capacity, bike touring. She made a mental note to convey that to him before the day was over. Margo smiled at Rhonda's finally getting the message across to an unwanted suitor and she hoped she wouldn't have that problem with Zachary.

When she pulled into the parking lot, Margo was amazed to see the crowd. Cyclists of all ages, shapes, and sizes were milling about with bicycles in a rainbow of colors. There must have been at least thirty people taking the tour from what she could see. David had *given* those bikes away? She had to learn not to appear so gauche at what rich people can do with their money.

She found a spot and parked. In minutes she was walking toward the crowd craning her neck to spot Zachary. As she walked, people greeted her with smiles and she caught the excitement that was in the air. A young woman about her age walked beside her.

"Hi, I'm Alana Montenegro." She smiled, glancing at Margo's bike. "First time, too, huh?"

Margo looked at the woman's friendly grin and sparkling black eyes. Her jet black hair was hanging loosely under a white and red helmet that matched her white bike.

"Does it show all that much?" she said, liking the woman already. Zachary had said to expect a friendly bunch.

"Uh-huh," Alana said. She tossed her head at the crowd. "But everybody here is in the same pickle, so don't feel like you're an outsider. Who's your mentor?"

"Mentor?"

"Yes, your supporter for the ride today," Alana said. "I'm in Zachary Dixon's group. He works with us out of the community center on Remsen Avenue."

"I'm here through Zachary," Margo said. "But I haven't been working with a group. I've only had the bike for a week."

Alana whistled. "Brand new," she said. "Had any street experience, yet?"

"Not that much. Just locally," Margo said, suddenly feeling apprehensive. She hadn't thought that there would be much street traffic involved.

Alana saw the look and said, "Don't worry, we'll be safe. Just stick with the group and follow the leader." She waved when she saw Zachary approaching them. "Hi."

Zachary smiled at the two women. "Hi. I see you two've met." To Margo he said, "You're going to have fun, so just relax. Alana is already a pro, so stick with her." His voice dropped. "Glad you came," he said warmly.

Margo saw the look and heard the voice and knew she'd been right. This was just the beginning for him and she made sure she would set things straight between them before too long. She and Alana waved to him as he walked away to call the group to order. She felt the excitement and was ready to see if she was just blowing wind.

The crowd was broken up into groups of eight or nine with mentors in between who were recognizable by bright orange helmets and white and orange body shirts. They set off from the pier and followed the winding exit from the parking lot onto the wide Rockaway Boulevard. They traveled for about ten blocks before they turned around and headed back the way they'd come. That had been the warm-up and now they were cycling along the Belt Parkway toward Jacob Riis Park. Margo felt a surge of energy and excitement as her legs pumped in tandem, the warm breeze tickling her nose and fanning her face. Alana rode just ahead of her and Margo wondered if she sat her bike as assuredly as the friendly woman did.

The sun was hot on her back as Margo rode but she wasn't complaining nor was she tired. She experienced nothing like she had last Sunday after she'd ridden for hours with David in Cunningham Park. When they reached their destination, just yards away from the bridge to Riis Park, they turned into the former site of Floyd Bennett Field and biked toward the administration building. There were tables and stands set up all ready for the hungry and thirsty cyclists. The refreshments were light, fresh fruit and soft drinks.

"Zachary told us to expect this," Alana said, parking her bike next to Margo's. "The real food is back at the pier after the tour. Come on, I see some friends I want you to meet."

They stayed for at least two hours eating and refreshing themselves and meeting new friends. Margo was surprised to see the people from all walks of life taking a first-time interest in cycling. There was a cycling club offering tips on safe cycling and extolling the joys of group touring. Already her brain was going like sixty planning on a sidebar piece about capturing the interest of those who've never given cycling a thought. Or it could be another ad, she thought, or a two-part commercial. She found herself gathering information from the new people she was meeting.

"You're really taking to this aren't you?" Alana said, quirking a brow at her new friend's enthusiasm. "Are you reporting or something?"

Margo laughed. "Or something," she joked, hardly ready to tell Alana how she'd gotten her shiny new bicycle. Before she knew it the time had fled and they were preparing to make the trek back to the pier where the tour would end.

It was just after one o'clock when the group turned into the parking lot of the pier. There in the picnic area, tables had been set up with an array of food and drinks. There was an ice cream stand and to beat all there was a DJ playing victory music as the cyclists entered the lot. There were spectators, family and friends of the cyclists, standing around cheering as the riders parked their bikes.

Happily tired Margo was caught up in the crowd as they milled about waiting for some announcements. Alana had gotten lost and while Margo was scanning the crowd she was surprised to see a familiar face at the table filled with merit badges. She walked over.

"Hi Cindy," she said.

The manager from Champion Wheels looked up. "Margo," she said in surprise. The two women shook hands. "You were on the tour?"

"Yes," Margo answered. "It was quite an experience."

Cindy frowned. "I didn't see your name on the list of beginners," she said.

"There was no need for it to be there," said Margo. "I only found out on Thursday about the tour from Zachary Dixon and he invited me. I'm glad he did." She noticed the frown. "Is there a problem?"

"No, except that I don't have a merit badge for you," Cindy said, really looking dismayed. "Zach should have called your name in as a last minute participant." She clucked like a mother hen that was missing one of her brood. "He knows that David is very particular about everyone being recognized."

"David?" Was he here? Margo wondered as she glanced around.

"Yes," Cindy answered. "He likes to be here to give out the badges. He almost missed this one because he'd been out of town but since he got back last night he said he'll be here." She gave her watch a worried look. "He should have been here by now." She frowned at the man who walked up to them. "Zach you should have called me about Margo being a participant," she said, clucking her tongue again.

Zachary slapped his forehead and turned to Margo. "I'm so sorry about that," he said. "I completely forgot about your badge."

"Oh, don't worry about it, Zachary," Margo said, seeing how upset he and Cindy were. She could see that they really placed a lot of importance on encouraging people. "I know what I did today and I'm proud of myself. I don't need a badge."

"I know what you did today, I was watching. You

were great," Zachary said. "So come let me give you a hug for being a trooper." He caught her by the shoulders and pulled her to his chest in a bear hug.

His hug was so exuberant that Margo's arms flung around his waist to keep her balance. Cindy laughed at the surprised expression on Margo's face. "Zach you're crushing her to death," she said. "Let her go before I have to get the medics over here." She looked at Margo who was gingerly feeling her ribs. "Are you okay, Margo? This big lug doesn't know his strength sometimes."

Margo looked up at Zachary who was smiling sheepishly. She hadn't known that the wiry man who was less than six feet wielded so much power in those slender arms.

"I'll live," she said, giving Zachary some space. "Just warn me next time."

He laughed and caught her by the hand. "I'm sorry about that," he said. "Come on, I think I owe you a treat to make up."

Margo waved to Cindy as Zachary led her toward the ice cream stand. Minutes later they were seated on a bench, she eating the gooiest sundae he could order. Alana and some other friends had joined them and they were all talking excitedly about their mean accomplishment for the day. Some were already planning the next tour, a longer one: thirty miles. Margo was caught up in the excitement and was planning right along with them. As she looked around at the diverse group she thought that a few weeks ago had she been told that she'd be sitting where she was she'd have called it the tall tale of the century. But she was loving every minute of it. Already she was devising a scheme on how to get Rhonda out and on a bicycle.

All heads turned as the announcement came that the

merit badges would be handed out in alphabetical order
and the announcer's voice was filled with excitement as
she said that David Blackshear would do the honors.

Applause and cheers rang out at the mention of the
benefactor's name and Margo along with everyone else
stood to get a look at the man who'd made the day possible. When she looked toward the area where Cindy
was with the badges she saw David.

Something she hadn't felt in a long time—as long
ago as when they'd first touched to be exact—swam
through her like a school of minnows causing her to
clasp her stomach. Butterflies? It was in that second that
she realized how much she'd missed him; missed his
voice with its low baritone explaining the details of his
business; laughing at her silly over-the-top bike wear
last week. Six days. If that's how she was affected in that
short period of time she wondered what six weeks
would do to her. A little voice told her that she was kidding herself and that the very astute Rhonda knew from
whence she spoke. She was attracted and there was no
more denying it.

But last Sunday she'd been so adamant about not dating him that it was no wonder that he'd turned away
from her as stiff as a wooden soldier. The next day she'd
thrown herself into the project and hadn't given their
conversation much thought until now. Now she wondered if there would be a next time where he'd ask her
out. The picture of the beauty on his arm crossed her
mind and she grimaced. Probably not, she thought.

David looked over the crowd and was pleased with
what he saw, relieved that the cyclists hadn't gotten tired
of waiting. He'd stalled for as long as he could, trying to
reach Margo to wish her birthday greetings. After leaving two messages he left the house, frustrated and
annoyed. He wondered if she'd possibly gone away for

a birthday weekend. If she did then he'd have to wait until at least Monday before he spoke to her and that thought was not sitting too well. Especially when he wondered whether she'd gone alone.

He did a double take when a woman resembling Margo Sterling came past his vision and he stared. No, it couldn't be. But there was no doubt. She was standing next to one of the male volunteers who seemed very intent on keeping her by his side. David's eyes narrowed and his lips thinned. *Who the hell is that?* he thought. *And is she with him?* When his eyes connected with hers, she smiled at him. He was so taken aback that he could only look from her to the man he now recognized as having met once or twice at volunteer meetings. He was a personable and likeable guy. Cindy's voice broke through his thoughts but all he could do was stare from Margo to the good-looking brother beside her.

"We're all set, David," Cindy said. "Here's the first group of badges. I'll start calling the names." She looked at him. "You ready?"

"Ready," David said. He turned away but not before he saw the smile die on Margo's lips.

Chapter Seven

"Have you seen Margo?" David asked Cindy after the last beginner was given her badge. It was nearly four and he scanned the thinning area hoping that she had only wandered off waiting until the proceedings ended. The volunteers had stayed behind until the end but he failed to see the one who'd been at Margo's side for the presentations.

"Um," Cindy said, packing up her paraphernalia. "I saw her in the parking lot a while ago. Guess she had to leave."

"Who was her mentor?" he asked.

"Zachary Dixon invited her but he never called in her name, which is why there was no badge prepared for her," Cindy answered, still miffed at Zach's oversight.

"Dixon," David muttered remembering the brother now. "Thanks, Cindy," he said. "You got it covered?" he asked, watching her pack.

"Sure, you go on. The rest of the guys are still here," Cindy answered, giving him a smile. "We're all glad you could make it. The cyclists loved it."

Driving on the Belt toward Queens, David was somber. What was going on? Did Margo leave because she had a date? Or did she leave because she didn't want to see him? He remembered the dying smile on her face and he now knew it was because he hadn't returned hers. He wondered if he had looked like some angry Neanderthal man, giving her the possessive eye as she stood beside Dixon.

Man you're messing up as bad as Mrs. O'Leary's cow. The great fire of Chicago started by that bovine was nothing compared to the fire in his belly when it came to Margo Sterling. She was blowing his mind and he'd be fodder for the loony bin if he allowed it to continue any longer without making his move. "Employer, employee, be damned," he muttered.

Deciding to make a couple of stops, he made a detour. More than an hour later he was back home. Once there, he stripped, showered and shaved, taking careful pains with his dress. It was after six o'clock.

Margo was at a loss for words. When she'd entered the building with her bicycle earlier the doorman had smiled discreetly when he pushed a giant white woven basket of flowers her way. The display was an enormous spread of roses, with bunches of soft white baby's breath nestled among the ruby red flowers. A building worker had delivered the basket to her apartment as she couldn't handle it and her bicycle too. She sat looking at the extravagance taking center stage in her living room on the coffee table. The card simply read, Happy Birthday. David.

The messages from him on her answering machine after she'd left this morning were also a surprise. He'd called before nine and again after eleven. The tone was surprised and then impatient. There was no "I'll call you later." Nothing. She didn't know whether to return his calls as his employee or just call to say thank you for the flowers, but she was pleased that he'd selected her birth month blossom.

She had luxuriated in a long therapeutic bath, soaking in extracts of eucalyptus, juniper and sage to soothe her muscles. Lighted candles flickered from the corners of her bathtub, from shelves overhead, and along the sage and cream tiled floor. She reluctantly left the warm and aromatic room after smoothing her skin with iris- and lavender-scented oils.

Dressed in a royal blue silk pant set, a gift from her parents, a birthday ago, she now sat with a cup of blackberry tea staring at her flowers, drinking in the sweet floral scent that filled the room. She stopped counting the blooms after she reached two dozen.

The doorbell intercom buzzed and she walked to the hall to answer it. After a moment she said, "Thank you. He can come up." She waited by the door and minutes later when the bell rang she let him in.

"David," she said.

"Margo," David said, almost losing himself in her beautiful dark eyes that were staring at him with shock. "May I come in?"

Stepping back, Margo let him in and closed the door, her heart thumping wildly in her chest. He looked like a chocolate dream dressed in a sharp navy blue suit and light gray shirt with a blue tie. And he smelled like a million bucks! That thought almost made her giddy with laughter.

"These are for you," David said. "Happy birthday."

Margo took a bottle of Krug champagne and a crystal vase of white orchids tied with a red medallion ribbon from his hands. "Winner" was printed in large white letters in the center of the medal. She looked puzzled.

"But you've sent me . . ."

"The roses are for your birthday," David said, giving her an intense stare. "The orchids are your merit badge. The champagne is for toasting you."

"But . . . but . . . thank you," Margo said, almost speechless.

David took the bottle from her and placed it on the kitchen counter where Margo had led them. He took the vase and set it next to the bottle. He stepped closer to her. "I need to know something," he said in a low voice. David wanted to touch her so badly he ached, and surely she could see what was happening to him if she lowered her eyes.

"Yes?" His nearness was causing havoc to her body yet she savored the warmth from his breath, imagining it fanning her lips like a gentle feather.

"Are you dating Zachary Dixon?"

"Zachary?"

"Are you?"

"No," Margo said, unable to fathom the question because all she could think of was his delectable lips and the way they moved so sensuously.

The word had hardly left her mouth before David moved in. He caught her face in both his hands and lowered his mouth to hers. The kiss was slow and soft, his lips moving over hers like a whisper, as if this was the only important thing in the world to do at this moment in time. And then time evaporated.

As if fondling the finest silk his fingers glided over her cheek, her jaw, that proud chin, and slid to the delicate softness of her throat where he could feel her fierce pulse. His lips left hers and tasted that softness there and when she leaned into him with tiny gurgles in her throat he captured her lips again, deeply and hungrily. He inhaled the sweetness of her, a flower garden of tropical scents invading his senses and he felt as though he were plunging into a floral sea when he pulled her into his arms.

Bewitching, thought Margo. *That's what I am. Be-*

witched him. One moment she was thinking of those warm delicious-looking lips caressing hers and then they were. She melted into David's kiss and was shocked at the greedy sounds emanating from deep within her. Her arms went around his neck in a tight embrace and his million-dollar smell tantalized her nostrils. She acted like a starving woman—or was it wanton? she thought crazily. Her lips opened to his as she invited his tongue to do more damage. Or was it assault?

He was hard as stone against her and his body craved her touch. David was at the edge of his sanity when his hand slipped inside her blousy silk top. She was braless and the shock of feeling the smooth round naked breast cupped in his hand, the turgid nipple quivering beneath his thumb, was like being drenched with ice water, stopping him short of losing it. He wanted her so badly, to make love with her as if the world was their Eden. The fierceness of what was happening to them so fast was sobering.

David released her mouth reluctantly, and depriving himself from the feel of her heavy satiny breast in his hand, gently closed her top. He kissed her brow, her eyelids, and her cheek before he took a step back, folding his arms across his chest. His breathing was nearly manageable as he murmured, "You know how long I've wanted to do that?"

"Since January," Margo whispered, bereft of his touch, his lips.

"Since January," repeated David, his breath near normal. He was relieved to feel his body settling down but if he touched her again he'd topple into the danger zone; the fall would be never-ending. His arms remained folded. "I've wanted you that long."

"I think I did, too," Margo said.

"I guessed that," David said.

"How could you?"

"You apologized for your rudeness to a stranger. I knew you hadn't forgotten me."

"I've thought of you."

"I never forgot you and only dreamed of seeing you again."

Margo exhaled, brushing a strand of hair from her eyes as she sought to grasp what was happening. "I think I'd be more comfortable sitting," she said. "My legs aren't very strong right now." She brushed by him, stilling the ache to touch him again. He followed.

The living room was perfumed with his gift to her. He joined her on a long, wide, straight-back sofa in navy with many plump pillows. Two identical club-type chairs in a sage and ivory print surrounded a square, warm dark wood table with a beveled edge glass top. The highly polished hardwood floor was covered with a room-size rug patterned in ivory and navy abstracts. It was like her. Sleek, sophisticated without the coldness. And simultaneously serene. Quietly beautiful.

"Why did you come, now?" Margo asked. She was calm and could ask sensible questions.

"I couldn't wait any longer," David said simply. "And I want to take you out to dinner for your birthday."

"A date?" Margo smiled.

"As in," David answered. He liked her sense of humor and the sparkle in her dark eyes that rivaled black diamonds. "Do you mind?"

Margo shook her head. "No," she said. "Will I still be your associate?"

He laughed. "That is a definite yes. Good help is rare these days."

"David, I don't know how this will work. I've never dated my boss before."

And you won't ever if it's not me, David vowed. Aloud he said, "I'm just David, a guy you're enjoying dinner with." He quirked a brow. "So is that a yes for tonight?"

"I can't." Margo glanced at the mini anniversary clock on an end table.

David stiffened. "Then you already have a date," he stated.

"Not exactly," she answered. "Rhonda baked me a cake and will be arriving with champagne by seven. She didn't want me to spend my birthday alone."

"Rhonda," he said, expelling a breath.

"Yes." Margo looked at him curiously. "I'd love to go out with you tonight. It would be special. But I promised."

"I understand," David said, though he was immensely disappointed. But he also admired her loyalty. He knew about that, recalling storms he'd weathered with Wesley and Jonathan. "Speaking of champagne, why don't we invite her over now so we can crack open the Krug before I leave." He stared at her. "I'd like to toast you also. Then you two ladies can have the rest of the night to yourselves. Think she'd mind my company for a hot minute?"

Margo thought about Rhonda's comments about him and she smiled. "No, I doubt she will mind, David, and I'd like that." It was nearly six thirty and Rhonda was probably relaxing until seven. She was always dead on schedule in everything she did. "Excuse me," she said. "I'll be right back. She's right across the hall."

David was scanning the pictures on the table. Her parents he guessed, seeing the resemblance in the older smiling couple. And Margo as a teenager. His eyebrows shot up in amazement. On a skateboard? He got up to take a closer look at the picture, never believing that Margo had been such a daredevil. Her caution and apprehension at just learning to ride a bicycle was no put-on. The beautiful teenager was smiling but there was something different about her. He was still staring at it when he heard Margo return.

She saw his interest in the picture he was holding. "My identical twin, Kai," she said softly.

David heard the sadness in her voice and the same shadows he'd wondered about before were in her eyes as she, too, gazed at the picture. He sensed the reason why but was silent.

"That's her at fourteen," Margo said. "She died two weeks after that was taken."

"You still miss her," David murmured. Such inadequate words were "I'm sorry."

"It was a long time ago," Margo said, taking the picture frame from his hands and setting it back on the table. She smiled. "Rhonda said she'll take your Krug over the Taittinger she bought. She'll be right over."

David wondered at Margo's reticence to talk about her twin but he didn't pry. She was smiling now and the sparkle was back in her eyes. "Hmm, maybe she'll bring that too and my hot minute will turn into sixty," he said.

"I heard that," Rhonda said. She entered the living room holding a large cake platter with a bottle tucked under one arm. The chocolate cake looked a mile high and just as dangerously decadent. "Whoa." Rhonda stopped, staring at the flowers. She'd been about to place her burden on the coffee table but there was no room.

Margo took the platter from her and David took the bottle of champagne, both amused by her reaction. "Aren't they beautiful?" Margo said, taking the platter to the kitchen.

Rhonda turned a wary eye on David. "Yes, they are," she said to him. "And an extravagant gift from boss to employee." Her eyes rested on the vase of orchids on a corner table. But she turned back to him and said, "I'm sure you know what red roses mean to a woman." She inclined her head toward the beautiful blooms. *"That* is not playtime."

"I never meant them to be," David said quietly, getting her drift and returning her hard stare with one of his own.

She remembered the way he'd looked at Margo last week. That was not lust. He was in this for the long haul and she could see that David Blackshear was a patient man. "You're on a quest," she said softly.

David was relieved that he'd passed and met the approval of Margo's defender and he silently exhaled. "I am," he agreed in a mild voice. They stared at one another with understanding.

Rhonda nodded her satisfaction. "Good luck," she said. She saw the hope in his eyes and knew she was right. But then her eyes speared his and her tone wasn't as light as it had been when she added, "I love that girl like my own."

Margo returned, looking at her two guests staring at each other. "Come on, cake's ready," she said. "Which bottle do we want to open first?"

Rhonda walked with her to the L-shaped kitchen with a dining area, where Margo had set the round glass table for three with crystal flutes, silver and white linen dinner napkins. She nodded at the bottle David was still holding. "Let's start with that first and then later you two can enjoy David's gift together after I'm gone and you've eaten dinner."

David was opening the Taittinger and he stopped. "Dinner?"

"Dinner?" Margo echoed.

Rhonda looked at them and smiled. "When Margo refused your invitation to take her out I butted in on your evening, David. You both need to eat, especially drinking bubbly on an empty stomach, so I ordered some nourishment. I hope you like Italian."

David poured the champagne in the three flutes. "Very much," he said, giving the older woman a direct look. She was helping him in his cause in a way that he hadn't expected. He raised his flute. "Happy birthday, Margo," he said. To Rhonda he said, "Thank you."

The intercom buzzed. "That'd be Conchetta's," Rhonda said when Margo went to answer it.

When the food arrived, the table was set with three plates after David and Margo insisted that Rhonda stay and eat with them. Giving in to their threats, Rhonda stayed, had a bite of lasagna, two glasses of champagne and a slice of cake before she stood.

"Early day, tomorrow," she said. "David, it was a nice evening. We'll meet again?"

"Plan on it," David said easily. He liked Rhonda Desmond—a lot.

"Good night, Rhonda," Margo said, embracing her friend with a tight hug. "Thank you for a wonderful birthday surprise. It was the best I've had in years." How many times had this day come and gone uncelebrated? she thought. She'd never forget her thirtieth.

"You deserve the best, honey, don't ever forget that," Rhonda said. She returned the hug and left after giving David a meaningful look.

"She's a good friend," David said as he helped Margo clear the table and put the remainder of the food away. The Taittinger was nearly finished and he emptied the rest in the sink. They'd each had two glasses and none of them even thought about cracking the Krug's, since David was driving.

"She is," Margo agreed. The dishwasher was humming and Margo turned to David who was watching her.

He'd removed his suit jacket and had rolled up his shirt sleeves and loosened his tie. He looked comfortable and uninhibited in her space and she couldn't believe that this was his first visit to her home. He seemed *at* home.

"Do you like coffee?" Margo asked.

He cocked his head. "When it's made right," he said. "You know how to make it or should I call Rhonda back here?"

Margo bristled but didn't miss the laughter in his eyes. "Listen, when you can't cook you learn how to get *something* right. Rhonda's is not as good as mine," she defended.

David held up a hand in mock surrender. "Then I'll have a mug of your java."

While she was making the coffee David excused himself and went to wash up. On the way back he glanced inside the room that was obviously her office. He couldn't miss the framed picture of Kai, and curious, he stood in the doorway looking at what were obviously more pictures, sketches of children at play.

"Did you find everything—?" Margo stopped in the hallway.

"Your work?" David said, giving her a quiet look. When she nodded, he said, "May I?"

"Yes," Margo murmured after seconds. She'd hesitated because no one had ever seen her secret passion. Not even Rhonda. Kai and her friends was her outlet from the pressures of her world, especially when the world threatened to swallow her up. But David somehow would understand. His outlet was his bicycles even though he'd turned it into a money-making business. She gestured for him to go ahead and she followed him into the room.

Quietly amazed at the level of talent in the sketches, David flipped through one drawing pad, reading with interest the escapades of the trio of friends and the morality lesson that was learned. He put it down and picked up others, seeing the progression of problems to solve as the kids matured. David put them down and looked around Margo's work space. Besides the children's stories he saw on the wide desk evidence of the Champion Wheels project, neatly organized in stacks ready to be worked on in an instant. The room was ordered messy with a comfortable rose-colored roomy chair tossed with a multicolored throw, a table and lamp beside it. Its place marked, a novel by a popular mystery writer lay waiting to be continued—an escape from the high-back desk chair, and work. A small vase of fresh violets on the table perfumed this personal refuge. Her bicycle with her helmet resting on the handlebars leaned against the window wall with its sill-length white curtains blowing gently in the evening summer breeze. A jacket rested on the seat and her sneakers were sprawled nearby. Days of newspapers lay on the floor beside the chair, and his eyelashes flickered at the Black weekly resting on top. There were more pictures of her parents and Kai. That was it for the personal. On the walls she'd hung art from some of his favorite black artists. An African-inspired ebony wooden fruit bowl sat atop the black metal three-drawer file cabinet holding a bunch of plump green grapes and an apple.

"You have no other siblings?" he asked quietly when he turned to her.

Margo shook her head. "There were just the two of us."

"Your parents are here?"

"They retired to Florida," Margo answered. "And you?" He'd mentioned a brother and she wondered if there were more.

"An older brother. My parents retired to Virginia." He

waved a hand over the desk. "This is wonderful work, Margo," he said. "Have you thought about publishing?"

"No. This is for my quiet time. I get away from it all in here." She looked at her work. "It helps."

She'd walked back to the door and noticing her dismissive tone David joined her and they returned to the kitchen. She was private about her life and he wondered that there were no other photos displayed. Of friends, lovers, even her good neighbor, Rhonda. He was curious about that part of her, suddenly realizing how much of herself she'd given to her career.

Pouring two steaming mugs of the aromatic coffee, Margo sat across from him. "There's milk and sugar there," she said, indicating the small white ceramic pitcher and bowl. "Help yourself."

David added a little milk and one sugar and tasted. She was watching and as he made a show of grimacing, her eyebrows shot up.

He swallowed and drank some more, then smiled. "Great stuff. Rivals my own."

Margo relaxed and drank. She was beginning to see that he liked to kid her and somehow she didn't mind. She sat back in her chair and looked at him oddly.

"What?" David said. "Don't believe me? You're invited anytime to see whether I lie or speak the truth."

His eyes gleamed and Margo didn't doubt the sincerity of his invitation. "I'm just wondering about something," she said.

"Wonder no more. Ask me," David said simply.

"Why did you ask me about Zachary, like that?" she said.

David frowned. "I was surprised to see you there number one, and second, from where I stood he looked as if he were an extension of your hip." He tilted his head. "I wasn't aware you two were acquainted," he said. "Cindy told me that he invited you."

"All coincidental." Margo explained about her meeting Zachary in the park. When she finished he gave her the same look as Rhonda had. She held up a hand. "I know exactly what you are thinking so don't even say it. I heard all about the irresponsibility of my actions from Rhonda," she said firmly.

"Did any of it sink in?" David asked, still incredulous she'd done something so rash.

"I don't make a habit of picking up men," Margo said defensively and added, "You should know."

"Ouch," David said, but inwardly he sighed with relief. It was all so innocent and he'd been about to wage war with an unsuspecting brother. "I apologize." He saw her circling her thumbs and he knew she was disturbed or doing some serious thinking about a problem. Intuitively he knew what was on her mind. "Go ahead, ask me," David said.

"What?"

"I have no reason to keep secrets from you, Margo," he said, holding her gaze. "Is there something you want to ask me about my trip to San Francisco?"

"You and the girl in the *Amsterdam News*." There, she'd gotten it out. "She accompanied you?"

David held her look. "That would imply that I was having a relationship," he said. "I told you there was no one in my life like that. And you called it right. She was just a girl, young enough to be planning her high school prom."

"Then how—"

"There are hundreds of pictures like that in any newspaper archive if you want to hunt for them." He shrugged. "Those women wait for the opportune time, rush up the second before the flash pops and voila, they're photographed with a celebrity. If you noticed they printed my name and 'unidentified beauty.' She disappeared and I never saw her again."

"Amazing," Margo said.

He nodded in agreement but said, "What else?"

Flushing, Margo said "How do you do that?"

"I've had a lot of experience these past few years reading people," David replied. "Learning how prevented me from getting rooked and making bad business deals." He gestured. "So you have another question?"

"Why in the world were you masquerading as a redcap in January?"

A slow smile spread over his generous mouth and finally he chuckled, shaking his head at the memory. "Wes and I never worked so hard in our lives for those tips."

"Wes?" She caught his infectious grin and was already fascinated by the story he was going to tell. A millionaire playing baggage handler!

"My best friend, Wesley Gray," David said. He threw her a wry look. "He was one of the guys with me that day in Penn Station. Well, anyway, Wes was a redcap working with AMTRAK. I was a Long Island Rail Road conductor. It was all a bet. Five years late but we were honoring a bet. When I hit those lucky numbers I was in la-la land. I waited a couple of days before letting on even to Wes and after I took care of business with the lottery biggies, I went to Wes's job, took his hand truck from him and politely handed it to his boss. Wes was ready to have me committed until I showed him my receipt for the winning numbers. His boss Joe nearly passed out." David enjoyed looking back on that day. "I told Wes he didn't have to tote another bag if he didn't want to. I was tickled to death."

"You could have cost him his job."

David stared at her. Quietly, he said, "Wes is like my blood, Margo. When I became a millionaire so did he." When her mouth softened into a tiny smile he wanted to reach over and catch her to him and take her right there on the sofa. With great effort he pulled his eyes from what lay beneath that blouse and went on with his story.

"Wes said he'd stay to the end of his shift. I was through and the supervisor smirked saying it was me who'd won and not Wes, and if he wanted to keep his job he'd better stay. That ticked me off but I knew Wes, and he was going to keep his word. I wanted to stick it to Joe so bad I could cry. Here I was about to bank millions and for my friend's sake I couldn't tell his boss where to chuck it. Then he said that I'd never known what it was to work as hard as Wes, working that crowd and grousing for miserly tips that sometimes never came and when they did, begrudgingly. I bet that man right then and there that I would come back and give him a full day's work. And every cent in tips that I got would be given to the rest of the guys. Wes said he'd join me."

"And you went back after five years?" Margo said.

"Took us that long, but we kept our word." David's voice lowered. "We were taking a break when I saw you."

Margo saw his eyes shadow and she wondered if he was remembering her cutting remarks. "You were laughing," she said.

"*They* were laughing," David said. "At me."

"Why?"

"Because I lost it when I looked over and you were there," David said, looking amazed that he was sitting beside her. "I went numb and Wes threatened to call 911 if I didn't snap out of it. Joe said I was crazy, that I'd only to give a whistle and I could have any woman I

wanted. He said, get up and speak, or get back to haul-
ing luggage; the crew was waiting for the tips. Then he
laughed and said a professional-looking babe like you
wouldn't give a redcap the time of day."

Margo flushed. "He was right wasn't he?" she said
softly.

David nodded. "He was."

"Seems like a long time ago."

"I remember it like it was an hour ago," he replied,
looking at her intently.

"But what you saw and heard didn't meet with your
illusions, did they? I was a disappointment." She had to
know. "Why have you thought about me all these
months after the way I treated you?"

David shrugged but his eyes never left hers. "Because
after five years I knew the woman I wanted. I stopped
looking for her the hour I spotted you." He added, "And
you've admitted you've thought of me."

Margo breathed deeply. "I wanted to apologize."

An eyebrow rose as David stared. "That all?"

All of her senses were heightened at his look, his
voice, his scent, and she wanted to taste him again, feel
his hard body against hers. But if she seduced him on
her sofa, where would they go from here? she wondered. Business as usual? Unconsciously her thumbs
moved nervously.

"Margo?" David knew she was disturbed and he
backed off hearing his brother's voice in his head. Intimidated. He knew if he pursued her now he'd be on the
losing end. Who said something about patience being
a virtue? Damn straight it was he breathed inwardly.

She looked at him. "Yes?"

"I'd better go," he said. "You've had a long day."
David leaned over and brushed a strand of hair away
from her face. His knuckles skimmed her soft cheek

and he inhaled. "Would you have dinner with me tomorrow night?"

Margo nodded. "I'd like that, David," she said easily. She didn't have to be a detective to understand what was happening. She wanted to be in his company, for whatever reason. When he stood and caught her hands, pulling her up, she felt the warm blush tingeing her insides again and she hoped she wouldn't melt in his arms. She was saved when he released her to roll down his sleeves. He slipped into his jacket, leaving his tie loose as he walked with her to the door.

David caught her chin in his hand, bent to kiss her lips lightly and then stepped back giving her a bemused look. "There's something else that was in your contract that you missed," he said.

"What?" Margo looked wary.

"You have to take a course on Monday."

"A course?"

"Uh-huh," David said. His eyes and voice turned serious. "Margo, you went on a serious tour unprotected. No, I don't mean your helmet," he said when he saw her protest. "There's more to it than that. You had no tools to repair a tire if you'd gotten a flat. No air pump. No first-aid kit. Things you need whenever you're out. If I'd thought you were going without me I'd have taught you all that so you'd have been prepared."

"Repair a tire? I don't know the first thing about fixing a flat!" Margo exclaimed.

David grinned. "Hence, your meeting with Cindy at the shop at ten A.M. sharp," he said, leaning down and kissing her again. This time he indulged himself, deepening the kiss and losing himself in her sweetness. He released her, not wishing to ride down in the elevator trying to hide the result of his greedy indulgence. "Five o'clock all right to pick you up tomorrow?" he breathed in her ear, nuzzling her delicate lobe.

"Five's fine," Margo murmured, leaning into him, stealing one last caress of her own from those delicious lips that did powerful things to her body.

When she closed the door she stood against it for several seconds trying to still her beating heart. Could it be possible that she was falling for a man she'd met only three weeks ago? A man she'd thought of seeing again—but wasn't it only to apologize? *Since when did you start telling lies to yourself, Margo,* the voice in her head said over and over. *Be true to yourself.* But what is the truth? She couldn't help but ask herself just what it was that a wealthy man like David Blackshear wanted of her. So many beautiful women came and went in his life. And then there was her. Why was he pursuing her?

Sleep came late into the night as, still haunted, she murmured, "What is the truth?"

Chapter Eight

"Incredible!" Margo wasn't surprised at her utterance when she received a mock-up of her work in the mail. In five weeks of working with David she'd come to think of him and everything he did in those terms. What she asked for she got. No matter the cost. When she'd opined that it would be great for the print ad to appear in the summer months, it was done. He actually stopped the presses! In August her ads would hit with a prominent spread in the popular bicycle magazine, *Cycling Away!* Champion Wheels would have the cover along with a feature story on David's beginner's tour.

In what would have taken two or three months, she was able to put everything in place in just two weeks. The magazine's team had cooperated fully and was enthusiastic about pulling it together. They'd interviewed David's staff, the tour volunteers and the bikers, taken photographs, and completed the story layout, including her sidebars.

It was now mid-July and Margo woke one Saturday morning without the pressing need to jump out of bed and start the day. She was taking a much needed break on her boss's orders before she started pulling her people together for the commercial that was finished and the layout on her computer. David had already secured the airtime for September, almost immediately following the release of the magazine spread.

Margo luxuriated for a while in being lazy, just thinking of all that had passed since she'd been fired from Mirken and Prusser. She'd gotten a fantastic new job, which led to her starting her own freelance company. She had a client, her boss actually, who wasn't threatened by her creativity or given to vindictive cruelty. Not bad for a woman who'd incurred the wrath of her former employer through no fault of her own.

But today she was filled with quiet excitement! David's call last night, his baritone voice tickling her ear and doing crazy things to her while she lay in bed was scintillating. Though they'd communicated by phone and e-mail she hadn't seen David for the last two weeks, not since they'd had a fabulous dinner at an elegantly quiet restaurant the day after her birthday. He'd been in and out of town on business and it was then she realized that biking was just one of the many enterprises that required his attention. She wondered if they would fall back into that relaxed way they'd had when they last were together, he leaving her with kiss-swollen lips as he whispered good night to her.

Margo slipped her legs over the side of the bed and sat, a worried frown marring her brow. David had insisted that she leave the computer off today. No working, just relaxing. But she wondered how easy that was going to be once she saw him. Even during those frenzied weeks he'd invaded her thoughts at the oddest times. And most definitely before she closed her eyes at night and when she opened them in the morning. She'd looked forward to his calls about what progress he'd made with the magazine people and she'd prolonged her calls to him when another cog had fallen into place.

Today his driver was picking her up at three o'clock.

David was having his brother and some friends over to kick back and enjoy some downtime together on a nice summer day. But Margo was apprehensive about seeing David, especially around strangers. She knew that her feelings for him went deeper than that of just two people sharing throaty kisses, and wondered if his ardor had cooled. It was written somewhere that absence made the heart grow fonder and she knew that *something* was happening to her heart. But how did he feel? And would his friends look at her and wonder if she was just another station-climbing female that David was making time with?

Still in a lounging mood, forgoing a quick shower, Margo drew a bath. She wanted time to think about what was truly in her heart. Was she falling in love with David? She'd seen the results of a man wielding such power making lightning decisions with monster results that the sheer impact of it all awed her. Or was she enamored just like the groupies who threw themselves at him wherever he went? She had to laugh at that thought having never jumped up and down at a concert like she was in the throes of mad sex!

She was thirty years old and had never before thought of her life as being unfulfilled because there wasn't a significant man in it. She'd had her career and had excelled and exalted in it. Men friends were just that, at least until the dull go-nowhere relationship she'd had with a man ended and he soon became nameless. No, that definitely wasn't, couldn't have been, love.

But now, thinking of David—was that normal when her skin tingled and her toes curled and her body shook with shivers when he fondled her breast and swallowed her tongue? Was it love when she worried that he wasn't eating right with his no-cooking self making do with his inventive peanut butter and jelly sandwiches? Or stressing himself to the point of exhaustion with never-ending meetings?

Margo laughed as she lathered her body with perfumed soap that smelled of a hyacinth-filled summer garden. "No, it just means that your mothering antenna is up, you silly!"

At half past two Margo was studying for the umpteenth time her choice of outfit. David had said dress was very casual as they'd be outdoors. As the July temp would hit ninety, a swimsuit would be ideal for cooling off in the pool, he'd said.

She'd nixed the bathing suit feeling that she'd be on display enough without baring skin to boot. So she chose a dressed-up casual outfit, something she'd be comfortable in wearing for a first-time meeting with his family and friends. The collared, deep pink, sleeveless button-front blouse had sashes that tied in front, and would be worn over an off-white calf-skimming capri pant, with an abstract print in shades of black and pink. She completed her outfit with a flat black strap sandal and carried a small black wrist clutch that held the essentials.

With the buzzing of the intercom announcing her ride she exhaled and left the apartment wondering if her body was going to behave and allow her to act like a dignified woman—instead of one who thought she was falling in love.

Jonathan watched his brother sitting alone by the in-ground pool watching people splash about or lounge in the sun. Although David appeared to be enjoying the scene, Jonathan knew better; he was as tense as a pulley on a conveyor belt. Jonathan was as eager as Wes to meet the woman David had fallen in love with so hard that it hurt to watch him trying to keep a cool head.

"Enjoying yourself?" David asked when his brother took a chair beside him.

"Uh-huh. Sorry you can't say the same."

David frowned. "What do you mean?" He glanced at his watch.

"That," Jonathan said, indicating the motion. "If you hurry you can transform your face before she gets here."

"Speak English," David said impatiently.

"I mean that you put on this unfettered serene mask for her but in private you have the same look you wore for four months—that of a haunted man," Jonathan said in a voice meant just for his brother. "You're afraid of pushing her too hard too quickly for fear that she'll bolt like a skittish colt. Why not be honest with her and yourself about your feelings. She's a grown woman and she might surprise you."

"She's something else, Jonathan," David said quietly, thinking about how much he'd agonized over being away from her for so many days. "Proud, independent." A sweep of his hand encompassed the beautiful grounds, the house, and the beautiful people. "I was wrong. I've concluded that this means nothing to her. She doesn't care about my money. She's all about work and getting back on top where she was before that jerk fired her. She wants to prove herself again."

"And you're afraid that once she finishes your projects she's off into the wind," Jonathan stated with a sharp understanding of the emotions his brother was feeling.

"Yes."

"Then you've decided she's not game-playing even knowing that your name on her résumé will be a powerful tool in getting recognition from potential clients."

"No, she's not playing," David answered thoughtfully. "I've told you I was wrong about that." He looked at his watch and stood. "She should be arriving now. I want to meet her out front."

Jonathan nodded and stood. "David?" he called. When his brother looked back Jonathan brushed a hand over his face and said, "The mask?" He grinned.

Feeling lighter than he had been, David returned the grin and then strode to the front of the house to wait for the woman he loved.

The flutter in her stomach as Margo caught sight of David standing by the driveway waiting for her was no surprise. It happened whenever she saw him and this time was no different. *Telling yourself a lie, Margo?* the voice in her head chastised. *Yes, I am,* Margo answered it. *A whopper!* The flutters *were* different: like giant butterflies that were sending her a clear message; she had indeed fallen in love with David Blackshear.

"Margo," David said, reaching for her hand and helping her from the car.

"Good to see you, David," she said, her heart tripping all over itself as her eyes locked with his.

David didn't release her hand but pulled her to his chest, burying his head in her soft black hair, and holding her tight, nearly bowled over with her fresh scent that he'd not forgotten. "I've missed you," he whispered. He lifted his head and then took her lips gently, tasting her sweet mouth as if he thirsted.

Unmindful of any watchful eyes, Margo melted against him. Her arms wound around his neck as she leaned into him and his kiss that was no longer gentle, but was craving, deep, and full of the passion that she was feeling. "I've missed *you*," she murmured when he moved his mouth from hers to nibble her ear. Her temperature soared to rival the midday heat.

"Am I seeing what I think I'm seeing?" Wes said in awe to Jonathan. The men were standing inside the open front door staring at the couple who were oblivious.

"It's not a vision," Jonathan responded, nodding his head with smug satisfaction. "Brother has loosened up and is going for the whole enchilada."

A low whistle escaped Wes as he continued to gape. The ice woman he'd seen briefly on a cold day in January was nothing like the woman who was like melted butter in his buddy's arms. Margo Sterling, whether she knew it or not, was a goner. His friend didn't lasso a woman like that unless he meant to keep her for the final roundup.

David's side vision caught his friend and brother and he broke away from Margo. "We have an audience," he whispered, reluctant to stop tasting her. "Want to continue the show?" he breathed, smoothing wisps away from her cheek.

"I do not!" Margo whispered fiercely, suddenly coloring. She saw the teasing look in David's eyes and said, "You'd really continue, wouldn't you?" He was holding her hand now and he clasped it tightly in his and she held on unsure of what to expect from his friends.

David felt her tense. "Don't be nervous," he said, giving her hand a tug as they walked up the steps. "They're cool."

"Margo, meet my brother Jonathan Blackshear and my friend Wesley Gray." He gave the two men a pointed stare. "Gentlemen, Margo Sterling."

She extended her hand to Jonathan, giving him a tiny smile. "Pleased to meet you, Jonathan." Her stare was direct and her chin tilted a little wondering just what stories he'd heard about her.

Jonathan didn't miss the nearly imperceptible action and he took her hand and smiled. "The pleasure's mine,

Margo," he said. He saw the tiny sigh of relief and he stepped back as she turned to Wes.

"Nice meeting you, Wesley," Margo said, coloring a little. He'd been present when she'd been at her worst.

"It's a pleasure, Margo," Wesley said. He was pleased at her firm handshake knowing that she was feeling a little uncomfortable with him. He reassured her by giving her hand an extra tug before he released it. "We're glad you're here."

"We certainly are!" Jonathan said, giving Wes a look.

David interrupted them before things got out of hand. "Okay you two, don't you have some guests to entertain? I'm going inside to introduce Margo to Inez. She wants to meet the lady who makes her mouth water for candied yams. See you guys out back." He led Margo inside.

When they were alone he said after brushing her lips with his, "Now that wasn't so bad, was it?" he whispered.

"No," Margo answered, kissing him back.

David stared at her. "I wish they would all go home," he said. "I don't like the idea of sharing you with anyone else, not now," he said with frustration.

"Why?"

"I think you know why," David said, spearing her with a look. "That is something we're going to discuss before I take you home tonight." He led her to the kitchen.

"Hey, Inez, meet Margo Sterling, the lady who took the last candied yam from my mouth." His eyes twinkled when he said, "Margo, Inez Lyons, my housekeeper."

Margo's eyes widened at his tease but she turned to the woman who was smiling, obviously pleased. "Hi," she said. "But they *were* out of this world." She made a face at him.

Inez lifted the cover of a casserole dish. "Then I'm glad I was able to deliver this special request for today," she said to Margo in a pleasant voice. "They're just about ready to go outside." She smiled. "Don't wait too long. They're piping hot," she said, leaving by the back door.

David and Margo both turned to see the woman who'd just left the bathroom. David didn't know she was here and he looked surprised. "Val? Glad you could make it," he said. "Jonathan thought you'd be tied up today." He thought she looked frightened and he frowned. "Everything okay?"

Valeria Kimball gave David a quick smile. "My party was canceled at the last minute so I told Jonathan I would come." She smiled at Margo. "Hello."

"Margo Sterling," she said and stuck out her hand. Margo looked closely at the woman who'd surely been crying.

"I'm sorry," David said, the frown deepening. "Margo, this is Valeria Kimball, Jonathan's friend."

Valeria nodded and said, "I'll see you later?" She hurried outside.

David stood watching Val as she mingled with some people by the pool. His brother was in a corner watching her. When David met Wes's eyes both men shrugged but each knew what the other was thinking.

Margo didn't miss the silent exchange between the two friends nor did she miss the woman's obvious distress. Lovers' spat? she thought. A glance at Jonathan told her that the happy man she saw moments before was gone. She'd never met the man before but she knew anguish when she saw it.

She was led to the buffet table and when they'd filled their plates, David guided her to a quiet spot in the shade away from the noisy pool crowd, where he introduced her to some friends.

"David?" He'd barely touched his food and for the last fifteen minutes Margo had been watching him watch his brother. When she had his attention she said quietly, "I'm in fine company and no one's going to whisk me away. I'll be here when you get back." She nodded across the lawn. "Go on."

Waves of love and desire for her warmed his body at her quick perception of what was going on. He leaned over and kissed her lightly on the cheek. "Thank you," he whispered. "I won't be long."

Jonathan saw him coming and walked across the lawn and into the house.

Knowing where he'd be, David strode to his library and closed the door. "What the hell happened?" he asked in a tight voice. "And where'd she get that bruise?" There was no mistaking the angry red welt on the soft beige skin of Valeria's neck.

Jonathan poured a Hennessy and handed one to his annoyed brother. "You don't miss much do you?" he said.

"Not and keep my millions intact and steadily growing," David said tightly. "Are you going to fill me in or what?" His eyes narrowed. "Did you do that?"

The look that flared in Jonathan's eyes was murderous and his hands tensed around his glass. "You'd ask me that?" he said in a hoarse voice.

"No, you wouldn't," David said, looking apologetic. "Forget I even asked that." If his father had even thought that his sons would raise a hand to a woman they'd been decorating a slab years ago. The respect and love that he and his brother had grown up around had been the hallmark by which they'd wanted love and marriage someday.

Waiting until his brother's inner anger subsided, David nursed his cognac. For the last weeks since Jonathan had returned from his trip to Venezuela without her, he and Valeria had been an item. David liked the self-assured businesswoman whose catering enterprise was taking off after only two years. He liked her sense of humor and he liked the way she looked at his brother. She was a woman falling in love.

"She won't tell me who did it," Jonathan finally said.

"When did it happen?" David asked quietly, glad that his brother wanted to talk.

"Last night. She heard a noise in the catering house and she went to investigate. You know what the setup is like, a separate building from her living quarters. When she got there, she found the place in shambles." Jonathan rubbed his brow. "Everything she'd prepared for the party today was in ruins."

"The cancellation," David said.

"Yes. She was crazy with worry about the party being ruined for the couple. It was an engagement affair. It was like bedlam for her to make things right, finally getting a friendly competitor to take over." Jonathan gave a wry grin. "Just like her to worry about the couple instead of the damage done and the money she lost, not to mention expected future business from the party itself."

"The bruise?"

His eyes blazed with fury. "She knows, and I can assume, but she won't admit anything."

"The old boyfriend?"

"That's my sure bet," Jonathan said. "He knows she's been seeing me and he has hassled her about it."

"Is he dangerous?"

"I didn't think so until this happened," Jonathan said, the anger heightening.

The whole scenario worried David. Jealous boyfriends who couldn't take no for an answer were not known to fade away quietly into oblivion. If Valeria was in danger she shouldn't be trying to slough it off as being nothing.

"So why aren't you two speaking out there?" David asked.

"Because she won't let me help," Jonathan answered. "Doesn't want the police involved thinking it'd be bad for her reputation and business. I offered to investigate quietly but she refused. I think she's afraid that there'll be retaliation against me if there's an arrest." He grimaced. "I called her stubborn."

David winced. He'd *known* stubborn, remembering eking a date out of the woman he loved. "You'll have to make her understand that it's dangerous out there. She lives alone, doesn't she?"

"All alone," Jonathan answered, tensing, envisioning Valeria walking through the deserted, dark space, investigating strange noises.

"Both of you sulking about it is not doing a thing to prevent it from happening again," David said firmly. "If it is the old boyfriend, then he has to be stopped before something drastic happens." He saw Jonathan's pained expression and knew he was thinking of his dead wife. He stood and clapped his brother on the shoulder. "Go on out there and make her see the danger of her denial of the situation."

When David returned to the party he saw Margo in animated discussion with Wes and some other friends. He stood back and watched her for a few seconds, swelling with pride. The woman he'd chosen to be in his life was all that he'd imagined she'd be. Beautiful, intelligent, with a sense of humor and the courage to jump back into life's fray when she'd been knocked down and made to suck on a mouthful of lemon drops. He drew in a breath and wished again that everyone would go home.

Margo glanced over and saw David watching her and she smiled. When he started walking toward her little group she flushed recognizing the look on his face and the undisguised desire in his eyes.

When David neared he slipped an arm around Margo's waist and kissed her cheek. "Hi," he said, whispering in her ear. "Missed you."

"You okay?" Margo asked quietly, closing her hand over his at her waist.

"We're good," David answered. He caught Wes's eye and the two men with just a glance understood that they would talk later. Both glanced at Jonathan and Valeria who were apparently talking seriously.

When the sun went down chilling the bathers who abandoned the pool, many people started to leave but not before consuming the last of the bountiful spread that Inez had prepared. Margo, as everyone else, had her fill of the delicious food, complimenting the cook again on her culinary skills. There was an abundance of the usual barbecue selections as well as a few interesting dishes that Margo enjoyed, rarely tasting the ambrosia salad and a taco salad that brought tears to her eyes.

By nine o'clock, David was saying good night to a straggling couple and returned to the living room where Wes, Jonathan and Valeria sat listening to CDs. He'd been thinking all evening about having Margo to himself and had put off broaching his plan for fear of her begging off to work. But he decided to throw it out there anyway.

"Hey folks," he said as he sat next to Margo on the sofa. They all looked at him and he was pleased to see that his brother and Valeria were holding hands. *Perfect,* he thought. "What do you say to spending some time at the beach tomorrow? I think we can all use the break in this heat."

Margo hadn't been to the beach in years and she wouldn't recognize the places she'd attended infrequently when she was still a college student. "Jones or Riis?" she asked, mentioning the two popular beaches. Four pairs of eyes looked at her inquiringly and she felt as though she'd said something out of place. Surely they'd partied there many times.

David could have kicked himself at seeing her discomfort. "Neither, Margo," he said, caressing the back of her hand. "Long Island. We all have houses on the beach in Sag Harbor and we summer there a lot." He squeezed her hand. "And none of us have gotten our feet wet out there yet. Have you guys?"

Jonathan, seeing the potential for disaster for his brother said easily, "Not me, and I'm about overdue. You, Wes?" he asked the perceptive private detective.

Wes shrugged. "Not me, but I'm raring to go."

"What do you say, Margo?" David said, still holding her hand tightly. "Would you like to go to the beach with me?" She'd gotten so quiet that he feared he'd messed up.

Margo felt a rush of insecurity but only for a moment. If she was going to be hanging around with the man she loved she'd better get used to the idea of his wealth. He was relaxed and comfortable with what he could buy and saw no reason to be ashamed of it, so why should she feel any different?

She felt the tug on her hand. "Margo?" David said. She tugged back and smiled. "There's nothing like the beach on a hot summer day in July," she said. "Certainly I'd love to go. What time do we leave?"

Wes and Jonathan shared a look and both felt relief

for David as he grinned and kissed Margo lightly on the lips.

"Seven." David looked around. "Seven okay with you guys?" he asked. "This way we'll have the whole day."

"Val?" Jonathan said to the quiet woman beside him. "What do you say? Can you make it?"

Valeria looked at Jonathan. "It'll be a great day out of the city," she said quietly. The wrinkle in her forehead came and went in a flash. "I'm looking forward to it."

David looked at Wes who shook his head. "Something came up in the last hour or so that demands my personal attention," Wes said with a wry grin.

"Don't want to wait until Monday?" David asked, already knowing the answer.

"Nah, I think sooner is better than later on this one," Wes answered. "I'll catch you guys another weekend," he said, lifting a shoulder. "Summer's still young."

Earlier David had gotten the name of Valeria's former boyfriend from Jonathan and had given it to Wes. His friend was now on the case.

"So are you all right with this, Margo?" David whispered against her cheek, as he pressed her up against her apartment door. He groaned with frustration at leaving her, wishing to stay and watch her fall asleep snuggled against his chest. The vision stirred him to burgeoning again and he stepped away remembering he still had to descend in the elevator.

Margo nodded. On the drive to her home David had asked her to stay at the beach for more than a day, maybe two. Her protests flew into the night when he said he had a laptop and a cell phone as did she.

"Yes," she murmured, nuzzling his neck with her

nose, inhaling his male smell that was pure intoxication.
"And I'll be sure to bring a suit this time."

"More than one," David replied, throwing caution to
the wind and slipping his hands back under her bra,
fondling her satiny breasts again. "You'll be living in it,"
he murmured. Regretting his decision, he dropped his
hands because he'd hardened into a staff of cement.
"You see what you're doing to me?" he agonized. With
one last peck to her lips he took a deep breath and
opened the door, praying that no one was about—least
of all Rhonda Desmond for whom there would be no
denials.

It was the fresh sea breeze that awakened Margo as
she opened her eyes to see that they'd arrived. David
reached over and brushed her cheek with his knuckles.
"We're here?" she said, looking at what he'd called a
cottage but resembled a full-grown house to her.

"Yep, and it looks like we're the first to get here," he
said, getting out of the SUV and going round to open
her door.

Margo breathed deep, the salt air tickling her nose,
and she anticipated cooling off in the Atlantic Ocean. It
was barely nine thirty and the temperature was already
at eighty. She was also hungry and for the first time
wondered about food for the day. Packing a picnic lunch
had never occurred to her when she was enjoying being
thoroughly kissed by David last night.

"It's a lovely house," she said, looking at the one-
story sprawling structure. It was in the middle of two
other houses, all respectable distances apart from the
other but near enough to greet a neighbor.

"Thanks," David said, pulling bags out of the back of

the car. "That should do it," he said, surveying the car for any forgotten bundles. "Ready?"

Margo looked at the surrounding area noticing a few more houses and said, "How far away are Wes and Jonathan?"

David pointed. "The house on the right is Jonathan's. The other is Wes's."

"Oh," Margo said. "That was convenient getting them all together like that."

"Yes," David agreed. "We were lucky." There was no need to go into how he'd acquired the properties all in a row. The owners were only too glad to accept an offer they couldn't refuse for his convenience to have his family near.

She was certain that it had involved more than luck but Margo silently accepted what were to be many more power moves she'd learn about this successful man.

Inside, David dropped their bags on the hall floor and led her to the kitchen. He looked around, nodded in satisfaction at what he saw and picked up a note left on the brown granite-topped center island surrounded by seating. He turned back to a counter near the sink and flipped the switch on the coffeepot and in seconds it began to gurgle.

"Coffee will be ready soon and there are some breakfast Danishes to nibble on as well as rolls and fruit. That should hold us over till lunch," he said.

"Mm, I'm not so sure." The coffee aroma was tantalizing her taste buds. "Don't tell me how you managed all this," Margo said.

"Okay." David opened the fridge and studied its contents.

"D-a-avid!"

He laughed and closed the door. "I called the service last night and they promised the place would smell like a rose and there'd be food to boot before we arrived," he said, giving her hair a tweak. "Annoyed?"

"Why would I be?" Margo answered in surprise.

"Oh, I thought that you would be miffed because you wouldn't get a chance to let me see you in action in the kitchen," he teased.

Margo laughed. "Surely there are takeouts out here in the boonies. I'd make sure we wouldn't starve."

David slipped his arm around her waist and pulled her close to his side. "Sure about that?" he whispered in her ear. "I'm hungry now and not for Danish." He shifted her easily, caught her by the shoulders and looked deeply into her eyes. "I want this." David bent his head and captured her mouth, his tongue tracing the softness of her lips. Slowly he deepened the kiss, taking his time savoring all her sweetness. When she leaned into him, parting her lips to taste more of him he groaned his pleasure.

"Margo," he murmured against her mouth, "I want you, sweetheart. I want to make love with you."

His hoarse voice stirred her soul as Margo wrapped her arms snugly around his torso, and when her hands wandered down to his firm buttocks she felt him stiffen against her belly. "David," she whispered. "Yes, yes."

"Oh, my God," David breathed, unsure of what he heard. "Yes?" He released her mouth to taste the softness of her throat and whispered again, "Yes?"

The sharp beep of a car horn made Margo jump from him and David groaned as he straightened her top and smoothed her hair. He gave her a wry grin. "Company," David said, kissing her gently one last time before his brother burst through the door. "You'd think a man would want to check out his own place first," he grumbled.

"You did say you wanted to spend the day together,"

Margo teased as she smoothed her shorts, wondering if the dampness between her thighs was telltale. "Come early and all that?"

"Yeah, yeah, I remember something like that," David said gruffly. "I'm not so sure that I want all that brotherly love right at this moment."

Jonathan came through the door with Valeria and both were smiling. "Coffee's ready, I smell," Jonathan said, sniffing the air. "Danishes too," he said, lifting a cake plate cover.

"Yeah, thought you might want to get *yours* going too, Brother," David said pointedly. "Hi, Val, you enjoy the ride out?"

"Yes, but I slept most of the way," Val said, smiling at Jonathan. "Your brother had me up before five." She suddenly flushed.

David looked at his brother who wore an impassive mask. "I rang Margo's bell earlier than expected, too," he said, trying to put Val at ease. "So don't feel bad." He cut a look at his brother who returned the stare and David knew the couple had made things right—at least for today.

Later, Margo and Valeria left the men burning ribs on the grill while they were in the kitchen putting together a green salad. The people who'd prepared everything for both houses had left very little for them to do. Salad fixins were chopped, mixed, ready to toss with dressing; meat marinated, cooked dishes left in the fridge and the freezer. All one had to do was unthaw, heat and grill.

Valeria spread a hand over the romaine lettuce leaf she was tearing apart. "Doesn't leave me much room to cook my way into my man's heart, does it?" she said.

Margo smiled at the woman who was more at ease than she'd been the day before. They'd felt comfortable right from the start and fell into easy conversation.

Margo liked her. "At least you know how to go that route," she said ruefully. She threw a leaf into the bowl. "I can do this much without disaster striking."

"Don't like the kitchen, huh?" Valeria said as if she understood.

"Never mastered cooking 101 enough to move on to 201 so I just put the basics together or eat out," Margo answered with a shrug. "So have you always liked to cook?"

"Only when I had to get out on my own and couldn't afford good restaurants," Valeria responded. "Once I found I could take a recipe and make it my own I sort of liked doing different things. Actually swooned over my own cooking." She laughed and the sound was deep and melodious. "Started out making dinners for family occasions, and then small parties and finally the weddings. When the calls started coming in I got serious about it and found a space, but didn't quit my day job until after the first year. It was pretty rough juggling the hours. I finally had the courage to jump all the way in and so far I've been lucky."

"I'm sure luck has nothing to do with it," Margo said with admiration. "What did you do before?"

"I was a third grade teacher in a public school." Valeria frowned. "I liked it but the last few years working with the kids left a bad taste in my mouth. No respect and even less from their parents. It was a challenge, but when two parents cornered me in a classroom ready to make me into chopped liver that hastened my decision to take the plunge into my own business." She tossed the salad, covered the bowl and put it in the fridge. "You know, cooking is not so bad," she said. "If you ever want to fix something special just let me know and I'll be glad to show you."

"Candied yams?" Margo said.

Valeria laughed. "Is that all?" she said. "Be glad to show you and guaranteed you'll be a pro by Thanksgiving."

"Now *there's* the challenge," Margo said, joining her in laughter.

David and Jonathan heard the laughter and they shared a pleased look before entering the house. "Hey, what's cooking in here? We're finished outside," David said.

"We're done in here, too," Valeria answered, admiring the two good-looking men.

"And just in time," Jonathan said as he slipped an arm around her waist. "We were thinking about taking another dip before lunch. Ready to get wet again?"

Valeria leaned into him with a wicked smile. "Sure," she said. "I'm ready for that."

Jonathan nearly choked as he guided her from the kitchen. "You two coming?" he muttered, steering Valeria out the door.

David was toying with the spaghetti strings at the waist of Margo's gauzy beach jacket. "Want to leave the ocean to them or stay and find something else to do with me?" he said, staring at the curve of her breast beneath the thin fabric. When she'd appeared earlier in her swimsuit he'd had a hard time keeping it together. The bloodred maillot with its deep V neckline accentuated every curve of her slender body. The thigh-high cut showed legs that were never-ending, and her tight bottom begged for his touch.

Margo caught his face in her hands and brought his mouth down to hers and tasted his lips. "Great idea you had about staying over," she murmured, after giving him one last quick flick of her warm tongue. Her eyes were full of delightful things to come as she raced out the door and down to the edge of the water, her laughter drifting back to David as she plunged into the cooling surf.

David couldn't walk much less run as he made his way slowly down the hot sand that paled in comparison to the fire in his groin. But his smile was wicked when he said, "Great men have great ideas."

Chapter Nine

Alone at last. David smiled smugly as he locked the doors and turned off the lights before walking toward his bedroom. Jonathan and Valeria had said their good nights at nine, begging off more cocktails as they were getting an early start in the morning. He hadn't missed the signs; they wanted to be alone, too.

Margo was in the bathroom and he heard soft humming in between the sounds of running water and gurgles as she brushed her teeth. He leaned against the wall breathing heavily while imagining her dress or lack of it after she'd showered. The faint scent of lilacs wafted to his nostrils and he couldn't stand it any longer. He knocked and called, "Decent?"

The door opened and Margo stood smiling at him dressed in a short sleeveless white cotton robe that clung to her moist skin. "Yes," she murmured, devouring him with sultry eyes.

David swallowed. "You are?" he croaked. He stepped inside and pulled her into his arms. "I can't wait any longer, Margo," he groaned against the sweet softness of her throat. "I want you now."

"I want you, David," she whispered, nibbling his ear. "Now." She gasped when his hands touched her breast and moaned when his lips closed over her hardened nipples. The sudden heat cloaking her body spread to the deep valley between her legs and the moistness was like a swollen river. "David, hurry," she murmured. When his fingers touched her there she nearly swooned in his arms but with one arm he held her tightly as he sent her to heaven.

She was hot and wet and David could feel the excited throbbing of her femininity and when she tightened around his finger and threw her head back with a scream he felt the dam burst as she climaxed. "Damn," he breathed, holding her and manipulating her as she spent herself.

The subsiding shudders passed through, settling in her toes, and like a rag doll Margo went limp in his arms, lifting her head to stare into his eyes. "David, I told you to hurry," she said weakly.

"I know you did, sweetheart, I had no idea," David said, feeling floored. She'd been so ready he'd forgotten his own needs in bringing her to orgasm. She rested her head against his chest and he held her until the last tremble. The robe had fallen off her shoulders and was hanging between them and David flicked the garment to the floor. He held her away from him and stared.

"Let me look at you, sweetheart," he whispered, tilting her chin and gazing into her eyes. She smiled at him and he melted all over again when he saw his desire for her reflected in her eyes and he wondered if she could see hers in his.

His eyes traveled slowly from her face down to her breasts that were round and full, the berry brown nipples still quivering slightly, and he longed to suckle them again. Her belly was flat and smooth as he'd known it would be under her sexy swimsuit. The sun had turned her tawny skin a deeper shade of pecan where the suit didn't cover and the two tones of satiny skin made his mouth water, ready to feed on all that chocolate candy.

"You're beautiful, Margo," he said, taking her hand and leading her down the hall. In his bedroom he gently laid her down on his bed. "Now let me love you." He pulled the tank top over his head and let it drop to the floor. He never took his eyes from hers as he unbuttoned and unzipped his tan shorts, pushed them down with his black briefs and kicked them aside. He'd vaulted out of his underwear like a spring and he stood watching her eyes wander over every inch of him.

Margo licked her lips as she stared. She'd felt and seen him bulging beneath his clothes before and had felt his penis against her belly. But she'd never expected to see him so big. She swallowed thinking of how she hadn't felt a man inside her in so long she wondered if she could take it all without acting like a skittish virgin. He was a beautiful man. His body was firm and his buttocks and thighs were sculpted granite. He had little hair on his chest that rose and fell with every heartbeat and the quivering nipples beckoned her to taste.

"I won't hurt you," David said softly, leaning over and removing a condom from the bedside table drawer. He sheathed himself.

Margo reached up and touched his chest, letting her hands run over his nakedness. They boldly snaked around his neck and she pulled him down on top of her. The shock and intimacy of hard flesh against soft sent sparks of fire through her once more, and her body was wantonly responding as it had moments before. She hungered to feel him inside her.

"I know you won't, David," she said, almost shyly, filled with desire as his shaft throbbed against her. "Love me." She guided him to where she would be fulfilled and he sank into her. Her hips lifted to meet his thrusts and she whimpered a little at the long unmet need, but the twinge didn't last as her body adjusted to his in the most normal and perfect fit.

No longer able to contain himself when her hand closed around his penis, David bucked, rising and falling, thrusting deeper and deeper each time as she caught his movements and they were soon in a fierce, passionate rhythm.

David was powerless as he answered her need to be loved. He could feel the heat passing from him to her and back, consuming body and soul. He was lost in a world he never knew existed when having sex: no, not sex. David was experiencing love for the first time in his life. The awe of making love with a woman he loved hit him with all the blast from a colossal furnace. No one had set him ablaze like this before. Very slowly he felt the fire ebbing, but the flames still licked at his groin as spent he fell against her heaving breasts. Her legs that had entwined him like vines now fell limply beside him. He rolled off her and lay on his back panting.

Margo was drained. She'd never been taken anywhere like that before. The man beside her was a powerful lover and she'd just been loved thoroughly. She stopped counting the orgasms she'd had and couldn't believe she wanted more. The blood was pounding in her head as she sought to still her thoughts. Did she just experience the action of a lusting man or one in love? she wondered. There was no lying to herself; *she* was a woman in love!

"Margo?"

Shivers of delight pierced her at his husky whisper in her ear. She turned to face him. "Hmm?" she murmured.

"Did I hurt you?" David asked, lifting a hand to smooth hair from her forehead.

"No," she replied in a dreamy voice. "Not at all."

"It seemed like a long time for you," he said, dipping his head and gently caressing her lips.

"It was," Margo answered. "I haven't been with anyone in three years," she said softly.

"Then I hope I made it good for you," he replied. "I know you took me places I've never been before."

A soft laugh escaped. "Then we were there together," Margo whispered, kissing him back.

"Serious?"

"Uh-huh," Margo said, snuggling against him. Her hands drifted over his nipples and he shivered. "Want to go there again?" She trailed her hand down his side and smoothed his buttocks. When she touched his inner thigh he flinched and groaned.

"You're ready?" David said hoarsely, though he was already removing the condom and reaching for a new one.

"Whenever you are," Margo said throatily in her best vamp voice, her hands busily exploring his contours.

Love more than desire swelled up in his heart as David flipped her over onto his belly. "Then let's go for a ride," he invited as he positioned her on top of him and thrust. When she sank down letting him take her fully he caught and held her gaze, his moans of excruciating pleasure mingling with hers as her rhythmic undulating sent him back into that other world.

Dawn and the quiet awoke Margo and after a fleeting moment of disorientation she smiled. The lingering sensation between her thighs was a reminder of how and where she'd fallen asleep; in her lover's arms in his king-size bed. David was sleeping soundly, his arm outstretched on her belly. She ran her fingers over it delighting in secretly touching him. She could feel the warmth already spreading through her body and the giddy thought of taking him while he slept made her feel like a femme fatale in training.

A car door slammed and the engine started. Jonathan and Valeria were leaving, and Margo found herself looking forward to being alone with David. Her thoughts left her breathless, and still naked after the long night of lovemaking she eased from the bed, and silently left the bedroom. In the guest room she'd been given she looked at the untouched bed and smiled knowingly.

Still naked she padded down the hall into the spacious guest bathroom and stepped into the shower. While she soaped her love-swollen body she relived the passionate night scenes. They'd fit so well together and made exquisite love like it was the most natural thing in the world. Yet a thought brought tiny wrinkles to her forehead. With all their burning desire and fierce loving spiced with lovers' endearments, why had neither uttered those committed words: I love you?

David heard the bathroom door close and then the water bouncing off the shower tiles. Thoughts of her tawny nakedness glistening with scented soap rekindled his desire. But instead of going to her he lay looking up at the ceiling. No one would ever be able to convince him that he was not a man in love with that woman in his shower. The one he'd spent loving through the night as if there was no tomorrow. With every breath he drew he loved her. So why hadn't he told her that? He'd said some of everything else, called her his sweetheart, his love, his darling. Three little words refused to take shape on his lips. Was he waiting for her to declare herself? he wondered. Were old thoughts of mistrust beginning to intrude?

The smell of coffee wafted to David's nostrils as he left the bathroom. Dressed in white swim trunks and a light blue tank top he entered the kitchen.

"Good morning," Margo said when she saw him. Her heart did flip-flops as she looked at his bronzed body, warming when remembering her legs wrapped around those strong thighs. "Ready for coffee?" she asked, knowing that was the last thing she wanted at the moment.

The bathing suit she wore today was a two-piece royal blue with halter straps. David drew in a breath and in two strides was by her side. He slipped his arms around her waist crushing her back to his chest while he fondled her breasts. David was already bulging against her. His hands on her bare midriff brought back vivid visions of what he'd had last night. "I want more of you," he said, nuzzling her neck. "Right here, and now. You're driving me crazy, sweetheart."

Margo closed her eyes and leaned into him and when his hands slid under her top cupping her bare breasts she gasped. "David," she murmured, "I—I want you too." A soft moan escaped her lips as she twisted in his arms, while tugging down his suit. At her touch he jumped and she whispered, "I want to love you, again." The weight of him in her hands was heavy as she fumbled with her bottoms trying to guide him inside.

David swore because he had no protection and he agonized over stopping her but sanity gripped him and he caught her hand. "Wait, love," he whispered. "I'm sorry for starting something I can't finish. Not here." Her eyes clouded and he said, "Oh, damn," kicking off his suit and pulling her with him into the bedroom. In seconds he was sheathed and she was naked. "That won't happen again, I promise you," he said harshly as he sank on top of her and buried his shaft deep inside. She thrust upward to meet his assault, screaming his name as he took her.

Their lovemaking was fierce and powerful, taking them to new heights. It was over as it began with Margo devouring his mouth as he ravaged her tongue. He fell back, shivers rippling his body, his mind blown at the intensity of their loving, as if this was the end of it all. Like hell, he laughed inwardly at the absurd thought.

Margo had shocked herself at the way her body was drawn to his magnetism. She'd practically attacked him in the kitchen and would have had him right there against the counter if he hadn't had presence of mind. Was it she who was the lustful one? she wondered. The thundering of her heart began to quiet as she lay limply beside him.

When he felt her relax David took her hand and she clasped his tightly, neither speaking but content, marveling in what they'd just shared.

By late-day, David and Margo had swum in the ocean, eaten leftovers and swam some more before changing clothes and riding bikes. Margo had been surprised to see David rolling bicycles and helmets from a shed out back. Soon she'd experienced riding on the different terrains of sand and unpaved back roads, something David said she'd need to know when she was ready to join more challenging tours.

Teasing each other about their cooking skills and neither daring to attempt the feat, at six o'clock they were enjoying a lobster dinner at one of David's favorite seafood eateries.

David loved looking at her and listening to her quiet voice, her dark eyes twinkling at some bit of humor. He watched her chewing on the last succulent morsel of the crustacean. She wiped the corners of her mouth and sipped some of her Krug, then looked at him expectantly.

Margo couldn't help but feel his penetrating stare during their meal and conversation. For the last few minutes they'd been silent while finishing their food. "What are you thinking?" she said.

"Just wondering if you're relaxed." David reached over and covered her hand with his.

"Very," Margo said, offering a smile. She flipped her hand so that she was clasping his. "I enjoyed this very much. The whole day was absolutely perfect."

"I thought so," David answered with a devilish grin.

She sighed and began to gather her purse. "If we're going to get an early start tomorrow I think we'd better turn in at a decent hour."

"Is there something pressing in the city?" David asked.

"My work," Margo said, looking surprised.

"Isn't everything for the commercial on disk, ready for the next stage of hiring actors and such?"

"Yes," Margo answered slowly. "I'm ready for that."

David shrugged. "Then why rush back?" He squeezed her hand. "You look like you're rested and enjoying yourself. And I like being with you."

Her laugh was gentle as she shook her head and pulled her hand from his. "I'm still a working girl, and I haven't earned a vacation yet," she said. But Margo would have liked nothing better than to stay on the beach for days on end with him.

"Stay with me, Margo," David said, holding her gaze. "At least for another day. Those things can be put in motion so easily with a few calls."

That was the part she wasn't used to, she thought. "I'm beginning to realize that," she said but there was no edge to her voice. "Are you sure *you* have nothing pressing? Don't make me the bad guy for your missed meetings."

"Then is that a yes?" When she nodded, he caught her hand in both of his. "I like this place but it's not where I want to be right now. What do you say we get out of here?" David said in a voice heavy with emotion.

Margo liked the invitation in his eyes, his voice and the promise in his touch. Her cheeks burned because she knew their thoughts were alike. "Let's go home," she whispered.

Home. Did she realize what she said? David wondered as he parked the car in his driveway. This will be one of her homes one day he vowed.

When they passed through the kitchen Margo gave him a rueful look. "We can't stay out here David," she said.

"Why not? What's wrong?" He frowned.

"Food. We'll starve."

Opening a drawer under the counter, David pulled out a sheaf of menus. "No, we won't," he said, pointing to one in particular. "They'll even come in to cook the whole shebang for us. Take your pick." His arm was circling her waist and he began nibbling the delicate skin of her neck, losing himself in her perfume and womanly smell. "Besides, who needs food?" he said, trapping her against a closet.

Margo turned in his arms her body already tingling from his touch, and wrapped her arms around his neck. "Only those mortals," she said before teasing his tongue with hers.

David unzipped the white, sleeveless body-hugging sheath she was wearing and slipped it off her shoulders. The lacy white bra cradling her breasts was unsnapped in a catch of a breath and in the next he was tasting his prize. "You're all I want, Margo," he murmured against the soft throbbing mounds and when he nipped the berry-like nipples her moans brought him to attention.

Before losing his clothes and shoes and kicking them away, David produced a condom. "I promised you," he said, pushing her dress over her hips along with her tiny white panties. She was naked and he filled his eyes with the glorious sight.

When he would put on the condom, Margo said, "Let me." She took it from him and slowly rolled it into place.

David groaned when she was finally through and her wicked smile told him she'd been teasing. "Never again," he muttered, pulling her into his arms.

As she feverishly guided him inside her, Margo gasped. "I just don't want it to end, my love," she said, arching her hips to accept him fully.

David was thrusting deeply when he nearly froze at her words. "It never has to, sweetheart. Never." He plunged and took her, giving her all the love in his soul.

Later, Margo would remember an overnight trip to the beach as a three-day unforgettable odyssey with the man she loved. It wasn't until Wednesday late in the day that she and David had returned on a mostly silent trip to the city, both filled with thoughts of their new relationship. Neither spoke of being in love though their feelings and action told the truth.

She'd unpacked and at three thirty was sorting her clothes for laundering in the basement utility room when the phone rang.

A smile was in her voice. "David."

"I miss you," he said.

"Miss you back."

There was a pause. "Were you thinking about it?" David asked in a low voice.

"It?" Margo answered.

"Us and where we are now."

"Where are we, David?"

"You know we're definitely not the same two people who left here on Sunday morning," he answered slowly. "We didn't speak on it but it's there between us. I felt it and I know you did too and I wondered why we didn't bring it out in the open." He hesitated. "Any regrets?"

She could almost hear him holding his breath. "None, David," she answered.

He was silent for a moment before he spoke. "I'm glad," he said finally. Clearing his throat he said, "You haven't changed your mind about riding Saturday morning?"

"No," she said softly. "I'm looking forward to it." She was excited because David told her she was ready to take on a longer bike tour. They were going to do a thirty miler through the city and she was eager to test her new skills. She'd learned how to fix a flat in record time and had learned to navigate the dangers of rutted and rocky roads and streets filled with potholes.

"Good," David said. "Margo, I'm sorry but I won't be coming by tomorrow like I promised. Something's come up that needs my attention and it will be one of those all-day into night sessions."

This meant she probably wouldn't see him until their trip. "That's okay."

"It's not okay with me," David said, wondering if she really meant what she'd said.

"It's only a figure of speech," Margo answered. She detected weariness in his voice. "I meant that business just happens."

"It does," he agreed. "Then I'll see you early Saturday?" When he hung up, David stayed with his hand on the receiver for a while as if maintaining the contact but he was wondering what Margo was really thinking. She'd sounded disappointed that he'd broken their dinner date for Thursday but he knew he'd be tied up with the problems that had met him full force when he'd arrived home this afternoon. He finally took a breath and pressed in a number.

"Why wasn't I called about this last night?" he said, trying to keep a level voice. "Is the child harmed?"

"No," Barbara Olivera answered. "Just frightened," she added.

David rubbed a hand across his throbbing temples. "Just frightened?" he said, the irritability finally seeping through. "A three-year-old toddler was locked up in a darkened nursery for hours and he was just frightened? Wouldn't you be?"

Barbara felt her boss's anger and frustration. "It wasn't done on purpose David," she answered. "The director of the nursery was the last to leave as she usually is but neglected to check all the cribs herself because her teachers told her that all the children had been picked up."

"Apparently that wasn't the case," David said dryly. He could not imagine the mother's fear when she'd arrived at the center only to find a locked and deserted building. The Building Blocks Day Care Center was only one of the like centers that he owned and operated around the city and was one of the businesses he was ardent about. During the years that he worked on the Long Island Rail Road and leaving his house at five and six in the morning he'd rush past women, and some fathers, pushing strollers or carrying their infants to baby-sitters. No matter the weather, snow, sleet, or rain they did what they must to support their families. When he'd come off his year-long euphoric high of spending his riches, opening those centers was one of the first things he'd done. His associate's voice was droning in his head.

". . . and the child was hungry and wet but happy to see his mother. Of course the press got wind of it and it will be on the TV news at six tonight. Your lawyer and your publicity people are speaking and will make a statement later today."

"What about the director?" David asked. He knew the woman must be terrified and ashamed that such a thing could have happened on her watch and he empathized with her. "Has she been contacted by the press?"

"Yes," Barbara answered. "But she's been advised not to give an interview—at least not until she speaks with you."

"Get her on the phone for me would you please?" David said. "And after that, do a three way with my lawyer and the PR people."

When Jonathan patiently said good-bye to his pleased customer he hurried into his gallery office and picked up the phone. He was quietly expectant.

"Hey, man, got what you needed."

"Did he admit it?" Jonathan asked, getting to the bottom line.

"Yes," Wes answered. "Mister Frederick Shankley is your man."

Jonathan breathed. "Thanks, Wes," he said.

Wesley hesitated. "That isn't going to change anything with Valeria though, is it?"

"It's got to. The man is crazy. He was seen around her place while we were away last Sunday as if what he'd done on Friday night wasn't enough."

"You know she has to get the police involved now if only to get a restraining order against him," Wesley said. "At least it'll be a start." He popped some jelly beans into his mouth. He knew the danger Valeria was in even if she didn't want to accept it. The man he'd confronted had cold dead eyes, the kind that gave Wesley the willies. He'd seen men with that look willing to pay with their lives while teaching their victims a lesson.

"I'll be going over there when I close the gallery," Jonathan said. "Maybe she'll be ready to listen. She was really upset when her neighbors told her he'd been around again."

"She's still alone?"

"I'll be staying the night."

"Oh." Wesley smiled. It took his friend a long time but he was finally looking toward brighter days with the woman he'd fallen for. She was everything that Cynthia wasn't and he was glad that Jonathan had not sought to replace his dead wife with a clone.

Jonathan changed the subject. He wasn't ready yet to share all that he felt for the new woman in his life though he knew his brother and Wes suspected how deep his feelings were. "Have you spoken to David?" he asked.

"Yeah, soon as I heard," Wesley answered. "He's ticked off."

"He's a right to be," Jonathan replied. "Somebody messed up big-time and will hear it from him. You know the media cuts its teeth on negative news and they'll be eating on this one for days or at least until another unfortunate celeb grabs their interest."

"I know that," Wesley said, thinking that David hardly needed this kind of trouble, especially with his new ad campaign about to hit. "I've faxed him a report about what went on with Shankley." He paused. "I'll be on top of this, but you're going to have to convince Valeria to take this more seriously than she's doing," he said. "Trust me on this."

"I'm on it, Wes," Jonathan said quietly. When he hung up he wondered how he was going to fix his mouth to ask Valeria to stay with him for a while. He already knew the answer to that and he frowned yet admired and recognized her need to stay a staunchly independent woman. Headstrong, but lovable and beautiful, he wouldn't change a thing about her. But Jonathan couldn't shake his deepening fear for her safety.

Margo was watching the six o'clock news with wrinkled brow. When the doorbell rang she knew Rhonda had heard. She got up to let her in and they went to the living room and finished watching in silence.

"Damn shame," Rhonda said when the news anchor switched the topic. "Can you imagine the fear in that child?" she said, anger flashing in her eyes. All the anxiety a mother feels for a child's well-being while out of her sight weakened her like a deflated balloon.

"No," Margo murmured. "I can't imagine. They must still be shaking from relief."

"I'm sure they are." Rhonda looked at her friend. "David never told you?"

"No." Margo wondered why but she didn't voice her feelings. But why should she feel hurt that he hadn't mentioned a thing that would definitely impact his life. Was she already developing feelings of possessiveness? she wondered. Feelings that David didn't share?

Rhonda saw her friend's thoughtful look. "He's been busy with his lawyers and the media, more than likely," she said. Smiling, she looked Margo up and down.

"Some tan you've got! So how was Sag Harbor? I've yet to get out there myself this summer but after looking at you, so rested and everything, I'm going to take some friends up on their offer to visit."

"It was fabulous," Margo said. "We had a great time. David's brother has a house next door and he came with his girlfriend. They're a lot of fun."

"Plan on spending more time out there with them?" Rhonda asked. "You're long overdue for some vacation time what with going right into this freelancing with David."

Margo nodded. "Yes, we talked about it and plan to get out there again soon. It is relaxing and as far as vacations go that will be about it for me." She gave Rhonda a rueful look. "I fell into this thing so fast I've yet to get my business plan together. In a way I'll be glad when I finish with David's projects so I can get started on my own. I'm revved up for that now, and ideas are coming to me like crazy."

"In a way?" Rhonda teased. "Does that mean you want to see him as man and woman and not boss and employee?"

Seeing that Margo was at a loss for words, Rhonda came to her rescue. "Don't mind me honey, I'm just playing mother hen here," she said. "I can see the signs. You like him don't you?"

"Very much," Margo said. Why confess that she was in love with the man? In a few weeks it would all be over and they both could get on with their lives. He'll have a successful ad campaign going on and she'll have jump-started a new business.

Rhonda leaned over and patted her hand. "Remember what I told you. You have to go after what you want in the love department as long as you believe it's for you. Just like you did when you saw the career you wanted and fought for it." She stood and walked to the door with Margo following. "I've seen you two together and whatever either of you is saying or not saying will get said eventually. Don't give up on it yet."

It was barely six thirty Thursday morning when Margo's phone rang.

"Hello?"

"It's David, Margo. Are you up?"

"What's wrong?" She sat up, her brow wrinkled. Thoughts of yesterday's news came to her. "Did something else happen?"

There was a short pause before he spoke. "I'm sorry I didn't call you. TV was no way you should have learned about that."

"I did wonder why you kept it from me," Margo said with candor. "What did you expect I'd do? Run from your trouble?"

Another pause. "I deserve that," David finally said. "I didn't want to burden you with my problems since we . . ." He let that thought die.

Since we're not committed lovers, Margo finished the thought in her head. "The child is okay?" she said.

"Yes," David answered. "I spoke with the mother yesterday and she's relieved and happy that he's back in her arms."

"How are you?" Margo asked, sensing there was something he wanted to say.

"Can I come over?" David asked in a quiet voice. "I want to see you."

The despair in his voice overwhelmed her and she realized how much to heart he'd taken the plight of that child and his mother.

"Margo?"

"Yes, David. I'll be here," she answered and before hanging up said, "Don't forget breakfast unless you can make do with a bowl of cheerios."

The gloom lifted as David laughed. "I'll bring breakfast," he said.

Forty-five minutes later, Margo was showered, dressed in a mauve lounging outfit and was pinning up her hair when she buzzed David up.

"Good morning." Her breath caught as she stared into his eyes thinking that only a night had passed yet she'd missed him as if it had been an eternity.

"Good morning," David said, his eyes feasting on her like a man starved. He walked to the kitchen and dropped his bundle on the kitchen table. She'd followed and he turned and took her in his arms and just held her, his chin resting on her hair, gently rocking her back and forth.

Margo's arms went around his waist and she held him tight. Neither spoke as they reveled in the feel of each other. Their closeness brought back visions of their three days together and her body stirred as if reacting to the vivid memories. She closed her eyes and wondered how she'd ever managed day by day without him in her life and the thought of them parting in mere weeks brought sheer misery to her heart.

David lifted his head and stepping back a few inches, raised her chin with his finger so that he was holding her gaze. "That won't happen again," he said softly. "I want to share everything with you." He ran his knuckles softly down her cheek. "I need you to understand that." He kissed her forehead, her throat, and then sought her lips in a slow, hungry kiss that had him panting to taste more of her charms. Instead, with great effort, he released her saying quietly, "I never want to hurt you, Margo."

Her heart was full of love for him as she raised her hand and caressed his cheek, and then traced the outline of his lips. "I know you don't." Having no desire to be released from his embrace she snuggled back against him, wrapping her arms around his neck. She repeated softly, "I know." Then she kissed him, deeply and hungrily, her tongue exploring the sweetness of his mouth. The soft moan that gurgled in his throat sent shock waves of desire through her body as she felt him rising against her. Margo was heady with love for him. Then she released him and with a yearning look eyed the bag on the table. "What did you bring?" she said. "I'm hungry." A tiny smile played about her mouth.

His body trembling with his need to have her, David fell back looking incredulous. "You're what?" he croaked.

Chapter Ten

David saw the twinkle in her eyes and the barely held back laughter and, catching her hand, pulled her to his chest. "I didn't know you were such a tease," he growled. He loosened the pins in her hair, kissing her neck as the soft waves cascaded to her shoulders. He caught her face between his hands. "Are you really hungry?" he said, smothering her with kisses. He slipped his hands inside her silky top and fondled her naked breasts. Dipping his head he kissed them, twirling his tongue around the soft brown areolae as if feasting on rich, chocolate ice cream.

"For you," Margo managed against the onslaught of his drugging kisses. She caught his hand and led him down the short hall to her bedroom. "I want to love you," she whispered.

David felt her need when she stepped away long enough to shrug off her top. He stayed her hand on her hips as she tugged on her trousers. "No." He slid the pants down her hips and when they dropped to the floor he could only stare at her beauty and wanted to love her where she stood. He trailed kisses from her neck to her shoulders where he tasted the soft, sweet skin and bending he caught her nipples in his mouth and suckled.

"David," Margo moaned, wanting to feel him inside her. She pulled his shirt from his pants and struggled with the belt buckle when he stopped her and pushed her gently on the bed. She looked at him with want.

"Shh, let me love you now," David said. His eyes holding hers, he undressed, then sat down beside her, stroking her thighs. He felt the moistness between her legs and his senses heightened as he cupped her velvety mound, but he held himself in check wanting nothing more than to give to her. He knelt to the floor at the foot of the bed and then caught her thighs and slowly pulled her to him, draping her legs over his shoulders. "Let me love you, sweetheart," he said. Tenderly, he kissed her thighs and as she wriggled beneath his hands on her buttocks, with his tongue he spread her lips and tickled her throbbing nub, tasting her sweetness, her womanly scent driving him insane. Her moans were but his name on her lips, as he flecked teasingly. When his tongue plunged deep inside she screamed and jolted her hips, and he caught her to his mouth as her love flowed.

Spent, and panting, Margo couldn't believe the raging journey her orgasm had taken her on. She must have climaxed more than once because her body descended and soared with each thrust of David's magical tongue. When he withdrew it she was sated. Slowly unwinding her legs from around his neck, she reached to smooth his hair. When he looked up at her she saw the love in his eyes and she nearly cried her heart was so full. She was surprised to feel the moistness on her eyelashes.

David rose and sat on the edge of the bed. He looked at her with wrinkled brow. "Tears?" he murmured. "Was I wrong in loving you like that?"

Margo shook her head. "It felt as right as anything could ever be," she said.

Reaching over to the nightstand he took a tissue and wiped her eyes. "Then what, sweetheart?" he whispered.

"I—I never wanted to be loved that way before," she murmured.

His thumb was caressing her lips as he stared down at her. "And now?"

"I loved the way you loved me," she said simply, but she could feel the warmth spreading over her cheeks.

He lay down beside her, cradling her in the corner of his shoulder. "I don't want what we have to ever end, Margo," he said.

She threw an arm across his chest and hugged him. She didn't answer because she wasn't sure of what they had, especially if it was going to remain unspoken between them. Margo decided she wasn't going to question anything, but would believe until her last breath that he loved her. Twisting in his arms, on one elbow she looked at him. "Ready?" she purred.

"For?" David asked, twirling her hair around his finger.

"For me to love you now," she said, but then started to slip out of bed. "But if you want breakfast instead . . ."

David caught her before her feet touched the floor. Holding her close so she couldn't wiggle free, he said, "You *are* a tease."

She laughed as he held her with one hand while fumbling around on the floor for his pants. Finding the condom and struggling to put it on, mission accomplished, he said with a devilish grin, "Are *you* ready?"

Sometime later Margo said, "Mm, that was good. Isn't there anything she makes that doesn't taste like you want more?"

"Not in my experience," David answered, finishing the last of the baked ham that Inez had prepared. She'd packed grits, bacon, biscuits and cups of fresh fruit. She'd made scrambled eggs but they were unpalatable by the time he and Margo had gotten around to breakfast. When Margo made some more they both laughed at the forlorn-looking lumps which followed Inez's into the trash.

Margo finished her second cup of David's coffee. "Not bad," she said. "You do make a mean pot of brew."

"Do I lie?" he said, winking at her, but quickly frowned. "Something's got to be done about this," he said.

"What?"

"Neither of us knowing what to do in the kitchen."

"Now why would that ever be a problem?" Margo asked lightly. "In a few weeks we'll go back to our old routines and never give a thought to our culinary skills or lack of." She smiled. "You have Inez and I have take-out menus."

David went still. "What do you mean?" His voice was dead calm.

Startled by the sudden current of electricity in the room, Margo looked at him. "I don't understand."

"You know exactly what I mean," David said in the same quiet voice. "You're not dense and you're not given to coyness. Tell me what's on your mind."

Margo lifted a shoulder. "My work with you is nearly finished. Once the commercial is put in the works, which will be today, then there is nothing more for me to do. My employment will be terminated as states my contract."

"Don't tell me what's in your contract, I wrote it." David's eyes were piercing.

"Then you know what I mean," Margo said, tilting her chin.

"That there's no more sleeping with the boss?" David said. "I didn't write that."

Cut by his remarks, Margo refused to show it. Instead, she looked away from the darkness in his eyes.

"Look at me."

She was drawn by the command to meet his probing stare. "What do you want of me, David?" she asked.

"An explanation," he said in a thin voice. "I just left your bed. You allowed me to love you like you've never been loved before. You gave yourself to me unconditionally and I to you and you ask what I want of you?"

She saw the hurt in his eyes and the pain on his face. Her shoulders drooped but she would not cave in. There was no way she was going to tell him that she loved him with every part of her being, only to be disillusioned when he remained noncommittal. Something was keeping him from admitting his deep feelings for her and she wasn't so sure that she wanted to know what distasteful flaw she had.

"I don't want you to walk out of my life, Margo," David said. Reaching across the table he caught her hand. "Is that what you want? To be rid of me?"

Her hand tightened in his as her heart churned with anguish. "After what we've shared, how could you ask that of me?" Her voice was barely above a whisper. "I want you in my life."

David stood, still holding her hand. "Come here," he said softly. He wrapped his arms around her as she clasped him around his waist. "Let me hold you," he murmured.

They stood clinging to each other for long silent moments. David was trembling with the thought of never seeing her again when she completed her contract. Yet he knew that she was more than ready to embark on her new career. Would there be a place for him then in her life?

Stirring in his arms, Margo lifted her head. "What are you thinking?" she asked.

He smoothed the wisps of hair from her forehead and

kissed her. "That I don't want to leave you but I must meet with my lawyers today."

"I know," she said, thinking of his problems. People used any situation to sue and David Blackshear was a huge target. She smoothed his brow, then kissed his lips. "Do you still want to take our cruise on Saturday?" The cruise, Cindy had taught, was a more difficult ride usually less than fifty miles with hilly and smooth terrain. Margo was more than ready to put her new skills to the test, excited to challenge more hills.

Seeing her anticipation, David grinned. "So ready, are you?" he asked, kissing the tip of her nose. "I wouldn't miss it." Sternly he said, "I'll be here before dawn so no playing with that computer all night."

When he was holding her by the front door, he studied her face. "Are we okay?"

Margo nodded. "We're fine, David."

A week later, Margo was standing at a Manhattan newsstand looking with pride and awe at her work. *Cycling Away!* had hit the stands as well as other print ads David had arranged for. Although she'd received advance copies she was thrilled to be able to purchase the magazine like thousands of other cycling enthusiasts. The commercial would air in two days and she was about to burst waiting for its debut.

Walking on air after taking care of some business and treating herself to a fine lunch, she decided to spend time in the city doing some shopping. She hadn't browsed in department stores or boutiques since she'd been fired and she missed that treat whenever she'd ventured out of her office to grab a bite to eat and take a breather. The midsummer sales had netted her two new swimsuits, a beach cover-up and a dress to wear to Jonathan's gallery showing.

Margo warmed at the thought of the cover-up. There was hardly any need for one because at the beach house in Sag Harbor she shed the suit to go naked to the shower or to David's bed. Or to the bed in the guest room. Or in the kitchen. They'd made love wherever their desire caught them. Sometimes they'd leave the city in early evening, dine at a fine restaurant and afterward lie on the beach under the midnight stars, only to leave at dawn.

Happily exhausted, Margo stopped in Penn Station to rest with an iced cappuccino. The first day of August arrived with steaming temps mirroring the nineties of July. She found herself at the same café that would always be a fond memory. It was where she'd first laid eyes on the man she'd grown to love. Looking at the hustle and bustle of the busy terminal and the baggage handlers hurrying by she smiled, knowing she'd never forget a man wearing a red cap while doing his job.

Reaching into her purse, Margo pulled out a card and studied it again, a sappy grin on her face. She'd picked up her business cards from the printer and she was still enthralled. Sterling Productions. Margo Sterling, CEO. The bold black letters sent delicious chills through her. Her company!

"Margo Sterling?"

She looked up at a woman who was sitting at a nearby table. "Pat?" It was the friendly sister who'd been her assistant at Mirken and Prusser, the only person who'd commiserated with Margo on her last day as she was packing her belongings. The woman came to sit with her. "How are you?"

Pat's smile was genuine as she shook hands with her former coworker. "I'm well," she said. "You look fabulous, Margo," she exclaimed, and then pursed her lips in a pout. "Not a word from you in these past months. You know we always got along; you could have kept in touch through cyberspace at least. Are you working in the neighborhood again?"

Pleased at Pat's unpretentious greeting, Margo smiled at the younger woman who seemed anxious to hear good news. "No, I haven't sought work with another firm, Pat. I've decided to freelance and things are looking up. I'm enjoying myself." Though bursting to share her news about her brand new company she chose to keep mum for now. Her former boss would know soon enough who was behind David's campaign. "What about you?" she said. "Has Lawrence seen fit to promote you yet?"

The smile disappeared as Pat glowered at the mention of her job. "Are you kidding?" she said with disgust and then, conspiratorially as if afraid of being overheard, said, "I'm floating résumés. It's time to move on. The place isn't the same without you but Lawrence will never admit that. Have you seen that feminine napkin commercial?" Without waiting for a reply she rushed on. "Probably not," she said. "It was on the air for as long as a New York minute! It was the pits!" She went on to describe it in detail.

"I think I saw something like that," Margo said, trying to remember. "It hardly aired."

"Exactly," Pat said gleefully. "The client fired us. That was Logan's work and scuttlebutt has it that he's scheduled to become the next victim of the firm's reorganization. And that's in quotes."

"Unbelievable." Margo could see the smug look on Eddie Logan's face the day he was given the Blackshear account. *Payback's a bitch,* she thought.

"I bet if Lawrence had it to do all over again he would

have treated you differently," Pat said. "It wasn't as if you *gave* Ty your idea to market to the competition! What a jerk Lawrence was to take that out on you." She shook her head. "That's another one who's getting his lumps."

"What do you mean?" Margo said, curious at Pat's look of delight. "Lawrence?"

"No, Ty," Pat said with a smirk. "Word is he's having a tough time and he's looking. He hasn't done anything since the perfume ad, so he's coming off looking like a flake. But get this. He had the nerve to call me the other day to find out where you'd gone. I told him to run the other way if he ever did bump into you." Her eyes widened. "Can you imagine?"

"No, I can't," Margo said. She couldn't help equate that bleak time with where she was sitting right now. She wondered had she not been fuming at the world and men in particular, if she would have taken refuge in a mug of hot coffee at this same café. Then she would have never been put in David's line of vision. *Wonderful fate,* she thought.

Pat gathered her purse and stood. "It's been great seeing you, Margo, but I've got to get back before I join that reorganization list before I want to." She smiled. "Remember I'm looking if you hear of anything. I'm getting desperate."

"I'll remember," Margo said and waved as Pat hurried away.

Wanting to feel some kind of sympathy for what was happening to her former colleagues, Margo just couldn't summon up the false emotion. It wasn't nice to gloat over another's troubles but somehow Logan's smug face and Lawrence's vitriolic words, and Ty's betrayal edged out any compassionate feelings she might

have had for them. This was her time now and she was
ready to take what she'd learned and fly.

Her business was already on the move. She'd sent out
some feelers and had gotten some positive feedback,
one, resulting in her first commitment since she'd finished David's campaign. The design and layout for her
client, a clothing manufacturer, was a reality, the signed
contract returned to her yesterday. She'd gotten help
with the legal stuff from Jonathan who'd been a lawyer
and had been more than pleased to give her much
needed advice.

It was with a jaunty step that Margo, laden with her
purchases, walked through Penn Station to catch the
Long Island Rail Road home.

"Looking good, Brother," Jonathan said after studying the magazine and reading the cover story. "Your girl
did her thing, I'd say," his voice full of admiration. He
looked at David who was sitting across from him in the
gallery office. "Thanks for bringing it by for a first
look."

David nodded. "No problem, man," he said, tapping
his copy of the magazine. "I think that this along with
the commercial will do what I want. In-your-face ads
that will stay in the head." He had decided to go for the
general-market consumer, with an African-American
spotlighted.

"So why the glum look?" Jonathan asked, though he
had an idea.

Shrugging, David looked away, and then shot a wry
look at his brother. "Just sorry that it's over. She was fun
to be with."

"Over? Was?" Jonathan said. "Where's this doom and

gloom coming from? I didn't know Margo was planning to leave town."

"You ought to know," David snapped. "You helped her with her first contract deal."

"Oh, so she'll be working, just not for you," Jonathan said. "You're begrudging her a little success?"

"Of course not," David bristled.

"I know things will be different," Jonathan said. "You can't be dropping by and at your whim take her riding on your little jaunts or whisking her out to the beach, because she'll be deep into building a business. But that doesn't mean you two still won't have that special thing going on. Anybody with less than twenty-twenty can see that." He paused. "That's still true, isn't it?"

"For me it is," David replied but he didn't smile. The day he'd dreaded was here and he often wondered how he was going to handle it. Obviously from the lecture he was getting he wasn't coming off looking too cool.

Changing the subject he said, "I haven't mentioned to Margo that the cocktail party I'm throwing Sunday is for her, sort of a victory celebration. ESPN will air the commercial between two and two thirty and I want her to see it for the first time with everyone there. Don't you and Valeria let on. I want her to be surprised."

"You got it," Jonathan said, knowing Margo would be flustered at the attention. He was happy for her and pleased that she and Valeria had hit it off, spending time together when either had a precious minute.

David studied the man who was looking mighty happy these days. "So has Valeria had any more problems?"

"Nah," Jonathan answered, and then grinned. "I guess with Wes up in his face and being issued the restraining order, Frederick Shankley is dust in the wind."

"Glad to hear it," David said. More relaxed than he'd

been when he got there he said, "Well, old man, what have you planned for your birthday this year?" He'd never seen a man look forward to celebrating a birthday as religiously as his brother. If he never took a sick day when he was with the law firm he did on his natal day, and he treated opening birthday presents with the same joy as a big happy kid on Christmas morning. David knew that for the first few birthdays after Cynthia's refusal to wear the jade butterfly for him, Jonathan had been a somber man. He was happy to see that he'd put that in the past.

"Old?" Jonathan scoffed. "Haven't you heard that the new old age is seventy? Hell, at thirty-nine I'm still an infant." He chuckled and waved his hand. "I'm thinking about making it coincide with my September showing."

"Why not keep them separate?" David asked.

"Business," Jonathan said with a big smile.

"Mercenary." David stood. "I've got to be in midtown in forty minutes," he said. "I'll see you Sunday?"

"Wouldn't miss it." He walked with David to the front door. "How did the day care center incident play out?" Jonathan asked. "Lawsuit?"

"Not yet," David answered, lifting a shoulder. "Who knows what's in a body's mind." He waved. "See ya."

At seven, Margo was dressed, waiting for David. A celebration dinner he'd said. When he appeared at her door she looked in amazement at his burden of bundles. Taking the vase of beautiful white and chartreuse flowers that she knew to be in the orchid family, she carried it to the living room as he followed and dropped his shopping bags on the floor.

David ran his eyes over her, drinking in her beauty. She wore a royal blue fluttery cap-sleeve dress, the fluttery hem inches above her knees. He kissed her lips. "You're gorgeous," he said. Then he stepped away and picked up one of the shopping bags and handed it to her. He sat on the sofa and watched.

"What is all this, David?" Margo demanded. "It's not my birthday."

"Some things I think you'll like," he said. "A thank you from me for a superb campaign."

"I was paid for that, David," she said.

"I know, sweetheart. This is something that I wanted to do," he said quietly while holding her gaze. "That's all."

"Oh," Margo exclaimed when she lifted cycling gear from the bag. A lightweight, weatherproof jacket in turquoise that when folded fit into a tiny pouch. Cycling shorts of which she needed another pair badly. She wouldn't think of riding without the padded and lined garment that prevented chafing. A turquoise and black short-sleeve cycling shirt made from a fabric that absorbed perspiration. In the other bag she found black biking shoes. And there was cold-weather clothing for a tour David planned in the fall: a thermal top and warm spandex tights in bright red and purple. She laughed when she pulled out a pair of fingerless, padded, black leather gloves.

"Remind you of something?" David said, getting a kick out of her reaction.

"Yes, and no teasing me about my getup the first time I learned to ride," she warned.

"I like teasing you," David said, running his knuckles over her flawless sun-kissed cheek. "It's one of the joys in my life."

"Thank you, David," she said, moving close and resting her head on his chest. They stayed like that for a while, both content in the embrace until Margo said. "I think we'd better leave. Dinner awaits."

"Must we?" David said, burying his chin in her hair and inhaling an intoxicating fragrance of exotic blossoms. "I like holding you," he said.

"Mm, me too," Margo murmured. "If you have time we can do some more of this when we get back."

He tilted her chin to stare into her eyes. "*If* I have time?" he questioned.

"Uh-huh," Margo teased. "Because I want to do more than just hold you, love," she said, her mouth curving into a smile. "But if you're going to be busy later on . . ."

She never finished as David crushed his mouth to hers. Later, when he released her swollen lips he said, "You mean busy like that?" he said, caressing her cheek.

Margo swallowed, while trying to float back to earth. "Exactly what I mean," she murmured. "Definitely what I had in mind."

On Sunday, when David escorted Margo into his living room she was surprised to see some of his closest friends. She always enjoyed their company and they accepted her as David's steady companion. Cindy and another manager from the bicycle shop were there as well as people she'd met at other affairs. Sensing an air of excitement not usually present at dull cocktail parties she was affected by the vivaciousness of the small group.

"You look great," Valeria said when she caught Margo alone.

"Thanks, you too," Margo said, returning the compliment, eyeing Valeria's simple yet chic, sleeveless baby blue skirt set, in a silk fabric with matching shoes. Looking around she said, "David never mentioned what the occasion was but I feel something's in the air. Any idea?"

Valeria smiled. "You know David," she said. "He likes to wine and dine his friends. Takes the pressure off. I think he's gearing up to train for that sixty-miler you guys will be taking in the fall so this will probably be the last one of these for a while." She studied Margo. "He'll be putting you through your paces until then. You think you're ready for such a tour?"

Margo nodded. "I will be," she said with enthusiasm. "I'm looking forward to it." She shook her head. "When I told my parents about it I think they wanted to fly up here to see whose spell I'd fallen under. They could *never* see me doing this." She laughed. "*I* couldn't see me doing this. I love everything about the sport." A devilish smile touched her lips. "Can't convince you to give it a try, huh?"

Valeria shuddered. "Not me," she said. "I can't see myself stopping wherever, fixing a flat in twenty minutes tops and go sailing off into the sunset again. I don't know how you do it. No, it's purely a spectator sport for me."

About two o'clock Margo looked at her watch. *What a dilemma,* she thought. How rude of her would it be if she sneaked off into David's library and turned on the TV in time to see the first airing of her commercial? Surely David was as pumped as she was to see the ad. But she knew he was enjoying entertaining his guests and she wouldn't deny him that, especially since she knew how hard he worked keeping all of his enterprises running smoothly.

"Got a date?" David asked, slipping his arm around her waist and kissing her cheek.

Margo flushed. "I'm where I want to be," she whispered in his ear.

"Good," David said, leading her into the huge great room where his giant plasma TV hogged one wall.

Surprised to see everyone watching ESPN, Margo spied a familiar face. "Rhonda!" she exclaimed.

Flashing a big smile Rhonda hurried over to give her friend a hug. "Wouldn't miss this honey," she said. "David made me promise not to tell."

David tightened his arm around an astounded Margo's waist. "Shh," he said. "Listen."

The commercial came on with fanfare music and a panoramic view of mountains, trees, lakes and a lone man racing on a winding trail riding the newest Champion Wheels road bike. The scenery was beautiful and there was something cosmic about this one human, being in the center of it all. Suddenly he reached the bottom of the mountain trail and he was no longer alone. There were groups of cyclists of all ages, ethnicities, families alike, with every kind of bike. Road bikes. Mountain bikes. Hybrids—all from David's line. The gist of the commercial was communing with nature while having the exhilarating experience of riding a quality product, be it alone or making it a family affair. The shot ended with two cyclists, black men, grinning and glistening with sweat, leaning on their road bikes, toasting each other with bottled water.

Watching the thirty-second spot with a critical eye, Margo was breathless as the scene faded into another commercial. She'd been apprehensive about trying to say too much in the allotted time but the commercial direction was excellent. There was silence in the room and then loud applause as people turned to salute Margo with flutes of champagne.

She looked up at the quiet man beside her who'd tightened his hold around her waist. "Did you like it?" she whispered.

Nearly speechless, David exhaled. "I had an idea of what it would be like but it exceeded my expectations," he said quietly, then kissed her lightly on the mouth. He took two flutes from the tray of a passing waiter. "Congratulations, sweetheart. We have a winner here."

Jonathan, Valeria, Rhonda, and others crowded in offering their congratulations and Margo looked at them accusingly. "You all certainly know how to keep secrets don't you," she said, while smiling her pleasure. "Thank you."

Minutes later, the commercial aired again and Margo knew the expense David had incurred and her heart filled, realizing that he'd had that much confidence in her abilities and vision.

The cake that was presented in her honor was from Valeria's kitchen and it was a big hit with everyone devouring the dark chocolate confection and clamoring for more.

"Thanks, Val," Margo said, unable to resist eating a second slice. "You've outdone yourself with this one."

"My pleasure," Valeria answered, giving her friend a hug.

Much later, after David had driven her home and she was pinning up her hair in front of the bathroom mirror, Margo stared at her image. She wasn't the same woman who only a few short months ago had stood here raging against the wrongs she'd been done. The look of contentment and happiness was genuine as she allowed herself to bask in the congratulatory remarks she'd heard this afternoon. The belief in her talents was real and she knew that doubt would never enter her mind as to what she could accomplish. Her desire to be a winner was stronger than ever and she would let nothing deter her from her goals—not ever again.

After her scented bath, instead of going to her bedroom to sleep, Margo found herself sitting in her office. She hadn't worked with Kai and her friends in some weeks now and she missed the small-fry getting into scrapes and eventually solving their problems.

One thing she had done weeks ago was to change the name of her newest character who had insinuated himself into the kids' lives. Dixon was no longer Dixon but had become Ellison because Zachary Dixon's face appeared every time she wrote the boy's name.

Unaware that she'd worked for hours the stiffness in her shoulders forced her to stop, surprising her that it was nearly two in the morning. But she looked at her finished tale and pride swelled up in her. The thought that suddenly came to her was sobering. All these years she'd never shared her work with others, except recently, David. This had been her refuge, her place to think, and to heal from the demands and pressures of her bread-winning career. But this was the private, creative side of her self. She realized that Kai, Antoine, Chloe and now Ellison had stories to share and morals and ethics to teach.

How many times had she begged for more books from her parents who only wanted her to get out into the sunshine with Kai? She'd resisted and they'd hopelessly given in, allowing her to spend hours reading her stories.

Margo asked herself why she shouldn't share her stories with so many other kids who would enjoy, and most of all learn, from the morality lessons? Suddenly she wanted to share her kids with other nine-to-twelve-year-olds whom she was certain experienced the same heartaches as her fictional little people.

Crammed with ideas on how to get started on this new venture, she forced herself out of the room and into bed. Her last thought was that she couldn't wait to share her idea with the man she loved.

David closed the artfully constructed book he just finished reading, but ran his fingers gently over the cover. Margo was watching him as they sat under the shade of an umbrella around his pool. "This is for me?"

"Yes." Margo answered.

The lump that appeared in his throat was hard to swallow. He knew that she'd given him a piece of the self that she'd kept hidden from him until a few weeks ago. But she'd never let him take one of the beautifully handcrafted books from her apartment.

His emotions were high as he said, "Thank you, love."

Oh, David, am I your love? Margo smiled. "I wanted you to have that one," she said.

The story was about eleven-year-old Ellison's losing his imperious air and learning the lesson of humility, when he accepted Kai's offer to teach him the intricacies of repairing a tire on his eighteen speed bicycle.

Margo saw the twinkle in his eyes and she said, "What?"

"That kid Ellison, moneybags and all that?" David said. "Any idea where he came from?" he asked

"Oh, isn't there a kid like that on every block who's got more than anyone else?"

"Um, I guess so," David said, growing serious. "But Ellison definitely isn't like me or Jonathan, though we did know a kid like that. Funny thing, he was likeable." Reaching over he caught her fingers and kissed them. "Just wanted you to know that," he said.

David picked up the *New York Times* that was already

turned to the society page. "I meant to show you the latest," he said and handed the paper to her.

Margo looked at it and made a face. "Isn't there anything they miss?" she said. The picture showed her and David coming from B. Smith's restaurant in Manhattan. She was holding his arm and smiling up at him. It wasn't the first picture taken of them around town on various occasions. One caption had begged the question, "Bye-bye bachelorhood for a multimillionaire?" "Rhonda showed me. I think she's kept every one."

Detecting an odd note in her voice, David said, "Do they bother you, Margo?"

She thought of the first picture she'd seen like that of David and the woman in San Francisco and she wondered if other people thought she was one of those insignificant women. He was looking at her expectantly. "Not at all," she answered, giving his hand a squeeze and pulling him up as she stood. "This heat is crazy. Let's swim."

David couldn't shake the uncomfortable feeling that she had just hidden another part of herself from him.

Weeks after Margo's second effort at freelancing, the business started to come in—not an avalanche but the trickle was enough to keep her smiling and hopeful. The one thing she didn't lament was the overhead of office space but she wondered how long she could keep that up. When she wanted to meet with someone it always had to be at a restaurant or at their place of business. Once she had a client come to her apartment and she was totally uncomfortable with that and nixed doing it again. But an office was the least of her worries. She was producing and she was happy doing her own thing.

One evening while pondering a decision she'd made,

the phone rang and she picked up never looking at the Caller ID display.

"God, girl, have *you* been doing things!"

Margo nearly dropped the phone and when she saw the name displayed she turned hot and cold. No one ever said *Gawd* like Ty Henderson!

Livid to the point of shaking, Margo took a deep breath. "What the devil do you want, Ty?" she said. Her teeth grated together and she winced. "I'm fresh out of ideas for you to steal."

Ty laughed. "Now come on, Margo, what happened is old news and you should be over it by now. What's one little idea between friends? You always had so many they spewed from your mouth like swarms of busy bees."

"They were *mine*, Ty," she spat. "How could you live with yourself? And how many other unsuspecting dupes like me have fallen for your helpless act?"

"I'm living very well, thanks to your brain," Ty said. "But the well's drying up and I wonder if you can throw something else my way."

"What!"

"Ah, come on Margo. I heard the news. You're flying high with your Champion Wheels ads all over the place. They're everywhere, and forget channel surfing. Just no escaping them." He chuckled. "Besides, I see in the papers the company you're running with. Why in the world are you working anyway? Doesn't Daddy Warbucks come across with the green?"

"Go to hell, Ty." Margo slammed the phone down. It was a full minute before she recovered enough to remember what she'd been doing.

Chapter Eleven

The call from Ty had unnerved her to near insanity. Margo couldn't sleep and the next day his image turned up on the computer screen, on her sketch pad, even in the mirror while brushing her teeth. His words singed her ears and she grew hot as molten lead. Dashing cold water on her face did little to quench her burning desire to smash his smirking face. Did she really have "stupid" written across her forehead? she fumed, that he dared to be so bold as to talk to her like that. Had he actually asked her to give him another idea? What a gullible fool she'd been to mistake her naiveté for friendliness.

For a whole day she tried working but her thoughts were dry, producing nothing, falling deeper into moroseness. She tried talking to herself reasoning that one unscrupulous creep shouldn't have such power over her, reducing her to a raging idiot. Wasn't she a new woman, strong, intelligent, and aggressive enough to trod new paths and become successful at it?

The answering machine recorded calls from Rhonda inviting her out to dinner and from David who said he'd call back when he returned from his overnight trip. In no state to talk intelligently to anyone, she didn't return their calls.

Though the day had been a hot one and defied strenuous outdoor exercise, at seven thirty when the sun was less brutal Margo dressed in cycling shorts and a tank top, took her helmet and left the apartment.

A pro now at maneuvering in street traffic, Margo biked unmindful that she wasn't protected by a steel shell pumping steadily alongside automobiles; she felt the tension begin to ease. Ignoring the silly whistles and shouts from some ignorant males, she rode until the perspiration soaked her shirt and only when she realized what she must have been exhibiting did she regret her choice of tops. But she rode on, liking the burn in her legs, her thighs, and arms as she skillfully sped through the streets. With each rotation of her pedals she was stamping out the voice of Ty Henderson. Soaked, the chill she felt brought Margo back to reality and she realized that she'd been riding for more than an hour. Close to nine o'clock, the sun was long gone. When she looked at her surroundings she was shocked to see that she'd taken the long stretch of Atlantic Avenue from Queens into Brooklyn.

Dismounting, she stopped and drank some water as she got her bearings. Recognizing the East New York area she shook her head ruefully. Unless she summoned a magic carpet she was going to have to take that ride back in the chilly night air on dark streets.

"Margo, Margo, Margo," she said aloud, a laugh escaping. One of the first rules Cindy had taught in her classes was about safety. Margo had thought she was only going to take a trek around her neighborhood and had broken many rules. She wasn't dressed properly. She hadn't told anyone where she was going. She had no cell phone and very little money. No food, though there were bodegas on nearly every street on the strip where she was. No map, though she didn't need one, but had she taken a route unknown to her she would have been in big trouble. And worse, she'd left her bike locks home.

Leaving a bike unattended, especially a high-end product like hers, even for a second, was dangerous business, but Margo was stopped by the security guard from bringing her bike inside a White Castle. Hungry and thirsty, even if she removed one wheel and carried it with her she couldn't be sure that the rest of the bike would still be waiting for her with no chain to secure it.

Spying a public phone, she made a call. Valeria lived about twenty blocks away and if she could make it there she would find herself back home one way or another. The line was busy so Margo guessed that Valeria was talking to a client as she never interrupted a customer's call. When she was set to ride, Margo mounted and rode toward Linden Boulevard.

David hung up, no longer annoyed that he couldn't reach Margo, but worried now. When he'd arrived home after eight o'clock this evening and she still didn't answer her phone his brow wrinkled. He'd even left a message on her cell. If she was working and just wasn't picking up that was one thing. She'd done that many times but had always called back saying she was in the middle of a thought. He understood that. But he'd been calling throughout the day with no response from her. Short of alarming Rhonda or even going over there, he forced himself to eat the meal Inez prepared for him and to settle his head. But afterward he couldn't remember a thing he ate.

Her legs feeling wooden, Margo mused that the sixty-miler she was preparing for with David was going to test her spirit for the sport. Then again, she'd done something foolish tonight, unprepared and alone and that wasn't going to happen with hundreds of other bikers on the tour.

Arriving at Valeria's, Margo wearily leaned on the bell hoping that her friend was off the phone and not in the catering house where she held small functions.

"Margo?" Valeria looked at the woman leaning against the door. "What in the world are you doing out like that? Get in here!" She took the bike and leaned it up against the wall and led Margo to the kitchen where she immediately put on the kettle. "You're shivering for God's sake. What happened?"

Grateful to be sitting on something wider than a bicycle saddle Margo eased onto the padded kitchen chair. "Hi, Val," she said, rubbing circulation back into her chilly legs and thighs. "Just got caught up in some venting and acted like a nut case." Warmed enough she stood, said "Excuse me," and headed to the bathroom. After washing up, dousing her face and arms with warm water, she felt the strength returning.

In the kitchen she found steaming tea and warm biscuits waiting for her and she drank and ate with gusto. Biting into the flaky bread she said with a smile, "Almost as good as mine," she teased.

"Oh, yeah?" Valeria said, but her eyes crinkled at the corners with pleasure. On Margo's visits she'd been making friends with the kitchen and the things she'd learned to cook tasted like seconds. Her candied yams were mean; the baked ham could take the prize.

Refreshed, Margo sat back and eyed her friend. "Explanation, huh?" she said.

"Uh-huh," Valeria answered. "Something like that." She finished the mug of tea. "Must have been a man," she grunted with disgust.

"How did you guess?" Margo said, making a face. "The moment's gone now though. I'm sane again."

"David?" Valeria tried to sound nonchalant because friction between her two friends wasn't normal and if something drove a wedge between them she knew both would be miserable.

"No!" Margo exclaimed. "Not David." A long sigh escaped. "Remember my mentioning the guy who treated me like a fool?"

"Your former boss?" Valeria's mouth twisted in distaste.

"No, the other jerk," Margo said. Calm while relating the phone conversation, she was warm at the tale's end.

"You couldn't have made that up," an amazed Valeria said. "Sounds like juicy material for another TV reality show. I hate to tell you what I'd name it," she said with passion.

Margo couldn't help but laugh at the look on Valeria's face. "If you feel so emotional about it maybe you have a marketable idea there." Just how would you package such hubris in a man? she wondered.

After joining in the laughter, Valeria became serious. "Can't blame you for your solo, vent-taking ride through the streets of Brooklyn and Queens, but you know how dumb that was, don't you? Anything could have happened."

"Yeah, stuff happens," Margo answered. "My angels were by my side."

"I'll get you some clothes to change into before you catch a chill in that wet stuff. When my cakes are finished I'll drive you home. Meanwhile why don't you stretch out on the sofa? I know your legs must be screaming for relief." The phone rang and Valeria looked at the display without surprise. To Margo she

said, "I probably won't be taking you home after all."
She picked up. "Hi, David."

"Val, have you heard from Margo today? I can't reach her," he said.

"She's here, hold on a sec." Handing the phone to Margo she said, "I'll be back with those clothes."

"Hello, David," Margo said, wondering how to gloss over her irresponsible actions.

Sagging from relief, David sat down at the kitchen table. "Hello, yourself," he said, trying hard to keep the tremors from his voice. "Is everything okay? All I got was your machine and your cell is off."

Margo sighed. There was no cool, intelligent way of getting around it. "I'm stranded," she said.

His pulse shot up again. "Your car broke down? Where?"

"No. I went riding this evening, got caught up and found myself here."

There was silence.

"You mean on your bike? To Brooklyn? At night?"

"Yes, all of those," Margo answered, knowing what his face looked like right now. She could hear the censure with every clipped word. "It's a long story that I can explain when I see you," she said, suddenly feeling very tired. "I'll be home in an hour or so."

There was another short silence. "Val is driving you?"

"Yes, as soon as she takes some cakes out of the oven."

"I'll be there in thirty minutes," David said. "Tell Val."

"David, you don't have to do that," she said.

"I know," he answered calmly. "I want to come get you." He paused. "I think Val would appreciate it too.

Her cakes can be iced and decorated sooner if she doesn't have to make the two trips," he added quietly.

Getting his drift, Margo said, "I'll tell her. Good-bye, David."

With her bike secured in his SUV, Margo waved to Valeria as David backed out of her driveway. They were silent while going east on Linden Boulevard. Once he maneuvered onto the South Conduit, Margo looked at him. She saw the muscles in his jaw working. When she'd met him at Val's door he'd stood looking at her, tall and silent, and she couldn't read the expression in his hooded eyes when he bent to touch her lips briefly with his. He'd only asked her if she was ready, but she hadn't missed his quick glance at the garments in her hand and the borrowed ones she was wearing.

"Did anything happen?" David finally said.

"You're angry," she stated.

He made a sound, and then cleared his throat. "No, I wouldn't call it that," he said slowly. After a glance at her outfit he said, "You went riding totally unprepared. Something happened to cause you to lose your common sense. All I'm asking is what was it?"

She heard the control in his voice and knew that he probably had been half out of his mind with worry when he hadn't heard from her. Margo knew that were the positions reversed she'd feel the same. She looked out of the window and then back at him.

"Ty called me last night."

"Who?" David said, trying to remember where he'd heard the name.

"My former colleague."

"Henderson?" David recalled the name and the situation from Margo's dossier Wes had compiled. He frowned. "Why?"

After Margo repeated the conversation verbatim she was silent trying to squelch the rage threatening to overcome her again.

David felt the tension and heard the anguish. He reached over and caught her hand in his, but he remained silent.

She leaned her head back and closed her eyes. Surprised to find David parking across the street from her building she said, "I fell asleep. I'm sorry."

"You were tired."

He rolled the bike into the apartment. After putting it in her office he followed her into the bedroom where she was sitting on the bed.

Margo looked up at him. "Thank you."

David folded his arms and stood looking at her. "None necessary."

"You're still angry," she said wearily, waving a limp hand at nothing. "I saw red and did a foolish thing. It won't ever happen again."

"I thought the worst," he said, still standing by the door, his voice very calm and low. A grimace contorted his face. "I wonder why that is? Why is it that we don't think positive thoughts in these situations? Like you doing a hair and nails thing. Or you could have lost your cell phone. Or you went on an impulsive shopping spree." He lifted a shoulder. "Those simple things never entered my mind," he said, rubbing a hand across his hair. "I care so much for you Margo that the thought of you being hurt made me a crazy man." After a moment and a deep breath his eyes roved over her body. "How are your legs?"

"Sore."

David pushed himself from the wall and walked to

the bed. "It's no wonder," he said. "You rode a lot of miles. I suppose without a warm-up?" When she nodded, his eyes narrowed. "You should be sore. Come on, get these off." He tugged on the jersey pants and pulled them down over her hips. "You need a massage before you fall asleep otherwise you won't be able to get out of bed in the morning. Finish undressing, I'll be right back."

The hurt he let her see in his eyes this time tore Margo up inside. All she wanted to do was hold him in her arms until she saw the familiar beautiful brown eyes instead of the black ones filled with pain. She heard the water running in the bathtub and she pulled off the rest of her clothes just as David walked back into the room.

Drawing a sharp breath when he saw her beautiful nakedness, David steeled himself against grabbing her because if he did he'd never let go. "Let me see your legs," he said tersely, and walked to the bed. He lifted one and studied it, while feeling from the toes to the thigh. He did the same to the other and then let it go. "There's no swelling yet. The water is hot so test it before stepping in." He pulled her up and for a moment held her against him before releasing her. "I'll be in the kitchen. Have you eaten anything at all?"

"Some," Margo answered, wondering how she was going to hold her head up in the tub. She wanted to sleep. The aromatic water tickled her nostrils and the soothing salts he'd poured in had a drugging effect. She closed her eyes.

"I thought so," David said, watching her from the doorway. "Margo, you can't sit in there and fall asleep," he said. "Do you want me to bathe you?"

"No, David. I'll be fine. Promise."

He stood and watched her for a second before leaving, but he left the door ajar.

When she pulled the plug and stepped out of the cooling water, she wrapped herself in the large bath towel and walked barefoot to her room.

David heard her and stopped what he was doing. "Here, let me do your back," he said. "Just pat yourself down; I want your skin moist." He disappeared and then returned with some bottles. With Margo lying stretched out on her stomach he rubbed her down with alcohol, massaging up and down and with strong circular motions, treating her legs and arms with special care. He turned her over and did the same to the front. When he finished he massaged therapeutic lotion all over.

"Margo?"

"I'm awake, David," she murmured. "I feel so much better."

"Thought you might. Come on, sit up and come to the kitchen. You should have a little something before going to sleep."

Putting on a short cotton robe she followed him. "I couldn't eat a thing, David. I'd choke on it."

"Just have some herbal tea. It'll relax you and then you can go off to dreamland."

She sat, sipping the hot beverage. He was having some too along with a toasted English muffin.

"Sure you don't want a muffin?" David asked. While she drank he was noticing her drooping shoulders. He finally felt the tension leave his own body. "You know you won't have any trouble covering the miles on that tour next month, don't you?"

The smile that reached his eyes, made Margo smile. He was himself again. "I'd thought about that after I realized what I'd done," she said.

"I think before we do anything else we better get you back in some more of Cindy's classes."

"Yes, the dumb stunts class," Margo said, stifling a yawn.

Giving her a look that said he agreed, David stood and cleared the table. "It's time for you to hit the sack," he said. "I'll be sitting talking to a zombie."

Margo caught his hand. "David, I'm sorry for scaring you like that." She slid into his arms and wrapping her arms around his waist, smoothed the taut muscles in his back, while inhaling his woodland scent. "I never want to hurt you." She lifted her head. "You do know that, don't you?" she murmured.

His arms tightened around her. "Yes," he answered, then kissing her lips lightly said, "Time for bed."

She stopped him in the hallway. "You're still troubled about something. What is it?"

They detoured into the living room and David pulled her down on the sofa beside him and held her in his arms. He let out a sigh. "Henderson," he said, huskily. "Did he threaten you in any way?"

"Threaten?" Margo was surprised but even through her sleepy haze she bristled. "No. He's simply an arrogant jackass who thinks he can get over on me again." A shudder racked her body. "I swear, David, I saw another side of myself today. If he'd been in the same room with me talking like that I would have used anything I could get my hands on to hurt him and face the consequences later. That's how I let my rage take over. It scared me."

"Then I'm glad he wasn't here, sweetheart," David said, kissing the top of her head. But his eyes darkened. Feeling her body slacken against him he shook her gently. "Margo, don't fall asleep here. You have to lock the door behind me."

"Mm, stay with me," Margo murmured.

"No, I can't, because I'll keep you up all night,"

David said, pulling her up and walking with her to the bedroom. "Take off your robe and put on a gown. You'll be more comfortable. And then come put the chain on the door." She moved slowly and he helped her slip the soft gown over her head.

"David, hold me," she said drowsily and lay down on the bed and closed her eyes.

He thought she was asleep before her head touched the pillow. David settled her under the covers and stood watching the soft rise and fall of her breasts, wanting to take her right then. Finally, bending, he kissed her lips first gently and then crushing as if he'd never get enough of tasting her. She stirred and muttered something that he could not make out. Smoothing her hair from her face he gave her one last kiss and with great effort, left the room.

In the living room, David kicked off his shoes and stepped out of his jeans and lay on the sofa. It was after midnight but he picked up the TV remote and pressed the power button. The images flashing across the screen were as nothing as he thought about the woman in the next room. If someone wanted to give her grief they were going to have to go through him. Ty Henderson was his last thought as his eyelids drooped heavily and he fell asleep.

The next morning Margo awoke to the smell of coffee. The sun was bright and she knew she'd slept long and hard. Frowning, she didn't remember putting on a gown or getting into bed. She didn't even remember locking the door after David. Then hearing the bathroom sounds she fell back against the pillows, a smile covering her face. He'd stayed with her. The memories of last night and all that he'd said and done flooded her brain.

"David, you say you care for me but I think you love me with your every breath." The sound of the words on her lips saddened her yet made her happy. She'd promised that she wasn't going to torture herself with what was going on in his brain. She knew what was in his heart and in hers.

Gingerly throwing off the covers and moving her legs she was surprised to feel no pain. There was no swelling either and Margo knew how lucky she was.

Images of her lover naked, his golden body glistening and slick, stirred things deep inside her womanly self. Wanting to love him as she never had, Margo slipped out of her gown and walked naked to the bathroom where she pushed open the door.

David felt the slight breeze as the shower curtain opened and then closed and he felt her hands on his shoulders smoothing and caressing him down to his buttocks. He hardened in an instant. "Good morning, sweetheart," he gasped

"Good morning, love," Margo whispered. Her hands closed over his penis and the yelp that escaped his lips made her smile. "Mm, you feel so good," she said, leaning her front into his back and rotating her hips but never letting go of him.

"Margo," David rasped. He dropped the soap and the wash cloth in the dish and wrapped his arms around his back, holding onto her bottom, straining to feel more of her. "You're killing me here," he managed through clenched teeth while turning the faucets off. "I have nothing on. Wait . . ."

"That's okay, love," Margo murmured. "You don't need to protect me." She slid slowly down his back, her breasts rubbing against him as she rained kisses on his slick body as she descended. When kneeling she kissed the taut muscles of his derriere and then turned him toward her and kissed his thighs while still holding him gently. She touched him with the tip of her tongue and felt him nearly jump out of her hands. "Shh," she said. "Let me love you like this."

The taste and smell of him was intoxicating as Margo twirled her tongue around and around playfully flecking the throbbing shaft with fleeting taps. His hands were entwined in her hair and she could feel the control he was exhibiting. Her heightening excitement met his as she slowly took him into her mouth.

"Margo," David groaned as her wet, warm mouth closed over him. He went spiraling into another world as she loved him.

His body trembled, then as if toppled from a summit, shattered into a thousand pieces. David was limp but had strength enough to grasp her shoulders and pull her up where he held her against his beating chest. She was wet and smooth and shaking with the powerful emotions she'd just displayed and he knew she was in love with him. His heart sang with a new song. He kissed her lips, her throat, and caressed her breasts, gently smoothing the throbbing brown berries. He wanted to plunge inside her where they stood but held himself in check until he was prepared.

On her toes, Margo sought his mouth and kissed him hard. Then she sighed and leaned against him, her head resting on his chest.

David tilted her chin and kissed her closed eyelids. When she looked at him he said, "Falling asleep on me again?"

Her eyes widened. "I did do that, didn't I?" she said. "Not while we were . . ."

He laughed and squeezed her waist. "No, we didn't

even get on the field much less score a home run," he said. "But we can do something about that now if you got a second."

"Is that all you have?" Margo teased.

"I meant to get my stuff," David growled. They were out of the shower, and toweled dry. "Don't blink. I'll be back."

He found her on the bed holding her eyelids open with her fingers. "You nut," he said, nearly cracking up. "How can I make love with you, laughing all over myself?"

Margo wrapped her arms around his neck and pulled him down on top of her, his sheathed penis taut against her mound. "Easily, my love," she said. "Just like this." She guided him into her and arched her hips. "Oh, yes, just like this," she whispered. She yelled his name as he plunged into her. "D-a-avid."

Hours later after sleeping, loving some more, they were sitting at the kitchen table. Margo marveled at the magical way David got things done. Not only in the bedroom but in everything he did. He'd made a call and in less than an hour he was being handed a duffel bag at her apartment door. Now shaved, smelling like a dream dressed in fresh khaki slacks and yellow short-sleeve shirt, she could only admire his air of confidence that one might label arrogant. That was definitely not the case. He knew who he was and what he wanted and wasted no time in going around the mulberry bush.

"What?" David said as he finished the last of his omelet, then poured more coffee. "Didn't you enjoy it?"

"Where'd you learn to do that?" She looked at his laughing eyes accusingly. "If I remember correctly the last time we tried to put an egg together we had to bury our sins." She finished her vegetable omelet and hungered for more. "It was out of this world."

Pleased with his newly learned skill, David drained his mug. "I thought that if we were going to be waking up like this, one of us had better get something going on in the kitchen department. There's nothing like eggs in the morning." He laughed at her flashing eyes. "Inez."

"Inez is teaching you to cook!?" Her jaw dropped. "You've been keeping secrets." Then she warmed at the reality of the situation. She was keeping secrets of her own. She coughed and then said, "You're an excellent student!" She wondered if he would say the same about her when she planned her holiday dinner for him.

"Thank you very much, love," David said, still grinning as if he were the cat who'd gotten the cream.

Lazing in the living room, David said, "Working today?" He was sitting on the sofa with Margo stretched out, her legs resting across his thighs. He was idly massaging her calves.

"Uh-uh," Margo answered. "I decided to take this Friday off," she said. "I'm going to select another Kai and Friends manuscript to send out. Maybe I'll have better luck with this one or start making some changes."

"Oh. You've been trying publishers?" David said with interest.

"Yep." Then Margo laughed. "I thought it took a year to get an answer back. When I received the first reply I couldn't wait to rip it open thinking they'd responded so quickly in order to be the first to buy." She shook her head. "Not so."

"They didn't like it?"

"Not so much that," Margo answered thoughtfully. "The criticism was constructive, which I'm grateful for, but the situations were too mature." She looked away for a minute. "Kai was old for her years," she said quietly.

David continued stroking her legs. "Not every ten-year-old acts like a ten-year-old. Why not try another publisher without making any changes and see what happens."

"Maybe I will," she said. "I rather like the way the kids are."

Quiet for a long moment, David finally said, "What about a day at the beach where you can think on what you want to do? You're free. I'm free. Just the way I like it." He tickled the bottom of her feet and laughed when she struggled to get away.

Sliding her feet to the floor, Margo stood. "Twice you need not ask," she said. "I love your beach."

Friday turned into Saturday at noon and David was lounging in a deck chair watching Margo swim. She waved and he waved back. Days and hours spent with her were golden and he never wanted them to end. It was time he did something about it but over the years he'd learned that timing was everything. Reluctantly he knew he had to wait until she was ready.

The phone rang. "Yeah, Wes," he said and then grinned. "I'm enjoying the summer out here so when the devil are you going to get out here and stay a while?"

Wesley could hear the happiness and he smiled. "Seems like every time I get out there you two have gone," he said. "Guess we'll have to make solid plans for a weekend together." Serious he said, "I've got that information you requested last night on Henderson."

"That was quick," David said, the smile fading from his face. "What'd you find?"

"The brother is insolvent," Wesley said. "When he first got the job with Mirken and Prusser he was like a starving artist. He'd recently left his parents' home to get a crib of his own. Rent too high but on top of the forty-eight-thousand-dollar college debt still owed, he ran up some more, furnishing his place to entertain, and then began living over the top. Appears he was flying high when he joined the firm that was paying him good money. But he wasn't producing and he needed a crisis thing to happen—fast." Wesley paused. "He did make something happen, though."

"Margo's idea," David said flatly.

"You got it," Wesley answered. "My man was living good, new job, new position with a substantial increase in the green. He's just about rock-bottom now and has contacted realtors looking for a cheaper place. Wouldn't be surprised if he ran back to the empty nest."

"Thanks, Wes," David said. "The check's in the mail, man."

"Chalk this one up, David," Wesley said. "If anybody even looks like breathing on her, they got big trouble. Do you want surveillance?"

"No, he's nonthreatening. She told him what was on her mind so he'll get the message."

Wesley wasn't so sure but if he had to he'd act. "Okay, whatever you say." He thought of the two of them out there and he couldn't help but feel happy for his friend. "Glad you two are doing okay," he said. Then, "So what are you waiting for?" he asked, a big grin parting his lips.

"Not understanding you," David said, but he'd begun to smile.

"Yeah, yeah. The senility game again. Okay, buddy, I hear you." Chuckling he hung up.

Getting up to turn the chicken on the grill, he sat back down to answer another call.

"Hello?" he said, frowning at the display. "What is it?" David listened without interruption while his jaw steadily tightened. Responding occasionally he mainly listened. After several minutes he said, "Yes, we can meet tonight. My home."

Margo shook the water off as she hurried up the beach to David. He'd been on the phone for so long she wondered if he was conducting business after promising he wouldn't. She stopped when she got close enough to see his face. It held no smile and he looked stricken. "David?" He reached for her and she sat on his lap and hugged him.

David lifted his head from her chest and kissed her lightly on the lips. "We have to get back." His voice was hoarse.

"Please, tell me. What happened?"

"I'm being sued. Two different charges hit my lawyer's desk today."

"What?"

"Remember the day care center incident?"

"She's suing after all this time?" Margo was incredulous. "Why?"

"It appears that the tot has been suffering from trauma."

"Oh, no," Margo breathed. She felt for the little boy and prayed that it wasn't true. She kissed his furrowed brow. "What is the other one?" she asked.

David held her gaze. "Paternity."

Chapter Twelve

A shudder raced through Margo's body as if she'd been jolted with a cattle prod. Suddenly she felt strange being in his arms. What was going on? Her hands dropped to her lap. All she could do was stare at him, unable to formulate a sensible sentence or even to question him. When he took her hand in his she felt nothing. Another shiver coursed through her.

David saw the look of pain on her face and his heart sank to his toes. He could see the mistrust enter her eyes and he knew that that was what hurt him worst of all. She doubted him. Easing her off his lap, he got up, reached for her cover-up and gave it to her.

"You're cold," he said. He went to the grill and removed the overdone chicken. Holding the platter he said, "Come on inside, Margo. You haven't eaten since breakfast and you need something before we start back. I'll finish the plates with the salads." He turned and went inside the house.

Margo was like a wooden soldier as she moved to the outdoor shower to wash away the sand. With the hand-held nozzle she sprayed the cold water over her face letting it cascade down her body as if she were floating away the shock. Now she knew why David had never committed to her, saying those words she longed to hear. He loved someone else. Who? One of those women in the tabloids? Someone who'd been in the same room with her at so many different gatherings?

He wasn't in the kitchen when she entered but saw that he'd left their food on the counter. She heard the shower and she went to the guest room where her bag lay on the bed. A soft laugh escaped. This room was only used to hold her clothes. Since that first day here, David's bedroom was where she'd always fallen asleep in his arms.

Dressed, her bag packed, she carried it into the kitchen and set it by the door. David was sitting outside on the patio eating, staring at the ocean. From the stiffness of his shoulders she could guess the look on his face. Impassive. Taking her plate she pushed open the screen door and joined him at the table.

"David," she said, but he continued to look at the water.

"Eat, Margo. We have to leave soon."

The salad tasted like grass and she toyed with the rubbery chicken. Pushing the plate away she drank the lemon Snapple that he left for her. She turned to watch the ocean, too, wondering if their intimate relationship was like the waves hitting the shore: dissipating with such finality, as if they'd never existed.

Setting his fork down, David drank deeply of his soft drink then wiped his mouth. Turning, he finally looked at the woman he loved. "You don't trust me." The statement was flat but his steely eyes defied her to look away from him.

"I was shocked," Margo said in a quiet voice. "I had no words."

"Do you now?" David asked.

Nodding her head, she said, "Yes."

"I'm listening."

"Is it true?"

His eyes shuttered briefly but he didn't look away. "No. The woman in question was someone I stopped seeing over a year and a half ago. The child that she says is mine is ten months old."

"Did you love her?"

"No. Our relationship was all of two meetings and I can't say that I remembered what she looked like with clothes on or how she wore her hair or whether she had a beautiful smile or even if she had a brain." His voice was brusque. "It was all sexual," he said bluntly. "Just plain old healthy, mutual lust."

"Then why now after all this time is she coming after you?"

"Dammit! Money! I guess I can afford to give her what she wants." He studied her. "And then there is you," he said.

"Me?"

"The pictures in the papers," David said watching Margo closely. "She has the idea that I'll be a married man soon so her big opportunity is now, without a wife and other kids in the picture."

How can you marry someone you can't admit to loving? Margo brushed a hand across her eyes and sighed deeply. "I'm sorry, David. For all of it," she said. "What are you going to do?"

Getting less than the response he expected, David shuttered the hurt in his eyes. "Right now?" he said, rising from the table, beginning to clear it off. "Get back to the city to meet with my lawyers." He grinned. "Got to develop a strategy you know. Prepare for the next knockout punch. Once these things start it's like a snowball turning into an avalanche. There's more to come."

Summer traffic made the drive longer than usual. Nearly three and a half hours later David was double-parked in front of Margo's building for lack of parking.

They'd been silent most of the way—conversation touching on unimportant things, neither speaking what was in their hearts. Now Margo wished she'd forgotten her own pain to try to vanquish his. She knew that she'd wounded him badly when she'd thought the worst and now he didn't know whether he could trust her.

"I'll be tied up for who knows how long," David said, handing her the small bag. They were standing beside the Mercedes and he leaned back and folded his arms. "When I know something I'll call you to fill you in," he said.

"Not until then?" Margo asked.

"What would you have me say?" He lifted a shoulder, but was hoping she'd say the words he wanted to hear as badly as he'd wanted anything else in the world.

"Nothing you wouldn't want to tell me." She imitated his shrug. "Guess I'll have to wait until you know *something*." After a second she said, "You'd better go prepare. See you," and walked away.

David watched her go and he felt as though she was taking part of him with her. He drove home wondering where he was going to summon the strength to face up to the possibility of living his life without her in it. A man and a woman together without trust are like pieces of driftwood floating in rancid waters. Jonathan's dead wife taught him that. His brother was a weakened man when he'd learned of Cynthia's deceit and it'd nearly destroyed him. David knew that he was innocent of the false charges that this woman was bringing against him. Yet Margo had tried and convicted him in her mind before he could offer her an explanation; her respect for him had died in an instant. There was no denying what he'd seen in her eyes. And there was no telling that she wouldn't spend the rest of their days together waiting for other wrathful former lovers to emerge like locusts.

That wasn't the kind of life he envisioned with her nor did he want it if mistrust simmered in her heart like an oozing wound.

But in the solitude of his home, thoughts of her were so intrusive he held his head in his hand trying to ease the drumming in his temples. She was everywhere. The whirlpool. His bed. The study. The kitchen. David missed her with every passing second and he agonized over how he was going to make it through the night.

For the first time that she could remember, they did not share a kiss on parting. Margo entered her apartment feeling weary. *How strange it is,* she thought, *how in an instant life can hand you lumps of sugar or sacks of coal without warning.* She and David had nothing in their lives to worry about when they'd set out to the beach. But hours later she was confronting her actions wondering if she'd lost her lover because of her inability to speak her mind. David's coldness toward her was eye-opening. She knew he was waiting to hear her words of comfort, of faith, and her eventual blowing off the whole thing as pure nonsense. But she hadn't and she wondered about her own insecurities and just where she fit in his life.

Soul-searching had forced Margo to look honestly at herself. What did she really expect to have in living a life with David? Asking herself that dozens of times left her with a feeling of discontent for her unforgiving behavior. She knew that David was an important, busy man working diligently to keep his many enterprises together. He was an intelligent businessman and once he'd joked that his seven years of night school studying business was mighty useful to an instant multimillionaire.

He'd learned to keep his millions steadily growing so that he could do whatever he desired.

Many didn't know that he was one of those silent philanthropists, giving unselfishly wherever or whenever the opportunities lay. She'd seen him do things without batting an eye, never wanting or waiting for any thanks. From the lone stranger to a charitable organization she'd seen his unselfish generosity. The immigrant selling wilted flowers in heavily trafficked streets was often handed a hundred dollars and looked befuddled as David drove off with a wave. The frustrated teenager walking an ancient bike with a busted tire and no tools to fix it was overjoyed when David stopped to repair the tube to get him home—and speechless when he was given money to buy a new bike.

Margo knew his passion for his chain of day care centers all over the five boroughs. Some of them were twenty-four-hour operations staffed with caring individuals who tended the children of hardworking parents. He'd told her that he'd never realized how many women refused better paying jobs because of the flexing hours. Baby-sitters who could adapt to fluctuating schedules were hard to come by.

It had been nearly a week since Margo had spoken to David. She'd busied herself working on a new client's print ad for facial cream. Word-of-mouth was turning out to be a good part of her business and she was enthused, puffed with pride that she was becoming a success in her own enterprise, steadily building relationships with new contacts and resources. She had learned to divide her time between work and relaxation knowing that inactivity would burn her out more often than not if she didn't exercise. So, early mornings would find her out riding in the park, heedful of her foolish trek that could have been disastrous. Refreshed, she returned home ready to work, new ideas clamoring for release into a project.

Quitting early one evening, Margo shut down the computer and went to the kitchen to prepare a meal. She was slowly dropping her bad eating habits thanks to Valeria's patient instruction and plenty of help from a slew of cookbooks. Mashed potatoes, stir-fried vegetables with a broiled lamb chop, not scorched, were on the menu tonight.

From her seat at the kitchen table Margo could see the big screen TV and she was enjoying her tasteful meal as she watched the six o'clock news. She nearly choked when a picture of David appeared and the news anchor began reporting the story of two lawsuits hitting the wealthy man. The mother and child were shown and then a picture of the woman who was David's accuser flashed briefly. Then the anchor introduced the reporter delivering a report on what had taken place earlier in the day. There were many parents and children parading around the day care center in question, holding placards and chanting. They were positive shouts extolling the value of the center, and how one incident, though unfortunate, should not be looked upon as a blemish. One parent was interviewed and she had nothing but good to say about the care her two children were getting. It was like a second home to them.

The lump in Margo's throat that prevented her from swallowing more food was but empathy for David and what he was feeling as he watched his private life being displayed so publicly. He'd never meant to do anything but good in his quiet ways and she knew that this kind of exposure was extremely painful to him. As for the woman and her paternity suit, Margo dismissed the ac-

cusation, knowing that David wouldn't have told her a
blatant lie about his relationship with her. He'd always
been straight up with her in everything he did or said. It
was just hearing it from him like that that had shocked
her senseless, immobilizing her like a mummy. *But he
was never straight about admitting that he loves you.*
Margo dismissed the intrusive laughing voice in her
head.

Why couldn't she have been a big enough person to
tell him that it was her own insecurities that had led her
to act so indifferently to what he was feeling?

Clearing the table and cleaning the kitchen were simple actions that captured Margo's attention so that she
could stop thinking about David and what he was going
through right now. She had abandoned him in his time
of need so why was she feeling sorry now? she asked
herself.

"You want some company?" Jonathan asked, while
watching the newscast. He was angry and his jaw muscles worked as he attempted to calm down.

David heard the controlled fury in his brother's voice.
"Nah," he said. "I'm okay here with Mister Hennessy."
He swallowed another mouthful of the cognac that
burned sliding down his throat. "Don't you have anything better to do than to watch that drivel? Take Val out
for a change. She's been working too hard." He finished
the glass and poured another.

Frowning at the dismay he heard and the beginning
of a slur in David's voice, Jonathan said, "I'm coming
over."

"No, don't do that, bro. I'm only feeling a little sorry
for myself and you know that that doesn't last long."
David sipped. "I mean it though. How many parties

does Val do in one week? If she caves in under pressure what's that going to do for the business? Go over there and take the spoon from her hand and get her out of the house."

"Val is building a business and you know what that takes," Jonathan said. "She'll be fine. Besides she'll be finished around midnight and I'll see her then. We're going out to the beach when I pick her up." He paused. "Want to come?"

Remembering the last time he was out there, he closed his eyes briefly. "No," he said. "I'm still having damage control phone and fax sessions with my lawyers. I'm sticking close. Maybe after your showing next week we'll get together."

There was a short silence before Jonathan spoke. "Have you heard from her?" He knew something had happened between Margo and David but his brother had zipped lips and wasn't talking. Jonathan had missed seeing her at the house whenever he dropped by. And he didn't miss the haunted look in David's eyes. Wesley was in the dark also.

"Margo's building a business and you know what that takes," David said wryly. The sharp curse in his ear stung.

"Okay, David. You know where I am. Just call," Jonathan said quietly. He hung up.

Inez had gone quietly about her work cleaning the dinner dishes and doing whatever she did in preparing for the next day while David was in the library. She'd come to say she was leaving and had offered him encouragement accompanied by a hopeful smile.

At midnight, David checked the front door, double-locking it when he heard a car in the driveway. Annoyed that his brother ignored his refusal of a visit he peered through the clear edge of the glass doors. His chest constricted. She sat there for a long time, her hands on the steering wheel, her forehead resting against her hands, and he wondered if she was having second thoughts about this unannounced visit. Seeing her rendered him senseless and suddenly all the longing for her surged up from his toes to clutch his throat. *No,* he thought, *she can't leave.* He unlocked the door.

Margo heard the door open and she looked up. Like a deer caught in headlights, she stared, unmoving.

Seeing her indecision, David held out his hand. "Margo."

His voice turned her body to jelly and she could barely move, but doing so in jerky movements climbing out of the car, beeping it locked, she walked up the steps to him. His arm was still outstretched and she took his hand, and as if no time had separated them, went into his arms.

David held her close, rocking her from side to side, murmuring her name and burying his head in her fragrant-smelling hair. He'd missed the scent of her, the feel of her breasts crushed against him, and he squeezed his eyes shut from the pain and pleasure that was overtaking him. Stepping inside backwards, never releasing her, he pushed the door shut with his foot and they stood there once again holding each other in silence.

Why had she tortured herself knowing that deep down this was where she wanted to be—even when she became gray and plump with age? In David's arms. Wasn't that what sharing life was all about? To take the good with the bad? The misfortune with the fortune? The tears with the laughter? Together?

She lifted her head and looked into his eyes and saw the mist in the corners. Reaching her arms around his neck, then on her toes, she pulled his head down to hers

where she kissed the corner of each damp eye. She
smoothed his cheek, and sighing she rested her head on
his chest again.

David saw her own tears and tilting her head he
kissed them, licking the salty wet, and then kissed her
forehead. After a while David took her hand and led her
into the living room where they sat on the sofa, his arm
around her shoulder, her arm hugging his middle.

"I'm sorry," Margo whispered, huddled against him.
She kissed the softness of his neck inhaling his scent,
almost losing herself in it. "David, I'm sorry for my lack
of trust in you, and for not telling you when you needed
to hear it the most. I was like the proverbial rat leaving
the sinking ship. Can you forgive me?"

Exhaling, David hugged her close, loving the feel of
her softness as his fingers skimmed her breasts. He
wanted to love her in the worst way.

"Yes, sweetheart," he murmured. There was nothing
else to say.

They didn't love, but were content to remain as they
were, holding each other tightly.

It was nearly one o'clock when David lifted his head.
She'd been so silent and he knew from the gentle rise
and fall of her breasts that she'd fallen asleep. He smiled
and eased out of her arms, planting stolen kisses on her
cheek and lips as he settled her on the long sofa. He left
the room and returned with a throw but then stared
down at her undecided. Taking a deep breath, he
aroused her. "Come, Margo, let's get you into bed," he
said.

Margo opened her eyes, half awake, wondering why
she was being led down the hall. "David?"

"You're knocked out and a few hours sleep here
won't harm you," David whispered while laying her
down on the bed in the guest room. He smiled, remem-

bering what a sound sleeper she was, especially after she'd stayed on that computer for the better part of a day and half the night, chuckling softly while he slid her slacks over her hips and lifted the T-shirt over her head. The billowing sheet settled over her, and without opening her eyes she smiled, snuggling against the pillows. He'd teased her that she burrowed into them as if she were a woodland creature. The smile was still on her face when she murmured, "Love you, David, my love."

As if frozen, David stared down at the sleep-drugged woman who'd uttered the words he'd yearned to hear. In sleep she'd finally bared her heart. In sleep, the truth be told.

Margo knew when she awoke that she was in unfamiliar surroundings. The illuminated digital clock on the bedside table read four thirteen. Her eyes accustomed to the shadows as she realized she'd never left David's home, and was in one of the guest bedrooms. The sheet was down around her hips baring her midriff, and skimming her midnight-blue sexy satin underwear. She rubbed her shoulders then flung her legs over the side of the bed. In the dark she found the bathroom and turned on the light after closing the door.

How could she have fallen asleep so hard that she hadn't budged when David put her to bed? Had they made love? Impossible! No way would she ever forget that—entwining her legs in his long strong ones, his hair tickling her skin as they moved passionately over one another. She splashed water over her face and brushed her teeth using one of the many new brushes from the vanity drawer. Refreshed, she turned out the light and left the room. She was no longer sleepy and didn't wish to wake David. After that news report she knew that fatigued as he was he'd be behind closed doors with his lawyers probably for days to come.

Wondering where her clothes and shoes were she padded through the shadowy, still house to the living room and gasped at the silhouette in the chair.

"It's me, Margo," David said, turning on the end table lamp.

"Oh, I thought you were sleeping," Margo said. "I was looking for my clothes." She felt odd standing in front of him half naked, his eyes roving over her in that familiar way she loved, yet her body was already sensing his nearness.

"Were you planning on leaving without saying goodbye?"

Her cheeks warmed, but she remembered the last time they parted, her arms feeling empty, and her lips cold and untouched. "I'm never leaving you again without a hug and a kiss."

"Are you leaving me again, Margo?" he said huskily. He was standing, watching her. She was beautiful, the soft shadows from the lone lamp playing over her sun-bronzed skin. He was close to her now and he could smell the mint on her warm breath as it came in small puffs.

"Only if that is your wish," she answered, already so weak in the knees that she nearly swooned into his arms.

He caught her shoulders then. "You *are* mad," he whispered. He bent his head and took her mouth, his tongue searching and tasting hers. He groaned his pleasure as his hands roamed down her back and caught her buttocks, pressing her against his arousal. "My sweet, mad, love," he moaned against her lips.

The dawn crept into the darkened bedroom, waking Margo. She was entwined in David's arms, her legs wrapped around his, her head nestled under his shoulder. He slept soundly. Disentangling herself as quietly as she could she eased to the edge of the bed, sitting there unmoving, watching the steady rise and fall of his chest. Vivid memories of how she'd gotten there warmed her cheeks as she saw herself shedding her panties and bra, stumbling naked up the stairs to his bedroom. The smell of warm heady sex and his maleness filled her nostrils. They'd loved in the wee hours of the morning oh, how they'd loved. She thought that they would never get enough of each other until she remembered that they'd fallen against the pillows both with triumphant smiles as if each had won the blue ribbon.

Running her fingers lightly as a feather along his chest she watched him stir, his handsome face devoid of that bleak look she'd seen when they last parted days before. He looked content even though she knew that his heart was heavy with what was looming over him. Margo loved touching him. She loved feeling his long firm length crushed against her, his chest hairs rubbing against her breast as he moved over her. She lifted his hand and softly kissed his fingers, her senses reacting almost violently to what they'd done to her. With one last shudder she placed his hand gently down across his stomach and sighing she got up leaving his room very quietly and went downstairs.

In the whirlpool Margo wondered just how she would manage her life without David in it. Not waking up with him day after day was a concept hard to take, especially with her body still humming from David's magnificent ministrations to it. But, she thought with her practical mind, she had her work and he had his. It wasn't as if they lived hours away from each other making theirs a long-distance relationship. "Yes, but early morning lov-

ing certainly starts the day on a high note," she muttered, grinning at her lascivious thoughts.

David reached for her but his arm fell onto an empty
space. Her smell, the cooling warmth of the pillow, was
evidence that he hadn't had a glorious dream, that indeed she'd spent the night in his bed in his arms after
allowing him to fill her with his love. Thoughts of how
they'd loved aroused him to the point where the sheet
was under attack. Groaning, he thought this would
never do. She was constantly in his thoughts and the
image of him conducting business in a suit and tie while
trying to hide evidence of where his mind was, was definitely not very funny.

She was not in his bathroom and he let the smell of
soft scented floral lead him to the downstairs bathroom.
The door was ajar and he pushed it open. She was murmuring to herself but she was nearly cracking up. He
couldn't help but wonder what was so hilarious.

"I hope it's not my performance that's humoring you
so," he said huskily, his eyes on her naked breasts glistening with soapy bubbles. He licked his lips.

Margo's eyes widened. He was naked and standing at
attention. She nearly had an orgasm just staring at him.
She swallowed. "Well, I don't know," she said, deep
frown lines wrinkling her forehead. "I was so sleepy I
can hardly remember what took place. Did you love me
at all?"

David was by the whirlpool in three long strides.
"What?" he croaked. His own body was still stinging,
his tender nipples a reminder of how she'd tasted and
suckled like a starving baby. "You honestly don't remember?" he said in a deadly calm voice. But he was
already stepping inside the big tub, standing over her,
his penis pulsing in anticipation.

Margo reached up and touched him. "It's coming

back to me," she said haltingly as she ran her hand alongside the rock-hard shaft.

"Aargh," David yelped and caught her hand. "Don't do that," he barely managed as he sat down. She was still holding him. "Margo, I want to be inside of you." The words barely made it through clenched teeth. "Now."

She smiled while caressing him then kissed his lips, tracing their outline with her tongue. "Mm, I want that too, love," she said. "But we're down here."

"So what does that mean?" David said harshly while sinking under her assault.

"No condoms," she said simply but her lips were curved into a mischievous smile as she continued to manipulate him.

David stopped fondling her nipples, the realization hitting him like a blow to his gut. But then he grinned as he reached to the overhead shelf and opened a small ceramic box. It was filled. "Never had any use for these in here before," he said hungrily, then looked at her with a grin. "Some foresight, huh?" he asked and then sheathed himself.

Margo watched in fascination and relief as she'd thought that she'd be deprived of feeling him inside her. Bracing herself, she stretched out her legs inviting him to cover her with his body.

David groaned and moved on to her, steadying himself by holding on to the edge of the tub. He groaned as her hand guided him and he slipped inside as easily as if he'd loved her like this all his life. His body was at home. Too long anticipating, his uncontrollable thrusts sent her upward as she arched her body to meet his desperate plunges.

She wrapped her hands around his middle to keep him from slipping away from her as she kept up with his frantic rhythm. The water lapping around them slapping at her thighs, ebbing and flowing with her gyrating hips was so sensuously captivating, that she felt as though she was one with the ocean. With a powerful thrust that sent her over the edge, she overflowed while screaming his name. Like a falling star she plummeted to the watery bed as swiftly as she'd been lifted to heaven.

Sliding off her, David sank to the bottom of the tub and then emerged shaking the water from his eyes and face. His breathing was rapid and he feared disaster would strike if he didn't get hold of himself. Slowly his breath was coming back to normal when he opened his eyes. Her eyes were still closed and the smile on her face made him grin, filling him with such a cocky boldness that he nearly crowed.

"Do you remember now?" he whispered, leaning over so that she could look into his eyes.

Margo couldn't help but laugh at his triumphant gloating. She reached up and put both hands on his head and pushed him down into the water, and then scrambled to get out of his way when he emerged shaking and growling like a wounded polar bear.

Shaking the water from his eyes, David found her on the other side of the whirlpool and went after her. Catching her he pulled her down with him holding her tightly. "You didn't answer me, sweetheart," he crooned.

Unable to escape him Margo surrendered, reaching up to caress his cheek. "I'll never forget us, love," she said. "Never."

Later, while Margo was putting the finishing touches on yet another Kai story she couldn't help but remember her words to her lover. She knew that she would never forget him, her mind and body was proof of her feelings. The thought of staying with him was heavy on her mind. She wondered if he asked, would she move in with him. Would she take what he had to offer without benefit of marriage? Did she even want to marry while making all the exciting career moves in her life right now?

Her mind raced with the possibility of their relationship cooling into one of complacency—seeing each other between his trips and her projects whenever time allowed and eventually drifting apart. The thought of that happening was mesmerizing and she could only scoff at such an absurdity.

"I'll never forget us, love," she repeated, her words to him echoing in the silence. They had come from her heart. She couldn't think of herself as being without him. He'd looked at her longingly when she got into her car, holding on to her hand as if it was his lifeline. His words had both warmed and chilled her and as she thought of them now, she shivered remembering how his eyes had darkened with anguish.

"Don't ever leave me, Margo. My life is nothing without you in it. It would be as if you killed me."

Chapter Thirteen

From a distance, Jonathan watched Margo talking animatedly with one of his guests, pointing to a particular photograph. He angled his head to see the one in question. A shadow crossed his face and he shuttered his eyes briefly. It was of a father's grief at losing his infant son to an accident. He strove to take himself out of that scenario. The theme of the show was Fathers and Sons. The gallery was filled on both levels with his photos of the men and boys in the lush dense forests of Venezuela as well as the cosmopolitan parts of the country. The show was well received and he felt a certain satisfaction that mingled with his sadness of what he'd almost had.

His eyes turned to Margo again and he smiled. He'd never seen her look more radiant than when she'd walked in on his brother's proud arm. She was beautiful in a soft, pale green sleeveless dress that whispered above her knees. David came into his view and turned his head to catch his stare. He smiled and Jonathan smiled back.

"They're a pair, aren't they?" Wesley had nothing but admiration in his voice as he stood by Jonathan watching the two people who were so obviously daft about one another that they'd blow the needle off the lie detector machine if they so denied it.

"Truer words, et cetera, et cetera," Jonathan said with

a grin. He looked at the plate of food Wes had and said, "Haven't you had enough? Stop feeding your face and go fill out your order. I want SOLD on every picture hanging up in here. Going to the Children's Home as you well know."

"Can't help it man," Wesley said. "Your lady outdoes herself every time." He shook his head. "Half this stuff I can't give a name to but it's smokin'."

"Fits the theme of the showing," Jonathan said, finding Valeria, and when their eyes locked, smiling at her.

"Any more incidents?" Wesley asked, seeing the exchange, and nodding his delight.

"From Shankley? Nah. Long gone," Jonathan said, relief filling his voice.

"Good." Wesley turned his attention back to David and Margo who'd walked off to the second level. They were holding hands and whispering like young lovers discovering the wonders of the opposite sex. "How far do you think this woman is going to go?" he asked Jonathan. Both knew the lawsuit was still in the air until the DNA test results were revealed in a matter of days. "Do you think she'll want the whole shebang if the child is David's?"

"That was a dumb question, Wes," Jonathan said with a scowl on his face. "Just what do you think?"

Wesley imitated his friend's dour look. "Yeah, you're right," he said. "Guess one good thing came out of this mess with that mother dropping her suit."

"Yeah, that's true," Jonathan said. He'd seen the relief on David's face when the lawyer had called with the news. Apparently the woman changed day care centers but when she saw the difference in caring, learned teachers and staff, and that her child was the one getting short shrift, she called David asking him to readmit her child to the center. She also knew that the valuable learning experience was costing her little or nothing compared with other schools. She wanted the best for her child. "Sometimes people get egged on and heated up to go against what they know is right." Wesley made a soft expletive and Jonathan looked at him.

"What the hell is he doing here?" Wesley mumbled.

"Who?"

"A worm fronting as a man."

Wesley and Jonathan watched as Margo released David's hand as someone spirited him away to a group of well-wishers. She waved at him and then wandered back down to the first level, hungry again and anxious to discover a new morsel that Valeria had cooked up. She bumped into a hefty back and when she looked, she stopped dead in her tracks. That neck!

Ty Henderson turned to face her. "Hello, Margo. Nice party." He bent to kiss her cheek and grinned when she stepped back. He caught her arm, steadying her. "Can't we go back to being friends?" he said. His square face was plastered with a smile.

Margo was stupefied. The good-looking husky man who had betrayed her was standing before her with that silly grin as if they'd parted yesterday. A big man, though not as tall as wide, was even wider than she'd remembered. His hand on her arm and the touch of his lips was so revolting that she feared she'd throw up.

"Get your hands off me, Ty," she said through clenched teeth.

Ty Henderson was holding her elbow and his grip tightened. "Now don't be like that, Margo, we were friends once. I'm only asking for a little favor and then I'll be out of your hair for good." He nodded his head at the pictures. "You're traveling in some kind of company, girl. Multimillionaires, for playmates."

Margo tried to get away from him. "You're sick. Let

me go!" When he grinned and held on she swung the flat of her left hand hard against his left cheek. "I said let me go!"

Wesley and Jonathan were across the room in an instant.

David was still on the second level. When he saw the two men running he sprinted down the ramp, thinking only of Margo and danger.

"Okay, Henderson," Wesley said. "I think it's time you got out of here while you're still able." He turned to Margo. "Are you all right?"

"What do you mean is she all right?" David said, reaching them, frowning at Margo rubbing her arm. "What the hell happened?" he asked. "Margo, what happened?" He glanced at the stranger hemmed in by Wesley and Jonathan.

"Seems Henderson here didn't take Margo's warning to leave her alone and she hauled off landing one smack dab in his kisser." Wesley rubbed his cheek. "Ouch!"

"Henderson?" Incredulous, David stared at the man and then what Wesley had said registered, and he studied Margo. "Did he hurt you?" His voice was deadly calm. Before he got an answer he turned to Henderson with balled fists but Jonathan stepped in front of him.

"We'll handle this David," he said quietly. "More lawsuits you don't need."

David's jaw muscles were working. He took Margo's hand and gripped it while staring at Henderson. "Stay away from her." Words left unspoken hit their mark as the man's eyes wavered before David's cold stare.

Jonathan, with Wesley on the other side of the man, walked with him to the entrance door. They stepped outside. "You won't have any more contact with Margo Sterling," he said in a steady voice. "Take it from me this is your only warning."

"And me," Wesley said, his eyes boring into the man's nervous ones.

David watched Henderson being escorted out of the gallery. When his breathing was even he looked at Margo, alarmed at the fury in her eyes. He'd never seen them so black. "Are you sure you're okay?" he asked in a low voice. He saw the red marks on her arm where she'd been held. "He hurt you." The statement was flat and angry.

"He can't hurt me again," Margo said. "I was just surprised that he'd turn up here with his arrogant self. Boy, some people have more brass than a chandelier."

"This is the first time you've seen or heard from him since that call?" David asked.

"Yes." Margo frowned. "I still can't believe he'd come here to ask me that."

"Ask what?"

"You know. The same crap. Wants another idea and he'd leave me alone after that."

"He threatened you?" David's eyes narrowed.

"Not really. Just said after one little favor he'd be out of my hair for good." She frowned. "That couldn't be taken as a threat against me, could it?"

He shook his head. "No," David answered. But he was furious. The man was a potential danger but he didn't want to scare her to death unless things took a different turn. Wesley's report had shown Henderson to be in dire straits. When a man is knocking on the door of poverty after living the high life, he can become irrational, liable to do anything.

Margo knew him well enough to know that he was holding back. "What is it David?" she asked.

"I had him checked out after that call he made to you," David answered.

Surprised, Margo said, "Why?"

"Because that call was out of the ordinary, and I wanted to make sure you weren't in any danger from a loose cannon."

A soft laugh escaped. "Ty? He's as sane as anyone else in this crazy world. I realized he's just a lazy man, unwilling to rely on his own talents to make it. Trying to threaten somebody will take up too much time and effort." She smiled and slipped her arm around David's waist. "Come on. Let's find some more of Val's mysterious nibbles. I'm starving."

David kissed her lightly. "You sure you're okay? Not frightened?" He rubbed the spot on her arm where the angry-looking marks were disappearing. His lips tightened but he remained silent.

"I'm fine," she insisted. "And the only thing frightening me right now is that I won't have enough strength for later on."

"What's happening later on?" Then he frowned at her. "You're going home to work tonight?" He'd anticipated her falling asleep in his arms.

"Of course."

"You can give it a rest for one day out of the week, Margo," David said, feeling a little peeved.

They'd reached the table filled with inviting edibles and Margo picked up a plate and began filling it. "Well, what I had in mind," she said in a low voice, "was to get a good workout." She smiled. "First in the whirlpool. Then in your bed. Then in the shower. Then in the living room. Then back to your bed and then maybe in . . ." Her words were smothered when he crushed her mouth with his.

"Okay, okay, you little tease," David whispered. "I got the message. So why are we still here? Sounds like what you have in mind will take hours."

"I hope so. I sure do hope so," Margo said, wickedly.

* * *

September arrived in a silky dress billowing with soft warm breezes trying to hold on to the hot summer. But the second week did a turnaround. The days were brisk yet the cool sun did not intimidate those hardy souls, sun-worshippers who delved into their sport with frenzied energy as though trying to hoard the memories to last through a cold bleak winter.

Cyclists were no exception with the excitement high in the air about the Tappan Zee Bike Tour. Margo especially was keyed up. For weeks she'd trained for this, getting up before dawn, stretching before setting out on a sweat-popping ride through her streets, winding down in Alley Pond Park and back again. She didn't consider herself a novice and was puffed as a pouter pigeon when David heaped high praise on her for her skillful maneuvering of her high-tech machine.

She'd long since given her borrowed bike back to Champion Wheels where it was donated to a group home. Her new hybrid bike, now broken in, was one of David's pride and joy models. She'd refused to let him pay for the expensive vivid royal blue bicycle, proud to pay for it with her own money. Of course the thousand-plus was part of the money she'd earned after doing his projects, she thought. But still, it was hers. David had only rolled his eyes at her stubborn streak of independence.

The charity bike tour sponsored by major corporations attracted hundreds of enthusiastic cyclists. Margo had been part of groups before but none larger than sixty. She couldn't fathom cycling among hundreds of riders. David had explained that this was a van-assisted tour, or as some called it, a sag wagon. Some of the cyclists rode to the site in vans while their bikes were transported in another van occupied by experienced bike technicians along for minor and major repairs. The sag wagon would travel the route picking up a cyclist whose bike had become immobilized. No one was left behind. There were also medical staff and group leaders ready to assist in case of trouble. The tours were always well-planned and organized. Some of the cyclists would bike the twenty miles to Rockland Lake State Park and back. But Margo looked forward to the scenic tour doing the full sixty-mile route to the Bear Mountain Bridge and back again to Tarrytown.

Margo was happily exhausted as she sat on the sofa sipping a cup of tea while waiting for David. She was packed and ready to leave from his house at four in the morning. But the excitement of the trip far outweighed losing a few hours of sleep. Frowning she reached over to pick up the phone.

"Hi, love," she said. "Running late?"

"Margo, something's come up."

The annoyance in his voice was evident. "You can't make the trip," she stated.

"I'm sorry," David said. "I know how much you looked forward to this but I have to fly to D.C. in the morning. Senator Young's calendar is full for the next month. He called suggesting a working Sunday brunch if I was agreeable. Otherwise my plans for the Battered Elderly program will sit another month or so before gaining any attention." Her sigh was almost inaudible. "This is my chance to have his undivided attention."

"Oh, David," Margo said with frustration.

"I know you're disappointed but there will be other tours we can take," he said, wishing he could make it up to her.

"Yes, you're right. But I understand. Your business is more important."

"Necessary, yes, but not more important than joining you on your first big tour," he said firmly.

"Will you be back tomorrow evening?" she asked, trying to keep the disappointment from her voice.

"Plan to," he replied. "How about dinner out, say around seven o'clock?"

"You're flying commercial?"

"No, I'll have better control over my time if I use my own transportation," he answered. "Then is seven okay?"

"That'll be fine. Have a safe trip."

The letdown was more than she expected. She'd looked forward to this, especially since the season would soon be over.

She got up to rinse her cup and looked at her bag and bike by the door with resignation. "Like the man said, Margo, there will be others."

But why not this one? she thought, her mind going like sixty. There were hundreds of people taking the tour and she knew at least two others who were going to meet her and David in Tarrytown. Alana and Zachary. Why couldn't she get a ride up with either of them? Or even follow in her car if necessary? Her mood was lightening as she reached for her telephone directory. Her only hope was that they could work out a plan.

"Zachary, it's Margo Sterling."

"Simply amazing!" There were so many people, bikes and vans assembled in the parking lot of a large corporation that Margo could hardly contain her excitement. "Incredible!" It was difficult trying to maneuver into a spot close to Zachary and his friends but she managed and was standing outside of her Mazda unhooking her bike.

Zachary walked over to her. "I'm sorry that I couldn't handle your bike on my rack, Margo, but three is the max." He grinned. "But you sure kept up."

"Listen, I can drive when I have to," Margo said. "I'm just glad I was able to hook up with you guys. A sense of direction I don't have and I'd probably still be riding around this town looking for you all."

"Hey, you two," Alana said, rolling her bike up to them. "I was hoping I'd hook up with you in this maze." She looked around. "Where's David?"

"He had business," Margo said. "He'll make the next one." She felt the excitement in the air as people began to mount. "Looks like we're on our way."

By nine thirty hundreds of cyclists were on the road. They were each given maps that would take them along the spray-painted path that zigzagged through small towns that would eventually lead into the park. Although she'd gotten separated from Alana and Zachary and his friends, she didn't mind. They were all going in the same direction and would meet in the same place, so she enjoyed the ride looking at the scenery, thrilled to pieces at this new adventure.

Before cycling Margo had never thought about the sport, driving being the quickest way to get anywhere. No one was more surprised than she when stopping along routes in a state where she'd lived all her life, she discovered some little-known but amazing facts.

She'd heard about Weeksville in Brooklyn, for instance, but had never seen the four wood-frame houses, vestiges of a once thriving free black community in the nineteenth century. The historic street had originally been an Indian trail. There were so many places steeped in history that she'd visited with David on so many rides throughout the five boroughs of the city.

The ride into Rockland Lake State park came quicker

than she'd expected, though she welcomed dismounting. Hunger gnawed at her and she began munching on the lunch she'd packed.

"Better hold off eating too much," Alana said. "Still got a lot of miles to cover, and cramping up is not what you want to experience today."

"My fault," Margo said. "Guess I was too excited to eat much of anything this morning." She finished her turkey sandwich and started on an apple.

An hour later they were on their way again. About twenty minutes into the ride, Margo clutched her stomach. "Oh, Lord," she said.

Hoping that her body wasn't telling her what she thought it was, she blocked it from her mind. There were no golden thrones on this wide open road. But it wasn't mind over matter to her regret. She was in trouble. Big trouble! Her stomach was griping to beat the band and if she didn't want to be embarrassed she'd better get back to civilization. She thought without humor now that many cyclists found a toilet wherever they were: behind a tree, a rock, another tree. No one wanted to be left behind because they were answering nature's call. But a tree was far from her solution.

She had her map and the spray paint was still on the ground. That little town they'd just left was only a five-minute ride back. Margo veered off and pumped hard in the opposite direction, waving to some cyclists who were waving at her. According to the map they would be on a straight road for a good stretch so it wouldn't be a problem finding them.

The restaurant was a welcome sight when Margo turned onto the same street that they'd passed before. She propped her bike against the brick wall and clutching her stomach hurried inside, trying to be sedate, but one look at her face and the cashier, with a knowing smile, pointed to the back.

Margo exhaled. Now a smile touched her lips as she wondered how to look calm and collected as she walked from the establishment. But happily no one paid her the slightest bit of attention as she slid out the door. A moment later, she sagged against the brick wall to keep from sinking to the ground as she stared. Her bike was gone!

Pounding her fist against the rough stone, Margo screamed in anger at herself. "Damn, damn, damn." *Never, never, leave your bike unattended! Lock it, lock it, lock it!* Lessons she'd learned. Suddenly laughing at the absurdity of her situation, Margo sat down on a bench outside the small restaurant.

"I know that you'd agree that taking the time to secure it was a highly tenuous decision, Cindy." Talking to herself gave her something to do while she pondered her situation. It wasn't as if she could call Val like she had once before. Or call David on his cell. *Would you please come get me, I'm stranded on a mountain in Upstate New York?*

Well, she'd have to call someone, she thought as she reached for her phone clipped to her waist. But her hand felt nothing but the strap of her fanny pouch. The car. She'd left the phone on the front seat of her car. "Oh, God," she said. "What in the world is wrong with me?"

Worried now, she looked at her surroundings. Somewhere around this quaint little peaceful-looking town there was a thief riding around on a very expensive piece of equipment, she fumed. Hoping that he or she went head first over the handlebars when applying the brakes, she felt an iota of comfort.

Maybe a sag wagon would be coming by she hoped, but knew they were long past this point and would be returning by another route. The contents of her pouch were sparse: sixty-three dollars and some change, a driver's license and registration, house and car keys, and a gas card. What else had she needed on an all-day bike ride? she defended.

Guessing that she was halfway between Bear Mountain and Tarrytown she stood and walked the few steps to the curbside pay phone, thinking that this marvelous wonder would soon become extinct. If she could catch a cab thirty or so miles back then she'd have it made. But how in the world was she going to explain this one to David? She could only imagine the changing looks on his face as she told her tale. He'd be surprised because she hadn't even called to tell him her plans before she went to bed last night. Well, she sighed, so much for getting in one last tour.

The driver of the car service didn't appear too happy about driving thirty miles, but Margo shrugged it off. He was getting paid wasn't he? After charging her fifty dollars she'd be practically penniless driving back to the city. The surly man took twists and turns making it back to the highway, and grateful that her ordeal was nearly over, she closed her eyes, suddenly feeling drained. She just hoped that she'd find some of the cyclists in the parking lot when she got there. The days were shorter now, the sun had gone down and the sky was looking gray—and the last thing she needed was to try to find her way back home in the dark.

She opened her eyes and blinked, after seeing the sign. "Hey, I said Tarrytown. You're going north," Margo said, angry at his blunder. For the first time she felt a flutter in her stomach when the man pulled over and turned to her, the disgruntled look now replaced with something she knew instinctively to fear. "Why are you stopping here? Turn around."

"What else do you have to pay me with beside money, honey?"

The last word was lost as Margo was out the door, fleeing unheedingly across the road, running in the opposite direction. There was a car coming and she waved frantically but it kept going. The cab had sped away, continuing north as breathless, she kept running, staying on the highway. Trying to remember the route the group was taking back from Bear Mountain, she was certain that it wasn't following the highway, but was taking a scenic road. She slowed to a quick walk, panting, but breathing easier. There was a stitch in her side but she ignored it.

It was dark enough for headlights now and she was hesitant about flagging down another car. The first time was out of fear and panic and the need to get away from that driver. Now she wasn't so sure that hitchhiking was such a good idea. So whenever she saw headlights in the distance, she stood far off the road out of the glare and waited until the car passed. If it took her until the break of day she'd be damned if she was going to put herself in any more danger with her Einstein decisions.

Trying to find humor in her situation, she smiled at David's granite face when he'd picked her up from Val's, had admonished her, rubbed her down and put her to bed. The next day they'd made delicious love. Those thoughts kept her walking as if she were walking right into his arms.

The terror she'd felt back there had not completely abated. The enormity of what could have happened had she not run on instinct was overpowering. If she'd acted like a dullard, he'd have been on her in an instant, and she wondered how long would it have taken for someone to have found her. And in what condition? Her fears were heightened when she envisioned David's tortured face. If the worst had happened he would never know what was in her heart. How foolish she was in not revealing her feelings. Now she knew that when she laid eyes on him again, he'd know.

"I love you, David Blackshear," she said aloud. "I'll always love you."

Zachary slowed as his head beams caught the movement darting to the side of the road. He swore. "So that's what she's been doing." He pulled over and inched along until he came to the spot where he'd seen her. He flashed his lights and blew his horn. "Margo?"

She got up from her crouch. "Zachary?"

"It's me," he said, getting out of the SUV. "Are you all right?"

"Now I am," Margo said, walking toward him. "Just tired." The headlights showed the concern on his face. "I'm okay, Zachary." She put her arms around his waist and hugged him. "Thanks for not leaving me on this mountain," she said.

"Are you kidding? I could never go home again." He laughed, while leading her to the car. "Let's get out of here. Where's your bike? What the hell happened?"

Margo buckled herself in. "It's a long story."

I love you Margo. Know that and hear me wherever you are.

David kept his mind on the positive while he waited. Thinking bad thoughts would make it difficult for him to react in a hurry if need be. He could only wait for a call.

Earlier when he'd arrived home and couldn't reach her, like one time before, he'd thought the worst, yet all he'd had to do then was drive to Brooklyn to get her. Now she was lost in the mountains of Upstate New York, which was a far cry from hopping to the next borough.

He hesitated to answer the phone when he saw the name on the display but he picked it up. "Anything?" he said, barely able to get the word out.

"I found her," Zachary said. "We're driving back to her car now. Hold on." He handed his cell phone to the exhausted woman sitting beside him.

"David?"

His body went limp with relief. "Margo. Are you all right?" he managed in a voice that strangely could not be his.

"I'm fine," Margo said, the sound of his voice tightening her throat. Tears sprang to her eyes. Her voice was a whisper. "David, I love you. I've always loved you."

The world spun. "I love you, Margo. I always have."

Chapter Fourteen

He'd been waiting in his car in front of her building when they arrived after nine o'clock. Zachary had driven her car while his buddy had driven his SUV. Not many words passed between the two men but David had shaken his hand, saying thanks. He couldn't say any more for what the brother had done. Not then.

Margo didn't protest when he drove her to his home. Once inside, all she wanted was a shower but he caught her and held her close. "I was scared," he said simply.

She leaned into him, wrapping her hands around his waist. "I'm sorry," she murmured.

After a moment he lifted his head. "I didn't realize you'd wanted it that much," he said. "Want to talk about it?"

How could she talk sensibly about her foolishness, now? She reached up and caressed his cheek. "Nature did me in." At his puzzled look she said, "Later, love. Much later."

Dawn found David awake in his bedroom, his arms over his head as he lay on his back staring at the ceiling. He hadn't slept well, though he couldn't understand why.

He turned his head and looked at the sleeping love of

his life who was dead to the world before her head hit the pillow. When he'd slid into bed beside her he'd held her so tightly that she protested until he loosened his hold. Now he wondered how he could ever let her out of his sight.

David was glad it was Sunday and his housekeeper's day off. He wanted to be alone with Margo. If he had anything to say about it she wouldn't be leaving for a good while. Before slipping from the bed he kissed the tip of her nose. He donned a robe and left the room.

Before Margo opened her eyes she knew where she was. She smelled the fresh woodsy scent that intermingled with his male scent that made him unique. The indentation in his pillow was still warm. She sat up, the covers falling away to bare her nakedness. Then she vaguely remembered the motions she'd gone through the night before, showering and then tumbling into his bed.

The coffee was ready and the aroma filled the room as he prepared a tray and carried it into the bedroom. She was awake and sitting up. He stopped a moment sucking in his breath at her beautiful bared breasts. He liked that she didn't try to cover up in front of him. Then he set the tray at the foot of the king-size bed.

"Good morning," he said.

"Good morning."

They could only stare at each other, their eyes telling a story.

Finally David lifted a mug and handed it to her. He took his own and carefully slid into bed, sitting up beside her. They sipped the hot brew in silence.

Margo savored the delicious coffee. "I never want another thing to eat in life," she said.

"Hmm," David said, giving her a look with raised

brow. "Learned your lesson, did you?" He could only smile when she'd told him of her dilemma.

She laughed and poked him in the arm with her elbow. "You're so smart. Why didn't you warn me that could happen?" When he didn't answer, but made a production of sipping the hot coffee, her eyes grew wide. "It happened to you, didn't it?" she accused.

Nodding, he chuckled. "About umpteen years ago when I was a green kid. Never forgot the experience."

Laughing, Margo set her mug on the nightstand, and then turned and slid an arm across his belly, slipping her hand under his robe. He was naked and she closed her eyes, relishing his touch and his smell. "I lost my beautiful bike," she murmured.

David set his own mug down and put his arm around her so that she was cradled against his shoulder. He kissed the top of her head. "Don't worry, I'll get you another." He felt her stiffen. "Let me do that for you, Margo," he whispered. "I want to."

Margo relaxed and sighed. "Okay, my love," she said. "If you want to."

"I want."

They were silent for several minutes, holding on to one another as if it was the most natural thing for her to wake up in his bed, in his arms. After a while they began to talk, of her ordeal and of many things: her business, his enterprises, and his next trip out of town. They talked of Jonathan and Valeria and how they were so in love, and of Wesley for whom Jonathan insisted on playing matchmaker. They talked of flying to Hawaii where Margo had never been and was intrigued by his description of the lush islands.

"When would you like to go?" David whispered, kissing her forehead.

"You mean in the near future?" Margo asked dreamily, thinking of a glorious vacation sometime next year.

"Tomorrow, the next day, whenever you want," David said. "If Hawaii isn't your desire I have a villa in Florence you might like."

"South Carolina?" Margo asked.

"Italy, smarty-pants," David said, tweaking her nose.

"What about St. Maarten? I love it and haven't been there in years."

"Yes, that can be arranged," David said. "My place is always ready."

Margo sat up and looked at him. "You actually have a place there too?"

David met her stare. "I do." He saw her frown. "Does that bother you?"

She stirred and settled back against him. "Not really."

Her voice was so quiet that it disturbed him. He lifted her chin so that he could look into her eyes. "Margo, I'm not ashamed of what I have or what I can do with my money. It came to me honestly. I know I didn't work for it but I do work at keeping it so that others can benefit from my good fortune. I am the happiest man in the world when I can do things for you. See the shine in your eyes when you're happy because of something I've given you. I want to shower you with things, hear your laugh at experiencing something new and different. I live for that." He kissed the tip of her nose. "So will you let me?"

Her heart was filled with love for him. She didn't care if he still wore working blues as a conductor on the Long Island Rail Road. He would still be the same man she'd fallen in love with.

"David?" She lay quietly against him.

"Hmm?"

"You told me that you loved me."

"I always have," David answered softly.

"I told you that I loved you."

"Yes, you did."

After a moment, Margo sat up and looked into his eyes. "Why did we do that?" she said.

"Do what?"

"Waste so much time pretending that our feelings didn't run so deeply," Margo answered. "I didn't know I had fallen in love. Not until I walked into Lawrence's office and you clasped my hand. Then I knew that all those months that I couldn't sleep it was because of the man in a red cap who'd given me a charming smile and a disarming hello that I returned with a nasty attitude."

He didn't answer but thought about what she'd said. How could he tell her the real reason without seeming a fool? That he'd been waiting to see if she was a schemer after his money or a woman after his heart. David knew that Margo was the woman he wanted to spend the rest of his life with and that such a relationship required trust on both sides. An earlier demonstration of her lack of trust in him had left him angry and cold. But revealing such a thing to her now went against his better instincts. There could be no easy way to speak the words so they'd fall softly on her ears. Deep down he knew that he'd keep that a secret between him and his conscience.

"I know," Margo said finally, feeling a strange sort of relief. Or was it guilt? "You don't have an answer and neither do I." After already exhibiting her lack of faith in him how could she confess to believing that he was stringing her along while loving someone else? Weren't some things best left unsaid in relationships?

* * *

Margo and David never got to St. Maarten or Hawaii or any other exotic vacation spot. Two days after Tarrytown, Margo's burgeoning business swelled to a pulsating crescendo that left her breathless, yet happily tired: the same feeling she'd had when working with Mirken and Prusser while at the top of her game, but only now the company was her own. Entrepreneurship was a whole new world and she was loving it.

But she was also frightened. How could she continue on her own like this? She knew at some point she'd have to make some changes—involve other creative and business minds. She couldn't work solo and be a success. As it was she was utilizing the services of people she knew in the business. She pondered her dilemma. Just how or when was she going to become an employer herself? A decision was necessary, and soon, before she lost all that she'd gained.

Was she really ready to compete with billion dollar agencies—several successful black-owned? Could she weather the competition of those long-established firms? Margo knew she had the talent and trying to stick to her plan, she continued to work hard, but prayed that it wouldn't all fall apart.

She and David had celebrated quietly when the paternity lawsuit was thrown out. The child was not his and the woman was made to look the scheming gold-digger that she was, and she'd slunk from the courtroom after the judge's stinging words. She was the worst kind of mother, being thoughtless, vile and selfish for subjecting her child to the distasteful publicity later in its life.

And David was on a fund-raising campaign which kept him on the move. The Blackshear Foundation for Battered Elderly money-raiser, was well under way, culminating in a black-tie affair at the end of the year.

He'd bought and renovated two eight-story buildings in Queens, offering comfortable housing to over a hundred senior families. Many of the occupants were singles who'd been displaced from their homes after losing a spouse. Most were rescued from bad home situations where they were abused either by family members or unscrupulous home care workers.

But when they were separated by distance a day didn't go by without either David or Margo communicating by phone or e-mail. Many times Margo would enter the building to the smiling face of the doorman, who would hand over a huge basket or vase of flowers. When they got together their time was sweet.

The one thing Margo regretted as fall was waning, the nippy days just a prelude to what winter would bring in two months, was the parking of her bicycle for the winter. Although some of her new friends, like Zachary, did winter bike tours, she wasn't that hardy a soul to dress like an Icelander trudging through the cold and ice to catch breathtaking views of snowcapped peaks on a mountain in Oshkosh. She'd make do with her forsaken exercise of walking the streets of her neighborhood.

Coming in from a meeting with some actors who would be starring in a facial cream commercial that she was setting up, Margo was feeling on top of the world, though tired. Happy that it was Thursday, she let out a contented sigh. She'd learned to temper her work hours with leisure and tried to end her workweek on Friday night leaving weekends for fun and time with David.

Not surprised, she smiled and took the glass vase from the doorman who raised a brow at the single red rose with the small white envelope pinned to its stem. In the elevator she chuckled. The doorman was probably thinking that finally her suitor's ardor was wearing off not to have spent a fortune on the constant spray of blooms. But her heart warmed at the sentimentality of the man she loved. A single rose spoke volumes.

At seven o'clock she looked at the Caller ID display and smiling, picked up the phone. "Hello, love," she said.

"Hi, sweetheart," David said. "Just got in?"

"Uh-uh. I've showered, and eaten, and I'm finishing up another Kai tale," Margo said.

"Oh? How's it coming?" David said, a cryptic smile touching his lips.

"Well, *I* like it," Margo said defensively. "I'm not giving up my dream of seeing Kai and Friends in print one day. Somewhere out there is an editor with vision." She chuckled if only to make herself feel better.

"Never give up on your dreams."

"I'm not. Just venting." She was lying on the living room sofa and she glanced over at the vase on the table. The delicate fragrance from the single flower scented the air around it. "Thanks for the rose, David," she said. "It was sweet."

David frowned. "Rose?"

"Yes. Did *you* ever surprise the doorman. He probably thinks your pockets are getting mighty low."

"I didn't send a single rose."

"But it's sitting right here," Margo said.

"Was there a card?"

"Of course, you always send a card." Margo sat up and reached for the vase. She unpinned the envelope from the stem and opened it. "Now don't think I never read your cards, love, I always do." She felt sheepish for skipping this one.

"But not this time," David said.

Margo was staring at the card. "No, not this time,"

she said slowly. She dropped it on the glass-top table. "I feel like an idiot. I-it's not for me. Joe made a mistake. It's for the apartment beneath mine." Her eyes were glued to the card.

"That's a first," David said. He detected a change in her voice. "Don't worry about it. I'm sure your neighbor will understand the honest error." She didn't answer right away. "Is there something wrong?"

"N-no. Nothing else." In a lighter tone she added, "It's just that I would be pretty ticked if she got my flowers."

After agreeing to meet for dinner tomorrow evening, Margo placed the phone in its base and only then did she allow the restrained shudders to overtake her. Her eyes were glued to the message on the card. *Just one more blockbuster. Will call. Ty.*

Margo felt nauseous. The broiled fillet of cod she'd eaten earlier was swirling around in her stomach, when spiraling like a tornado, it reached her throat. She made it to the bathroom in time. The cold water on her face threatened to freeze as she chilled at the ringing of the telephone. Racing to her bedroom she knew what she'd see on the display. Ty Henderson. She didn't answer. His voice was hypnotic.

"Ty here, Margo. My rose was a thank-you in advance. Will see you soon to discuss our new venture. Hugs."

She backed out of the bedroom, her hands outstretched as if warding off something evil. See him? Where? Her brain didn't comprehend that, yet she hurried to the front door and put on the chain lock. Then, walking to the living room she snatched the vase from the table, and rushed to the kitchen where she spilled the water into the sink. She tossed it and the rose into the trash can.

* * *

David watched Margo with a keen eye. She'd barely
tasted the Indian cuisine that she went nuts over. He
reached across the table and touched her forehead with
the back of his hand. "Not coming down with something are you?"

"What?" Margo said, his voice startling her. "I'm
sorry?"

He frowned. "You're not eating. Lost your appetite?"
A shadow flitted across her face and the weak smile she
gave him was so unlike her that he felt as if he were dining with a stranger. "Want to talk about it?" he said.

Margo pushed her plate away. "There's nothing to
talk about, I'm fine. Didn't realize what a hectic week
it was and I'm glad to take two days off doing nothing."
She smiled. "Stop worrying about me, because everything is okay."

She was lying. Or deliberately evading the truth.
"Doing nothing?" David said. She gave him an odd
look. "We planned to go to the charity auction tomorrow evening. Have you forgotten?" He held her gaze.
"Or have you changed your mind about attending?"

"Oh," Margo said. "Of course I'm going. Why would
you ask me that?"

David shrugged. "Because it's apparent that you don't
want to be where you are right now so I thought present
company was responsible."

Margo's head throbbed and every nerve ending tingled until she couldn't stand it any longer. She hadn't
slept all night and all day she was on tenterhooks waiting for the phone to ring or listening for the doorbell
intercom. Now the man she loved thought she'd rather
be anywhere but with him. She had to pull it together.

"Please, don't ever say that again," Margo said quietly while holding his gaze. "I love you and there's no place I'd rather be than with you."

He listened to her words and heard the sincerity in her voice but David saw the shadows in her dark eyes that did not smile. "Then tell me you're trying to work out a problem, sweetheart, but don't tell me nothing's wrong," he said. "Believe it or not I know when something's not right with the woman I love. Give me a little credit in the sensitivity department."

Margo's cheeks burned. But she knew if she revealed her fears David would be courting another lawsuit if he went after Ty.

"Are we having an argument?" Margo said, smiling, and injecting a sparkle in her voice, hoping the smile was in her eyes.

David gave Margo a hard look. "Don't do that," he said harshly. Phoniness didn't become her. His eyes darkened. "I haven't convinced you, have I?" he said. Before she answered, he signaled for the check. "Let's get out of here. I'll take you home. Maybe whatever's bothering you can be solved while you're alone."

They walked into her apartment building and Margo almost dreaded looking at Joe the doorman for fear he would hand her another surprise. When he spoke, she stiffened.

"Evening, Ms. Sterling. You have a delivery." He reached down to the floor and lifted a vase with a single rose. "Here you go. Have a good evening."

Margo nearly went limp as she stared at the tiny envelope. "Joe, are you certain this is for me?"

"Sure. Your name and apartment. Identical to the one you received yesterday." The phone rang and he said, "Excuse me."

David watched the exchange in silence. He didn't speak until they were inside her apartment, standing in the kitchen where he'd followed her. He leaned against a counter, ankles crossed, and stared.

"Identical?"

Margo nodded, feeling miserable.

"You lied to me last night?" David almost didn't want a response, his mind too numb to understand what was happening.

She nodded again. Didn't one lie necessitate another?

"And downstairs, you wanted me to think Joe had made another mistake."

"Yes."

Staring at the vase that she was still holding, David's lips tightened. "Why, Margo?"

Pouring the water into the sink, Margo repeated her actions of last night and tossed the vase and rose into the garbage can. She turned to David. "Because I don't want you to become involved in something that can hurt you," she said. "I couldn't live with myself if anything happened to you because of me."

David had been steeling himself for the worst. When she spoke he felt as weak as a bear cub. "Hurt *me*?" he said, his breath released in a whoosh.

"Yes," Margo whispered.

Retrieving the envelope, David tore it open. He read the message and his eyes narrowed as he held the card toward her. "What does this mean?" His voice was like steel.

Margo took the note from him and read.

Got tied up. Will keep that date tomorrow. Hugs, Ty.

After dropping the note on the table Margo left the room. It was hard to know whether she was shaking from anger or fear for David, knowing he wouldn't let this go by. She'd seen the fury on his face at the gallery when Jonathan had kept him away from Ty.

David followed her and sat next to her on the sofa. He

didn't touch her because he could see the warring within. "Talk to me, Margo," he said in a quiet voice.

"This is the second one he's sent," she said. "The one that came last night said he was ready for another blockbuster. He followed it up with a phone call which the machine picked up. He said he would see me soon." She shuddered and hugged her arms.

"Like hell he will," David murmured.

She shook her head. "Please don't get involved. He's just full of talk and will fade away soon enough." She silently wished she could believe her own words.

He shot her an incredulous look. "Too late for that isn't it? Loving you gives me the right to be involved. Would you really have me turn my back, leaving you to deal with a nut job? The man is obviously becoming unstrung."

Inwardly, Margo realized that and it was scaring the hell out of her. She gave him a steady look, and nodded. "That's it exactly," she said. "I don't want you hurt because of the actions of a madman. Who knows what he could do? Taking out his misguided anger on someone I love." She shook her head. "*That* would be the tragedy."

"Don't you think I have sense enough to get out of the way of danger when I see it coming?"

"That's just it," Margo said. "Besides the physical danger, he can hurt your reputation in so many ways. Slander. A trumped up lawsuit for whatever scheme enters his mind."

"So what's one more," David said in disgust. "He can get in line."

Margo looked at him with surprise. "What are you talking about?" she said.

David sat back and closed his eyes briefly. When he

looked at her he said, "There are three more allegations, all filed within days of each other."

"What?" Margo said in disbelief. "When?"

"Last week," David answered.

"And you didn't tell me?"

He heard the hurt in her voice. "You were caught up in your work and I felt it would be a burden. Something you didn't have to think of or worry about."

A short laugh escaped. "I don't believe I'm hearing this," she said.

"Margo, I was just sparing you some unnecessary headache."

"Well, it would seem to me that that was what *I* was doing here."

"They don't compare," David said impatiently. "You might be looking at potentially bodily harm."

"And yours just hits you in the wallet," Margo said heatedly.

"That's unfair," David said.

"More paternity suits?"

"Sexual harassment, race discrimination, and unfair firing."

"All here in New York?" Margo asked, already wishing she could ease his anger. She could only think that the floodgates had opened and this was a mere ripple of the torrents to come.

"Only one," David said. "The firing. The discrimination is in Chicago. The sexual harassment is in California."

"I'm sorry, David," Margo said.

"Me, too." After a moment he said, "I know you lost sleep over Henderson's call last night and must be feeling it now. I'm going to go so you can get some rest." He caught her hand and pulled her up with him. "I want a promise from you," he said.

"What's that?"

"Don't talk to Henderson. If he shows up here don't even think about having him come up. There's no way he's going to listen to any rational talk. Okay?" He bent and kissed her lightly. "Do that for me?"

Margo returned his kiss. "I can't see myself entertaining Ty in here, so there's no need to worry about that," she said.

"Good." He kissed her again. "I'll pick you up tomorrow at four thirty."

In the elevator, David erupted into a cold sweat. The queer sensations that he'd gotten when seeing that single rose had deeply disturbed him. Why had he been so quick to think that there was another man in the picture? Was he truly over those ill thoughts that he'd first had when meeting her? That Margo Sterling was less than honest and after his money belt? His evil thoughts had made him feel, not like a man in love, but like one who needed to delouse himself. He knew that Margo was wondering why he hadn't stayed, to fall asleep together after a night of passionate loving. But he couldn't stay and make love to her knowing where his mind had been.

Driving home he had the sobering thought that if she ever learned what he'd thought about her, she would walk away and never look back.

Early Saturday morning, Margo was in Valeria's catering kitchen, her hands full of dough.

"No, no, gently," Valeria said, unable to hold back a chuckle. "You're going at the poor little ball of innocent dough like you're wielding a sledge hammer. Knead softly until it's like putty in your hands." She gave her friend a sidelong glance. "Rough week?" she asked. "You're in a foul mood this morning."

Margo followed instructions and was kneading the dough gently. Making pie crusts was a knack she wasn't getting and she was determined to have homemade pies on the menu when she made Thanksgiving dinner for David. Thoughts of him sent a chill through her. Why hadn't he stayed last night? She'd wanted him to love all the fears from her. What was wrong with them? she wondered.

"Hello, hello, in there," Valeria called. "We're on earth in Val's Catering, not on far-off planet Jupiter."

"Sorry, Val," Margo said. "It's been a little crazy this week." She smiled and said, "But that's not a complaint you hear, mind you. I'm happy as a rooster in a hen house with the way my business has grown in such a short time. I can't and shouldn't ask for a better beginning." She gestured around the kitchen. "I think you can say the same about your business, too. You hardly have time to go out with us anymore."

Val smiled. "Yes, and I'm also a happy camper. Business is the best it's been since I started."

"That's great," Margo said. "No more sightings of Mr. Shankley?" The familiarity had become normal in their fast and close friendship.

"Oh, I saw him once at a party I catered. He tried to talk to me until I reminded him that he was too close and he backed away, looking like I'd stabbed him with the long-handled fork I was holding." Val chuckled. "Scared rabbit." She stuck the cake pans in the oven and turned to Margo. "Now don't change the subject. We were talking about you. Everything okay with you and David?"

"Uh-huh," Margo said, concentrating on rolling out the ball of dough.

"Is that a yes, or an I-don't-know, kind of answer," Val said.

Margo stopped and looked at her. "You and Jonathan are in love. David and I are in love."

Valeria laughed. "This is front-page news?"

"Do you keep secrets from the man you love?"

A sobering look settled over Valeria's pretty features. "That depends," she said slowly.

"On what?" Margo asked, perplexed.

"Well, for one thing there's no sense in dredging up every little thing that went on in past relationships. And that's not really keeping secrets because it was before either knew the other existed. Does that make any sense to you?"

"Of course, but I don't mean that," Margo answered.

"Then tell me what's on your mind," Valeria said in a quiet tone. "Maybe I'll better understand how to answer you."

"Ty Henderson's trying to contact me again," she said.

"Has he threatened you?"

Margo explained the call and the notes and David's reaction.

Valeria stopped greasing a pan. "That's a secret best out in the open for safety's sake. As you realized, one lie leads to another. Besides, a man takes exception to being lied to, especially from the woman he loves," she said. "Wouldn't you?"

"But I was only trying to protect him," Margo said.

"He wants to be your protector, Margo."

"From someone who is acting crazy? Wouldn't you think that should be a matter for the law?" Margo said. "You got a restraining order. If it came to that, I can do the same, so there is no need for David to even go near Ty."

* * *

On Sunday morning, Margo hung up the phone after telling David to have a safe trip. He would be in San Francisco with his lawyers on the sexual harassment charge and would be away for a few days. Margo was already missing his voice, his nearness and the feel of his arms around her. She hadn't felt them since he'd kissed her good night at her door after coming home from the charity auction. It hadn't been that late although he'd insisted on ending the evening early so that she could get some rest. Margo had been surprised and felt a little hurt at his actions. What she did need and want was to love him until the wee hours of the morning. There was no better rest than that coming after good loving, she thought, thinking of the many times she'd awakened feeling as if she could conquer mountains.

Yet, she couldn't shake the feeling that they were growing apart. And it hadn't started when he'd caught her in a lie on Friday night. She felt as if something was missing in their relationship ever since they'd both admitted their love for one another, the morning after her Bear Mountain ordeal. Had that been a mistake? she wondered. Before that they'd been living in a perfect world. But she felt as though a steel girder was wedged between them keeping their passion at bay. She sensed that David was regretting his confession in an unguarded, passionate moment. But why would he? she asked herself. What could have been so wrong?

When he had told her about the sexual harassment charge, she'd been stunned. But soon the doubts entered her mind. How and when could it have happened? She convinced herself that it had to've occurred long before they'd met. After all that they had meant to each other, sharing their love and their bodies, had she been wrong about him? Could he have been a player all along, romancing women on his travels and deceiving her?

No, she couldn't, wouldn't believe that. David loved her and she loved him and to deny it would be to lose one's tongue for voicing the lie.

By noon, Margo was feeling hemmed in by her constant wayward thoughts. Even working with Kai and her friends didn't seem to relieve her of her dire thoughts. She dropped her sketch pad and pushed away from the desk.

"What would you think about this if it were you?" she said, looking at Kai's laughing face. Margo grimaced. "It's a good bet that you'd have washed your hands of the whole man affair and taken off to the next adventure."

Dressed in warm biking gear, Margo wheeled her bicycle from the bedroom and out of the apartment. In the elevator she couldn't help thinking that by the time she finished her ride, she'd have come up with a solution. She was fast coming to the conclusion that keeping secrets was not always the best remedy for certain problems. When David came home she would tell him all about her errant thoughts. A rested heart, she thought, was far better to live with than a troubled heart.

Three hours later, Margo was biking slowly down Hillside Avenue turning onto her street, Midland Parkway, feeling exhilarated by her ride. The burn in her legs and thighs was indicative of the thirty miles she'd covered over flat terrain to the Brooklyn Museum and back. The ride had accomplished what she'd set out to do: to clear her mind of troubling thoughts. And she had. Come what may, she would open her heart to David and prayed that she wouldn't lose the love of her life.

A block from her building Margo dismounted to stretch her legs, walking the rest of the way. Within yards of the entrance, she stopped, gripping the handle-bars as she stared at the figure leaning against a car. She felt the first stab of fear that was soon displaced with white-hot heat. She rolled her bike and stood inches from his face.

"What the hell do you think you're playing at?" she fumed.

Ty Henderson looked her up and down. Then giving her a dark look, said, "This is no game, Margo. This is my life. Now where are we going to talk? Here or up-stairs?"

Chapter Fifteen

"You wish!" Margo said, heat and anger consuming her until she felt her nostrils flaring like an enraged bull. How she could have even let this pitiful man intimidate her was beyond her good reason. He was nothing! "Ty, we haven't a thing in this world to talk about. Not now or until the day I die. Go get a life and leave me the hell alone. If you tried working on your own merits maybe you'd find you have something worthwhile to offer somebody and you can make a decent living! You're like a sniveling, senseless little boy who peed his pants, waiting for his mama to give him a change of drawers. You're disgusting!" She was clutching the handlebars of her bike so hard the leather of her fingerless gloves was stretched taut. She turned the wheel to go into her building.

Ty's mouth twisted into a mean slash. He grabbed the bicycle frame and effortlessly held it with one hand, preventing Margo from moving forward. "You arrogant bitch," he said, spittle dripping from the corner of his lip like froth sliding down a glass of beer. He clenched and unclenched his other fist, controlling his urge to pummel that beautiful face. "I heard your little speech and it's just a puff of smoke. Now, I ask you again," he said, speaking with hushed rage. "Where do you want to have our conversation? I prefer upstairs, though. Your work is probably all over the place and I can just take my pick of projects."

"Get your hands off," Margo said without regard to who heard. "You've done lost your mind." Incredulous at his gall, she wrenched the bike away but it didn't budge. His grip was like the Jaws of Life and for the first time she became alarmed. He was a big man, just at six feet, surely weighing well over two hundred. He was strong and his strength showed as he held her hostage seemingly without breaking a sweat. She struggled to get her bike loose from him.

With his other hand, Ty grabbed her forearm. "I'm not here blowing in the wind, Margo," he said. "Now, if you don't want to make a scene, let's go on upstairs."

Seeing red, Margo let go of her bike and swung. The blow was unexpected and Ty dropped her arm and the bike, stepping back in surprise, holding the side of his head where she struck. She grabbed her bike and started to walk away when he caught her arm and held tight. He was squeezing so hard the blood seemed to pool in one place. "You're hurting me!" she exclaimed, her eyes smarting from the pain.

"That's the intent, sweets," he said, his lips parting in a gleeful smirk at her surprise. "You don't get it do you? I'll do anything to get what I want. A-n-y-thing!"

His threat got her attention and Margo's eyes widened. For the first time she felt fear. "What the devil are you talking about?"

"Ms. Sterling?" Joe, the doorman, was walking towards them. "Having some trouble ma'am?" He looked from Ty to Margo. "Need some help with your bike?"

Ty stepped back as the man who didn't match him in size, but wore a calm look that said I-got-something-for-you. He backed away.

"Joe," Margo said, relief and disbelief at what was

happening tingeing her voice. "I'm coming and he's leaving. Aren't you, Ty?"

Tyrone threw her a glance and after another look at Joe, turned and walked away.

Margo watched until he disappeared around a corner.

"I saw what was happening, Ms. Sterling, but I was on a call or I'd have come out sooner," Joe said. "Did he hurt you? Want to report it to the security patrol?"

Shaken, Margo walked to the building. "No, Joe," she said. "I don't think he'll be coming back. Thanks a lot. That could have turned nasty."

"No problem," Joe said. "If there's any more trouble let me know and security will be right on it."

Inside the apartment, Margo let the fear she'd felt at that last moment overtake her, and she sagged against the wall like an overused, empty burlap sack. Until his last words she'd thought Ty was acting like an overgrown crybaby trying to scare the hell out of her. *Anything!* That word was running across her brain like a scratched CD. What did he mean by anything?

Dragging herself to the bedroom she pulled off her long-sleeve biking top and looked at her arm. The angry red marks had turned into welts, and looking at them gave her serious pause as she recalled David's words. She, too, now had the same thoughts. Ty was not joking. He was seriously unhinged, and becoming dangerous.

Repulsed by his touch, Margo stripped and hurried into the shower where she tried to scrub away the feel of his hand even though he'd never touched her skin. Looking at the bruise after she'd toweled dry, it appeared more angry-looking than before.

Later, dressed in tank top and jeans, Margo was returning to her apartment from the compactor room. Even though the building was secure with Joe at the front desk, she jumped when she heard a door opening.

Hurrying around the bend, she bumped into a body. Her skin became gooseflesh.

"Whoa," Rhonda said, catching hold of Margo's arm before she toppled backwards. "What's wrong?" she said with a laugh. "Missing *Alias*? I'm watching that too."

"Ouch," Margo said, gingerly trying to extract her arm.

Rhonda felt the raised skin and frowned. "What the hell happened to you?" she said with narrowed eyes. If she didn't know any better she could just make out fingerprints. Big ones. "What's that?" she asked, giving Margo a strange look.

Margo walked down the hall. "Nothing," she said. "A little accident." At the door she unlocked it, meeting the glance of her surprised friend.

Rhonda stared. Who locked their door just going to throw out the garbage? "Since when?" she said, gesturing at the motion. She joked. "Joe quit?"

"Can't be too careful, what with break-ins all over the place," Margo said.

"In here?"

"No, but you never know," Margo said.

"That's weak, Margo Sterling, and you know it. Who the devil did that to you?" She found it hard to believe that David had anything to do with it. If he did, her judgment of human nature had gone south.

Pushing open the door, Margo stepped inside. "I told you, just an accident. I was riding with a friend and nearly fell when he grabbed me before I tumbled on my head. I'll be okay. The bruise is fading already." She looked down at it. "It's not nearly as bad as it was," she said. *Lies, more lies,* she thought. *How easily they come.*

"So that's why you screamed when I touched it," Rhonda said with a skeptical look. Margo was silent.

"Okay," she said resignedly. "If you say so, but you know as well as I do that to tolerate abuse is a dangerous thing." She touched her friend's shoulder. "If you need me I'm a holler away." She opened her door and went inside.

Margo felt relieved. If she'd told Rhonda what had happened she was certain that her friend would act. Confront David. Or confide in him. Either would be to protect her. So Margo thought it best to say nothing to anyone. She'd handle it, vowing that no one was ever going to get hurt because of her. She was as sure about that as death is a part of living.

Later, while watching TV, Margo could find some tiny bit of humor in what had occurred and she laughed softly at Joe's address to her. At turning thirty she was now a ma'am?

Ty Henderson was sitting at a restaurant bar, still in the Jamaica Estates area. He had downed two shots of scotch, but neither had the numbing effect he sought. How dare she? he thought. He rubbed the side of his head that had received the brunt of her punch. That was the second time Margo had landed him one upside his head. It was going to be her last. And she'd had the bad sense to play the mama game with him. He signaled for another hit and as he drank he sobered, angered at the lack of numbness. He didn't want to feel!

There was nowhere for him to turn. For months he'd floundered at work, after riding the golden wave of his success when first joining the company. He'd been given his props and was looked upon as new lifeblood for the firm. But the bomb of a commercial that he'd produced had his colleagues giving him sly looks at team meetings and had his boss shunning him. He knew what that had meant and it had come as no surprise when he'd been pink-slipped.

Ty had always known that he didn't have Margo's talent and vision, but had thought that he could do well enough on his own if given a break. He'd had his break and fifteen minutes of fame, but those fleeting minutes didn't cut it. He wanted to ride the crest of the waves for far longer than that. He wanted what Margo had. With her talent she'd never needed a break or a man to prove her worth. Hell, he'd wondered why she didn't strike out on her own long ago. Yet, she'd hooked a gold mine, running with a crowd that boasted bottomless pockets. A damn multimillionaire! She surely didn't need the money she earned on her own; she could marry it. Tapping her brain for another moneymaker wasn't too much to ask. Shoot, if he could get her to throw some of her business his way he'd have it made. A partnership!

He looked evilly at the TV screen when her latest hit commercial aired. It'd been running for weeks now and obviously was selling a lot of cologne for the happy client, the same as her genius bicycle ads had done for her wealthy boyfriend. Money begot money, he always knew, but it rankled him that Margo was quickly rising to the top again while he had fallen out of the loop. She'd started her own company and the scuttlebutt had it that Sterling Productions was going to be around for a long time.

His mood darkened as he compared lives. He had no job, no apartment, and was living back home with his parents. His life was crumbling and he saw no way to make it whole again other than to "borrow" another attention-getter idea from his former colleague, as his passport into another firm. Ty knew that he was going to have to make her know that he was a desperate man.

"And desperate men don't play games, Margo," he

mumbled into his glass as he drained it. Ty traded glare for glare at the bartender who removed his glass, refusing to replenish the whiskey. Rising from the stool, stumbling, he teetered to the door.

Days later, when Margo entered the apartment, she looked at the Caller ID display in the kitchen with trepidation as she slipped out of her lightweight jacket. There were several messages, including one as usual from David, and she breathed easy. Ty hadn't called or made another surprise visit. With a weight finally lifted she walked lightly to the bedroom to undress, thinking that the man was getting some sense. He'd been blowing smoke dreams all along.

She'd had a successful meeting with a new client and was already mentally clicking off the ideas she had for a sportswear print ad. After a light meal she would begin bringing them to life. Her only peeve at the moment was that David's business in San Francisco was taking far too long. She missed him and couldn't wait to see him when he returned in two days.

Dressed in jeans and pulling a short-sleeve sweatshirt over her head, Margo paused as the phone rang. Letting the machine answer she continued down the hall to prepare her dinner when she stopped mid-stride as Ty's voice chilled her.

"Let's meet, Margo. You really didn't think I'd done gone and left town did you? I have something that will make you change your mind. I saw you come in so I know you're listening. Be down at that dinky little restaurant bar on the corner of 184th Street, in fifteen minutes."

Anything. She remembered his words and now they pumped fear into her as she stood in the hall between the bedroom and the kitchen, the wall holding her weight. "Ty, what have you done?" she said. In the silent

apartment, her voice was that of a stranger, harsh and
sour as though she'd sucked on a rusty spoon. For the
first time in her life, she felt helpless.

At first, she didn't see him but when she peered down
the far end of the bar she spotted the unmistakable figure sitting at a nearby table. She walked to Ty and stood
peering down at him.

"Sit down, Margo," Ty said. "This won't take long."
He gestured to the chair on the other side of the small
table. "Go on."

Margo hesitated, looking around at the sparse crowd.
There were two men and two women at the bar and two
tables of patrons eating dinner. Everyone was minding
their own business trying to talk over the music that she
thought was just a little too loud for such a small place.
She didn't feel threatened in her own neighborhood and
besides, Ty would be crazy if he did try anything stupid
with so many witnesses. She'd seen how he'd backed
away from Joe. She sat.

Her voice was strong when she said, "So, what's this
big thing you have that will change my mind about you
stealing from me again, Ty?" She refused to show him
fear.

"No, no, no, Margo. You have it all wrong." He
cocked his head to one side as if thinking. "I do believe,
the first time, I did use a little skullduggery to get your
idea. But this time, you're going to willingly share." He
smiled.

"Oh, really? And what makes you think that?" Even
in the soft light she could see the deadliness in his black
eyes. In all the years they'd worked together she'd never
seen such a look. He'd always been so full of good
humor and worked so well with everyone that the staff

had looked at him as being a big teddy bear. Something stirred in her soul. *Be afraid, girl.* She listened to that inner voice, and was alert to Ty's every movement. When he reached down to the seat next to him she was poised to run.

"Settle down, Margo," Ty said. "We're just talking—for now." He opened a large envelope and dumped a slew of photographs on the table. He spread them apart, almost lovingly as he smiled again and looked at her. "Now which of these people do you love the most?" he said. Then he laughed. "Now you know I don't mean your main squeeze, but he's not exempt."

"What are you talking about?" Margo said in a voice that had lost its verve. She stared at the table plastered with the faces of her friends.

Rhonda Desmond coming and going from her apartment building. Rhonda entering the bank where she worked. Rhonda at her desk.

Her stomach had suddenly become a parade ground for a platoon of marching bugs. She held down the nausea as she sifted through the others. Jonathan. Wesley. Valeria. Cindy Walden. Zachary. Inez. All in various poses either at work or play. Inez in the supermarket, setting the garbage cans at the curb. Wesley getting in his car in front of his business. Wesley and Jonathan having a beer together in a bar. Jonathan and Valeria kissing on her front steps. Valeria loading her catering van for an affair. Zachary in what looked like Cunningham Park. Cindy and her staff selling bicycles.

They were all there, her friends that she'd come to know and love. But there was one missing and she glared at Ty.

"I know, I know," Ty said with a humorless smile on his face. "David is in San Francisco and I hardly had the funds to fly out there and photograph him, too," he said.

"But I think you get the picture." He shuffled the photos around, as he laughed at his own joke.

"You're a sick man, Ty," Margo said, wondering if she was having a nightmare. "You honestly want me to believe that you'd harm people because you're too damn lazy to get a job?" Her anger got the better of her but she couldn't help it. What he was doing was trying to blackmail her and any fool knew that the first time giving in would not be the last. It was a never-ending vicious cycle. Her face was flushed with the warmth she was feeling and trying to keep her voice low, said, "You need help and my suggestion to you is to get it—and fast."

Ty looked at her in disbelief, his jaw dropping at the spitfire sitting across from him. She was showing a side he'd never seen and he was startled; but only for a second. He pulled the photographs together and stuffed them back in the large envelope.

Standing, he looked down at her with fury distorting his features. His voice was deadly when he said, "I never took you for a fool, Margo." Ty turned and his long strides carried his large frame out of the restaurant so fast a cool breeze fanned the jacket tail of the man sitting on the bar stool.

Alone, Margo was still shaking with controlled rage when her cell phone vibrated against her waist. It was David.

"Hi, love," David said when Margo answered. "Been trying to reach you. Not at home yet?"

"Hi, love," Margo said. "No, I had to come back out. Are you wrapping things up there?" She managed to keep her teeth from chattering.

David frowned and moved the phone away from her raised voice. He heard the music in the background. "Pretty much," he said. "I'm hoping that we can finish on schedule, but this woman is tough, sticking to her story that I touched her."

"I'm sorry," Margo said, feeling downhearted. She needed him here with her. She thought it ironic that David, with his desire to help so many people, had his good efforts thrown back in his face. The woman involved had asked for assistance in keeping her nonprofit Boys and Girls Club from closing its doors. He'd complied but not only financially. He'd spent time with her showing her what she needed to do to get and keep the politicos interested in her program, and to finesse the art of fund-raising. When he'd left San Francisco that was the last he'd seen or heard from her until he was hit with her lawsuit.

"Margo?"

"I'm sorry," Margo said. "What did you say?"

"I said, it looks like tough going and I might be longer than expected." He listened to the music. "Where are you?" She told him. "Eating?" His stomach squirmed at the thought.

"N—no, I stopped in for a moment to—to meet a client," she said quickly. *Lies, more lies.*

"Why would you meet a client there?" David asked. "You must not have wanted the business very much," he joked. "What line is he in?"

"Wigs."

David's lips tightened. He knew Margo's moods, her up times and down times and the times she needed her space to do her thing. He'd understood that and appreciated when she allowed him to do the same. She'd always been honest about what she wanted and needed. Now, the inflection in her voice clued him in that his lady was being evasive. No—lying to him. He closed his eyes against intrusive thoughts and powerfully pushed them from his brain, refusing to go there once more. The door to the room he was waiting in opened.

"Mr. Blackshear," the woman said from the doorway. "The attorneys are ready for you again."

"Margo, I have to go," David said, his whole mood suddenly changed, with a few echoed cadences to her voice. He knew the woman he loved. Or did he? "I'll call you later."

"Sure, that's fine," Margo said. They disconnected.

Margo hurried from the restaurant, wishing she had driven the five blocks. She looked around as if she would spy Ty stealthily aiming a camera lens on her. It was with fear, not anger, that she hurried into the building and entered the elevator, her heart keeping time with the whir of the elevator gears. In her apartment she chained the door and leaned against it, wondering what in the world she had done.

By defying Ty, she'd unleashed something in him that now scared her silly. She'd seen the demon in his eyes as he'd given her that dark look. A horrible chill settled over her. She'd felt such coldness before and she hoped never to experience it again. She would never again place flowers in another mausoleum.

As she undressed her head was a jumble of thoughts on what she should do. She knew that David didn't buy her lies. There was no way that she could tell him what was going on, not with all the outside drama that was suddenly thrust into his life these past few months. For once a person could say that money didn't buy happiness. His current troubles were proof of that. How many more lawsuits could the man take, for surely he'd land in jail for busting Ty's jaw. Or worse. She closed her eyes and mind to what the ultimate scenario would be: David's death at the hands of a madman.

Her stomach churned with what she knew she had to

do. So what if Ty wanted to pick her brain again? Couldn't she give him what he wanted to make him go away? Her conscience warred with her good sense. If she did meet Ty's demands, would she be able to look herself in the eye again?

The faces of her friends swam before her. Ty had been that close to all of them. It must have taken days for him to seek them out and follow them around sight unseen, stalking them like some feral animal. Just what did he have in mind? The thought of what a crazed person might do caused her chest to constrict as though a giant fist was squeezing her heart. Could she live with herself if harm came to any of them because she refused to be intimidated or used again?

Midnight found her sitting by the bedroom window staring out at the darkness. There was a war going on inside and she didn't know how to make it stop, yet she knew she had to make a life-altering decision. It frightened her that it might lose her the love of her life but she would be a shell of the woman he had fallen in love with if she didn't follow her heart.

Something inside her just wouldn't let a madman dictate her life to her. She'd worked long and hard to become who she was and she liked herself. Bending over for Ty Henderson would make it difficult to look in the mirror each morning. She knew very well that one request would balloon into three, four and evermore. He'd become as a festering sore, rotting into eternity.

In bed, Margo's last thought was that she'd rather keep her self-esteem than knuckle under to a piece of slime. She'd keep her ideas to herself. Ty's dreams of fame and fortune on her back would soon wither as he learned to deal with her restraining order. His idle threats against her friends were just that—will-o'-the-wisps disintegrating in the wind. Margo closed her eyes and slept.

The genuine pearls lay on the bed of black velvet, giving a soft glow as luminescent as the full moon. David picked up the single strand and let the graduated beads glide over his palm. They were cool to the touch yet felt so alive. He laid them back in the box, but instead of closing them from view he continued to stare at them. Imagining how they'd lie against her smooth tanned skin he inhaled, his pulses quickening at the thought of touching her as he placed them around her elegant neck.

David had never given jewels to a woman. Before his good fortune he couldn't afford expensive gifts on his conductor's salary. Any extra cash he had after paying school loans went to his survival needs. Afterward, when he could afford the luxury items, he had no desire to shower inconsequential dates and one-night stands with costly baubles. He'd been soured on that after his brother's experiences. One day, when he met that special lady, then nothing would be too costly for the love of his life.

David had stood by the grave site with Jonathan watching him throw away what had been so precious to him. David had stayed behind and when Jonathan was out of sight, he reached among the flowers and plucked out the jade butterfly along with a few other jewels Jonathan had tossed. Later, David had given the jewels to their mother who'd cried, saying she'd always keep them. One day maybe her son would find it in his heart to forgive Cynthia.

Closing the box, David packed it in his briefcase. He'd purchased the pearls during a break in the proceedings and had wandered into a well-known jeweler's where he'd spied the beads of beauty. He could see them gracing his lady love and his acquiring of them had made him step lightly.

It must have been a good omen because when he'd returned to the courtroom, after a statement read by his lawyer and a witness catching up his accuser in her lies, the judge dismissed the charges. There was no hefty settlement, which the woman had expected, and he sadly shook his head at her as defeated, she left the room trying to save face, yet giving David a hateful look.

Back in his hotel room he'd wanted to share his joy and had called Margo on her cell phone. After hanging up, he'd been deflated. What had caused her to lie to him? Meeting a potential client in a neighborhood greasy spoon at night was not only the epitome of poor taste but a stupid act. He remembered the first and only time he knew of her lying to him and a dreaded thought hounded him; was Henderson back, badgering her? The only way to find out was to ask outright. Afterward, with the air cleared he would take her away. They both needed some downtime alone. No daily stresses to get in the way of their relationship. She'd been working long hard hours and would never admit to being too tired. Any affair that he wanted her to attend with him she was always ready, looking as beautiful as ever with a pleasant smile, and was quick to converse easily with all.

There was nothing he wouldn't do to make things perfect between them, and he'd start as soon as he landed at La Guardia airport in the morning. He picked up the phone and after speaking briskly and briefly he hung up. Though satisfied with the plans he'd made there was still a small area of uncertainty jabbing at his

brain that threatened to topple that delicate balance between trust and distrust.

"David," Margo said, "I missed you. Where are you?"

"Me too, sweetheart," he answered. "My driver just
dropped me off at home. After I get cleaned up a bit
I'll be over. Want a quiet meal in or do you want to go
out?" He paused. "I know what I want," he murmured
as he kicked off his shoes and loosened his tie. He
wanted to love her madly.

Margo heard the desire and it was infectious as her
body heat rose, making the October air feel like the
middle of summer. She knew what would happen if they
had takeout in her apartment. Though her body yearned
for his, common sense prevailed.

"Out," she said and heard the intake of his breath.
"David, you know what'll happen if you stay here
tonight. You'll be dead-tired tomorrow and I'm not taking any chances on missing our flight to St. Martin."

David laughed. "It's a charter, Margo. It runs when I
say it runs." But he knew she spoke the truth. If he had
his way they'd just be closing their eyes at dawn, and
their flight was due to leave at nine in the morning.

Margo checked the time. "You've been up in the air
for over five hours and you must be exhausted. Your
body could use the rest. Why don't you get some sleep
for a few hours and we'll meet at seven for dinner. How
does that sound?" she asked.

"Sensible." David groaned at putting off holding her
in his arms. "You're right, my love," he said, "but you're
wrong about one thing."

"Wrong?"

"I know what always makes my body feel rested and

it's not this mattress," he said huskily. "Seven it is, my love," he murmured, and hung up.

Margo was breathless as she exited the private car David had waiting for them at the Princess Juliana International Airport after the four hour flight from New York. When flying over the Caribbean she'd always been enthralled at the beauty of the aquamarine waters and the white sand beaches. Wherever she'd stayed, she'd enjoyed the luxury accommodations from the high-rise hotel to the one-level casita.

The sprawling private home she was staring at stood alone as if on its own private island. In actuality it was on a plane by itself, high on a mountaintop in Dutch St. Maarten. The brick and pastel-stone structure was surrounded by green vegetation and colorful island flowers, hibiscus and bougainvillea. Other flowers waved proudly in the gentle breeze as if to say, *Look at us; we survived.* From previous visits Margo didn't expect lushness because she knew, depending on how recently the last rain had fallen, whether she would see beautiful deep greenery or parched brown earth and shrubs.

"It's beautiful," she murmured, turning to David who was gazing at her with a look she couldn't fathom but he shaded his eyes so she wondered if she'd been mistaken. He was probably still tired. Two plane trips in as many days were grueling, even for someone with David's drive and stamina.

A young woman appeared from around the side of the house and David greeted her. "Hello, Virgie. How've you been?" He looked over her shoulder. "You're alone?"

"Hello, Mr. Blackshear," she answered with a bright

smile and a lilting speech. "Yes, my mother had to leave but she sends greetings and we'll be back tomorrow. But if there's anything you need before then, just call. I think you'll find everything in order." She turned to Margo. "Hello."

"Margo, this is Virgie. She and her mother Rosalie are the caretakers for the property while I'm away."

"Hello," Margo said, extending her hand. "The landscaping is simply gorgeous."

"Thank you," Virgie said. "My mother and I love flowers." She turned to her employer. "I'll be leaving now. Good day." She waved and walked down the path to her car and drove away.

Before allowing David to lead her inside the house, Margo walked around the side and to the back. She exclaimed loudly at the panoramic view from the mountaintop looking down at the verdant valley and out onto the blue-green water thinking that the rain must have been plentiful. Nestled in the distant hillside were tiny pastel-colored homes and clumps of colorful wildflowers growing rampantly in the hills. She turned her gaze to the swimming pool and the hot tub beside it. The screened-in patio ran the length of the house and at the end were floor to ceiling double glass doors.

"It's paradise," she murmured.

David had his hand around her waist. He bent to kiss her lips. "Now, it is," he said.

Margo turned into his arms and kissed him long and hard. "I've missed you," she said. "So much." She leaned into him and reveled in his exploration of her curves, and when he slipped his hand beneath her top to squeeze her satin-covered breasts she moaned against him, nibbling his neck. "I missed *that*," she said dreamily.

David responded by kissing her neck, her eyelids—

their soft velvet lashes tickling his lips—her cheeks, her delicate earlobes and found her mouth again and devoured it, chasing her tongue in a mad cat and mouse dance. He was hard against her and wanted nothing more than to plunge deep inside. But as he did last night when he'd said good night at her front door he held himself in check. "No more than I, sweetheart," he whispered against her fragrant hair as he held her tight.

She wanted to stay in his arms here and in this place, to escape all that she'd left behind for a few days. Knowing what lay ahead back home was not going to spoil this precious interlude.

"Let's go in," he said and took her hand.

"Oh," Margo said when he stepped aside to let her pass by into a stone-clad hallway with a glass ceiling. She walked to the large kitchen where again half the ceiling was glass, letting in an explosion of natural light. It was really a dual setup with a combined kitchen and living area designed to keep host and guests connected while preparing meals.

"It's lovely, David," she said. He had her by the waist and was leading her away. Around a wide limestone wall, open on either side, she stepped into another large area.

"The great room. In here you do nothing," David said.

The panoramic windows framed the view of the valley she'd seen from the back. The high vaulted ceilings and skylights allowed the changing outside elements to set the mood in the room. A large, muted red stone fireplace was a focal point of the huge space. The furniture was oversize in keeping with the expansiveness of the bold, strong architecture. The casualness was understated elegance. Margo could sit in any one of the rust-colored, Indian cotton-fabric armchairs and feel she was outdoors.

"Come, you'll see the rest later," David said. "Thirsty?" Without waiting for a reply, David left and returned with a tray holding a pitcher and two tall glasses. He poured the rose-colored liquid and handed her a glass.

"Delicious. What is it?" Margo asked, taking another long sip.

"Something that Rosalie makes from flowers," he said. He set his glass down and sat next to her on the large sofa.

"Something's worrying you," she said quietly. He'd hooded his eyes again.

David nodded as his gaze held hers. "Wigs, Margo?"

She didn't pretend to be surprised for she'd known he'd suspected she was lying that night he'd called her in the restaurant. Margo shook her head. "It was the only thing I could think of at the time," she said simply.

"What was wrong with the truth?" When he realized the pressure he was giving to the crystal glass, he relaxed his hold.

Margo met his stare. She'd vowed not to reveal her meeting with Ty and at risk of experiencing her lover's anger, she wouldn't. There was no way she was going to be responsible for David losing everything because of her.

"I didn't think you'd believe the truth," she said.

"Want to try me?"

Lies, lies. Where do they come from? "I was wrestling with another rejection of a Kai story and I got depressed," she said, wishing that she could cross her fingers and her toes. "Instead of riding my anger off, I walked instead. Found myself on Hillside and ran into a

guy I used to date in high school. We talked. It just so
happened we were in front of that bar and we decided to
go inside to compare our lives after all these years. He
was in the middle of a divorce, was laid off his job and
he needed to vent. I listened."

David stared at his lover who'd just told him the cra-
ziest lie he'd ever heard from her beautiful lips. What in
the world was happening to them? His stomach lurched
and he held down the nausea when he said, "An old
boyfriend. That's it?"

She nodded.

"Are you seeing someone else, Margo?" He nearly
melted when the tears sprang into the corner of her eyes
but he steeled himself against grabbing her into his
arms. "I need you to tell me now." God help him, he still
loved her. He honestly felt she could tell him as many
crazy lies as she wanted. He didn't understand what was
going on in that secret side of her, but he would love her
with his last breath.

He didn't believe her. Inwardly, she laughed at their
absurdity. *Dear, intelligent, sweet David, why don't you
rant and rave, give me one of your steely stares and
send me packing?* Margo felt the tears form slowly and
before she knew it, she was sobbing softly. He hadn't
moved to touch her or to console her so she sat and
hugged herself, wrapping her arms around her waist.

"David, there's something I have to do. You can't help
me in this. It's a solo act." Failing miserably in her attempt at lightheartedness, she inhaled and let her breath
out slowly. "If we're going to be together, I have to do
this thing, without you. I love you with all my soul and
I would never do anything to harm you. Believe me, I'd
die first." She held his gaze. "I've never been in love before and doubt that I will ever again after you. I need
you to trust me."

"After me?" He didn't recognize his own voice.

Her heart felt like a mop being wrung out to dry. She dropped her eyes and wished she was down in the valley catching a plane far away from him and the agony she saw in his face.

"Are you ill?" Fear stabbed him.

"No," she said, raising her eyes. "Would that I were, I could handle that."

"Dammit, Margo. What in hell's wrong with you? Don't say that." His voice was like chalk scraping over a blackboard. As fast as he could manage he slid to her side and pulling her against his chest, said, "Don't talk like that, do you hear me?"

As he enfolded her against him, his head buried in her hair, he couldn't tell who was trembling more. He held on tight.

Chapter Sixteen

David lifted his head after kissing her hair, unwilling to release her. Somehow deep inside he felt they weren't going to leave this mountain the same two people. A foreshadowing caused a slight tremor.

"Hungry?" he asked, touching his lips to her damp eyelashes.

She lifted her head to gaze into his eyes. What she saw there made her heart tremble with fear. How could she live her life without him? she wondered. For as surely as the moon would appear tonight she knew she was going to have to leave him. His life and the life of his family and friends depended on her making the momentous decision. She would make these precious days with him a time to look back upon as being the happiest in her life.

Taken aback by the sudden look of sadness in her eyes, he shifted until he was sitting up holding her by the shoulders, staring at her intensely.

"What are you thinking?" he said softly. "You're scaring me."

Margo leaned over and kissed his lips lightly. The tip of her tongue slid between his lips to dance tenderly with his. She heard his intake of breath, knowing that was erotic for him. She laughed softly. "Yes, love, I'm hungry. For you. And I'm thinking of doing more things like this," she said. "Tonight, under the stars, in your pool, in your hot tub. I want to make love with you everywhere."

David was touched in more ways than one at her sudden boldness. Her mood had lightened and did he only imagine the tears and the seriousness of a moment ago? He wanted her so badly, he felt himself burgeoning in his beige linen slacks.

"You can have your wish tonight, sweetheart, but what's wrong with the sun being high in the sky?" He began to unbutton the soft white blouse she was wearing, holding her gaze intently. He kissed the tip of her nose, her chin, and nuzzled her neck while deftly unhooking her bra, pushing the garments away until they pooled in her lap.

Taking in her nakedness, David exhaled as though he'd waited an eternity to have her again. Cupping each soft mound in his hands he moaned as he bent to swirl his tongue around the tips that had stiffened upon their release. "You're so beautiful, Margo," he murmured against her perfumed skin. She smelled of warm grasses and jasmine and he couldn't get enough of her scent. He nipped the turgid brown buds until she whimpered and squirmed, leaning into him for more.

Her hands were at his waist fumbling to release the belt so that she could feel him in her hands. "David," she whispered. "Help me."

"God," David breathed. He stood and took her hand and hurried to the bedroom. He wouldn't remember later how he stood naked and shoeless before her while she stripped to the tiny bit of lace covering her mound. He pulled that over her hips and they landed on the bed in a tumble of heat. David had promised himself that he would never again stop her in the throes of mad passion and he was true to his word when he produced a condom from the nightstand drawer, sheathing himself instantly.

Her eyes closed, soft moans emanating from her lips, Margo never released her hold on any part of his body while he prepared himself. She squeezed his nipples, delighted and excited at his yelps of pleasure-pain. Wiggling until she was atop him, she stretched her body over his length, thrilled at the feel of his full, throbbing penis pulsing beneath her own trembling secret places. She kissed the hairs on his chest, gently pulling at them with her lips until he moaned and writhed trying to make her stop yet reveling in it. She licked his plumped-up nipples, delighting in the instant quivers. She moved upward inhaling his male scent, now warm with the anticipation of making love with her.

"Margo," David rasped. "You're killing me, sweetheart." When her hand closed around his thick shaft he yelled her name, and flipped her over.

"Love me now, David," Margo managed before his mouth clamped down over hers and he slid into her and thrust with a strong, powerful motion that brought her hips up off the mattress. "David," she screamed. Then she was lost as he moved inside her with all the force of a roiling sea. She moved with him, thinking giddily that she was on a mountaintop with her lover and he was indeed taking her to new heights with the masterful command of his hard body. She soared as a bird, skyrocketing to distant places, while hating to descend from this magic he was doing to her. Her legs were wrapped around him so tightly that she feared letting him go or she would fall to earth. The sound in the room was tearing from her throat, she realized, as he sent her soaring again with a renewed pounding into her. He, like her, she knew, never wanted this moment to end. Sated, unable to remain in flight, she felt herself drop, her hips landing with a soft thud, David clinging to her so that they were as one body.

David's tormented groans as he lay atop her were mingled with her short gasps of delight and satisfaction. He buried his head in her neck, tasting the sweet salt of her skin and thrilled again at her smell of heated sex and woman. He wanted her again. He slid from her and lay by her side.

Margo lay panting, her hands above her head as she luxuriated in the feel of her body. She had been loved thoroughly.

Dipping his head to kiss the soft undersides of her arm, David felt himself rising. "I love you, sweetheart," he whispered.

She opened her eyes to see him staring at her, his beautiful deep brown eyes swimming with desire. "I want you, love," she murmured.

"Now?" David's heart lurched in his chest with the beauty and the pain of his love for her.

She touched a kiss to his lips with her fingers. "Now," Margo said. "With the sun still high in the sky." Her tiny laugh was as a bird's song as she brought his head down to hers.

"David?" Margo sipped her champagne as she twirled her other hand in the tepid water of the whirlpool.

"Hmm," he answered, playing tag with her toes. Draining his flute he set it down in a cup holder on the ledge of the large hot tub. David looked surprised when she stood and climbed out. "Had enough?" he asked.

Margo reached inside her robe pocket and pulled out a paper square that shone in the soft light surrounding them. Slowly she tore it open and then glanced dreamily at the black velvet sky. "There are stars," she said softly, turning to him while silently pushing down the bottoms of her bikini. She was topless. Margo placed an oversize towel on the smooth stone patio and lay down, her arms over her head, body wet and glistening.

Her invitation hardened him until he was throbbing, aching to be relieved. He climbed out of the tub and was standing naked by her side. "Yes, there are, sweetheart," he said, huskily.

Margo sat up and, taking hold of his shaft, gently sheathed him. "Love me, now?" she whispered.

A soft moan escaped at the feel of her hands holding him so tenderly. "Never ask, love. I'll always be here for you. Always." He settled himself over her and when she guided him inside, he did as she desired. He loved her.

Five days had passed all too quickly. Tomorrow they would be leaving their idyllic interlude. Margo couldn't remember a time when she had felt so free and uninhibited. David's mountaintop retreat was nirvana for the tired and troubled soul.

On the second day she could see the stress in his face dissolve, even as she felt her own mind begin to absorb the healing powers of the serene surroundings. The magic could have been inhaling clean fresh air or just the simple joy of being awakened by a bright welcoming sun. After a day and night of lovemaking when they'd first arrived, Margo had awakened in a dream world. Whereas all she could see and think about was her lover during the night, she curiously looked around to see where he'd loved her so exquisitely.

David's master suite and bathroom could have been out of a duPont Registry magazine. It was as huge as any room in the large house, but intimate in its design. Its many windows and skylights opened to spectacular views of the mountain foliage, the clear blue sky, aquamarine waters, and the moon at night. There were long white gauzy curtains for privacy if he so wished but they were never closed. The bare wooden floors were of bleached oak. The huge bed was custom-made, dark tan burl ash with matching nightstands, and linens in white and beige and brown. A fireplace set in beige and white mottled stone covered one wall, offering a sense of intimacy. The master bath with Spanish limestone floors followed the color scheme of the bedroom. A bay window looked out on the forest, while twin beige marble-topped vanities separated the steam shower.

At night they liked to lie in the king-size bed and watch the hundreds of twinkling lights below. During the day they would breakfast outside his bedroom patio and watch the majestic ships and sailboats floating by.

"Truly a paradise," Margo murmured as she settled deeply into the patio lounge chair. She was alone. After Rosalie and her daughter who always came to cook and clean left, David had gone for a ride. The first time he'd taken her biking on the mountainous, narrow roads, she'd begged off, frightened to death. He'd teased her, acquiescing to her wishes, saying if she could ride in New York City she could ride anywhere.

She'd eaten lunch alone, taken a swim and had soaked in the hot tub. Lulled into a dreamlike sleep she'd awakened to find she'd slept for over an hour. It was past two o'clock. The crunch of tires on the gravel path leading to the house told of David's arrival. Margo's eyes lit up and she felt the blush warm her cheeks as she stared at him. Never in life would she tire of looking at the sight of those long muscled legs and thighs. There was no way of staring and not remembering how they felt wrapped around her.

"Hey," David said when he saw her. After resting his bicycle, and joining her, he removed his helmet while bending to kiss her lips. "I need a wash."

His body glistened with sweat and his tank top was soaked through. Margo licked her lips, tasting the salt from his.

"Hey." David was staring at the tip of her pink tongue. "No fair," he said huskily. "I'm funky."

Margo tugged on his shirt until he had to sit or fall. She put her hands around his neck and brought his lips back to hers, kissing him long and hard. "But you sure do taste good," she murmured. It was a very long kiss.

Later, David checked himself out in the mirror of the room-size walk-in closet. Satisfied he reached for the small rectangular box on the shelf, then left in search of Margo. This, their last night on the mountain, he wanted to make special for her. Inwardly he meant to make it just as memorable for himself. He didn't know why but he knew it would be important.

Dressed for their last evening dinner on the island, Margo studied herself in the mirror of one of the guest rooms. Her glance slid to the undisturbed bed and she smiled. As in his beach home on Sag Harbor this bed had never known her body. She smoothed the sheer rose-colored, sleeveless georgette dress with its deep V neckline over her hips. Her shoes were a deeper rose high heel sandal.

She found him in the great room standing by the windows, hand in one pocket. Margo stared at his rigid back for a long moment before joining him. Since he'd returned from his ride earlier he had been quiet, almost subdued as they spent the rest of the day lounging around the pool. All too soon the time came to pack and then prepare for their dinner reservations at one of David's favorite places with superb island cuisine.

David turned to see her watching him. Holding out his hand she came to him, sliding her hand in his. They both turned to watch the breathtaking view of the valley.

"I'll miss this," Margo said. "I've had a marvelous time, easily the most memorable."

"Then we'll have to make this a habit, won't we?" David answered, squeezing her hand. He felt the slight stiffening of her body but he chose to ignore it knowing it had to do with her secret. Releasing her he handed her the black box. "For you," he said.

Margo stared in surprise at the beautiful pearls nestling in the folds of black velvet. The luminous beads rivaled the pale, majestic light of the moon.

"Oh, my," she whispered. "They're gorgeous." She ran a finger over the smooth spheres, gently, tenderly, as if the mollusks that had produced them were still alive.

David removed them from the velvet bed and setting the box on a table placed the shimmering strand around her neck. She had her back to him holding up her soft, fragrant hair. He kissed the nape of her neck, then slipped his arms around her waist and held her close to his chest. He closed his eyes briefly, wishing to hold her like this for eternity. She twisted around and slid her arms around his neck.

"Thank you for such a precious gift," Margo said. She kissed his lips gently.

His mouth lingered over hers while he held her tightly. When he released her he said, "You do them proud, love." His hand around her waist, he said, "We'll be late. Time to go."

* * *

Pearls, her birthstone, had never been part of Margo's jewelry wardrobe, not because she couldn't afford them, but she loved the shimmer and sparkle of colorful semi- and precious stones. Her favorite was the royal-looking lavender tanzanite of which she owned a ring and a pendant, set in gold. She knew that the strand of beads around her neck were indeed precious and nearly priceless. The look on his face when she returned them to David would bring more misery. Removing them she placed the strand in its soft bed and closed the box, placing it in her lingerie drawer.

She'd gone through the ritual of taking them out and putting them back for the two days that she had been back home. It wasn't hard getting back into a working mood because she loved her job. Business had slowed but she had enough projects to keep her budding company moving forward. Next year she expected to see a steadier increase in both clients and profits.

It was Wednesday evening and David had just left promising to call her in the morning. Since they'd returned he'd been working out of his midtown office and would be there for the balance of the week. They'd had dinner together, either out or takeout at her place. No home cooking for a while, he'd said, because Inez had fractured her arm while they were away. When putting out the garbage, she'd tripped over a hose that the gardener must have left across the drive, so she had to keep her arm immobile for a number of weeks. Tomorrow, he was going to try his hand at his new cooking skills and he'd given her a list of items to purchase at the supermarket.

Margo had turned out the light in her study, preparing to watch the evening news before readying for bed when she picked up the phone in her bedroom.

"Alana?" she said in surprise. It was late and Margo's brow furrowed. "How are you?"

"Tired," Alana Montenegro said. "I've been in the emergency room all night with Zachary. I wanted you to know in case you wanted to call or visit him at Mary Immaculate Hospital."

"What?" Margo's breath was a hiccup.

"Yeah. A bike thief jumped him and stole his bike. He took the security chain from around his waist and beat him with it. He has a slight concussion and a busted ankle."

"My Lord," Margo whispered, her heart nearly stopping. "Where?"

"He was finishing his ride in Cunningham and didn't make it out of the park."

"Is he crazy?" Margo said, suddenly fuming at such a stupid act in mid-October. "It's freezing out there, dark, and deserted. What was he thinking?" she said.

"You know him," Alana said. "A die-hard enthusiast, hating for the season to end."

"A crazy enthusiast you mean. He can get his jollies in a gym until spring."

When she hung up, Margo was angry, not at Zachary but at the thieves who'd hurt him. Since she'd been riding she'd learned the safety rules—the do's and don'ts of cycling especially in the city. Safety was priority. When she thought of her night ride to Brooklyn only afterward had she realized the sheer foolishness of such behavior. Not only was his expensive machine gone, Zachary could have been hurt far worse.

Stealing high-end bikes was common and not enough was done by law enforcement to crack down on the thievery, which was big business, Cindy had informed her classes. Rented trucks drive through the city every day with loads of stolen bikes to be sold. Many riders camouflaged their bikes by personalizing them with logos and crazy designs, making it undesirable for a "buyer" to purchase a stolen bike.

Tomorrow she would visit Zachary and try her best to cheer him up. Maybe as a consolation gift she'd buy him a couple of weeks at a gym where he could ride stationary racing cycles to his heart's content until next April.

On Thursday at one o'clock in the afternoon, David, Jonathan and Wesley were in the emergency room of Long Island College Hospital in downtown Brooklyn. They were waiting for the doctor to sign Wesley's release papers.

"Damn," Wesley said. "I never saw it coming." He touched the bandage over his right eye.

"Could have been a hell of a lot worse," David said harshly. "Where was your head?" He acted angry but in reality he was scared. If anything happened to that man or the one sitting next to him he'd lose it. Jonathan and Wesley were two of the three most important people in his life besides his parents. Margo was his life's blood.

Jonathan shook his head. "Walking on clouds, my man?" he asked, squinting at his friend. When he'd gotten the call from Wesley's secretary that he'd been in a car accident and was taken to the hospital in an ambulance he'd raced from the gallery. A world without Wesley Gray would be bleak indeed. "You finally fell in love or something earth-shattering like that?" His breathing was easy now that he saw the big man sitting and talking sensibly with them.

"Nothing so dramatic, man," Wesley said. "You and David got the good women all sewn up."

Quietly, David asked, "What really happened, Wes?"

Wesley lifted a muscled shoulder. "Sheer idiocy, I guess. One minute I'm heading for my car and boom—out of nowhere I'm lying in the street. I wasn't paying attention and I got sideswiped. Heard the van at the last minute and when I turned, its mirror clocked me good in the head. All I saw was red and next thing I was waking up in the street."

Jonathan frowned. "The van was mighty close," he said. "The driver kept going?"

"Beats me," said Wesley. "All I saw was the emergency ambulance workers and the usual crowd when stuff happens."

"Hit and run." David grew angry at what could have happened. "No witnesses I suppose."

"Now that, I'll find out when I get to the office."

"Not today, you won't," David said. "I believe the man said rest for a day or so?"

Wesley grinned. "You know better than that. Something about cold trails?"

Jonathan and David eyed one another when the nurse came and gave Wesley written instructions and left. They had the same thought as they walked on either side of their friend: was one of Gray's Investigations cases turning nasty?

Margo was happy—and content. She'd shopped at the Pathmark for all the things David had on his list, noting the ambitious dinner he planned for them tonight. She loved scalloped potatoes when they were done right, not hard and burned or soupy like she'd always managed to do. Cabbage was a walk in the park as Val had shown her. Smothered pork chops and mushrooms whetted her appetite. The trick to that she knew was knowing the difference between a little browning and burnt! Inez was really doing her thing with David in the kitchen.

Speaking to her and wishing her well had Margo thinking about Inez's accident. She pushed an ugly thought from her mind. Ty Henderson hadn't shown up or called since before she went to St. Maarten. She was feeling comfortable with the fact that her plan she'd devised to end her relationship with David was now in the trash. As she'd known, her former colleague was nothing but a flake. There were no more ridiculous thoughts of her managing to live a life without David in it.

The most vexing thing on Margo's mind now was finding the perfect outfit to wear to Jonathan's birthday gala next weekend. The semiformal affair was invitational and was being held at the beautiful Brooklyn Marriott. She and Val had made plans to go shopping together on Friday at a little boutique in Brooklyn that had fabulous clothes for little money. That suited Margo's aim to bank some of her hard-won earnings.

David had promised to call after his afternoon meeting. When she hadn't heard from him by two, she wondered if dinner was still on for tonight. She called his cell phone number but there was no answer. Busying herself with putting her groceries away and washing the meat in preparation for cooking, she dried her hands to answer the phone. It was David's cell on the display.

"Hi, I just called. Everything okay?" Margo said.

"I'm in Brooklyn, just leaving the hospital," David said. "I have to return to Manhattan so I'll be a little late getting dinner started tonight."

"Hospital? Who's sick?" Margo asked.

"Wesley was hurt in a freak car accident," David said.

"He's going to be fine. Jonathan is driving him home." He heard her gasp. "Margo, I said he'll be okay."

"There are no freak accidents, David. Just accidents." Yes, like Inez and Zachary.

He didn't like the sound of her voice. Maybe she'd gotten the thought he and his brother had; Wes's business dealings were somehow involved. "If it wasn't an accident, Wes's firm will get to the bottom of it, you can be sure of that. Usually in hit and runs there are plenty of witnesses."

"Hit and run?" She shuttered her eyes.

David frowned. "Yeah, but like I said the doctor gave him the all-clear. He just has to take it easy for a day or so. Are you all right?" he added.

"Yes, I'm fine, just surprised and concerned for Wes." Margo sat down because her knees had gotten weak. "If you're not up to cooking for us tonight we can wait until tomorrow."

"I think that would be best," David said. "Going to Brooklyn backed me up and there are things I have to finish up today, so I probably won't get in until late."

"Do what you have to do, then go home and get some rest," Margo answered. "I'll see you tomorrow. Love you." She disconnected.

Busying herself in the kitchen, Margo refused to allow negativity to ruin the serenity of the last few weeks. The items she'd left out for David's meal preparation, she put away. Storing the chops in freezer bags she left one out to broil for her own dinner. Only a salad would accompany it because her appetite had suddenly disappeared.

After aimlessly searching the tube for anything distracting, she turned the TV off and left the living room. In her study she pulled out an unfinished Kai and Friends story.

It was midnight before Margo climbed into bed but sleep was elusive. She got out of bed and sat in her usual chair by the window. The night sky was black and starless and she wished she was back on a faraway mountaintop looking at blue-black velvety skies alight with shimmering diamonds as companions.

Friday morning at eight the phone rang bringing Margo from the bathroom.

"Hi Val," she said looking at the display. "I'm just getting ready."

"You wouldn't believe that jackass showed up here last night."

"Shankley?" Margo frowned. So what good was that piece of paper she had on him. "At your door?"

"No, he sat in the car watching the house as if he could scare me, the jerk."

But she was scared. Margo heard it in Valeria's voice. "So what are you going to do?"

"I probably will call the precinct and report it. He's in violation." Val paused. "I'm real sorry about messing up our shopping trip, but I want to stay here to see if he's going to show up again. Why don't you go on anyway? The shop is really a find and you're bound to walk away with several gorgeous outfits."

"No, no fun without you," Margo said. "I'll probably rummage through this closet here and come up with something. You be careful of that nut case and I'll call you later to see how you made out."

Later, it wasn't Valeria but David calling. "Hey, love," he said. "How are you?"

"What's wrong?" Margo knew the moment he spoke that he had bad news. "Are you okay?" she asked warily.

"Val is hurt and I'm on my way to Brookdale Hospital."

"What?" Margo's throat went dry. "B—but how? What happened?"

"She was going from the house to the catering hall and someone jumped her from behind." David's face was twisted into a grimace that almost rendered him speechless, he was so angry.

"H—how badly is she hurt? Should I meet you there?"

"No," he answered. "Jonathan said they will be releasing her so she'll be gone by the time you get here. They took X-rays of her stomach where she took some heavy blows. They show no damage."

"Shankley was there," she said in a low voice. "Did she tell Jonathan?"

"Yeah," David answered. "He's wondering why she didn't call the precinct last night when she first spotted him."

"Was it Shankley who attacked her?"

"Val thinks it was. It was a quick attack. She never saw a face, but she feels it was him, especially since he was so bold letting her get a look at him the night before. That's all she knows." He hesitated. "Looks like I'll never get to cook for you sweetheart, but I'll make it up to you."

"Okay, David. Call me tonight. Love you."

Restraining orders! What good were they? Look where she was now. Margo's anger was hard to let go when she thought of the fear in Valeria's voice. There was no doubt in her mind that the man who beat Val was the man who obviously wanted her so badly he was willing to flaunt the law. Margo knew that her friend was protecting her lover by not admitting the truth. If Jonathan went after Frederick Shankley, the result would be disastrous.

Margo laughed but really found no humor in the

irony of it all. Valeria was doing just as she was doing herself—lying to David about Ty's meaningless threats.

Life can be beautiful Margo mused, but how beautiful would it be without the man she loved? She would continue to lie for as long as she had to—as long as it kept David safe.

Chapter Seventeen

October was unpredictable. It'd started out summery and balmy, turned cold in mid-month and was mild nearing its end with tomorrow being the last Saturday and Jonathan's birthday bash. She'd never gotten to shop for a dress for the party, deciding to wear a little-used outfit from her closet.

Margo's business had lost some steam, but she was content that the bills were still being paid and she had food to eat so she wasn't really ready to dust off her résumés. David had finally cooked her a meal and it was so successful that she feared not being able to reciprocate with just as an impressive Thanksgiving dinner. She'd mastered the making of crusts and had tried a delicious apple pie on Rhonda who'd been duly impressed.

These days she was content but ever mindful that things could change in an instant, so she never was really careless about her actions and was always cognizant of who was around her. There had been no sign or word from the man she'd come to dislike with a passion so intense that it scared her. She'd never realized she could be filled with something so close to hating another human being.

Just past ten o'clock in the morning she was on her second cup of coffee when she picked up the phone in her study. "Hello?" She didn't recognize the name or the number and she sounded reserved.

"Margo Sterling, please."

"Speaking," Margo said, delighted for more new business.

"Margo, this is Miriam Koster, editor at Milestones, Books for Children. We all love your manuscript here and I'm calling to make an offer if you're still interested."

"Excuse me?" Margo would have fallen if she wasn't already sitting in her chair. "What manuscript is that?"

"Your Kai and Friends is delightful and we would like to see more of your work. This is so fresh and unique; I'm hoping you will consider our offer."

Margo went flat with disbelief, listening as the pleasant-voiced woman skimmed over the details to be finalized later. "So think it over and get back to me as soon as possible so we can look forward to setting a publishing date."

When she hung up Margo was as limp as a baby just learning the functions of its body. A weak "wow!" was all she could muster as she rewound the conversation in her head. Pushing aside her bread-and-butter work, she pulled out her folder of Kai and Friends tales.

Frowning, she couldn't find the story that the woman wanted to publish. She pulled out another folder that contained all the publishers and the stories that she had submitted. This woman and her company were absent.

"Now I know I'm not losing it," Margo muttered, going through everything. She turned to the computer and pulled up her Kai files. Maybe she'd entered the information, but hadn't made a hard copy for her hands-on files, she thought.

Nothing. She sat back staring at the volume of stories. Then she picked up the folder she didn't want to see—the one that held her rejections. Margo could only stare. There it was. The tale she'd sent to this same editor who'd rejected it. This was one that had been returned without criticism, positive or negative, only the sterile "does not meet our needs," comment. Perplexed, she sat back, pondering what was going on.

"David!" It finally computed. The story that the woman was so excited about was the one she had given to David a while back. The one she'd shared with him because it was so dear to her heart. She'd even made it into a book, lovingly doing her own drawings of Kai going through her trials and tribulations in her small world.

Margo was in denial. "No, you didn't do that to me, David." Suddenly she felt as deflated as a tire gone flat on a highway and she had to struggle for control of the tons of steel. She felt she was losing control of her own life. How dare David take what was so precious to her and use it that way? He'd betrayed her love and confidence. He knew that she prided herself in making it on her own. She'd not accepted any help from him financially or otherwise while trying to build her business. His contacts were legion and he could have paved the way for her, removing stumbling blocks if she'd so desired. But he'd respected her wishes and stayed out of her business life. The only suggestion she'd taken from him was to seek Jonathan's legal expertise in getting started.

After her initial shock dissipated, Margo felt angry and then sad. She'd thought that she had accepted him for who and what he was. She had laughed and shrugged her shoulders helplessly watching him work his show with his money. To her it was a bottomless pit. Money needed, money gotten, with the snap of a finger or a few brief words into a cell phone. No matter where, when, or the hour of day, his money accomplished things quickly, whereas the average person would think nothing of a year passing by before achieving the same.

Melancholy interrupted her earlier mood of contentment and excitement. She left the study and put on another pot of coffee, something she rarely did. Three or more cups were a rarity and she only resorted to the caffeine when she was irritated—as she had that day in January. So long ago it seemed, after all that had happened in her life since then. She'd fallen in love with a fabulous man who had only one flaw: money.

As Margo sipped her hot coffee, she sat huddled up under a huge ivory throw on her living room sofa, absentmindedly watching the tube. Why had he done that? All feelings of anger had subsided leaving her feeling empty. She didn't get that satisfied, smug sappy grin on her face as she usually did when her work appeared. In the space of several minutes she'd seen her cologne ad and her facial cream commercial. Those she'd done by her own sweat and creativity. No help needed thank you very much from the coffers of David Blackshear.

She'd often wondered during their relationship how she could live a life not having to worry about money, or namely, the lack of. If she were married to David, she knew that all she need do was to ask and every desire would be satisfied. But what did that do for her creativity? Would he want her to be doll-like, smiling and entertaining his friends or at a moment's notice fly off to wherever to dedicate a new wing of a hospital or accept another humanitarian award, swathed in the furs and jewels he'd given her? That kind of woman no longer existed in her mind. If she did, Margo couldn't fathom a woman being so empty-headed and as window dressing, waiting to be summoned to duty by her mate. The talents of many women came to mind who were doing their thing: television personalities, movie stars, and entertainers. Some were married but many were single. Those that were married had wealthy husbands. Now she wondered just how much help those same women had gotten from their powerful mate and had accepted it with aplomb. Was she being a silly child for her reaction to David's interfering?

Reality set in and it chilled her. She liked her life as it was—the one she was building on her own, using her brain to create a fledgling business and watching it grow into a sound enterprise. That was what she wanted as her legacy: Sterling Productions.

She looked at the phone when it rang but she was too numb to answer. She listened.

"Hi, sweetheart," David said. "You got out early, I see. We're on our way to New Jersey for the luncheon ceremonies for the new PAL center in Wayne. It's a full day of events culminating with dinner so I'll call you this evening when I return. Love you."

"Will always love you, David," Margo murmured. After a while she stirred, and found her way back to the bed where she pulled the covers around her and closed her eyes. The day was dreary and so was her mood. All she wanted to do was to sleep away her dismal thoughts. There was no deep thinking involved in sleep. Only troubling dreams.

The next evening Margo took the pearls from around her neck and placed the beautiful strand back in its box. She couldn't wear them. Not after she'd decided what she must do. Returning them would bring tears when she saw the hurt in his eyes. But she'd made up her

mind. Even when David had called her last night when
he'd gotten home, she felt that he had sensed that something was wrong. But you didn't end a relationship sight
unseen by phone or e-mail. That was a coward's way.

She lifted the only other expensive piece of jewelry
from her box. She'd bought the precious tanzanite pendant when she'd gone on a cruise to St. Thomas with
Rhonda. Later she'd treated herself to a matching ring.
She stared at the pendant.

The violet jewel sparkled delicately against her deep
tan. She fingered it knowing the absence of the pearls
would affect him keenly. Since the night he'd given
them to her she hadn't worn them. Her fingers closed
around the pear-shaped stone as if she were willing it to
be her strength.

David held her coat while she shrugged into the
smart black garment. His eyes flickered once more at
the sparkling jewel at her throat. He only said, "You
look beautiful. Ready?"

"Yes," she murmured and her heart sank at the hurt in
his eyes and the stiffness in his hand at the small of her
back.

The black Lexus limousine was double-parked and
one of his drivers opened and closed the door and pulled
off, easily maneuvering the big car toward Union Turn-
pike.

With the partition closed, David felt free to speak.
"What's on your mind, Margo?" He'd meant to sound
calm but the words had come harshly.

She didn't answer immediately but instead looked out
the darkened window. When she finally spoke she continued to stare out the window at the slowly moving
traffic.

"Why did you do that to me, David?" she said. She turned to him. "It hurt."

What he'd expected to hear and what he heard made him look at her as if she was a being magically materializing before his eyes. "Hurt you? What in God's name are you talking about?"

"Miriam Koster wants to buy my book." Margo's voice was low as she tried to keep the anger out of it. "She called yesterday."

An expelled breath. "Is that all?"

"All?" Margo shouldn't have been surprised. Her laugh was short and caustic. "You would say something like that." Before he spoke she said, "She rejected my submission but accepted it later because David Blackshear demanded it. What gave you the right to do that?"

He felt her pain and he was surprised, yet angered by it. The world he lived in these past five years was a life's learning lesson and he was still going to school. Deals—life-changing deals—were made every second that passed. No one who had a chance to make it turned it down, but was instead eternally grateful for a helping hand up. He'd thought he was giving Margo that nudge that so many others yearned for.

"It was something you wanted," he said, his anger at bay.

"Yes, it was," Margo answered. "It was something that I wanted to achieve by myself, to see if I could channel my creativity into something new, and different, and rewarding. I love my company. The work is hard but I'm hanging in. I owe that to you for giving me a chance—for believing in me."

"You owe me nothing. You were paid," David said, his voice heavy with emotion.

Margo closed her eyes against his hurt. "Yes, I was," she said. "Handsomely. But you know something, I was worth it." A tiny smile touched her lips. "Lawrence Pearsall finally saw the light after your campaign and other projects he's either seen or heard about. He called, offering me what he thought I wouldn't possibly refuse."

"Pearsall?" David said in surprise.

"Yes. He was willing to 'work things out' as he put it." Her laugh was humorless. "Maybe in the next world."

Silent, the revelation rocked him. She'd never mentioned it. More secrets.

Minutes ticked by.

"Your anger is the reason you refused to wear your pearls for me tonight?" His voice was tight.

Margo couldn't tell him why—not now. After his brother's party would be the right time. The two men were so close they could read each other's thoughts— feel each other's pain as though they were born of the same egg.

"The tanzanite was a better choice. It matches my outfit," Margo said.

Had he heard right? The world started to spin and he felt as though he'd been transported back to a time six years ago. Jonathan's birthday party! His head throbbed with the memory of that night and those same words uttered to Jonathan by his wife.

"The tanzanite matches my outfit."

Later, Jonathan had been crushed and in disbelief when he related the story to David. Instead of his jade gift to her she'd worn something else—a jewel he'd never seen her wear before. Only later Jonathan learned that the stone—the tanzanite—was a gift from her lover.

This can't be happening again, David thought as he sat still beside her. *Life doesn't throw curves like this.* The woman he loved wasn't wearing his gift to her because she was wearing a jewel from her lover. Is that her secret—the thing she had to work out by herself? To find a way to tell him that she was leaving him for someone else?

Cold realization chilled him, turning his heart as frigid as the raw October weather threatening to frost the car windows. How inventive. To pretend she was angry over his interference—when all she needed to do was think up an excuse. He could have laughed if he didn't think the sound would burst a window, he was so furious. He'd provided her with the perfect out! Justified outrage!

The silence stretched into a millennium when he said with a deadly calm, "Then wear your tanzanite, Margo. You've dazzled me."

She turned to him, a puzzled look on her face at his choice of words. She had no response.

When they arrived at the Brooklyn Marriott they entered the ballroom filled with people feting Jonathan Blackshear. They saw him and waved, walking toward him with tight lips and unsmiling eyes.

Jonathan felt like a kid in Toyland as he grinned and greeted his friends. He'd always enjoyed throwing parties, even as a young man when his parents couldn't afford them, excited about opening the colorfully wrapped gifts. He'd convince his mother to buy a bunch of dogs and buns, some chips and soda and bake some cakes. With a blob of ice cream his young friends were happy. It was quite a different story when in high school—his football-playing friends demanded "real food" and he'd had to give up his little cheap get-togethers. That was when the gifts stopped, too. But now he just enjoyed his friends coming together for a good time, able to leave behind for just a little while the troubles and worries that weighed on their minds. Although there was nothing he wanted or needed, they insisted on coming bearing gifts. Secretly he enjoyed some of the things he received though later he donated most of them to his charities.

"You can't wait, can you?" Wesley said in his ear.

Jonathan's grin widened. "Yeah, but don't tell nobody." As his brother and the beautiful woman by his side neared, the smile died.

"Uh-oh," Wesley said, a low whistle escaping.

"Hmm, you're right." Jonathan looked at David's grim face and Margo's taut one. "Why tonight? It's my birthday." He tried to joke but he knew that something was terribly wrong. As Margo stopped in front of him, his brown eyes darkened, and he looked swiftly and in disbelief at his brother who stared at him stoically. His eyes drawn again to her neck, his lips tightened as dank memories threatened to rob his joy. *Tanzanite?*

"Happy birthday, man," David said, clasping his brother in a manly hug. "Some party. What's it going to be next year when the big four-oh zaps you?"

"Happy birthday, Jonathan." Margo, on her toes, kissed his cheek.

Jonathan recoiled visibly. "Thanks," he said, his lips barely moving.

Wesley and Valeria exchanged knowing looks then stared at the three people so dear to them.

Margo was taken aback and hurt by Jonathan's response to her. Yet didn't she know that if anyone bothered his brother the wrath would be returned? How could he have guessed that anything was wrong? And why had he stared at her pendant as if she was sporting a python around her neck?

The thought of what she would be losing when she

left David hit her like an anvil being slammed into her stomach. All her friends whom she cared about would be gone. Jonathan had become like a brother to her, as Wesley. Val would think her crazy and uncaring and would refuse to bother with such nonsense. Her whole world as she knew it now would become a void and she could see herself as before—a recluse, the workaholic who Rhonda would have to cajole and prod to come out of her shell like a tired old tortoise. She'd no sooner sat than she excused herself, the tears at the corner of her eyes stinging as she walked to where she thought the powder room would be.

The other guests sitting at the table wore puzzled looks, and all were uncomfortable as they looked at the grim-faced brothers. As the music started, they used it as an excuse to get up and dance. The two friends remained.

"Jonathan," Val said softly. "Can we help?" She laid a hand on his shoulder, knowing what had happened the minute she saw Margo's jewelry.

He shook his head, but reached up to clutch her hand.

Wesley said to his friends, "Look, why don't you two find a quiet place to talk. We'll keep the party going for you." David and Jonathan stared at him, nodded, and silently left. "Would you explain to Margo?" Wesley asked Val. She nodded and went to look for her friend.

The bar was full but a secluded table afforded some privacy as they sat, each with a cognac.

Jonathan was the first to speak after he drank some more of the amber liquid. "This is my birthday six years ago, man. Why are you reliving my story?" He laughed. "Always wanted to emulate big brother, huh?"

David liked the zing of the Hennessy sliding down his throat. "You wish," he said in a voice as rough as gravel.

"Mine was green jade and yours is pearls," said Jonathan. "But oh, man, that tanzanite. Where the hell does it come from that it dazzles them like that? Just freaks them out!" He rubbed a hand over his face. "Oh, man." After a second, he said, "I couldn't help myself in there. The minute I saw your face I knew the world had dropped out from under you. When I spied the necklace, I about lost it. The same song was playing, only six years later it wasn't for me but for you. I'm sorry." He studied his brother. "The pearls. Why didn't she wear them for you tonight?"

"They didn't match her outfit." David's tone was wooden as he held his brother's stare.

"God!" His head spun. *Cynthia's exact words*. Recovered, he said, "There's someone else, too?"

"There was this secret thing she had to work out," David said. He lifted a shoulder. "I guess tonight, leaving the pearls home was her way of telling me that she'd worked it out." He drained his glass and gave the sign to the waiter for two refills.

"You found out tonight?" Jonathan asked.

David nodded. "On the way here."

"Damn," Jonathan breathed. "Life's a bitch." He remembered laughing at his brother grinning with that smug, silly-in-love look as David described the way the pearls had looked around Margo's neck. "Who's the guy?"

"Does it matter?"

Concerned at the dead voice and the empty look, Jonathan said, "What are you going to do?" He couldn't help but think about earlier this year when his brother had that same vacant stare and lifeless tone.

"Work," David said. "What would you have me do now? Is there anything else to do but make my millions grow?"

* * *

Valeria found her in the lounge. "Hi," she said, sitting in a chair beside her. "You look beautiful. Now don't give me that story that it was something you just pulled out of the closet." She loved the silk and satin lavender pantsuit with the deep V neck. The jewel at her throat sparkled like fire.

"Okay, I won't," Margo said, smiling at her friend.

"I know you're puzzled at what happened with Jonathan just now," Valeria said softly. "I want to tell you a story, if you'll listen."

"I'll listen," she said. What choice did she have if she wanted to learn how she'd hurt Jonathan without uttering a word.

"You know Jonathan was crazy about his wife Cynthia," Val said, speaking softly yet tenderly when she mentioned her lover's name. "He'd do anything for her, everyone loved her and David idolized her."

Margo knew that Jonathan was a widower and that he'd lost his wife in a tragic accident. Yet she'd never heard much else. She waited for Val to continue.

"Cynthia's passion was jewelry and she went crazy over mint green jade in every form. She even had carvings of the gemstone in her home. When Jonathan wanted something special for her David had told him about the jade butterfly. He'd read somewhere about a legend that proclaimed it as a symbol of the deepest love. David was proud of himself when Jonathan called excitedly one day saying that he'd found a pendant in Manhattan's Chinatown. Bringing happiness to the two most favorite people in his life meant a lot to David, and he was glad to have played a part in his brother's surprise. The night of Jonathan's birthday party she wore a lavender dress but didn't wear the jade butterfly because it didn't go with her outfit, that the tanzanite pendant was a better match."

Margo looked at Valeria as if her words were spouting from her mouth like water from a park fountain sculpture. She looked down at the soft folds of her clothing and then touched her jewel.

Valeria nodded. "Exactly," she said. "The same color outfit, the same jewel."

"And the same words," Margo whispered.

"What?"

"I didn't wear David's pearls tonight. I told him the tanzanite was a better match." She didn't tell her friend any more.

"Uncanny," Valeria said.

"That's why David looked so stricken," Margo said. "And when he heard my words he was about to lose it. I could never have guessed." She stared at Val. "The same jewel?" Incredibly spooky, she thought.

"Yes," Valeria said.

"I would never have hurt Jonathan, you know that, Val," Margo said.

"I know. But he was shocked. The minute we saw you two walk in we all knew something had gone down between you and David. Your jewelry did it for Jonathan. You see, the incident happened the night of his birthday party. He wanted her to show off the butterfly."

"Oh."

"Soon after, Cynthia was shot in that jewelry store robbery. It was only later when she lay dead in the hospital that Jonathan found out that she'd been pregnant."

"A child?" Margo hadn't known that.

Valeria nodded. "Jonathan was certain that he couldn't have fathered a child. Cynthia was more career oriented and wasn't ready for children. Weeks later, the tests proved him right. The son she would have had was not his."

"Dear, God," Margo murmured. What he must have gone through, she thought. And tonight the memory was so vivid in his mind when he'd looked at her. He must have thought he was reliving a nightmare.

They were silent, each thinking about the bizarre coincidence.

"Will you and David be able to get past this thing between you?" Val asked.

Margo shook her head. "I don't think so, Val."

Her sigh was desolate as Valeria put an arm around her friend's shoulders and squeezed. "You two won't be the same, I know it." She stood and pulled Margo up with her. "I'm praying that a lightning bolt will strike some sense into both of you. Come on, let's get back inside."

Holding back, Margo said, "In a bit. Let me stay a while longer. I don't want to be the cause of spoiling Jonathan's party. He looked so happy when I first saw him. You go on, I'll be in shortly."

Slipping into her coat she was standing in the lobby waiting for the next taxi when she felt someone standing at her elbow. She turned.

"I never took you for a coward, Margo," Wesley said.

"You never can tell about people, can you?" she said. Margo had never seen his eyes so sad. She turned from them, knowing she was the cause. In the space of an hour she'd managed to hurt all the people she loved.

"I wouldn't say that," he said easily. "Otherwise I'd have had to close my agency doors years ago."

She noticed he was dressed in his overcoat. Was he leaving his two friends?

"Forget the taxi Margo, I'm taking you home."

"Why?"

"Let's just say I think you could use a friend right now." He took her elbow. "My driver is waiting." He led her outside to his black limousine.

"Val told you?"

"Yes."

"Some story, huh?"

"Yes."

"Why, Margo?"

There was no trying to act with this intelligent, very astute friend of David's. "Wesley, I think what I'm doing is best left my business," she said gently. "And best for all concerned if no one is to get hurt."

He laughed. "Oh, you think so, do you?" But he reached into his pocket and popped some jelly beans.

"Yes." She smiled at his habit, knowing he was agitated.

"Margo, don't you know that you left at least three hurt souls back there?" He paused. "And one of them is so wounded that the earth will have to shift for him to even consider moving on."

She sank into the corner of the soft leather seat and closed her eyes. David was strong, tougher than any man she'd known. He would survive this. But she wondered about herself. Was she as strong?

The sparse traffic was moving so smoothly that Margo was surprised when the car entered her neighborhood. She would be home in seconds. Turning to the quiet man beside her, she said, "I'm sorry, Wesley. Please don't ask me anymore. I—I must take care of this myself." The car stopped, double-parked in front of her building. Unmoving, the driver waited for a word from his boss.

Wesley was not giving up. "Okay," he said. "I'll drop it for now. But I want a promise from you." He forced her to look at him. "If this thing—whatever it is—gets too big for you I want you to call me. Anytime is the right time. No matter where you are. Call and I'll come. Understand?"

David knew Wesley was seeing Margo home safely. When Val had returned without her he guessed that she wouldn't step foot into the ballroom again. No words were spoken between him and his friend when he caught Wesley's eye. The big man had smiled and left the table.

That night he was restless. Rambling around the house going from room to room he stopped in each one that held a memory of her. The things they'd said and done. The funny antics and tricks she'd played on him. Her playfulness in the whirlpool, and their making love wherever their desire caught them, made him wince. He sat on the edge of the bed, kicking off his shoes as he smoothed his hand over the comforter, sniffing faintly as if she were near.

Lying down on top of the covers in the dark, he wondered if he would stay here as much, torturing himself with the past. Eventually, like a rose past its time, her scent would fade from his home, his memory. He couldn't help remembering that last night on the mountaintop in St. Maarten. He'd had a feeling of something monumental taking place in his life. Tonight had been colossal!

David wondered if another woman would ever invade his heart, ambush him so unexpectedly as Margo Sterling had. The harsh laugh rattled around the silent room as if chortling at the bad joke.

Margo was undressed, standing barefoot in black panties and bra in front of her dresser. She unhooked the gold chain, and gently placed the jewel in its velvet pouch. Closing the lid of the jewelry box, her hand lingered on the polished cherry wood with its carved rose design on top. Would she ever wear it again? she wondered.

With a robe over cotton pajamas Margo went into the study. Turning on the computer she went to e-mail. Finding his address she brought it up and typed a message but before turning off the computer, she printed it. She dropped the page on her desk, turned off the computer and left the room. Tomorrow she would deal with the consequences of her actions.

When do you want to meet?

Ty looked at the message. "I always knew you to do the right thing, Margo." A malevolent grin slashed his face. "But you waited too long."

Chapter Eighteen

The waiting was wearing on her nerves. All day Sunday, she'd waited for Ty to respond with an e-mail or worse, show up in the lobby getting into an altercation with Joe. What was he waiting for? she wondered. He was getting what he wanted, wasn't he?

She now knew what had been deep in her gut: that those mishaps weren't accidents. The gardener leaving the hose for an unsuspecting Inez was Ty. Zachary had been unexpectedly accosted in a friendly environment by Ty. Wesley's attack could have only been Ty. Hadn't Val cracked up when describing her encounter with Shankley while holding a carving fork? No, she was mugged by Ty.

All warnings to Margo. She chose to ignore her instincts and had sloughed them off as awful coincidences. When she realized his plan it had unnerved her. He was moving from the least important to the most dearly loved person in her life. Was Cindy or Rhonda exempt or were they next? Or Jonathan? Then there was David.

It was Wednesday and she was nearly tied up in knots while waiting. Margo couldn't believe how fate worked to her advantage. The pearls; Miriam Koster. They were on time! The perfect out, for her to enrage David. He could walk away from her with a clear conscience, knowing that she was the one who'd failed in the relationship.

The offer from a publisher who'd rejected her was still hurtful. She'd yet to send a response to the woman but she knew that if the book was published it wouldn't be with that company. She still had every intention of making it on her own, even if she went the route of self-publishing. Her tales for young children held a message and she felt strongly about getting it out there. *Everything in its own time,* she thought.

She was still furious with David for interfering. Yet she knew that in time, she would have forgiven him, refused his offers of help, and continued to love him. Hadn't she laughingly declined other gifts he'd tried to shower her with? Another bicycle, furs that she had no desire to own, a new top-of-the-line Cadillac?

Curiously, David had never bought her jewelry. The exquisite strand of pearls was the first bauble he'd presented to her and when she remembered the love in his eyes when he stared at them around her neck, her heart thumped with compassion. Never before had she thought about that, not until the night of the party and she'd been told the story of Cynthia's deceit. The gift of the pearls was the gift of himself to her. His symbol of trust in a woman. She'd been that woman who'd chipped at the block of ice around his heart until it'd melted. Now she was the woman who'd betrayed that love and trust.

Knowing that the pearls were terribly expensive, she couldn't let their life and luster die from lingering in her lingerie drawer. She had to give them to David and mailing them was out of the question. There was no way that any postal insurance would cover their value should they become lost. Unwilling to see David she knew it was something she had to bite the bullet and take care of right away.

His home machine kicked in and unwilling to talk to it she hung up. She called his cell. Refusing to leave a message she disconnected. Trying one more place she dialed his midtown office.

"It's Margo Sterling," she said when the efficient Barbara Olivera answered. They'd never gotten past the surname stage and Margo had wondered why they'd never warmed to each other. Possibly the mature woman thought she was just another passing fancy in his life. "Is Mr. Blackshear available?" she said.

"Mr. Blackshear is in a board meeting and can't be disturbed, Ms. Sterling. Would you care to leave a message?"

"No, no message, other than I called. Thank you." Margo hung up with the distinct impression that the right hand of Blackshear enterprises had considered the call a disturbance and was anxious to get back to more important business.

It was past five when he strode toward his office from the conference room, the last board member following him in order to get his point across. Annoyed, David dismissed the man. If he couldn't open his mouth after an all-day session, then he didn't have anything important to say or it could wait until the next meeting.

"No calls, Barbara," he said tersely. He paused with his hand on the doorknob. "Any messages?"

"Two. Mr. Blackshear and Ms. Sterling."

His mouth twisted in a grimace. "Mr. Blackshear from Virginia or Mr. Blackshear from Brooklyn, New York?"

Barbara gave him stare for stare. "Your father." He

turned to go when she said, "The tickets you ordered for tonight's performance of *The Lion King* arrived. They're on your desk."

"What did my father want?"

"Mr. Blackshear said he and Mrs. Blackshear decided to go on a monthlong cruise and won't be coming up for Thanksgiving. He said he'll call you tonight at home."

"Ms. Sterling?"

"No message. Just that she called."

In his office he strode to the desk, picked up the envelope and went back out. "I won't be needing these," he said. "Maybe you can use them." He caught the older woman's eye. "Barbara, I'm sorry."

"I know. Good night, David. And thanks for the tickets. I'll use them."

His mood was foul and he knew it. But barking at the woman who was his lifeline at work wouldn't cut it. He had to get a grip.

Three days it had taken her to think about him. Three days he'd lived in hell. Day and night. The nights were worse. The days were filled with numbers and problems and people bending his ear on the phone, at lunches, catching him in the hall or cajoling Barbara to let them in for "just a minute" of his time. It wasn't even six yet and he was already looking for a project to keep him here until midnight. But Barbara had taken care of that he thought, looking at his bare desk. Nothing to sign, or to peruse for his comments. Finally settling down he stared at the phone. He reached for it and then pulled his hand back as if it had come alive and bitten him.

"You won't learn, Blackshear, will you?" He steeled himself against picking up that phone. He wouldn't do it. The pain was still fierce and it was all he could do to act sane, going through the mundane motions of existing. He'd gotten this far into the week without hearing her voice or looking at the face he saw in his dreams. The big beautiful brown eyes that spoke to him, sending him promises that made him drool like a lovesick bull. No one walked like she did, her firm, rounded butt jiggling just a little beneath the soft silky dresses she liked to wear.

His mouth tightened into a grim slash as he dragged his hand over his face. Who was he? David tortured himself with questions. Who was the stranger? Or was he a stranger? Could have been in the same room dozens of times at any event they'd attended. He conjured up images of men he'd seen her talking and laughing with. His friends. His acquaintances. Did they first meet in his home? When? Why wasn't he aware of what was happening between them? Questions. Questions. Questions. Too many with no possible answers.

"Damn, damn, damn!" When was it going to stop? He thought about his brother six years ago. If he thought he'd known what Jonathan was feeling then, he was dead wrong. There was no way he could have imagined this kind of pain—as if his heart was slowly becoming encased in cement.

But life goes on, he thought. "And so will I." The words were startling in the quiet room, so when the phone rang he looked at it in surprise. It kept ringing until he realized Barbara had gone.

"Blackshear." He'd punched the speakerphone button.

"David, it's Margo." Her heart wrenched at the sound of his voice.

He couldn't speak. As if to be closer to her he picked up the phone.

"David?"

"I'm here, Margo." He closed his eyes briefly. Keeping his voice even he said. "You called before."

"Yes."

"Why?"

"I—I want to return the pearls to you and I didn't want to just leave them with Inez."

His lips thinned. "I trust her," he said.

The implication was not missed. "I'll drop them off tonight."

"There's no one there," David said. "Inez is away for the rest of the month. She'll be back after Thanksgiving." He paused. "Besides, there's no reason for you to come by. The pearls are yours. They were a gift."

"I can't keep such a gift, since we, since I . . ." Finally, "I can't keep them."

He couldn't help himself. "Why, Margo?"

"Because they're priceless and I shouldn't keep them."

"Not the damn pearls," David said, his voice raspy with emotion. "Why did you do this to us? Was it your scheme all along? What kind of game were you playing with me? Tell me because I'm trying to understand. Was everything you said and did with me a lie?" He wished now that he'd confronted her, gone to her. He wanted to see the lies in her eyes.

Her breath caught in her throat as she listened to the bewilderment in his voice and it was like a knife being twisted in her stomach.

When she didn't answer David said, calmer now, "Do I know him?" Why did he torture himself with that? What the hell difference did it make? But the burning desire to know was consuming him.

"What?" she said.

"The man you're dealing with while loving me,"

David said. "Did you go to his bed while mine was still wet and warm with your love?"

Without warning the keening cry erupted from her mouth, his words stinging her ears. "There is no one else," she managed.

"Stop. Spare me the lies!" Seconds passed. "Don't bring the pearls by Margo." How could he lay eyes on her now? "I'll send a driver around to pick them up tonight."

When he disconnected, Margo could only sit and stare at the phone. *He thinks I have a lover!* How could he after all they'd meant to each other? The thought left her feeling dirty. Shuddering, she moved from the desk to the comfortable upholstered chair, wrapping herself in a throw.

"What would you have done?" She was looking at the photo of the laughing Kai. "Staying with him would be a threat to his life and anyone he cares for. Right?"

Wishing to talk to someone she left the room to go next door when she stopped. Rhonda was in California visiting her daughter for two weeks. She'd left the morning of Jonathan's party saying how sorry she was to have missed the gala.

Calling Val would be an interruption, besides, she knew her friend was still giving her time to come to her senses.

Feeling desolate, Margo went to her bedroom where she retrieved the black box from her drawer and carried it to the kitchen, ready to be taken downstairs. She opened it and looked at the beautiful white balls once more. So gorgeous, she thought. She couldn't help but wonder what David would do with them. Give them to another? That thought made her wince. They were hers. Laughing at herself she closed the box. "You gave them up when you shut him out of your life, girl."

* * *

Winter was Jonathan's least favorite season. It was getting a ferocious start with early November's arctic winds. The gallery staff had long since gone and he was finishing up some last-minute problems with misplaced inventory. He'd stalled long enough, hating to get out there even though the walk to his car behind the building was but a few short steps.

All day he'd had Margo on his mind. How he could have been so wrong about a person he'd never know. She'd completely fooled him, not to mention what she'd done to his brother. Only Wesley and Val thought something was strange about her actions, neither wanting to believe Margo was involved with another man. Wesley was adamant about something not smelling right. At first, Jonathan had tuned him out, not wanting to hear his theory on why a woman did what she did. But now, that something wouldn't let him rest all day. He believed that the woman he'd come to love like a sister was hiding something. He was determined to find out what it was if it killed him. Because it sure as hell was killing David. Agreeing to meet tonight with Wesley to thrash things out, even to the point of paying her a visit, he felt hopeful. Maybe the two of them could delve into the mystery together and find a solution that would bring David back.

Closing and locking the door to his office, he stopped. The large outer space was dark except for a nightlight leading to the back door and his car. Upstairs was dark but he knew he'd heard a sound up there.

"Hello?" he called. There was another small office upstairs that housed a staff room, a bathroom and was used by his assistant. "Nick?" he called, walking across the dark room and up the ramp. "I thought you'd gone, man," he said, seeing the light shining from under the door. "Come on, man, it's ten o'clock and the hawk is out there. Call it a night and let's get outta here." He shook his head as the light went out and he turned and started back down the ramp. "Workaholic," he mused. He didn't turn at the footsteps behind him so he never saw the blade coming down in an arc toward his back.

"Damn," Jonathan swore as his hand reflexively went behind his back, but the pain rendered his legs useless and he slumped to the floor. "What the hell . . ." His eyes closed.

At ten thirty David sat watching the sports channel. He was drinking. Not the usual warm cognac that he enjoyed. Whiskey and soda, the eighty proof stuff. He was on his second.

He knew why he'd never sent his driver around to pick up the necklace. He wanted to retrieve it himself. An excuse to see her again. To see her eyes, to lose himself in them once more. The whiskey was helping him to fortify his heart, to keep him from making a fool of himself.

His glance at the display on the phone brought a frown. "Yeah, what's up?"

Wesley heard the slur. "You're drinking," he said quietly.

"Want to join me?" David said.

"Call your driver and get over to Long Island College Hospital," Wesley said. "Jonathan's been hurt."

David's head snapped back like he'd been sucker punched. The glass rolled out of his hand. "What did you say?" Silence. "Dammit, Wes, what the hell happened?"

"Hurry, David. He was stabbed."

* * *

At midnight, the intercom woke Margo and stumbling to the hall, she pressed the button. "Yes? What is it, Hank?"

"A Mr. Gray wants to speak to you, Ms. Sterling," the night relief said.

"Wesley?" She clenched her fist to her chest.

"Margo," Wes said. "Get dressed and come down now. I have my car here to take you to Brooklyn."

"Brooklyn?" Why not Holliswood where David was? she thought giddily.

"Hurry. Jonathan's hurt. It looks bad."

"God, no," Margo whispered as she sagged against the wall. "No."

The driver moved the big Mercedes through the quiet streets as easily as he would have sitting on a tractor mowing his lawn. As agitated as Wesley was he didn't need to be doing the driving. Jelly beans were produced as fast as he could chew. She sat, her thumbs going circle over circle. His voice made her jump.

"What?"

"Why didn't you tell me? Or warn David?"

He knew.

Wesley stared at her blanched face. "I don't know how I missed that." He laughed but it was a sharp bitter sound. "I couldn't have kept this agency going all these years missing something so obvious that it was kicking me in the rump and I couldn't even feel it." He sucked the sugar coating off a green jelly bean, and then chomped down on the gummy ball. "What does Henderson have on you?"

She was stunned and couldn't answer.

"Was it worth so many people getting hurt—or killed? Is David next?"

"Oh, God," Margo whispered. "Is Jonathan dying?"

"I hope not today." Wesley's long lashes shuttered his eyes and his mouth was grim.

"Why did you come for me?" she said. "Did David send you?"

"No. He doesn't know what I suspected and you just confirmed with your silence. I thought you might want to tell him yourself and to see Jonathan. He's sedated and won't know you're there. But after this is all over I think it'll mean something to everyone that you showed up tonight."

"What happened to him?" Margo said, crying inside for Jonathan's pain.

"Took a deep knife wound in the back, almost bled to death." He paused and looked out the window. "I found him in the gallery," Wesley said, as if still in shock. "We'd talked about coming to see you, to get to the bottom of what was going on. But tonight was too late I guess." He turned to her. "I wish you'd confided in me. I told you I'd be there for you, Margo." He heaved a sigh. "Want to tell me about it?"

What a rush!

Ty was in the basement apartment his parents had fixed up for him since he'd returned to their Corona home. When he'd gotten in, he warmed the meal his mother had left in the microwave, carried the plate downstairs, and locked the door. Setting the food down he stripped and stepped into the portable stall shower that had been installed. It was small and hardly held his bulk. It infuriated him further that he had to live like this after what he'd once had. Humiliated at having to give up his luxurious digs and selling off some of his massive furniture, he loathed his old home.

Hardworking people, his parents had struggled to buy their little three-bedroom house. The structure was old and needed repair but there was no money for new siding or cosmetic touch-ups. A clerk in an insurance company, and a bakery shop worker. That's who they were.

Ty knew he should have helped them financially when he was able, but he was always waiting for that huge break. They'd been so ecstatic about his successful career, bragging about their well-to-do son who made television commercials.

He wolfed down his food and was still hungry, but he refused to go back upstairs where he might be questioned by his nosy mother. Always asking him questions. *Where've you been? Have you found anything yet?* His large hands clenched and unclenched. But then his body relaxed as he felt warm all over. Something like he'd felt back in the gallery.

That knife sinking into that flesh was like sliding into a chocolate cream pie—so smooth and easy. When Jonathan reached back to see what had happened to him, he'd almost pulled it out and stuck him again, just to feel that sensation. It was almost like getting high. Like all the others he'd only wanted to tease, to hurt a little, not to kill. But something came over him at that last second. Blackshear had it all, the good life: things he didn't have and craved, and would do anything to get. It was then he'd wanted to really hurt him bad to see the rich man helpless at his feet.

Ty chuckled as he thought about it. He'd wished there was light enough so he could see what a millionaire's face looked like all scrunched up in pain and gasping for air like a fish out of water.

The laughter stopped when he thought about Margo. Was Ms. Thang acting like the spitfire now? he wondered, waiting too long to call, ignoring his warnings. Did she think he was spinning his wheels? He laughed out loud. "Yeah, I'm spinning Champion Wheels." Pleased with his humor, he said, "Maybe I'll send Chris Rock some of my material." His big shoulders shook with laughter.

Watching his brother's still form, David was numb with disbelief and fear. What the hell had happened? Who'd want to hurt him so bad as to try to kill him? There was nothing stolen so what was it? If Wes hadn't gotten there in time, Jonathan would have bled to death. He dropped his head in his hand and rubbed his forehead, kneading his temples. Jonathan had to recover from this. He didn't think past that thought. Looking toward the door when they appeared, he sat unmoving.

"Val left?" Wesley said, walking into the room.

"Yes. I sent her home. She was losing it." He looked at Margo but couldn't speak.

Margo turned from David and walked to the bed and looked down at Jonathan. He was sleeping. She didn't know what she'd expected, probably all wires and tubes coming from everywhere but he only had an IV attached to a pole by the bedside. His thin mustache moved slightly when he stirred but then he settled deeper into sleep. Touching his hand she smoothed it and then squeezed. "Jonathan, I'm so sorry," she whispered.

Her curious words caused David to send her and then Wesley a puzzled stare.

Wesley said in a low voice, "Margo has something to tell you." He jerked his head toward the door. "Not in here."

In a lounge not too far away from Jonathan's room,

David sat across from Margo. She hadn't spoken since those words she'd whispered to his brother.

"What is it that you have to tell me?"

"It's my fault," Margo murmured. "All of it." She raised her eyes to his. "I didn't know he'd go this far."

His heart constricted. "You mean you know who nearly killed my brother? And what do you mean by 'all of it'? What?"

"I didn't tell you the truth about Ty Henderson," she said. "He threatened me again and I didn't believe him." She saw thunder in David's eyes and she shuddered. "Before we went to St. Maarten, he accosted me. I told him to get lost and he did. I didn't hear from him for days and I thought I'd won, that he would leave me alone. Then the night you called my cell, the night I was in the bar, he'd just left."

David sat as if encased in stone, but he never spoke. He listened as she told him about the threats and the pictures and her voice hurt his ears. How could she have let this happen? To take the threats of a madman so lightly after he'd warned her?

"Inez?" David said. "And all the rest—Zachary, Val, Wes?" He shuttered his eyes. "And now Jonathan who was left to die?"

"Yes," Margo murmured. "I contacted Ty willing to work with him, but he never called." She felt sick as she gestured toward the room where Jonathan lay. "I was too late. I guess he was teaching me a lesson for ignoring him."

"My brother in there was the result of that hard-learned lesson now, isn't he?" David said harshly.

"I'm sorry I didn't trust you enough to confide in you, David. I thought I could handle it by myself."

"So you pretended to be angry about the book deal to

push me out of your life. To keep me safe." David held her gaze. "Is that so?"

"Partly," Margo answered. "I was angry with you because you were using your wealth and pull to get what you wanted." She didn't look away from his angry eyes. "Money isn't everything, David. Even though people like Ty think so. Everybody would be willing to admit it does make life a hell of a lot more pleasant, but it sure doesn't take the place of love and happiness." She paused. "But, yes, it came at the right time for me to use as the perfect excuse to say good-bye."

"And the pearls?"

"I knew you'd be hurt if I didn't wear them. It was the preamble to my ending the relationship."

"An understatement."

"I didn't know the meaning of the lavender, the tanzanite, how they played such a terrible part in Jonathan's life. That was totally uncanny."

After a minute, David said, "You're not the woman I thought you were."

"What kind is that?" Margo asked.

"A schemer. A gold-digger."

Surprised, Margo said, "Why would you think that?"

"Penn Station and the way a beautiful woman blew off a hardworking baggage handler. After that brush-off I thought you were the kind who would only let yourself be picked up by a briefcase and a three-piece suit." A tiny smile tugged at the corner of his mouth. "Later, when we met and I had a chance to say hello again, I thought you were running a game on me after you found out who that redcap really was. After we got involved, I had to wait and see who you really were before I . . ."

"Declared your love," Margo finished for him. She closed her eyes for a split second. "Aren't we a pair," she said.

"What do you mean?"

"After you left me that day in Pearsall's office, I thought you'd used your money to track me down," she said. "I needed to be sure of you, to see if you were really being honest about your feelings for me, before . . ."

"Declaring your love."

They were both quiet.

A laugh from David finally broke the silence.

"We were gaming each other all that time," David said. "Until Tarrytown," he said thoughtfully. "Am I right about that?"

After the danger of Tarrytown they'd finally spoken those three little words. Inside, Margo was hurting so badly she could hardly breathe. "Until then," she barely managed.

David murmured, "Yes, aren't we a pair."

Wesley was standing in the doorway. "He's awake." He looked from the man to the woman and he knew it hadn't gone well.

Margo stood and walked to the door behind David when he stopped her.

"No," he said. "Not now." He turned on his heel and his long strides carried him quietly down the hall.

Wesley looked at the stricken woman. "I'll have my driver take you home."

Numb, Margo nodded.

Passing by the room she saw David bending over talking to Jonathan. She paused and he looked up and caught her stare. Without any expression he turned back to his brother.

At nearly two in the morning Margo was on the living room sofa filling her stomach with chamomile tea in hopes of bringing on sleep. She'd asked and answered a million questions.

Now she understood why Ty hadn't returned her call. He was fixing her, teaching her a lesson. Why had she been so stupid, so arrogant as to think she could go up against a man who had gone off the deep end. She knew nothing about the workings of a sick mind but did have a sixth sense. The night she'd seen the demonic look in his eyes should have been clue enough that she was dealing with something that was beyond her comprehension, or if it came to that, the ability to ward off danger.

Because of that Jonathan had nearly died and others that she cared for were hurt. Without a doubt she knew that Ty was past reasoning with. Her fears heightened when she realized that David was not safe.

But knowing what she did, how was Ty going to be stopped with no proof of what he'd done, except for her suspicions? Wesley had figured it out but she knew he was helpless to go after Ty with no evidence except speculation. The authorities would think her crazy with her story.

The calming effect of the herb was working. Her drooping eyelids flew open when the phone rang. The name displayed caused her to come awake and a chill went through her yet mixed with feelings of reprieve as she reached for the phone; she was being given a second chance! There was only one person left who he could hurt and she had it in her power to see that that would never come to pass.

"Ty," she said woodenly. "Where do you want to meet?"

Chapter Nineteen

The twenty-something blue-collar working man with the idiot grin on his face holding up his check brought a snort from David. The onlookers who dreamed of standing in his shoes enviously clapped their good wishes while the silly announcer asked what the guy was going to do with his check for nineteen million.

How in hell does he know what he's going to do with nineteen million bucks? David thought. The most cash he's probably held in his hands was the thousand dollar jackpot he hit on the slots in Atlantic City. You know damn well he's going to pay the electric bill and the last three months rent to hold off the landlord's dispossess. Then he's going to get a Hummer or two or three and some other super expensive cars for his homies. Maybe there's a plan in there to lay some dough on his folks.

"Happy Thanksgiving, brother." David raised his glass to the TV screen. "I sure hope you're ready for prime time!"

The glass was empty and David filled it again with the VSOP and moving from the bar, stretched out on the sofa in his library. He continued to watch television, idly flipping from channel to channel. His new Champion Wheels commercial aired: the one he'd hired another company to make. It was a follow-up idea and one Margo had suggested that he consider in the future. The Christmas sales were through the roof.

Restless, he continued to flip channels in the hope that something would catch his interest or bore him silly so that he could fall asleep without thinking. For the last three weeks his brain was in overdrive and he knew he had to halt or go over the edge. He'd thought about flying to the mountaintop but there were too many memories there and he wasn't into masochistic behavior.

He'd had time to think about him and his wealth. He wished he could talk to that young brother who'd just won the jackpot of his life. Take him to school on the do's and don'ts of keeping friends and lovers and not making a complete jackass of himself.

Amazing how he'd deduced that without the help from a shrink. He'd thought that he'd matured during the years after winning; that he had learned to be humble and compassionate, unassuming in his dealings with others. After that first year of vain loftiness when demandingly he'd walked into an establishment as if he were King Tut, he'd learned to act sane and normal. Not grandstanding by dropping big bills on the table or picking up a tab that could have been an average man's monthly salary.

When his anger and hurt had dissipated after Jonathan was out of the woods, he'd taken stock of himself. Really looked inside to see what kind of person he was. Almost losing his brother gave him a chance to look at his own mortality and the legacy he would leave behind.

Where he thought it the most normal thing in the world to have visited that editor bringing with him Margo's handcrafted book, he thought that Margo would have gone berserk with pleasure and excitement.

That simple act—simple to him at least—had driven a wedge between them that was immovable.

He'd hurt her. He didn't even stop to think what his actions might mean to her. All he knew was that he'd lost the love of his life because he hadn't thought about her feelings. All she wanted was to prove herself, that she could get back her self-esteem and confidence doing something on her own. Although he'd given her that chance which resulted in Sterling Productions, he knew that she was on a mission to excel in other areas—again, on her own. And here he came, smugly expecting her to throw herself into his arms, thanking him with breathless kisses. Was he ever wrong about the woman he thought he knew!

For a week he'd stayed by Jonathan's side in the hospital, taking turns with Val and Wes so that someone was always there. They knew he was getting better when one day he threw them all out because all he wanted to do was get some sleep. At first David was angry because Jonathan was nearly put to sleep permanently, but then he'd laughed at his silliness. The man was going to be okay and that was all that mattered.

Once, Jonathan noticed Margo's absence and had asked for her. No one answered until finally he explained what had been going on and Jonathan had been strangely quiet.

He stirred, thinking about them, and hoping they were taking it easy in Mexico. New York was dismal with snow, ice and rain and was no place to recuperate. Two days after Jonathan's release from the hospital David had convinced him to take Val and go warm his bones in sunny climes.

David had missed them especially since Thanksgiving was tomorrow and he would be without family for the first time in years. His parents were still on the cruise and Wesley was visiting his folks in Georgia. That was his whole family. He didn't like the idea of being alone, eating alone, but he supposed he'd get through it. There were always peanut butter sandwiches.

He thought about all the plans he'd made for tomorrow—before he'd turned his back on the woman he still loved. He had been going to surprise her with the best Thanksgiving dinner she'd ever tasted, complete with Inez's candied yams recipe. David hadn't cooked anything worth talking about in weeks. With Inez still away he'd made do with eating out or delivery—whichever was more convenient.

The phone rang and David reached to the table for it. He grinned. "Y'all missing me, huh?" He sat up, feeling uplifted. "So what are you guys up to? Getting homesick?"

Jonathan listened and then looked at Val, shaking his head. As he'd guessed, David was in a funk. "What are you doing tomorrow?" he said. "Having dinner with friends?"

"Yes, as a matter of fact I am," David lied. "What about you two?"

"With who?"

"What do you mean who?" David said, annoyed. "Just some people I'm meeting at Bambou."

"A restaurant?" Jonathan frowned, knowing many eateries closed on Thanksgiving, that family holiday. His brother was lying. "I thought you were all set to show off your culinary skills that you've been bragging about."

"That was for family and you guys aren't here so what's the point?"

"Margo's there," Jonathan said. "You haven't called her," he stated.

Silence.

"David, you've already admitted to us that you were wrong, so how about admitting it to her. She'd like to hear that." He paused. "Besides, that whole thing with Henderson has gone away. I guess the brother was scared out of his mind when he thought he'd almost committed murder. He's probably living like a monk in the Appalachians, crossing you off his hit list."

"I still want him caught for what he's done," David said tight-lipped. He didn't know how Jonathan and Valeria were willing to let the matter drop instead of trying to find some proof, holding the man accountable for the things he'd done, not to mention attempted murder.

"We've hashed and rehashed that," Jonathan said quietly. "There's not a shred of evidence that the man did any of those things. We can suspect and point fingers until the cows come home and it wouldn't do a damn thing. You know that, so get over it. I sure as hell am moving on and you should, too."

When he was finished, David said, "You're right. And I'm sure Margo has done just that. Moved on with her life and not even thinking of looking back."

"You know that, do you?" Jonathan said. There was no answer, and he said, "I think you're wrong. Think about the time wasted. Life can be so short, David. Six years ago you and I both found that out. It took me a long time to come to terms with what Cynthia had done but now I'm glad the past is where it should be. Not forgotten but relegated to its rightful place in my subconscious. Allowing my hate for her to consume my life was wrong. And you were wrong for putting her on a pedestal so high that you felt as betrayed as I did. I've put the past behind me, and with what I have now with Valeria, I'll never regret it." He paused. "Be damned sure about what you're letting slip away."

When David disconnected, he went upstairs and

pulled a duffel bag out of his closet. He couldn't stay
here in this house. At least not tomorrow. The sound of
her laughter in the kitchen when he told her about his
gourmet peanut butter sandwiches made him wince.
Inez laughing at his burnt fingers and scorched pots and
pans brought a wistful smile to his lips. There would be
no puffed chest as he watched her eating his candied
yams.

He made a call giving instructions and then hung up.
The door locked and house secured, he got into the SUV
and pulled out of the driveway.

Sag Harbor in the winter was a lonely place. Even
lonelier on a Thanksgiving Day that had dawned damp
and cold. The call he'd made last night before leaving
Queens resulted in a sumptuous breakfast and a Thanksgiving meal that had been just delivered, hot and ready
to eat. It was two o'clock in the afternoon and David
hadn't seen or heard a soul since he'd arrived at close to
one A.M. except for the catering people.

Eating his breakfast alone at the island counter had
been a mistake. It was there that he could hear her
squeals of impatience when she wanted loving and he'd
stopped because there was no condom. He could see
her, smell her, and feel the satiny texture of those long
tawny thighs kissed to deeper beige by the hot summer
sun.

How could he have thought he was getting away
when she was all over the place?

David left the food on the counter, pulled on a jacket
and went outside. He walked the beach, seeing for the
first time a couple jogging by. They waved at each other
and he kept walking. The sky was a pale, gloomy gray,
and he wished for the bright blue sunny skies that he remembered. Since buying this place he'd never been
happier than those times he'd been here with her. Down

by the edge the icy waters lapped at his feet soaking his sneakers, but he stood there looking out over the horizon seeing nothing but more clouds and dull skies.

She wasn't seeing anyone. Those words had resounded in his head until he begged for mercy for the cacophony to stop. He knew that now. How could she have? He'd taken up her time until she'd begged to get back to her work. She had a business to run. There had been no one else and when he'd accused her he'd realized it when her cry had pierced his soul. But then, he'd only been thinking of his own hurt.

Pride. Nothing but foolish pride was keeping him from going to her. As he told his brother she'd probably moved on with her life. Maybe one day she'd find that guy who deserved her trust. Margo loved hard and with all her heart and soul. He would never find anything like that again nor was he inclined to go looking. He'd had it all and lost it.

His Thanksgiving Day meal was prepared exquisitely, including all the traditional fixings. The favorite part for him was always the crisp, browned turkey wing and savory stuffing. The dessert came second. All the rest was just food. When he bit into the yams he pushed his plate away and he felt the sadness wash over his face like a wet dish rag. All the leftovers were trashed, the fridge made bare, for he would be leaving in the morning. He couldn't stay here another day let alone the weekend as he'd planned.

Instead of lazing around he'd go to Champion Wheels, the only one of his offices that would be open tomorrow. The Friday after Thanksgiving was a moneymaker and he knew his bicycles would be rolling out of the store. The warehouse inventory had told the tale. Cindy and her staff were ecstatic and all were looking forward to an early opening and late closing. That would take care of Friday, he thought. But what about the rest of the weekend and the days after that?

David wondered just how long or where he could go that his memories of her wouldn't haunt him like some-body's bad dream.

"I don't believe you just started doing this, honey." Rhonda put her fork down after getting her fill of blended apple and peach pie with a crust that cried to be eaten. "On second thought," she said, and sliced another piece and slid it onto her plate, with another scoop of vanilla ice cream. "Shoot, we all become little piggies for one day. It's a tradition!" She ate dreamily, making faces of delight at her friend.

Margo laughed at Rhonda's foolishness but she was inwardly pleased that the meal had been a success. Nothing was burned, singed, overcooked or soggy. She got up and poured more tea for them both and sat back across from her friend. The table was all dressed up in snow-white cloth and orange and red runners. A center-piece of colorful flowers with orange and yellow mums gave the table a festive air. She'd used the crystal and china her parents had given her eons ago when she'd first set up her own apartment. Then, she'd laughed telling them they should have saved their money. She had spoken to them earlier apologizing for staying home on the holiday but she begged off because tomorrow she had to get cracking with her work. Business had slacked off alarmingly so that she wondered if she should sit back and take stock. Perhaps she needed to seek some advice.

Rhonda pushed away from the table, but she was slid-ing looks to her friend. "That was just out of this world,

Margo," she said. "I'm proud of you. This was no easy feat you pulled off."

"Thanks, I like hearing that." She cocked her head sideways with a frown. "Is that all? More, more."

They both laughed, settling into a comfortable silence. Carrying teacups they moved into the living room and Margo turned on the TV.

"I wish Brenda could have come," Margo said. "She would have died!"

Rhonda laughed. "You know she would have. She's as bad as you were, not knowing how long to cook a two-minute egg."

When their laughter subsided, Rhonda gave Margo a speculative look. "So you've made up your mind?"

Margo didn't bother to play dumb. She knew very well this conversation was inevitable. "I think it's best that we move on with our lives. We just fell in love with the wrong people is all." *Liar.*

"I don't believe that you believe that," Rhonda said. "At least not from what I've seen. You came alive the minute that man walked into Pearsall's office, handing you the project of a lifetime. As for him he was already bewitched."

"You don't understand," Margo said. "I like my work and want to keep on doing it. If every time I hit a stone wall it's broken to bits just so I can walk blithely through the debris, all because he spoke, literally moving mountains, where's the challenge and reward in doing anything?"

"He can knock down walls for me anytime he likes," Rhonda said after a soft chuckle. Then, "I think you're placing too much into what he did. Since he knows how you feel about it do you think he'd just continue? I don't think so."

"Well, I guess we'll never know now," Margo said.

Rhonda stood. "Come on, let's get the kitchen squared away. Much as I'd like to get an early jump on shopping like the rest of the city I have to go in. What about you? Taking a breather yourself?"

"I was thinking about it," Margo said as she cleared the table, putting food away. "But what do I really have to buy?" she said with a small shrug. "You, who have everything! Fuggedaboutdit! I just pull my hair out wondering what to get. Shoot, I bet I've given you the same thing time and again and you've never said a word. Brenda always can use the cash. Then there are my folks." She shook her head. "My mother is happy with a gift certificate from Nordstrom. My father just looks for more pieces to add to his train collection." She stacked the dishwasher. When finished, she said, "Christmas shopping is no fun for me anymore. Not like it used to be." What she would have gotten for him she couldn't even imagine.

Drying her hands, Rhonda turned to her with a smile, and then patted her back. "It will be one day when you have your own family. You'll see." At the door, she said, "Let's plan a night out before the holidays get too hectic. Dinner in Manhattan, maybe take in a show or something. Who knows, we might decide to go to one of the jazz cabarets in Harlem. We haven't done that in eons. What do you think?"

"Sounds like a plan," Margo said. "We'll talk about a date." She watched until Rhonda unlocked her door and they waved good night. Margo turned out the light and returned to the living room where she turned on the TV. Tonight had been fun and different, showing off her newly learned skills in the kitchen. She'd actually enjoyed herself and could see a repeat performance. Although her turkey was a small bird, only twelve pounds, it'd been cooked to golden brown perfection. She was proud of herself.

Though she'd promised she wouldn't, her mind strayed to thoughts of David. How had he spent his day? If like her, he'd laid it on thick, showing off for Jonathan and Wesley and Valeria, cooking up a blue streak.

She'd known when Jonathan had been released from the hospital. Each day she'd called and was given the general response of, "He's stable," and then finally, "He's been discharged." Valeria had called her a couple of times, leaving messages, but Margo never returned the calls. Why try to continue a friendship that would be a hurtful reminder to everyone? To have a clean break was the best way, but she wished the hurt inside would soon subside.

Turning off the TV Margo went to the study where she opened an envelope and double-checked the contents. Satisfied with what she read she returned the pages.

"That should do it for another good while," she said, but anger crept up into her throat as she stifled a groan. This was an idea that she'd had long ago but never had a chance to use. The time just wasn't right. Now she was giving it away, knowing the attention it would get. The consequence if she balked again was something she didn't want to consider. A forced calm settled over her.

Trying to lighten her mood, she smiled. Wasn't there a song about "the things we do for love"? She turned out the light leaving the envelope on the desk. Tomorrow night it would be in his hands and she could breathe for another few weeks.

She ran a bath and poured in soothing salts. The aroma filled the room and a smile curled at the corner of her mouth as the scent tickled her nose. It was the catalyst for the bath oil print ad that she knew would take off—to say nothing of the follow-up ad.

When she sank down, her shoulders covered with the warmest water she could stand, she closed her eyes thinking about the way people changed their minds. She'd thought she would be all tough and steely; no, she would never be the one to submit to blackmail. Not her!

Closing her eyes she allowed the water to lap over her breasts, tickling her nipples, the sensation stirring long dormant feelings. She imagined his fingers skimming over her, playing a little tattoo on her smooth skin, teasing, taunting her, like he loved to do. She opened her eyes and the feeling vanished. No mountaintop hot tub. No whirlpool in Holliswood. She was here on Midland Parkway, alone with her thoughts. A smart, professional woman, who was living her life under the thumbnail of a blackmailer. All for love. "All for you, David," she murmured. "To save you from a madman." If she never saw David lying in a hospital bed with a punctured lung like his brother, she would work, racking her brain to keep shoveling work the madman's way. With her last breath she would knuckle under.

Margo had never known what it was to be humbled. In the face of fear—not for herself—but for others, especially the man she loved; she would do anything to keep them safe. She'd seen the devil in Ty's eyes the night after she'd come from Jonathan's hospital bed. That night she would have sacrificed her life if that was what he wanted.

All these weeks she'd been carrying on a charade with Rhonda, allowing her to think the breakup with David was over his money. What a joke that was. She'd take David with his money or David with no money in a heartbeat. But sharing her feelings with her friend would be wrong. No sense in involving another innocent person who might be a potential victim. Besides, Rhonda was apt to give David an earful and that was just what Margo wanted to avoid.

At all costs David would never know the lie she was living. Never.

The decision to leave Mexico early this morning had been a rushed one. Though a bit tired he was glad he was home. He needed to be here.

Jonathan couldn't wrap his mind around the thought that David and Margo had split. For the life of him he couldn't, wouldn't buy the weak reason of David's interference. His feelings hadn't changed since that night he was attacked—that Margo was hiding something, yet he couldn't believe that she was cutting out on David. He'd tried to equate her actions with Cynthia's, believing that she was as deceitful, but he couldn't.

He hadn't seen his wife's deception coming, never believed she would do that to him, and after all these years he was still baffled by her betrayal. What signs should he have seen that would have warned him? But his gut feeling told him that Margo and Cynthia were two entirely different people with very different agendas.

Though David never mentioned the night she'd come to the hospital, Wes had told him that she'd nearly lost it when she heard. Her shock and grief were genuine, nothing put-on there, and Jonathan knew Wes wasn't just talking to hear the sound of his own voice.

His plan to visit her before the attack was still a plan. It'd been weeks now and his gut feelings hadn't changed, intensifying since speaking to David last night. If anything was going to be done he had to initiate it before his brother went nuts with grief over losing the one thing that had been so precious to him. It was past ten o'clock when he left the house.

David was beat, though smiling as he reclined, stocking-feet up on the sofa arm in his library. The day at Champion Wheels had been long, but profitable. They'd closed at eight o'clock and he and his managers didn't leave until after nine with Cindy being escorted to make the night deposit. Leaving the driving to someone less sleepy than he, he dozed in the back of his limo during the ride back home on the congested parkways.

Dinner had been Thanksgiving leftovers that Cindy had brought in for the staff and while eating he'd had a moment of sadness, thinking that he could have been at his home with Margo laughing over his culinary efforts. He'd shaken off the gray moment and dived into selling his product to eager new customers, many of whom had waxed poetic about his ad campaigns the last months.

His relaxed posture didn't last as he swung his legs to the floor and sat up. He was miserable. Like a man in a trance he left the room and went upstairs to his bedroom and in the most unlikely place for a priceless object he took the box off his cherry wood highboy dresser and carried it to the bed where he opened it.

The day the pearls had arrived by bonded courier, he'd been more deflated than surprised. Somehow, with the pearls still in her possession he had an excuse for going to see her. Now, he had nothing but the memory of the night he'd fastened them around her neck. He stared at them and frowned. They didn't seem as bright, appearing to have lost some luster. Was it possible that they needed air and light and warmth to hold that incomparable glow? He'd have to inquire about that. If he'd been sold a bill of goods someone was going to pay. But if that were the case—that they came alive only when worn—he knew where they belonged.

Twenty minutes later, at eleven fifteen, he was in the Mercedes, driving toward Jamaica Estates.

Margo was angry. Why he chose such a late hour to meet, she didn't know, but she immediately recanted that. She did know. Less people around. Ty, in his sick, cunning way, knew what he was doing. There was no double-parking for him, or coming practically into the building. He remembered his altercation with Joe. So she had to meet him a block away on a darkened corner where he'd parked unobtrusively, looking normal to the security patrol.

It was raw, cold and blustery, another snowstorm forecast for the wee hours. The streets were still wet and slimy with dirty ice and gray snowbanks blocking the sidewalks, making it hard for pedestrians to cross and for motorists looking for curbside parking.

Just twenty-five after the hour, Margo was standing in the warmth of the lobby waiting the few minutes before leaving the building. She'd misjudged the time, but she'd be damned if she was going to stand out there in that mess waiting for him. The nylon parka she had tossed on over her jeans was lightweight but she wasn't going to be out long, though her feet would probably freeze in the worn sneakers she'd tied on. The envelope fell out of the shallow pocket and she picked it up and began slapping it against her thigh. Hank, the night desk man, threw her a discreet look and she had to smile knowing he probably thought her daft.

* * *

Jonathan reached Margo's block and swore at the lack of parking. He drove around twice before he found a dug-out spot between two mounds of dirty snow, two blocks away. He bowed his head into the wind and began walking.

David could have sworn he saw Jonathan's dark BMW but shook his head. There were a thousand and one just like it on every street in New York City. His brother, the lucky so-and-so, was sitting on a sunny beach in Mexico and David wished he was there with him and Val. He found a spot, parking a block away from the building and was soon bracing against the stiff wind.

She's late, Ty fumed as he checked the clock on his dash. Eleven thirty and some seconds. Not good. The sound escaping from his clenched jaw was meant to be humorous but would've sounded maniacal to all ears but his.

Things were looking up. Those last ideas she'd given him were on the money. He'd worked them up as his own and had presented them in a job interview. Today, he'd gotten a call-back for another interview on Monday. When he walked in that door he'd have something else to lay on them and he'd be in. A job! The thought of working again, to be the shot in the arm to a stagnant team, was refreshing. Just like before when he'd stolen another gem of an idea from her. He was pumped. Ty laughed again. He'd been right to follow his mind, sticking it to her friends. It had taken her a while but she'd wizened up after he'd done Blackshear. A warm rush came over him as he thought about that night. He'd

wanted so badly to do it all over again. He almost
wished she hadn't been scared to death because he sure
would have liked to stick it to the main man. If that had
happened he could only wonder at what that meant. A
partnership for life!

Ty's chuckle turned to a strangled sound when his
mind raced. Where was she? If she thought she was
through, that she'd had enough, then she was dead
wrong. The thought that she wasn't going to show began
a slow burn in his gut. Not realizing he was suddenly
salivating, he reached for the glove compartment but
stopped, frown lines wrinkling his forehead. *What the
hell are you up to, Margo? Messing things up now when
I'm so close?*

"I'll fix this right now." Reaching for the glove box
he opened it, slipped the knife in his pocket. Seconds
later he got out of the car but stopped when he saw her
hurrying toward him. His hand gripped the knife.
Maybe she did have second thoughts but got smart at
the last minute. Well, he'd have to teach Miss High and
Mighty that he wasn't to be toyed with. He got back in
the car and waited.

David was walking across the street approaching the
building when he stopped and stared. Margo was hurrying from the lobby, clutching an envelope as if it
contained gold, walking quickly down the block. His
eyes disbelieving, he watched. Where in the world was
she going this time of night, dressed as if for a walk in
the park on a balmy day? The wind was fierce and he
saw her hunch her shoulders and continue her quick
walk, nearly slipping on the ice in her slick sneakers. He
swore. After the shock wore off he followed, staying
well behind on the opposite sidewalk of the deserted
street. When she rounded the corner, he didn't cross
over to follow but watched, his brow furrowed, when

she stopped beside a car and opened the door, the soft light illuminating the face of a man. David stiffened. Ty Henderson!

Jonathan reached the corner at the moment Margo opened the door and climbed inside the car. He saw his brother freeze and heard the expletive escape his lips as he was about to move.

"David," he said softly. "Wait."

Spinning around, David could only stare. "What the hell . . ." Was the whole world going crazy? "What's going on? Where'd you come from?" He didn't know whether to laugh or cry or go out of control, unable to think clearly, seeing his brother standing in front of him on a dark cold corner in Queens. He was in Mexico!

"Shh," Jonathan said. "I knew it. I suspected that slime bucket was involved. Shh, don't move yet. Let's wait this out." Jonathan was holding his brother's arm tightly.

David was nearly limp. If not for his brother's grip he would have flopped down on a filthy snowbank looking for answers from God-only-knew-where. "What's happening Jonathan?" he asked as if there could be no logical explanation.

"Look." Jonathan's lips curled in a knowing smile when he saw the piece of paper in her hand.

Margo handed him the envelope and was about to get out of the car when Ty pulled her back, tossing the envelope back at her. The door was ajar and she had one foot outside. The overhead car light made her happy that they weren't in the dark but the crazed look on his face made her wish she hadn't seen those bedeviled eyes, turning her knees to jelly.

Ty had gone over the edge. Swallowing was painful for lack of saliva in her mouth. "What the hell is wrong with you? Get your hands off me. You've got what you

wanted, now leave me alone." She tried to sound tough
and brave but she knew as well as he did that the quiver
in her voice was pure fear.

"You were late, Margo," Ty said, almost crooning as
if to a cranky infant. "Having second thoughts about our
little program, are you?"

"What are you talking about?" She picked up the envelope and swatted at the hand that held her arm like a
vise. "You're hurting me. Let go."

Ty enjoyed watching her squirm. Her little fist did
nothing to affect him and her hits were only as annoy-
ing as the mere lighting of a fly. Without warning, the
dull ache that had hounded him all day seemed to ex-
plode like rockets in his head. He was nearly dizzy with
anticipation and his blood flowed hotly through his
veins.

Somehow what Margo was there for seemed so inconsequential when he thought about what he could do
to her. He was so strong and she was like putty in his
hands. He wondered what she would look like if he
stuck her. He'd wondered about the look on Blackshear's face, but it'd been so dark. Now he had a chance
to see the fear of death on a human's face. Would she
cry? Would those big beautiful brown eyes plead with
him? Or widen in fear? He felt so in control! With his
free hand he reached in his pocket and felt the hard steel
of the knife, so cold, so smooth. He caressed it momentarily with his fingers, and then pulled it from his
pocket. Ty held it up to her face and slowly smoothed
the flat edge across her cheek, up and down, back and
forth. Smiling, unaware of the spittle at the corner of his
lips, he turned the tip of the blade inward.

Margo screamed.

The glint of the knife suddenly appearing nearly immobilized David. Yet, he flung his brother's arm away

and was across the street in seconds, slipping and sliding on the slick streets until he was by the car and yanking open the door.

"H-e-n-d-e-r-s-o-n," he yelled. With one strong hand he grabbed the man's beefy neck and pulled. With his other hand he began to choke the surprised man who'd dropped the knife to clutch at his throat, trying to turn to see what had hold of him.

Margo jumped away, kicking open the door and sliding out of the car and to the ground. Big hands caught her, lifting her up, holding her. She looked up. "Jonathan?"

David had dragged the big man out of the car and onto the street. He was beating the man's face blow after blow, unmindful of the SUV that swerved and skidded on the wet asphalt to keep from running over the tussling bodies. "You scum," David yelled, "I'll kill you." Suddenly he had a death hold around Ty's neck, squeezing, wishing the man would stay still. He wanted him to stop moving. "I'll kill you," he said, all the anger and fear for what Henderson was about to do to Margo, surging into his hands, making them a powerful vise, squeezing, squeezing, joyful when the man no longer clutched at his hands, his struggles beginning to ebb. David was losing himself in a dark world when he suddenly felt her touch.

"David, please." Margo's hands were on his as she knelt down in the street. "Please, let him go. He's not worth losing you forever, my love. Please." With her other hand she touched his face, running her fingers over his cheek, his lips. "David," she whispered.

"Come on, David," Jonathan said, pulling at David's shoulders. "I've got him. Let him go. He's not going anywhere." His foot was in the man's stomach and he was staring at Ty with a hatred he didn't know he could feel. The man opened his eyes and stared back at him and even in the dim light from the car he could see the crazed look in the wild stare. Jonathan was taken aback. And suddenly he knew. The man had cracked. The implication at what could have happened to Margo if he hadn't followed his hunch was daunting.

Two security cars appeared and each driver jumped out, nightsticks drawn, and one was already radioing for assistance from the NYPD. The handcuffs on the big man, who looked and sounded pitiful with his animalistic yelps, Jonathan stepped back.

David was trembling violently against the car, his hands hanging limply at his sides. Chin buried in his chest, eyes closed, he was numb. What he'd nearly done was like a jolt of electricity coursing through his veins. The enormity of it was chilling. Could he really have killed a man with his bare hands? The shudders tore through him. He felt her arms enfold him and she leaned into him, offering her body warmth.

Margo's arms were wrapped around his waist, her head pressed against his chest. His chin dug into the top of her head and she made soothing sounds as if to bring him back to a sane world.

Finally, the voices and commotion broke through his consciousness and David opened his eyes. Police were everywhere. Henderson was gone. Jonathan was giving a statement. But David looked down into Margo's soft dark eyes, and saw the love there. He inhaled and his senses went back to a time that seemed like an eternity ago, when he'd smelled summer breezes in the dead of winter.

David closed his eyes briefly, and then kissed the tip of her nose. "Hello, again."

Chapter Twenty

Everyone has an animal side. David knew that now. It was something he'd heard once or twice in his lifetime. A Jekyll and Hyde. To have experienced it at this point in his life was humbling. There was nothing he could ask for in life. He had it all, the money, the cars, and the women in his bed, the enterprises that the average man could only dream about; there was nothing he yearned for, yet he was willing to blow it all in one mad moment of lunacy. Ready to slide over the edge like Henderson. The man was lost. It made no sense to David. Try as he would he couldn't get it to compute. Sheer idiocy. He heard a scrape of a chair and looked across the table at his brother.

"You okay now, man?" said Jonathan. "I'll be leaving, before she finishes. You two need some time."

They both heard the shower stop. He stared at his brother. "How did you figure out what was going on?" David said. "Why didn't you let on?"

"Because we knew what happened to you tonight would have happened," Jonathan said. He stood. "Besides, me and Wes didn't want to have to spend our weekends bringing you home baked chocolate cookies and goulash and stuff like that."

David stood and followed Jonathan to the door, his throat tight with emotion. "See you tomorrow?"

"Bet on it. Wes is on his way back. We'll talk."

* * *

The bathroom door opened and a scent of sweet floral wafted to his nose in the living room where he was waiting. When she appeared he stood and went to her. Without a word she came into his arms and he held her.

David didn't deign to think himself worthy of her love but he knew that he would spend the rest of his life making her know her worth to him. Eyes closed, he rocked her, kissing the softness of her nape. Inhaling deeply, a shudder went through him as images of a madman with a knife kept obscuring his vision. He rubbed his cheek against hers—that smooth beautiful skin that might have been marred.

Holding him tightly, Margo smoothed the taut muscles of his back through the thin cotton of his shirt. She knew his thoughts and she sought to ease the pain and guilt he was feeling. "Don't, love," she murmured against his chest. "It's all over."

He lifted his head. "I've never stopped loving you," he whispered. "Never."

Margo took his hand and led him to the sofa. They sat; she snuggled against his shoulder, his arm draped around her waist. She ran her fingers over the strong hand that tonight was as a death instrument. Briefly she shuttered her eyes against that scene. The violence in him had frightened her.

Feeling her tremor, David tightened his hold. He kissed her forehead. Almost as if he knew her thoughts he said, "You'll never see me that way again, Margo. I swear that to you. You have to believe that." But he prayed that no one would ever come that close to hurting her again for he knew his promise would be broken.

She squeezed his hand. "I do, David."

"Margo?"

He sounded so serious. She eased herself up to look at him. "What is it, David?"

"I need a promise from you." When he had her complete attention he said, "Don't ever keep something like that from me again, sweetheart. Blackmail is one of the vilest of crimes. It never ends and before it's all over the poison touches some of everyone in its path." His knuckles glided over her cheek and his fingers caressed her lips. "I expect that in my lifetime, with all the dealings I do, that some joker will try that with me. I pray to God that whatever is being held over my head, I can weather it without becoming a victim. Or that it won't touch those that I love." His gaze was penetrating. "Promise me?"

She shook her head. "Never again," she said. Her voice was curious when she said, "How was it that you showed up tonight? I couldn't believe my eyes when you jerked that car door open."

"I kicked pride out the door and came running," David said. "I was a fool and if you don't forgive me my life is over. I accused you of seeing another man with nothing more to go on than the uncanny utterance of some identical words spoken long ago by a deceitful woman. If I hadn't been so into my own hurt and anger I would have seen right then that I was wrong. It was only later when I had time to think about it, I would have never accused you of such a thing."

"Why?"

"Because I heard that cry, as if I'd kicked you in the stomach." He smiled at her and kissed her lips. "You couldn't have faked that sound even if you were acting like the great Hattie McDaniel."

"Who's that?" Margo teased, knowing he was an avid student of African-American history and could give lectures on the subject.

"Funny lady. Come here." David kissed her lips long and hard before he lifted his head. He wanted more, much more; he wanted to plunder her, love her like he'd never had. "I was bringing something back to you." Easing out of her arms and walking to the chair where his jacket lay, he dug in his pocket and pulled out the cool, smooth spheres. When he sat beside her he caught her hand and let them drop into it.

The pearls spilled into her palm. Margo's eyes glistened. "I really never wanted to give them up. They're so beautiful," she murmured.

David watched the strand lying against her fine brown skin. They were where they belonged at last. He caught her hand and the pearls in his. "Margo?"

"Yes, David?"

"You know I'm never going to let you go, don't you?"

She smiled. "You're so serious. I'm not going anywhere, love."

"No, look at me," David said firmly, taking both her hands in his. "I mean you're not going to stay here alone. I'm not going to stay in my place alone. I want us to be together from now on, no matter where it is."

Margo caught her breath. "You mean live together?" she said.

"As my wife. Will you marry me?" His breath was shallow as he waited for her to speak. But her gaze dropped to their hands entwined around the pearls and his heart sank as the smile left her face. She didn't want him!

She'd wondered what she would say if it'd come to this. All the reasons that she had for not becoming Mrs. David Blackshear just went south as she thought of what might have been tonight. Nothing else mattered then that they lived their lives together.

He watched and waited. He'd hurt her badly and now

he was going to pay the price of losing her, an empty existence for the rest of his life. His shoulders drooped but when she touched his lips with her fingers he looked into her eyes and he knew.

"No matter where?" she said softly.

He nodded. "Anywhere."

"Then take me to your mountaintop, love," she whispered.

David exhaled. "Then you will?" He caught her face in his hands, looking into her eyes that shone with love. His heart hurt.

Her soft tinkle of laughter was lost against his mouth as she kissed him, the tip of her tongue dancing with his. "I think that's a yes, love," she murmured.

"The mountaintop it is, sweetheart," he gasped, clasping her to him tightly.

Epilogue

One year later

"I think Inez is mad at you," David whispered in his wife's ear. "She's also afraid she's lost her title of kitchen goddess." He chuckled. "So what do you say? Want me to fire her?"

Margo jabbed him in his ribs with her elbow but she smiled. "You do, and you'll regret it," she said. But she looked at the contented faces of her guests after eating her sumptuous Thanksgiving dinner. She'd allowed David equal time though, letting him prepare a golden goose that was a hit, and had him grinning from ear to ear. The presence of her family and friends brought mist to her eyes. Her parents as well as David's parents were there, looking like happy expectant grandparents. Jonathan and Valeria were engaged to marry in the spring. Wesley was still the most eligible bachelor in Brooklyn, and Rhonda was there with the new man in her life. Margo looked at her friend and smiled knowingly and to her surprise, Rhonda, the woman who had it all together, flushed warmly and Margo knew that the woman had fallen in love.

Ty Henderson, a sad excuse for a man, she was still trying to forget as the one who'd brought pain to her friends and threatened to take her away from her love.

He was charged with attempted murder and was now being held pending medical reports on his mental state to stand trial.

"Happy, sweetheart?" David said. They had wandered into the library, leaving their guests arguing amiably about the name for the baby. Neither he nor Margo wanted to know the gender, wanting to be surprised at the New Year's arrival. "No regrets?" he asked.

Surprised, she looked at him. "Over?"

"Our wedding. Your business. The baby coming so soon. It's a lot of stuff going on in such a short time. I was wondering if you'll regret turning the business over to your old colleagues like that, although Pat was an excellent choice to run things." David thought she'd gotten the last laugh on her old boss, stealing away some of his most talented staff to run Margo's new company. She'd realized she couldn't go it alone single-handedly like she'd been doing and had made the decision to reorganize and form a new firm.

"No regrets," Margo said. "I'm not president and CEO of Margo Sterling Advertising but I keep a hand in as creative consultant. I'm good with that." She slipped an arm around his waist. "Besides, I'm so busy with Kai and Friends now that I don't miss the agency. I much prefer working with the young people. Reading the tales and seeing their delighted expressions is my reward." Never would she have dreamed that her stories would have taken off so fast. The day after Christmas she'd received a call from a publisher offering to buy the manuscript she'd sent in months before; the one where Dixon-turned-Ellison had made his debut. It'd been one of her favorites. She'd been writing ever since then and she loved her new career.

Kai, what do you think of all this?

David saw the smile on her face and knew her twin

had crossed her mind. He knew those things about her now. He hugged her.

"You don't think the trip tomorrow is too much?" David asked. St. Maarten was where he'd taken her for their honeymoon and like her he hadn't wanted to leave.

Margo reached up and caressed the strong lines of his jaw, her thumb skimming his full mouth. She'd never stop wanting to look at him, to touch and feel the length of him next to her. "Going to the mountaintop again will never be too much, love. It's my most favorite place in the world to be with you."

David closed his eyes. *Thank you, God.*

Dear Reader,

Instant riches. Money, that is, is something many dream about but few attain. This story came to me one day while I was in Penn Station in New York and I found myself people-watching. The one constant as travelers came and went, rushing for trains and finding their way to the myriad exits, was the presence of the Redcap, a New York mainstay for many years, those baggage handlers who readily assist those with too many bags and those who are grateful for their help. I couldn't help but notice the camaraderie between a redcap and a man dressed in the uniform of a Long Island Rail Road conductor. They were obviously buddies. Already a story was formulating. When I saw the conductor smile at a very professional woman, suited-down, briefcase, haughty air, and his buddy shaking his head as if to say, "No way," David Blackshear and Margo Sterling were born.

I hope you enjoyed David's story as he made the attempt to remain grounded with enormous wealth, such as he'd never fathomed in life. He had his trials as he learned that ill-blowing winds do not pass a rich man by, and that his money could not buy real dreams and happiness. Margo learned to accept the love of a good man who only wanted to please her, not control or stifle her energy and creativity, and that accepting a helping hand in good faith, love and trust is not a sign of weakness or incompetence.

To my readers who've supported me over the years, I thank you and hope you've enjoyed these two lovers and their story. As always, I appreciate hearing from you. For a reply, please include a self-addressed, stamped envelope.

Doris Johnson
P.O. Box 130370
Springfield Gardens, NY 11413
E-mail: Bessdj@aol.com

About the Author

Doris Johnson lives in Queens, New York, with her husband. An award-winning author of ten novels and two novellas, she writes full-time while sharing good times with family, friends, and four beautiful grandchildren. Her interests include traveling and collecting gemstones.